THE
SHADOW
OF
FIRE

Published by Acorn Independent Press Ltd, 2014.

ISBN 978-1-909122-56-7

Acorn Independent Press

THE
SHADOW
OF
FIRE

DAMIEN WAUGH

This one is for Howard and Kathy.

*"All the world is a storm
and we are but ants in the fray."*

CONTENTS

PART 1

PART 2

PART 3

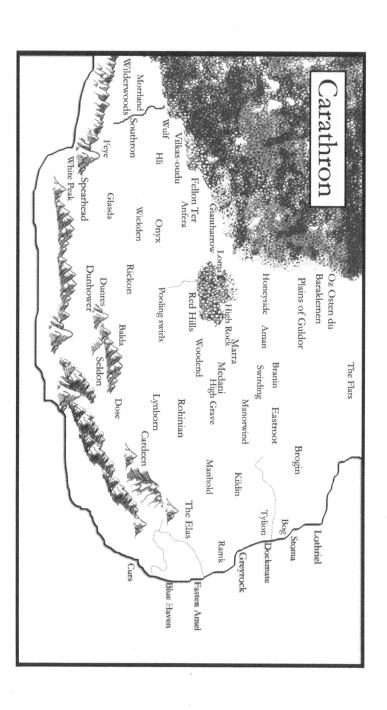

Carathron

The Flas

Oz Osten du Baraklemen
Plains of Guldor

Morland Southron
Wilderwoods
Wulf
Hli
Vilkas-oudu
Fellon Ter
Anfera
Gianharrow
Loma
High Rock
Marra
Medani
High Grave
Honeyside
Aman
Swirding
Branin
Eastroot
Manorwind
Kildin

Feye
White Peak
Spearhead
Glasda
Wicken
Onyx
Rickon
Pooling swirls
Red Hills
Woodend
Lynborn
Rohinian
Manhold
Brogin
Bog
Tylion
Dockmate
Storna
Lothriel

Dunres
Dunhower
Seldon
Balda
Dose
Carden
The Elas
Rank
Greyrock

Curs
Blue Haven
Fasten Amel

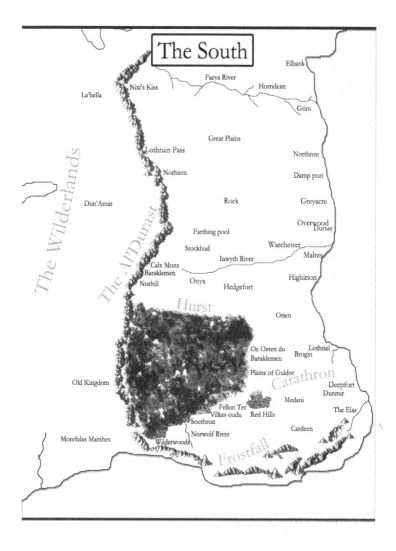

The South

Elbank

Faeya River

Nixi's Kiss

La'bella

Horndean

Grim

Great Plains

Northron

Lothruin Pass

Damp port

Norhiem

The Wilderlands

Dun'Amar

Roek

Greyacre

Overwood
Dursay

Farthing pool

Stockhud

Warchester

The ArDurast

Inwyth River

Malres

Calx Mons
Baraklemen

Onyx

Highirion

Norhill

Hedgefort

Hurst

Orien

Oz Osten du
Baraklemen

Brogin

Lothriel

Old Kingdom

Plains of Guldor

Carathron

Deepfort
Dunmir

Medani

The Elas

Fellon Ter
Vilkas-oudu

Red Hills

Morefalas Marshes

Southron

Norwolf River

Cardeen

Wilderwoods

Frostfall

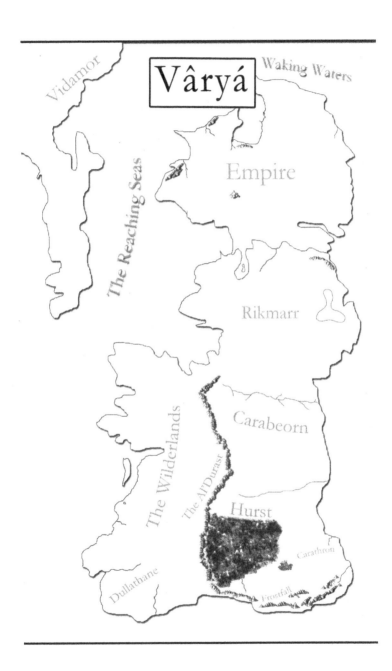

PART 1

"The only things ever heard in peace are whispers of love and war."

CHAPTER ONE

TORN FLESH
Loan caro

This is the end.

The darkness that had been lurking at the corner of his eyes encroached and, as it did, he felt death's icy fingers tighten around his dying heart. The events of the last few hours had played the card of death, and that fate had not gone unanswered. *I am going to die!*

The towers of Medani grew large as Thormir Darkin rode towards his hometown. The city was the last true capital east of The Al'Durast, the mountain range that divided the realm. To the north was the black city of Orien, and to the south was The Frostfall, the great realm of snow and ice – a place only the dead could describe. The Frostfall; home to mountains that spat out huge geysers of ice from their summits, and massive glaciers that swallowed all in their path. It was no place for a man who took The Green.

Thormir felt Shadow's hoofs beat against the ground. She ran towards the city at a tremendous pace, and Thormir marvelled at the fact that a beast could move so fast. Of course, he knew that

1

dragons could outstrip them in a wing beat, but those ancient creatures had not been seen for one thousand years; so Thormir had decided long ago that Shadow was the fastest animal from Hurst to Orien.

Looking up, he could see the city shining like a jewel that sparkled crimson in the light of dawn. Thormir had ridden all night from The Red Forest, panicking about the news he would soon deliver to his father.

This is all I need! If I am wrong then father will have me whipped, but he will not believe what I am to tell him, so . . . His train of thought broke off as he remembered what he had seen and felt deep within the forest at The Red Hills: a flash of black fur, and then being pushed flat onto his back. The smell of pine needles seemed to float back to him as the memory played out. One gigantic paw had pinned him to the ground. He couldn't move. He had clutched at the paw trying to shift it either way. Slowly he had raised his gaze to meet that of the warg. He had looked into eyes full of hatred, but as he stared he had seen sorrow too, and . . . was it fear? The next second he had felt an explosion of searing pain within his chest and arm. Then his vision blurred, his arms twitched, and he passed out.

When he awoke, it was not the purple-black bruising across his ribs that had scared him, but the small thorn sticking out of the side of his arm. It was an innocent, bright green colour and, at first glance, Thormir had known exactly what it was: the thorn of the miraki plant. Its poison would soon spread. He took out his hunting knife, which he had sharpened only the night before, and cut an X across the area of flesh where the thorn was embedded. Hot, thin blood spilled from his arm. The cut was deeper than expected, but it was all he could do to keep the poison at bay.

Thormir pulled himself back to the present. The city was close now, but he could feel himself slipping, giving in to his pain. *Death has come for me.* Darkness already impaired a large amount of his eyesight and he could feel that promised fever drawing ever closer. He winced and opened his mind so that he could sense the thoughts and feelings of the animals close to him. He extended a tendril of thought to Shadow, who understood his urgency and picked up the pace. Time was becoming blurred now. Had he been riding for a week or had he only just mounted? When would they be there? The city was close, but it would take another fortnight to reach the capital of Carathron. *So far.*

The cobbled road clacked under Shadow's hooves as she slowed to a trot. As always, the stables smelled of horses, but the odour was pleasant and familiar to Thormir. The huge doors of the barn and the stable house were both engraved with a horseshoe turned towards the sky – a sign of luck in these dark times. Bir, the stable master, was sitting in a gigantic, carved, wooden chair. He was so huge in height and girth that he seemed to melt into the chair, casting a massive and distorted shadow in the morning light. As he slept his tangled beard had the appearance of thick, black, hanging moss, from which the end of his long pipe sprouted. As Thormir squinted in pain, he saw the smouldering ashes of Crab-Leaf curling in the barrel of the pipe's head. *Smoking again. I always tell him, but he never listens!*

Thormir turned his head away from Bir's brown apron, which rose and fell with the long beat of his deep breathing. Spitting some fresh blood from his mouth and settling himself more securely in his saddle, Thormir again opened his mind, searching for a familiar consciousness amongst the hundreds of people within the western district of Medani. Finally, he found who he was looking for. The mind that he was touching suddenly recognised his presence and sensed his pain – Fern.

"*Fern, I need . . .*" A shudder of pain ripped through Thormir as he maintained the link between minds. "*I need your help!*" With that, Thormir severed the connection between them, slumped in his saddle, and fell from Shadow with a despairing finality.

For the second time in as many days, Thormir returned from the unconscious. As he opened his eyes, he saw that everything was distorted; the world was sideways. A grey fog seemed to cloud his vision. A rush of sounds and images flooded his mind and the memory of where he was and what had happened returned to him. He sat upright and yelled out in pain. Looking down, he saw that the bandages he had applied had come undone, and that he was bleeding profusely. As well as the pain in his shoulder, he heard a thumping in his ears, before realising that it was the sound of Fern running down the cobbled road. A sense of relief filled him as he saw the colossal dog streaking towards him. Fern was jet black and had a furry mane that was pushed flat by his speed. As the dog drew closer, still running with great strides, his size could truly be appreciated. He was taller than the waist of many men and he was capable of carrying a rider when on all fours. Thormir knew that Fern had powerful sabre-like teeth that could crush the skull of any beast he could imagine. As Fern padded up to him, his teeth were bared and he was snarling. Thormir knew that this was out of concern for him. In a blur of seamless grey and black the huge dog morphed into a boy of nineteen years.

Fern shouted in dismay at seeing Thormir's wounds. "We must get you up to the healers!" he said in his rough accent. "By all the gods, look at your shoulder! You are torn apart. What did this you? Never mind, I'll carry you to Mary, the old healer who tells those odd stories – quick." Then Fern touched Thormir's mind, "*Ava letha du lysá, bronus. Do not leave me, brother.*" Thormir felt his heart warm a little as he heard the phrase they had made up together and used when they needed each other, a phrase of love and joy, spoken in Nolwin, the ancient tongue of the first ones – a language forsaken by man.

With that, Fern lifted Thormir onto his shoulders and morphed into his dog-like self. Thormir could feel the soft fur of Fern's mane pressing against his face. He felt another stab of pain,

4

the rhythm of Fern's gait, then, as he heard the howl of a wolf far in the distance, he fell into darkness.

* * *

Fear has no place in a warg's heart, yet still he felt it – dark, terrible fear. He looked out over the craggy precipice and bit into the night.

The warg knows that fear is a poison carried on the whispers of the wind. The only trouble with wind is that it survives; it can survive even after all life is extinguished. The ages of this world pass and time devours the rest. The wind observes the passing of great rulers and the crippling of powerful kingdoms, and yet it never intervenes, it is just a mocking audience, laughing at beings that deem themselves powerful, for they too will pass in time. Beyond time's maw, the wind shall remain. But, as with all things within this terrible cycle of destiny, the wind served a purpose. It had a job to carry out – the will of fate, and that will had changed.

The wind was now blowing in a different direction, and with it the fear, which heralded the arrival of war and death. A storm would brew in the east and soon fate would be drenched in the blood shed by its own hand. The Darkness and the fear. They came from over the peaks of The Al'Durast and encroached upon the eastern kingdoms, poisoning the dark forests and turning the bubbling springs foul. The hunt had become scarce and rancid, and a plague swept the villages. Days had become short, retiring to watchful nights. Those nights drenched the sky in a darkness deeper and more frightening than blackness itself. That was when the chill set in. The pitch of night and an iciness worthy of the most deadly winter was invading the South. The smiles of young children had begun to fade to looks of doubt and suspicion as they gathered behind the backs of their mothers, who shut newly bolted doors, but no one could stop The Darkness – all surrendered to its will. The North was the first to fall under its influence and then it had slithered down, pressing further south. The Darkness hammered at the minds of men, and beat against the lone warg that stood upon a great, jagged rock looking over The Red Hills. It seemed that the warg was waiting for dawn, which should have broken a good two hours earlier, but the watchful night remained, the dark wind carrying the scent of change.

The only sign that morning was approaching was the dark vault above, which had begun to fade into lesser shades of black. It was now light enough to make out the face of the warg. The wetness of daybreak sat upon the glistening coat of the handsome warg, but the small droplets of water did not refract any rays of morning light, as they would have done in the times before The Darkness. Pure white fangs were half-revealed as the warg snarled with eagerness. The lips of the warg's muzzle curled, showing healthy red and pink gums that dripped with saliva.

Soon it will be time. He scanned the landscape for any predators but none revealed themselves to his keen gaze. His attention lingered on a human farmer far in the distance. The farmer was carrying what looked like a long, knotted staff and a solitary lantern aloft in front of him, guiding him through the morning darkness. The warg regarded the bobbing lantern for a moment longer. Just before he turned his head away, he saw the fire inside the glass casing flash green and blue, only to return to the swish of the orange flame. A strange scent tainted the wind.

A howl quivered upon the air and then died as a fresh breeze ruffled the warg's coat. He tasted the howl upon the wind, and it was one of pain and urgency. It was time. Quick as the fastest Night Hunter, the warg turned and fled down the crag. He ran so fast that he made no imprint upon the short grass. The only sign he had ever ascended the peak was the whispers of the stones –

whispers that told of a new coming, a coming of dark things, and the rebirth of old powers.

As the warg reached the edge of the Red Forest, he looked back to see a single golden ray of sunlight smash into the peak, revealing all the majesty of High Rock – the great seat that looked out over all of the tundra (the word habitually used to describe the lands of Carathron). This was not the barren, icy wastes of The Frostfall, but a great expanse of dark green, rolling hills splashed white with the heavy drifts of winter. Splendid plains reached out for the horizons and other towering peaks scattered around the southern realms. Growling with approval, the warg turned and began to weave his way through the still dark forest, and as he felt the wind in his fur he took pleasure in the chase. However, something still played on his mind – an old worry resurfaced. The nights now lasted longer – or at least the darkness did. No more did the nights shine with the yellow sky wolves, as they had become blocked by that darkness. It had come from the west, over the mountains, from The Wilderlands. The Wilderlands. He had heard tales of those lands – a vast expanse beyond Hurst Forest and the great peaks of The Al'Durast, and from whence no man or warg had ever returned. They were cursed lands, only home to shadows and the bad hunt. However, every wolfkin east of The Al'Durast and even the lions in the empire's Burning North knew of the Dacarrus. They lived in those lands – doing what, he did not know, but there was a reason nobody spoke of the Dacarrus. There was a reason the dire wolves still watched the mountain passes, and there was a reason that men still built their high walls and armed their gates with fists and metal. The stories of the Dacarrus were not forgotten – how they had once taken the east, burned the forests, slaughtered the wolves, raped human cubs, and enslaved their alphas. It was said that the terrors in the West would only return with true darkness.

The warg burst through a clutch of branches that whipped his back as he passed, but he was moving too fast to care. The forest watched this cunning predator slide between trunks and rocks that had fallen from weathered cliffs. The fierce eyes of the warg glittered in the shadowed forest and as he descended a slope, launching himself between the conifers that climbed the valley, the full majesty of his appearance was revealed between the branches. A white scar slashed across his right eye but did not take away from who he really was. He was a vicious, brutal killer, but one who was running towards his mate. He knew she was in trouble.

Before long, the birthing den came into view. The warg picked up her scent far before he saw her, but she was not the only warg that trod the forest this night. There was another with her. A foreign smell surrounded him, and yet it seemed to be familiar – like a hazy dream. He brushed away a few small stones and entered the small clearing. There was his mate, her coat glistening silver grey, and her yellow eyes burning with life. The alpha looked at the small bundle that was upon her belly and growled in fury, baring the full grandeur of his sharp teeth. A human child lay upon his mate's belly, suckling on a single teat.

"Human," he growled. And he bore down upon it, ready to rip the infant limb from limb. He would taste man-blood upon his lips. He opened his mouth wide, ready to snap the child's neck. Without warning, his mate rose and bit him twice upon the neck, hard enough to make him stop.

"The infant is yours." The bright eyes of his female burned with passion. "We can shift, the time has come."

The warg looked in shock at his mate and then the infant, but now the human child had become warg kin again and stared upon him with a strong, handsome face, much like his own, all except for the ring of white that surrounded his right eye.

Only with magic are we able to shift. This can only mean . . .
Then the warg thought of the human he had seen earlier that day. Why had he come? Was it for this reason? Humans did not usually venture this far from their walls. Together with his mate, he let out a deep-throated howl that pierced the night and could be heard for miles around. As he let the howl fade, he tasted the air for any game that he could plunge his fangs into this night, but all he sensed was a horse far in the distance carrying a bleeding rider; a rider who was close to death.

CHAPTER TWO

FEVER
Villa

A woman was muttering overhead. It seemed her words were directed more to herself than anyone in particular. Thormir could tell that she was some sort of healer, as not only did his arm feel a little better, but she spoke what Thormir thought must be the names of plants and herbs as she worked, as if checking off a list.

"*Durcasi, imporidium, nexti, mecen . . .* A thorn for sure," she said. "Nothing like I've ever seen, but then I have not seen much." The woman chuckled then paused. "But never a rose without a prick, I always say." She laughed and continued, "The winds are changing, the world has changed course, and so much of what was lost will return anew – magic, I feel it returning. My bones ache for the elder days, when magic ran wild and free – dancing around the oldest of trees, which were yet samplings, and making bubbling brooks and rolling dales sing and hum with life. Now the forest birds sing but they cannot remember what they yearn, for to them magic is a long forgotten memory. It is only through the whispers of the stones and deep-rooted trees that the memory is kept alive. But I wonder what their hushed tones say now, for from the oldest rock to the eldest tree, all must feel it – the ancient power of magic. It is returning."

As she leaned over him, he picked up the smell of onions and garlic mixed in with the pungent smell of cooking sherry. He could feel her breath close to the open wound and he braced himself for the pain that was sure to come.

Thormir gasped as he felt Mary's fingernails open his wound, sprinkle something in, seal it, and press a wet cloth against his forehead. As it had done before, time blurred and fog clouded his eyes and mind so that reality passed in a haze of whispering smoke, burning incense and wandering dreams. Thormir had lost count of how many days or hours he had been in Mary's cabin. He had yet to see her in person, as whenever he opened his eyes she was gone, but a plate of bread, a cup of mead, and a bowl of stew lay waiting for him. The stew. *This is disgusting, and it makes me feel no better – if anything I get worse after every bowl.* It comprised of what looked to be oxen, horse blood, red wine, and various chunky oddments that floated around in the small, brown pool. *The old bat must have forbidden visitors or otherwise Fern would surely have come to save me from this hellhole. This is horse dung,* he thought, anger swelling up inside of him. *This is ridiculous! I am the king's son, the last of the Darkin bloodline, and descendant of Benor himself – I should not be treated like this!* He despised himself for thinking that. Ever since he was little, he hated being the son of the king. There was so much to live up to, and so many choices that weren't his own. He had no control over his future, just a destiny to become king. He had run away several times over the years, but each time the guards found and brought him back to endure the disappointed gaze of his father. His father. No matter where he went, and no matter how far he rode, he never forgot his father's gaze. Thormir knew his father cared for him, but the bond between them was not one of love and affection, but one of achievement. Thormir closed his eyes.

11

Childbirth had taken his mother, and he had always thought that some of the anger his father often bore towards him was because he blamed his son for taking his wife from him. Thormir carried the guilt with him. It was his fault that he had not had anyone to tuck him into his sheets on winter nights, or read him the tales of the heroes who fought bravely in the battles over Tyrber and Safria, or how the great kingdom of Dullathane dissolved and collapsed into ruin. He was quite young when he had decided to look for her within himself, and eventually he had imagined her as he thought she would have been in real life. He had burned her image deep within his mind so that she would never leave him – and every night he would stare up at her, looking into her crystal blue eyes, and only when she smiled back, her chin creasing in the middle, did he feel safe to fall asleep. Abruptly, he felt a tear curve his cheek and he flicked it off, angry with himself for allowing any weakness to show.

Fern had always told him to bite his tongue when he had an axe to grind with his father, but he never could and the shouts of a blazing row could often be heard echoing around the palace. Even the heat from the eleven stone hearths in The Great Hall could not match the fire that passed between father and son on such nights.

The way he saw it, the only upside to being the king's son was that he had Fern for company. At an early age Fern had been adopted to be the second son of the king. As the story went, Fern was a foundling, abandoned by his mother in the middle of the crowd upon Hanging Day, and it had always been assumed that his mother was the skinny woman who swung limp, second in the line of five. But Thormir knew this was the story that had been passed around as gossip to be made truth, for the truth was much darker still, and if people knew they would not feel the same way about the king's adopted son.

FEVER

Fern was found near the old ruins that bordered the east side of Hurst Forest. The fall had come quick and the promise of the coming winter had tightened its grip upon the South. That day the horses had fought hard against the snow, and the patrol through the ruins had made slow progress. This was fortunate, as otherwise they would not have spotted the naked baby on the side of the road, resting upon the frosty, stone blocks of an ancient tower. It was the king who spotted the bundle and when he looked into the green and yellow eyes of the child, he smiled and deemed the child his. Only when he brushed away the unusually long hair from the babe's eyes did he see the smudged mark of a fern leaf upon his brow. Upon seeing the mark, the men deemed the babe an ill omen, however the king would have none of it. The ravens of Hurst would not feast on that child that night.

Fern had been taken back to the palace as the king's second son and second in line to the throne. Thormir and Fern soon became inseparable as brothers and friends. They did everything together, and at the age of fifteen, Thormir convinced his father to let Fern and him work in the stables with Bir, tending to the horses and animals that were housed there.

Working there with them was a middle-aged man named Tangar, who often dressed in an artistic array of clothes. He was in charge of the books and healing the wounded animals. On occasion, the livestock would come back from the fields, wounded from attacks by creatures of the tundra, or injured from slips over a moss-covered boulder or a disguised pothole. Either way, it was Tangar who healed their wounds so they could brave the grasslands of the southern tundra once more.

As Thormir got to know Tangar, he realised that there was much more to him than he had first suspected. While he was just a stable house healer, he seemed to know all the stories of the ancient scriptures. He often recited the saga of Cinarett, singing softly to the horses, who seemed to understand, and mourn the loss of the elves as his sorrowful words fell from his tongue. However, Tangar would also tell tales of how the first men battled creatures born of darkness to cross The Al'Durast and form new kingdoms, built from gold and silver. One tale that Bir often requested told of a hero from Silverhaven, Teor. Born high of house he was raised to hunt with horse and ride by hound. He defeated many foes on his travels, and through his victories won undying loyalty from his men. Despite the devotion of his shield mates and brothers in arms, Teor still felt the pain of loneliness beating a thousand drums within his chest. Long did he walk, under lost leaves and woven trees, looking for a light in his lonely shadow. For seven years he wandered the woods, avoiding the winter's wolf and the summer's sun. He had abandoned his city and his men to dwell in the rolling forest, ever walking in his waking dreams. Always searching – searching for a sign of the one.

Then Teor came to a ringed pond through a misty grove. Looking into the silver pond he heard music and the whispering of 100 voices – they told of a great beauty to the south. Faeya was her name, and she dwelt in the city of Helios. Teor travelled over heaving hills of dark green, where winter had laid a slick of ice so thick that even he, who was sure of foot and keen of eye, had trouble crossing the tattered land. Eventually he came to Silverhaven and many were glad to see his return and good health. His renown and the loyalty from his men had not faded into dust and shadow but still remained shining even after those seven years. Teor was thankful for this, and he raised an army, asking them to follow him south – to find the fair Faeya of Helios. Many came – and they built three gigantic bridges that reached across The World's Vein. There, the White Bridges of Teor remained unconcerned with the fierce waters that churned below. As Teor crossed with his men, he knew that he would soon lay eyes upon Faeya. His army crossed the river but soon came under attack from savages from the western shores. Teor's silver spears and flying white banners were not enough to stop the prick of dark arrows or the bite of poisoned swords. Yet, he and some of his company survived, only to greet harsh weather that laid bare many of the remaining men who had travelled with him. Hearing of his bravery, Faeya rode forth from Helios to find Teor. She searched valleys, groves, and wooded hills, until she found him lying beside a fair river under a golden sunrise. He was broken and battered, with the horn of a giant ox buried in his side. He bore many bloody cuts from arrows and swords, yet still he had life to look upon her. When Faeya looked into his dying eyes, she saw his heart. For two days she sung to him in the ancient language of Nolwin, forsaking the language of her own people, and in that time such a love formed between them that she went with him to the afterlife, where they still lie – tenderly singing together, their voices flowing with splendour like the river that bore them away.

Rarely, and only when the dusk was winking at the night, would Tangar tell darker and more sinister tales of the many wars between the Lord of Darkness and the four allies: men, elves, dwarves, and dragons. These wars resulted in the downfall of magic and the end of the Age of Vanar upon The Fields of Celiton. All of these stories were gone now – fading from this world, only to be remembered between the yellowy pages of dusty books.

As well as his thorough knowledge of history, Tangar knew a great deal about weaponry. He was especially handy with a bow. Tangar had taught Thormir, who proved to be an excellent student. *What use is a bow now?* Thormir thought as he lay on his back. He licked his lips, fighting back the desire for food and drink.

As well as training Thormir in archery, Tangar shared his knowledge of the plants of the forests and the tundra. He showed Thormir which plants could be foraged for food, which held the key to life in dire situations, and which plants could be used as poisons. He always insisted that knowledge was a far more deadly weapon than any arrow or sharpened blade.

Often Tangar would adopt the dress of the Tangri people, the wandering tribes of the North, and would play a small harp, reciting verse long-forgotten by the troubadours that roamed the streets of Medani during the waning summers.

Thormir worked at the stables in the morning and the evenings, as lessons in the palace consumed his days like an ever-hungry beast that had set out to make his life miserable. When would he need to know about bridge-building methods? He did not need to know about geography and the wind patterns of The Al'Durast. However, there was one lesson he liked and that he often found a use for. The class concerned the application of mind touching; the opening of one's mind so that one could sense and communicate with others. He realised that he had grown somewhat accomplished at it when he learned he could touch the minds of animals as well as humans. Shadow, his great, black mare, was, quite apart from the opportunity to escape the pressure of the palace, what he loved about the stables. Although of course he could not read her mind through language, he could sense her thoughts and feelings. When he touched her mind it was if they became one, and when riding her, it was as if he was the horse and she the rider. Sometimes he had imagined he had seen through her eyes, only to be reminded by his two feet that he was Thormir, stable boy and the Prince of Carathron.

Thormir opened his eyes again. He was sick of thinking. Opening his mind, he tried to search for Fern or even his father, but he made no such contact.

Instead, a voice came out of the darkness. It crackled and was hard on the ear, but he recognised it as the healer's voice. "It's no good trying to do your mind business in here, youngling. No good trying to contact that dog friend of yours either. I've sent him on a little errand. It's good to see you've woken up – your father will be here any minute."

A sense of foreboding overcame him. He was not sure he could withstand the strength of his father's gaze at the moment. The healer moved out of her shadowy corner and looked at him. She had crystal blue eyes that emanated peace and serenity, but there was a coldness that seemed to glaze over everything else. As she continued to stare at him, her brow furrowed, creating deeper ravines in her already-creased skin. Her nose was perfectly straight and seemed to highlight her facial symmetry. She wore her red hair in a sort of bun that flared out at the end like the tail of a peacock that clashed violently with her orange robes, which she wore in the manner of the Tangri people, which was unusual for she had lived in Medani as long as he could remember. This, he thought, demonstrated his knowledge of useless information. He glanced at her robes again and confirmed the twist of garment in the middle and the overhand throw of her cloth that was particular to the wandering tribes of the burning north.

She caught him glancing at her garb and said in a soft voice, "There are many things that you don't know about Mary the Healer, youngling."

Thormir heard a thumping at the door of the hut. The blows were so powerful that they seemed to push and swirl the aromas of the herbs and potions so that they became more pungent and apparent to Thormir. Sniffing in discomfort, he looked over at the healer, who stood by a small table. A candle sat upon the table, flickering blue and green, casting gentle light upon a painting that hung above it. The light seemed to give life to the painting, causing the stalks of wheat in the painted field to sway in a breeze. Upon the fourth strike of the door, the healer blew out the candle, which cast a blanket of darkness over Thormir.

She opened the door swiftly, just before the fifth hammer of the man's fist fell and she said, "Yes, I did hear you. You'd better come in, my king, but I would prefer it if your men stayed where they are." Thormir heard his father say a few words of instruction to his companions before entering the house.

His father's hulking figure consumed the light of the doorway then passed through it, taking a seat at the round table in the middle of the house. Mary walked over to the seat closest to his bed and turned her back so that she shielded him from sight.

"Where's the boy?" the king said. He looked around but seemed unable to see Thormir resting, quiet upon the corner bed. His voice was deep and sounded like a wooden instrument, oaky and fluid. "Where's the boy?" he said again, his eyes narrowing – a familiar expression to Thormir. But there too was a look of deep concern; was it worry and fright?

Maybe I've been gone longer than I thought.

"Never you mind, the youngling is resting. We have matters to discuss and . . ." began Mary dismissively, but she was interrupted by the king.

With a gigantic wave that almost hit the lantern hanging from the oak beam, the king said, "The matter of your payment is settled. I will give you fifty gold crowns for your work. But, before we talk I must ask you what is wrong with him and what happened during his absence?"

"Yes, yes," said Mary, waving a bony hand at the king as her other scuttled over the table to a jug of red wine. Spider-like, she grabbed the handle and poured a goblet for both the king and herself, before taking them over and plonking down her fat bottom on the opposite chair. She smacked her lips. "From what I can gather your son had ridden to The Red Hills and was hunting within the forest there."

"Arrgh, how many times do I have to tell him not to go near that forest? For once in his life why doesn't he just listen?"

"He is young, my king, he will do as he will. I remember when you were in your twentieth year and you were exactly as your son is, if not more so."

"Yes, but I grew up, I took on more responsibility, and I certainly didn't ride into the face of danger without due consideration."

Thormir didn't think it possible, but his father's frown burrowed even more deeply into his face in frustration. Thormir knew this sign. Over the years he had learned to gauge his father's anger and frustration by how far his brow furrowed when talking. His father sighed.

"So how did he come by his wounds?"

"Well, as I have said, he was hunting in the forest . . ."

"How did you come by this information, Mary? If you intruded into the mind of my son . . ."

"No, my king, your son talks in his sleep."

The king grunted.

"Hunting in the Red Forest, it seems he came upon a deer – the story gets a bit blurred here, but the next discernible bit of information I could piece together was that he was tackled by a warg of Hurst. My king, I fear the boy speaks the truth. The wargs are awakening. Disappearances have been noted around Carathron. The week past, you yourself have received reports from Southron and Vilkas-oudu that people and livestock have gone missing. The town closest to The Red Hills, Vilkas-oudu, has had the most disappearances. Thormir was attacked in the forest near The Red Hills; it remains a mystery as to why the warg let him go."

"They cannot be returning – wargs can only survive when magic surrounds them, otherwise they are just mindless wolves. Mary, I have not forgotten my scripture. Even at my age I remember the accounts of the downfall of magic, the slaughter of the elves, and the crippling of the first alliance. Much that once was has been forgotten and destroyed, never to return."

"Really? Then is it not for nothing that the line of kings holds the tradition of patrolling the old ruins, protecting us from the horrors of Hurst? King Darkin, do you really think I would lie about these things?" Mary took from the pocket of her orange robes a flint and struck it hard. Sparks leapt into the air and Mary went over to a small candle that stood sentinel under the wall painting. She struck the flint again and the sparks took to the wick and the candle caught. Red and gold flame swayed in time to an invisible to and fro of air, before the flame flickered green, then blue, and back to orange. Mary looked at the king. "Only in times of magic does fire change its skin."

Thormir's father was staring deep into the flame. Mary continued to speak and her tone contained great urgency. "My king, you must know of the happenings in the North. Your station as the king has required you to guard the realm of Carathron from The Frostfall in the South, but it is to the North that you must look now. The empire is expanding. The emperor is spreading word of a new religion that will save man from these dark times and lead them to prosperity. He has moved to take Elgaroth and the Carabeorn, and aims to move south until the lands east of The Al'Durast are his. My king, you will notice that he has only taken the cities that lie along the lines of Doreil, the great lines of power, where magic is at its strongest. Do you not think this is a coincidence? The emperor knows that the world is changing – that magic is returning. He will seek to use this and take all the free cities of men. If you do not believe me, look at a map." Mary took a worn, frayed map from her wall. She blew on it once and a cloud of dust enveloped her before she emerged, swiping at the gunk with her spidery hands. "See here," her sharp nail cut into the parchment and landed on a name south of The World's Vein, La'Bometh. "Now, why would he deliberately miss this city? La'Bometh has the most trade, it is the wealthiest city, it has a vast army, *and* it's a strong, strategic point, particularly if he were interested in taking Safria, or even Tyber. He knows. He knows that with the cities that lie upon the lines of Doreil, upon the lines of power, he will more than likely have the use of magic under his control. Change is coming, my king, and you must find allies where you can. My counsel would be to offer an alliance to Lord Bath of Orien. Whatever his crimes, he might consider your appeal since his city will be the first city in the South to fall beneath the emperor's iron fist. Then send word to the towns beneath the shadow of The Al'Durast, where you might find unexpected support for the cause."

Still looking at the flame, which was flickering between blue and green, the king had taken his dagger and was etching out the dirt from under his fingernails. "You speak of things that have only happened in ages past – magic, wargs, great wars of men. There has been no such trouble for a thousand years. We have lived in relative peace, despite the The Darkness that has clouded our minds; I will not go searching for trouble where there is none. True, there have been disappearances. True, there have been reports of troubles in the North, of cities bowing under the word and iron fist of the emperor. But all this is far to the north – we should not trouble ourselves with such things. It is my job to serve Carathron, to serve The Green, not to manage affairs in different kingdoms. As for the colour of the flame, it remains to be seen if magic is truly rising. The only thing I will do now is send word to the six Warlords of Carathron and tell them to prepare their armies, to stand aware, and keep a keen eye. No warg of Hurst or soldier of the empire shall enter Carathron while I remain king. Now, let me ask you this, Mary the Healer; if the claimed *warg* did not harm him, what did?"

Mary sighed and muttered, "Only in death are we the wisest." Then she looked up and her eyes were once again that cold crystal blue. "Come, come then, when Thormir was attacked by the warg . . ."

Thormir shifted in his bed to see an annoyed expression flash over his father's features.

". . . he somehow fell backwards and onto the stem of a miraki plant. One thorn penetrated his skin. It seems that upon realising this, he cut into his arm in order to withdraw some of the poison before it spread. Unfortunately, the poison still spread throughout his body and is taking effect. He continues to have seizures in the night and his mind is beginning to cloud with haze and confusion. I doubt he could draw a bow in this state." She raised her chin and, with her long fingers, plucked a white hair lodged above a flap of old skin. Sniffing, she continued, "But maybe he shall get better in time . . . and it is only time that will tell." Her voice grumbled off into a curse and she spat on the floor.

Thormir lay in the dark, silent, still, and sombre. He felt as if he were broken inside, crippled by his mind. Now he would live in constant fear of an attack, and if it were to be in front of an audience, what then? How was he supposed to take the king's seat if he was as weak and vulnerable as he felt now? He could already hear his epithet being whispered by imagined future subjects, "The Crippled King". He could hear them mocking him, exposing his weakness like raw flesh to the frost. That's what they would call him, "The Crippled King" – too afraid to rise from his seat for fear of an attack. A tear slid reluctantly from the corner of his left eye and more soon followed it. There he lay, silently crying. But no one placed a gentle hand upon his brow or chest to calm his breathing and soothe him. So he did what he had always done when sadness tightened its grip upon his heart; he thought of his mother. He had never known her, but now she was as real as a warm hand upon his brow. And as he lay there, he could feel that hand and the gentle kiss and whisper of reassurance that everything would be all right. He lay still for a long while, holding on as hard as he could to the feel of his mother's hand and her soft breathing. As he felt her, a warmth that had not been there before spread throughout his heart and he felt his breathing soften and his tears ease off. He stared at his mother, devouring every detail, making sure he could remember her for next time. The short, dark hair, the kind, blue eyes, and the way her chin creased when she smiled. She had come. His mother smiled at him and he smiled back. *If only she were really here.* With that thought he saw his mother's smile flicker and the next moment she kissed him softly between the eyes and departed, leaving him in the dark. *Don't go! Don't leave me!* he screamed silently, but no voice came back.

Thormir opened his eyes and saw his father still talking with Mary the Healer. The look of worry upon his father's face was evident as he cast a gaze in Thormir's direction. *I didn't think he cared for me . . . and now . . .*

He heard the king speak, voice cracked, eyes steely. "My son is stronger than you think, Mary. He will weather this storm and will come out of this . . . this shadow cast upon him. My son, the future King of Carathron, will not fall victim to the poison of a plant's thorn!"

Looking up at Mary and nodding, the king said in firmer voice, one Thormir was more use to, "Come, Thormir, all is not lost. We have your birthday celebrations tonight." Brushing away his grey mane of hair, he exited the house.

CHAPTER THREE

FERN
Fern

Fern lifted his head, smelling the air. He could tell horses were nearby, although they weren't moving. The smell of human sweat was vile upon the air. The south winds were still so the scent couldn't have carried far.

Fern was sitting upon a flat slab of rock that formed an outlook over The Long Road leading into Medani. The Long Road had been laid down when the Sons of Artur and the House of Benor had come to the South. It had acted as the main road between Orien and Medani, but now it had been reduced to a mere trail in the snow, occasionally bearing the tracks of cart wheels but more often the footprints of a weary traveller or hoof-prints of elk crossing. Although there was no wind, a winter chill was in the air. The tundra looked cold and uninviting. It stared back at him, telling him his presence was unwelcome. Fern looked at the heavens and saw his mood reflected in the slightly overcast greying sky. Gloomy clouds loomed over the plain, ready to unleash their power of thunder and lightning.

Fern pricked up his ears. Something had caught his attention, but he could not put his paw on it. Then he heard the clash of steel upon steel. Fern looked for where the sound might be coming from, but he saw nothing. He shivered again, shaking his shaggy mane – he tried to ignore the cold. He peered into the heavy fog that obscured the road. Blinking some ice from his eyes, he focused on a stopped caravan that could be seen through a patch in the fog. Men were hurrying around the cavalcade of carts and wagons, trying to calm the horses, at the same time pulling swords and knives from their leather belts.

The man closest to the hill where Fern sat went over to a horse. His brow was furrowed with concern and he began whispering into the horse's ear and stroking the length of its head. Fern was pleased to see that the horse's breathing slowed as the man muttered loving words of peace in its ear.

Inspecting the man more closely, Fern could see from his apparel that he was a trader. He wore plain grey robes tied with a thick leather belt. With his good eyesight, Fern could see that several items hung around his waist. Directly below his navel was a gold piece, slightly larger than a coin and round like a small plate. On the flat face of the gold was an etching of a mountain and an oak tree within a star, the insignia of the traders. Next to this small plate were smaller attachments including a leather hilt, inlaid with silver thread, which was protruding from a plain sheath that obviously housed the blade of a small knife. He could also see a vial of purple liquid. The bottle had been used recently, as it was not secure in its clasp. On the trader's other hip was a small flute, a whip, and a roll of parchment. As the stocky trader stroked the horse, Fern noticed his hand was shaking. He grasped the neck of the bottle attached to his hip and pulled. The bottle came free and made its way to the trader's lips. He arched his back as he drank, savouring the purple liquor.

A spear erupted from his chest. Chunks of flesh and tissue sprayed forth, bursting out of his breast. A spurt of blood surged forward, drenching the horse. The shaft of the spear stopped halfway through the trader's body. The barbed metal head of the spear held what appeared to be part of his lung, drooping limply from the spike. Still on his feet, he took a few steps forward and collapsed in a lifeless heap.

More shouts came from the fog shrouding other caravans. Fern, springing to his feet, leapt down the hill, his great paws pounding the soft grass. Mary the Healer had said to watch over the road and the surrounding area, but she had said not to move if anything out of the ordinary happened. Angrily, he pushed the thought aside and continued to the bottom of the hill. As he drew closer, he saw another trader showered in blood as he buried a sharp, curved axe between the splintering ribs of an ugly thug.

As Fern moved towards the centre of the fight, streaking past three or four wooden vans, he saw a woman and her baby being backed into a corner by three snarling bandits. But was this just a band of raiders, or something else? Fern looked at them carefully. They were unlike any humans he had ever seen. These men were tall, taller than any a man of the South. Each had grey-brown wild hair that fell to their broad shoulders. Two of the men had bright green eyes that shone from their dirty faces like emeralds, but the third had eyes of dark orange, flecked with red shards. The same dark tattoo covered their right arms.

Tribal in design, it could be many different shapes at once and it seemed to move, the ink blotches shifting around under their skin. He had heard of 'the moving tattoo' in his lore lessons with Thormir; and in those lessons he was taught that only one people used that technique, one that had not been seen since The Great Banishment, when the Dacarrus had fled to the west. The Dacarrus, the wild people from across the mountains, had developed the tattoo technique. It seemed the mountain passes were no longer guarded by the dire wolves which, Fern realised, meant only one thing: the Dacarrus had returned.

Fern quickly changed course, leaping over the bodies of two traders and noting that both were still alive but badly injured. Fear now rose up, deadly as any sword, and tried to seize hold of Fern. He had no idea what to expect; he was about to engage with an enemy that he thought had passed into legend. As Fern stopped and began circling the three bandits, he heard one say to the quivering mother, "That's a pretty baby you've got there. Maybe we'll take it as a souvenir."

With that, anger surged in Fern. He leapt over the mother and child, landing squarely in front of them, shielding them from harm. The leering faces of the Dacarrus turned into snarls as they faced the hulking form of the black dog. They showed black and yellow teeth and swore at him in deep, guttural sounds, cursing in their own language. The largest of the three men charged, raising his double-handed axe high above his head. As he did so, the other two ran at Fern, lowering their own axes to swing at Fern's ribs. Rearing onto his hind legs, Fern swung one of his massive paws at the two men, breaking their necks. The blow of the first axe missed by an inch and before the man could recover, Fern had pounced, placing one paw over his soft, unprotected neck. Spluttering, trying to find his breath, the man uttered a barely distinguishable sentence, as he seemed to be speaking in a dark, mutated form of Estarion, "The West has risen . . . The Dacarrus are coming. Darkness shall fall."

Not today. Fern punctured the bandit's throat and watched him die. The Dacarrus, not unhappy to leave this world, lay there feeling his own blood spill from the fleshy hole in his throat. He began to laugh, enjoying the look on the dog's face. *He, his friends, and his family shall soon suffer the wrath of my own people. Through burning fire and bloody metal we shall come, and we will take the South for our own.* Eyes rolling to the back of his head, the Dacarrus spluttered and heaved before becoming another bloodied corpse lying on the ground.

Fern slowly turned his head towards the mother and child, growling. Realising he was scaring them, he stopped and calmed himself. He padded over to them, and winked with one great eye to reassure her. He would have morphed, but he did not want to be seen in his human form by an unknown merchant for the traders shared words as well as goods.

Like the winds before a storm, he heard them coming before they struck. A whistle of deadly arrows hissed through the air and a second later five metal arrowheads buried themselves in the roof of an upturned caravan. Fern barked loudly at the mother and child and, understanding his warning, they fled. He twisted around. On the brow of a small hill was a group of five archers. His muscles tensed as he saw that they were reloading their bows with black arrows, every one of which was about to be trained upon him. In the seconds it took them to reach for their quiver and fit an arrow, a small axe whizzed up the hill and split the horned helmet of the farthest archer. Panicking at the presence of a new enemy, the archers turned, chaotically releasing a hail of arrows. Fern ran, pounding up the hillside. On the opposite side of the hill, two traders rounded the corner of a van and threw four axes directly at the hillside archers. Two of them hit. A gush of blood spurted from one archer, the force of the axe knocking him backwards down the hillside, smearing the yellow and blue tundra flowers with a coating of wet blood and entrails. The third archer had a cleaner death, as the head and shaft of the axe passed right through him, leaving a gaping hole, devoid of innards.

Enraged by their companions' deaths, the two remaining hilltop men flew down the hillside towards the traders. Remaining calm despite the furious charge of the Dacarrus, who stood near seven feet tall, the two traders drew short swords and began to run. As they matched the Dacarrus' pace and were about to clash, they leapt into the air. Fern, who had stopped at the top of the hill, watched as the two airborne men rammed their swords simultaneously into the open mouths of the shouting monsters, the points of their swords emerging victorious from the rear of the Dacarrus' feral heads. Fern tossed his head back and gave a blood-curdling howl. He lowered his head and saw the two men withdraw their short swords, spraying the dewy grass with blood and gore.

The men turned, faces full of concern, as they heard the rear of the line of caravans being attacked. They hurried away, a stream of unfamiliar curses tumbling from their mouths. Fern followed. The party of three found other traders engaged in a furious battle with the rest of the Dacarrus. Fern heard a whisper of footsteps to his left and turned in time to see a huge iron hammer fly towards him. Bright lights erupted before his eyes as the flat of the hammer-head collided with his skull. Fighting through the pain, he used his sabre-like teeth, wrapping his jaw around the man's neck. With a loud crack, it snapped.

The battle was not going well for the other traders. There were forty of them against about one hundred Dacarrus, some of which rode on the backs of ugly creatures that Fern had not seen before. The creatures were horse-like in their height and appearance and had red and grey shaggy fur. Fern could see they had sharp, razor-like teeth that bent inwards, which likely proved useful in close-quarter combat. Around the horses lay slain traders and their fallen riders. The Dacarrus did not care either for friend or foe, making them all the more deadly. Fern decided to attack from above, as this way he would have the advantage. Spitting blood from his mouth, he pounced onto one of the parked caravans and the wood groaned under the weight of his landing. Fern once more began to run full speed towards oncoming danger. Less than a spear's throw away, he saw the leader of the Dacarrus change direction, and spur his steed towards him. With only the thought of protecting the mother and child, Fern leapt into the air, soaring towards the leader's brutish form.

Time seemed to slow for Fern as he leapt. He could hear the leader say in a rasping voice, "Today you die!" and in an instant the two of them collided. He struck the Dacarrus clean off his steed, and Fern tumbled and fell to the unforgiving ground of the tundra. The two landed in a heap but they were soon fighting furiously at close quarters. The Dacarrus warrior was on top of him. He was strong – stronger than Fern had expected. His two hands were firmly planted around Fern's huge throat, compressing and closing his windpipe. Fern whimpered for the first time. *So this is how I die.*

Fern rolled around trying to find footing, and began to lose feeling in his front paws. As if knowing this, the man grinned, exposing his yellow and brown teeth, which were covered in saliva and the blood of an enemy.

Without warning, the Dacarrus bellowed, emptying his lungs of air. The sharp teeth of his steed were locked mercilessly around his upper arm, shredding the top layers of his forearm and biceps. It was a credit to his strength that he kept his other hand firm and unyielding upon Fern's throat. As his arm was wrenched upward, an arrow shot by a trader from a stolen bow pierced the skin below his armpit. He howled in pain and the hand that was pinning Fern down flew to the arrow buried in his bleeding torso. Seizing the moment, Fern shot towards him, biting down on his rib cage. Blood and viscera poured into Fern's mouth. Pulling his maw away from the limp and broken corpse, Fern spat out the bones and tissue. He now saw the other Dacarrus fleeing at the sight of their fallen leader. The traders, who seemed to have mostly recovered from the fight, were shooting and picking off the last of the Dacarrus with the bows and arrows that they had left behind.

The din of battle soon died down. As he watched the men place the sick and wounded in the back of the wagons, Fern noticed there were some larger vans at the back, towards the end of the line. Padding over the blood-stained road, he saw that the carriages were barred and a whimpering sound was coming from within one of them. He wanted to dismiss it, reassuring himself that the traders often brought wild animals to Medani, to show and to parade to the crowds. However, there was something that distressed him about the noise, and only when the sound of orders to move out were given did he continue on his way.

As Fern turned away, his mind cleared surprisingly quickly. He had to get back to Mary. He broke into a run, and as he did so, his muscles protested and screamed, but he sprinted past the men and women that silently trundled towards Medani, carrying goods and supplies to sell there.

Before leaving the caravan, Fern noticed the pile of bodies on the side of the road. The Dacarrus, the foul ones, seemed to mock him even in death, but their much-feared tattoos were now still at last.

CHAPTER FOUR

REVELATIONS
Purgansenus

The Great Hall. It was more of a cathedral than a hall. Majestic, arching beams made from the great musk trees of Hurst traversed the width of the palace. Up close, each beam and each grand pillar was elegantly engraved with glyphs and pictures that told stories of Medani's great kings and wars that were fought in their name. The roof of the building was wooden as well, but its texture did not match the hard tone of the Musk wood. No planks spanned the roof; instead, it was a carved hollow trunk of a single, long-forgotten tree. The knots in the wood were as beautiful as the grain that flowed around them.

Towering pillars were made up of carved vines, twirling around each other to form graceful yet wild columns of sculpted wood. Buried within the wooden vines were tiny strips of silver and gold that could be traced up to the rooftop. In the light of the fire, the styled inlay shimmered, coming to motionless life. The pillars seemed to breathe as the eternal flame gave light to the hall. Even the magnificent tapestries that hung in each corner seemed to breathe in the life of the hall. Immense stone statues stood watch; the permanent memory of the ten kings who had ruled Carathron.

Torches were held in brackets all along the hall, but these were only lit at night; during the day, the room was lit by light that entered the hall through two huge mosaicked, jewelled stained-glass windows at the rear. The left pane depicted a king, in his armour, holding his crown high above him as if to place it on his head. The eyes of the king, called the Window King, were two sapphires that pierced the soul of whoever looked into them. Upon his breast was a coat-of-arms of a silver leaf, itself depicted in silver veins across the window. Next to this symbol was a glowing anvil that seemed to be continually alight, both burning in the darkness of night and in vivid daylight. Below both of these, and surrounded by a triangle that enclosed all the symbols, was a white hand with an outstretched palm. The symbols within the triangle were the insignia of three races: those of the elves, the dwarves, and of men. The window had shown the strength of unity between them as it had been in ages past, but now it spoke only of sadness, and kingdoms divided and fallen.

The right window had been more simply rendered. It showed the shape of a great red eagle, the emblem of Medani. Through the brilliant glass it was possible to see over the entire city, and even to the edge of Hurst Forest, where the dark green blur of trees rested on the horizon.

Between the heights of the massive windows sat the throne of Medani. Made out of pure gold, it shone within The Great Hall, drawing every eye. Despite its dominance, the throne gave off a sense of calm, peace and serenity.

This was The Great Hall. Everything about it shouted royalty, but it was more than that. It was also a place of joy and humility, a place of peace and tranquillity. Any citizen of Medani was welcome within the hall, and many public proceedings took place within its walls. Judgements were passed, orders were given, and new contracts were made, all under the gaze of the Window King. However, on this night, a more private event was taking place. Thormir Darkin, last of the Darkin bloodline, was becoming a man. He stood beside his father, who was in the process of delivering a slow, and considered speech to a small crowd.

". . . We are here tonight honouring those who came before us." He paused. "But more than that, we have gathered to celebrate the return of my son and rejoice in him becoming a man."

Thormir looked out at the crowd. Fifty faces stared back at him, some in recognition and respect for the future king, and some just seeing a boy growing up. Through the shimmering heat emanating from the fire burning in the centre of the hall, Thormir could see a few familiar faces. Amongst the nobles and scholars gathered, giving their undivided attention to his father, were some of his friends. At the back of the crowd stood a few of the maids and lads that had helped around the palace over the years. They looked at him, faces full of joy and admiration, and nodded in recognition of the celebration. For an instant he felt weak at the knees, and a thought flashed through his head: *Oh God, I am going to have another one of my seizures!* The thorn had left more than a mark on his shoulder – it had blemished his very core – his soul. He stood perfectly still, trying to fight off the urge to collapse to the floor and, just as suddenly as it had begun, the feeling passed and once again he was able to gaze at the faces of the crowd that stood before him.

The King of Carathron looked upon his subjects and, with a deep voice, began the ritual. He had clasped his shaggy mane of hair back in a silver brace and he was wearing the ceremonial royal chains. All of his jewels and royal adornments would one day be Thormir's, but for now they flashed in the firelight. Thormir looked out over the hall once more as his father was speaking and caught sight of the ten stone kings staring back at him. He wondered how many men and boys they had seen adopt their titles here, under their watchful eyes.

"To your knees, son."

Thormir winced and flinched as he bent to his knees and remained there as his father spoke over him.

"Blood of my blood." Beginning again, the king took from his belt a thin silver knife, and with one quick motion the king sliced his hand open. Opening his fist, his father leant closer to Thormir and let his blood spill onto his cheeks. Thormir closed his eyes, as he knew he should, and he felt the newly-formed crimson rivers run down his face. Only when he could not feel the drops of blood falling upon his skin did he open his eyes, to see his father smiling at him with a pride not shown towards him until now. Thormir gave a tentative smile back but he could not stop himself and it soon transformed into a loving one.

His father once more turned to the audience. "The Darkins have ruled Carathron since the Sons of Artur and the House of Benor came from the north, and today we still stand as powerful and as resolute as we did then. With my son taking the mantle with the line of kings, he must take the test to see if he is truly a king."

Thormir's father came over and whispered in his ear. "Not to worry, boy, once the spirit is raised you won't have to do anything." He paused. "You are a man now." Then considering his next words carefully, he grumbled, "You are my son".

Standing up, and looking to the crowd, he spoke to what Thormir had taken to be a bundle of rags – an oddity in the impressive room. "It is time."

A crackled voice came from under a fold of the rags. "Aye, that it is . . ." Mary the Healer was removing what Thormir now saw to be a hood. "That it is," she said again, smiling. "The youngling shall no more be a youngling; although young he will remain." She pondered her statement for a moment, and then approached.

Thormir was scared. He hated the feeling. He felt exposed to the outside world, vulnerable. He saw Mary approach and then felt her hand on his good shoulder. He felt a consciousness intrude upon his mind and heard Mary's voice inside his head. *It will be all right, calm yourself. Be calm.*

"So it begins," she said, addressing the crowd gathered in anticipation.

Thormir felt their minds touch again. *I will start by raising the spirit. It will seek to grant you your manhood. Do not worry, this has been the tradition for many a generation. I performed your father's spirit celebration when he was a youngling. If all goes well the spirit will then heal your wounds, although I suspect they will never fully recover. Are you ready?*

Yes, he responded in kind.

Upon his answer, Mary began to chant to the fire in a melodic voice unlike her own.

> *Spirits of the deep hear me now,*
> *for I call upon your strength.*
> *Grant this child of mine the will,*
> *grant him a star upon his brow.*
>
> *Across the sea and wind I call,*
> *come to me, come to me!*
> *Through the rain and fog I call,*
> *come to me, come to me!*
>
> *Forget his injuries, heal them now.*
> *Brush away his ignorance, his night of mind,*
> *for he is young with much to learn,*
> *make him whole as he takes his vow.*

REVELATIONS

Bow in hand, sword and shield,
he rides in the night,
blood of blood, and blood again he lives,
Thormir, son of Dormir, will never yield in fight.

Then Mary switched her verse and in a softer tone she sung, "*Elya en dalon, faeth en scel, krona na enrion ona aran*". Chills ran through Thormir as he heard the oldest and first language ever spoken amongst those who walked upon the earth – the language of Nolwin. There was a time when that language was used to control magic but that time had passed; the language was barely remembered now, and magic no longer played a part in the world. However as he thought this the air in the room seemed to quiver *or was that the smoke?* A silence followed the end of Mary's song and Thormir had just translated the verse roughly to mean, *Day and Night, Fire and Dark, crown this prince into a man*, when he saw Mary bow and exclaim high and in clear Estarion, the first true language used only by men, "Haren gwineth!" *May your road be blessed.*

As Mary's last utterance flew through the air, the fire burst into silver-white flames, filling the hall with brilliant light. The fire changed colour, writhing green and blue, with huge flames flashing at the centre of the hall. Thormir could see the metal spit that hung within the fire turn a glowing red that contrasted with the blue flames, as the heat melted the core metal. All the wood within the circular hearth had disintegrated, leaving hot, glowing coals. Then, as the fire turned a crimson blood red, a spectral blue and red phoenix rose out of the flames. Its wingspan was at least eight feet across; it seemed to be the epitome of power and beauty. Its spiritual form seemed solid, but Thormir could tell that it was beautiful, an ethereal shadow of light. While it scared Thormir, its presence also seemed to calm him. The phoenix flapped its giant wings and the hair stood up on Thormir's neck as hot air rushed over him. The phoenix approached, taking slow deliberate steps, and touched Thormir's chest with the tip of its wing. A tremendous heat rushed through Thormir. He closed his eyes and, as he did so, he felt his wound knitting. He resisted the temptation to scratch as he felt tissue crosshatch and mend itself.

He opened his eyes as he felt the phoenix remove its wing. It stared at him for what felt like an age, and then just as he was about to look away, the phoenix reached out again and gently brushed Thormir's forehead with top of its beak, as if kissing him upon the brow. Heat and energy exploded simultaneously within him. He wanted to scream, but he couldn't. Something held him in place – a power beyond anything he had ever seen or felt – bound him to the ground with invisible ropes. Then he felt another consciousness press against his own. A huge expanse of alien memories resided in his mind. A sea of thoughts whirled through his head until he felt that he would explode. Then, just as quickly as this feeling had seized him, the phoenix released its grip upon his mind and withdrew. Thormir looked in amazement at the phoenix. Winking one intelligent eye, the bird burst into a shower of white flames that were flecked with sparks of blue and red. As he gazed helplessly into the fiery explosion, Thormir thought he saw the wisp-shape of the phoenix plunge back into the fire.

The crowd was staring at Thormir in amazement. A freckled, miserable, old man was gaping at him in shock, his mouth open in a comical 'O' shape. A copper-skinned, young woman had both her hands over her mouth, fright plainly showing in her eyes. An expressively-dressed, fair-haired man looked upset and sneeringly surprised. A small boy was tugging on his mother's sleeve and pointing at Thormir open-mouthed. Thormir was puzzled as to what they were so rudely gaping at. He looked to his father to see a man frightened and stunned by his son's appearance. Thormir looked down, trying to hide his embarrassment and disgrace, and he saw, curling around his forearm, a thin snake of blue energy. He screamed and tried to shake it off but its rotations only increased. Soon the energy faded, leaving a clear burn mark along his arm.

Thormir looked around again, this time his attention was drawn to Mary. The healer was looking at him; her cold hawk-like stare had now been replaced with a gleam of excitement. He reddened under her gaze. In a sharp voice she said, "Come". Doing anything to escape the gaze of his peers, he followed her at a sprint.

After five minutes they made it out of the palace courtyard, passing through the two carved dragons. Like the hall itself, they were old beyond memory and had seen many criminals pass through their gates, as well as the processions of many high ceremonies, but this was the first time that a boy of twenty years had burst out of The Great Hall with an old lady, particularly with one of them shouting. The stone dragons silently chastised Thormir for his loud voice as he turned and yelled at Mary.

"Where are we going and why are we running?"

He noticed that she could move surprisingly fast despite her age. He had never tried to guess how old she was. She seemed to have a face that had seen many winters yet, in all the time he'd known her, it seemed as though she had not aged a day.

"We must hurry, youngling," she paused as an excited frown creased her brownish face, "because that little stunt you pulled back there has got you noticed. What you have just performed was magic and the sort that has not been seen in an age. Magic is returning to the world and the evidence has begun with you. If I am not mistaken, which I rarely am, you are the pebble that causes the avalanche, and you, Thormir, have been Flametouched. But there is no time to explain what all this means. To cut words short, magic has returned, you are Flametouched, and you and your family – indeed, the city – are in great danger."

"But why? Is someone coming for us?" From his time he had spent in Mary's cabin he thought he might know – and dread filled his heart. As soon as he had become Flametouched he had become a target. The worries of southern invasion, of darkness to the west, northmen, and wargs, were as nothing now – for the world had changed and now he himself was the hunted."

"Were you not listening when you were lying in my cabin? The emperor commands his general, The Crow, to move further south, taking cities, and securing the great lines of power. He wants all the main cities under his control: Scree, Stormcarg, Elgaroth, Cainspire, Elbank, Silverhaven. The cities of the North will surely bow to his will. All of those cities lie where magic is strong. Do you see now? When magic does arise, he will be able to find those people who can wield it, and he will use them. In ages past, magic was used for good and bettering the world, but, as with all things, evil took root, and magic became a weapon; great wars took place and the power of magic destroyed the realms of men, and the kingdoms of the last alliance. The first battle of the alliance took place at The Split. Many died there and the stand at The World's Vein became a futile attempt to halt the march of the enemy. Battles spread out across the Carabeorn and soon fire and ash consumed all the villages and towns that dwelt across those lands. The stand at what used to be the majestic city of Roek was to be the final hope, a hope that was to fail. The last battle of that age took place upon The Fields of Celiton. All gathered there – men, elves, and dwarves – all fighting a dark lord of terrible power. He took the name Vandr, and he ruled the lands, setting fire to all that was green and good, for a black evil had taken root in his heart, turning it to ash and coal. In one hand he wielded great armies of men, fallen under his spell of wicked words and glorified promises, and in the other hand he held his unmatched skill in magic. Blood flowed in great torrents on that day and the nights were writhed in fires of burning crimson and fierce colours of blue and green that licked at the sky. The last alliance fell, and all hope seemed to have fallen from the world, leaving only terror and fear. It was amongst the swirling flames and churning blood that the elves choose to suppress the power of magic, banishing it from that age. And so it pasted into lore and legend. If magic be raised again, do you really think the emperor will use it to better the lives of those below him? Youngling, we must get you to safety before he finds you. What he could do with your power . . . it would be dire indeed. And, make no mistake, he would bend you to his will. You will need to learn much – healing that which is sick and killing that which is harmful. Many things are afoot and we must do everything we can to protect those who need protecting. Your father will understand this in time."

A look of worry and pain crossed Mary's face. Thormir gazed at her then his mind turned to his family and friends, to Fern. Where was he? As he began to run on, he asked Mary about Fern. Her face was contorted in concentration. For several minutes they ran side by side, their footsteps beating into the red-grey dust that had gathered on the road. The winds had been hard the night before. It had been said that darkness too had been carried upon the Doriel's breath – The Darkness coming from the west.

"This road is rather steep. I think the palace should have been built on a flat part of Medani, not on some huge, ugly hill. Oh well, nothing we can do about that, I suppose. Now," she said, and turned her head towards him, the wind whipping her hair violently in the breeze, "Fern will meet us outside the city. I told him to stay put and watch for anything suspicious." She laughed a short bark. "He was already doing that anyway. He says the weather is a little foggy but otherwise the road seems clear. So, that answers your first question. Your second question that you were going to ask was 'Where are we going?' Well, I need to get a few things from my house, and pick up supplies in The Eastern District."

Thormir looked at her for a moment longer before turning his head towards the horizon. The sun was sitting halfway across the sky, its heat failing to make it through the cold winds that swept the tundra. It would be dusk soon and then he would have to leave, turning his back on his home and all that he knew. *What have I gotten myself into? What does this mean? What about all I've known? What about my people? What will I tell my father?*

*   *   *

Thormir slowed. Mary had told him to cover his face with his hood as they entered The Eastern District. It would not do to make his presence known here. Thormir had never really explored the eastern district of Medani. He had always heard that it was filthy, and filled with scum and thieves. However, Thormir did know that most of the district was taken up by a huge market. It was an expanse of sprawling stalls, booths and stands, all selling products to passers-by. Fern had once told him that you could get almost everything within the market. Once he had brought back a flask of clear liquid. When Thormir tasted it, it had burnt and stung his throat, leaving warmth within his chest. Despite the curiosity the market held for him, he had never explored the area. It had a dark reputation – thieves and bastards lived there, smuggling goods in from the upper east coast.

Mary stumbled forward, grumbled something to the guard standing at the entrance and motioned for Thormir to follow her. Thormir's eyes were quick enough to detect Mary's sleight of hand – he saw her exchange gold with the guard before they passed through. A nervous-looking man with a shallow face emerged from a side street as they made their way under the gate. He cast Mary a withering look and walked away, pulling on the leash of a small dog. The man shouted at the creature and kicked it so it would hurry up.

"If it weren't for Elisa I would put you down, you stupid mutt." The shallow-faced man jerked on the chain and turned a corner, muttering something about his daughter's love of animals.

Thormir took an instant dislike to him, thinking of what Fern would say about the dog being treated like that. He smiled to himself as the comic image of Fern being put on a leash entered his mind.

Mary turned down side streets with familiarity, nodding to a cast of suspicious and nefarious-looking characters – obviously she knew where she was going. The streets here were dark and the tall, decrepit houses that lined the cobbled stone roads bent in on them, their windows glaring down at them as they walked past. Thormir soon concluded that Mary was taking shortcuts. He was sure the healer would not have used these streets if this were a normal venture to the markets. At a certain point in the trip Mary stopped, looked around, and then whistled a clear, high-pitched note.

There was a scuffling sound, and from a doorway in the corridor between two houses emerged a woman. She had deep-set eyes that appeared grey in shadow. Her slick black hair passed over her face in a wave. Curling one black lock around a thick forefinger, she said, "Arrrr, Mary." Her voice was warm and seductive but within the charm there was a note of deceit. Thormir noticed that her smile did not extend all the way to her eyes. A golden ring sat firmly upon her wedding finger, and it flashed as she spun her hand around her hair. Thormir found it highly distracting, irritating even. "It's good to see you. You have not come for,,, supplies for a while. I was getting worried you'd forgotten me."

"Never," said Mary, matching the honeyed tone of the woman's voice. Thormir looked at Mary but she gave him a glare, warning him not to talk. "I would never forget you, Giselle. Indeed, I was wondering if you did have any . . . supplies."

The woman pulled back part of her shawl and showed Mary some sort of herb. It had the appearance of a dried leaf that had been frayed at the edges; the sort of herb you might chew or perhaps smoke. Gold passed between them, and Mary stuffed the herb into the leather bag slung over her hunched back. Thormir pondered what he had just seen.

As Thormir and Mary entered the main street that divided The Eastern District, a blast of sound bombarded his ears. People, so many people; they swarmed like ants around the day-to-day necessities and treasures, the likes of which he had never seen. As they passed store after store, Thormir saw beautiful paintings, coloured tapestries, intricate mosaics, elegant sculptures, wooden carvings, and many other exotic trinkets. He stopped at one stall and touched the finely-carved petals of a redwood rose. Ten paces behind Mary, he continued to marvel at the art on display. Looking at a small etching of a hummingbird, he decided that if he ever returned to the markets of Medani, he would buy it. Regretfully, he turned his back on the art stalls and continued down the market street. As he went further down, he noticed the stalls were less crowded and those that were more popular had patrons that did not seem good-natured. They looked dangerous and formidable, knives sticking out from under leather belts, always a hand over a hilt – a silent warning to would-be thieves. Bows of Elmar wood were slung over men's backs as they inspected some item or device.

Thormir felt a tug on his arm and he turned quickly to lash out. He stopped his fist just in time. Mary had a firm grip on his wrist. He felt her presence in his mind as she said, *Come on! We cannot linger.* She bustled forward, holding her chin high, avoiding the gaze of a red-headed young man who bore a well-muscled, tattooed chest.

Finally, they arrived at a stall that boasted some shade – a small overhang prevented light from entering the wagon. A man was bent over his parchment, reading with obvious intensity. Thormir could not see his face, just the top of his head. A strangled grey mop of hair fell forward onto the table top. He shifted as they approached, and Thormir caught a glimpse of a charm carefully wrapped around his wrist. There was nothing on the band except an engraved gemstone. An open eye crossed with two swords was embossed on the flat side of the gem, glinting red in the setting sun.

"Aye," The grey mop of hair spoke, "What ye like, Mary the Healer? Western district ye be comin' from, no?" His voice was unlike anything Thormir had ever heard; each word carried its own music. "And with a boy? Interesting that you should come at this late hour, no? Aye well, ye be here. So what can I get you, in exchange? I presume you have the leaf?"

Mary removed the leaf from her satchel and slid it cross the table. The man picked up the leaf, crumpled it into a ball, and popped it in his mouth. He threw his head back and gargled, savouring the taste. Staring at Mary, he said, "Arrr, beautiful stuff, that. My price be paid." He barely looked at Thormir, treating him like a shadow in the dark.

"I would like to see what you have, Dusthane."

Responding to Mary's request, he pulled back a purple rug – what Thormir had considered until then to be part of the table top. Underneath was a glass case. Using one bony and gnarled hand, Dusthane flicked a switch in the shape of a hawk's beak and Thormir watched as the glass case tilted, sliding drawers upon drawers out of the unit. Each drawer was made of chestnut that had been finely carved. Inside the glass case, they gleamed. Within every drawer was a weapon, tools of blood and war. One weapon caught Thormir's eye. It was a short sword. Quite thin at the hilt, the blade widened in the middle then came to a sharp point, all with an elegance that did not betray its deadly nature.

The hilt of the weapon was pure white, with unfamiliar runes engraved into it. A sapphire had been set into the pommel of the sword like a giant unblinking eye.

The other cases housed similarly gilded weapons, each with its own unique characteristics. One axe head was completely hollow; another sword had two barbs on the end, designed to shred the insides of whoever was unlucky enough to face it. In one corner was a spear, its two-headed blade glinting menacingly, the reflection of a line of bows displayed on the opposite wall, mirrored in the cold metal.

Thormir looked over at the bows. They were many and varied. One was a simple flatbow, a length of Elmar wood bent into a U. These bows were famous for their power. They were effective shooters and generally of a good weight. With the right arrow and a strong arm, the bowshot was approximately half a mile. Shot correctly these bows could pierce armour and break bones. Another more elegant selection was a recurve bow, which was painted with gold. The two curves in the bow were shaped like wings, and where the curves joined the grip, the wood had been carved to form points. Though shorter than the long bow, this one looked like it could shoot farther. Further along the rack was a bow unlike any other. It was pure white, like the hilt of the short sword, but it had lines of pitch black that traced and followed the gentle curve. Everything about it screamed his name. This was a bow that had been waiting for him all along, and it was now ready for its rightful owner. Wrenching his gaze from the bow, Thormir reached for his money bag. As he did so, he saw Dusthane talking with Mary, and hand her a long staff along with a bundle of blankets and rags.

Thormir walked up to the counter, "How much for the bow on the end?"

Mary shot him a glance but he ignored it.

"That'll be 1,000 crowns, kid."

He did not have that much money, he thought, letting go of the coin purse. Agitated, he fiddled with his hands, carving the dirt out from his forefinger. Then an idea came to him. His gold ring. Pulling it off his finger, he set it on the table. "Is that enough?" he said pleasantly, as Mary watched him beady-eyed.

"Aye, that be enough," said Dusthane, his eyes widening. He slipped it on his own finger, and seeing that it fit well, he added, "And here be the arrows." He took down the bow and handed it to Thormir, along with a sizeable quiver of arrows. It must have held around sixty, maybe more. The arrows were made of the same white wood with black metal heads attached at the end, each one shaped like a teardrop; a teardrop meant for piercing mail, metal, and flesh.

Thormir placed his left hand on the grip and felt it slide into place. It was like it had been made just for him. He wriggled his fingers and felt each of them fall back into place. The bow weighed little more than his hunting bow. It truly was a remarkable piece of craftsmanship, feeling like an extension of his arm. He raised the bow, drew the string, and fired a non-existent arrow into the darkening sky. A musical 'twang' emanated from the bow before his mind's arrow disappeared into the clouds. Thormir beamed and turned to face Mary. *You have just bought the most expensive bow in the district with a priceless ring. When will you learn to think, child – this has got you noticed.* Mary's voice was loud within his head and Thormir tried not to flinch.

Why didn't you stop me, then? he retorted angrily. Mary thought for a second and then wheeled on the spot, saying: *You need a weapon.*

Thormir smiled and followed her out, securing his hood over his head. He traced the curve of his bow, grinned, and walked on.

CHAPTER FIVE

FLIGHT
Vindir Renna

As Mary and Thormir hurried back through The Western District they were stopped as Jurkin, a palace guard, stepped out in front of them. Jurkin had a slightly devious look about him, with eyes slanting upward and thin lips that curled at one corner. He was not good-looking, but Thormir could see how his angular face could appeal to some of Medani's women.

"You may not pass," he said crisply, securing his grasp upon his spear. "There has been an incident."

Mary stepped forward. "If you do not let us pass, I will personally make sure that you turn into a toad by the full moon."

Thormir thought this was a rather feeble threat but Jurkin's eyes widened with fear and he stepped aside, his green and gold cloak billowing around his legs. Mary strode forward, her new staff punching a hole in the dust and grime. Straining to see why all the guards were crowded around Mary's hut, he could see nothing, but as a guard shifted his position, buffeting a citizen, Thormir caught a glimpse of a red shape marked on Mary's oak door. The shape was drawing a great deal of attention. Passers-by were stopping and gaping at the symbol, mothers pulled their children closer to them, and many men rubbed the pommel of their swords.

As they drew closer, they could see that it was a red handprint. Drops of blood wept from the shape so the wood appeared to be wounded and bleeding. Thormir looked in horror at the macabre sight. He had only ever read about the red hand in thick, dusty, leather-bound books that told of darker times than these. Times when great evils were born unto this world, and when the red hand found themselves strong and emerged powerful, hungry for prey. The red hand was the sigil of The Pale Riders. They had many names, and always resurfaced from the dark places of the world when evil and shadows rise in the hearts of all things. The Pale Riders sense when the powerful arise, but what they crave more than anything else is magic. They feed off it to stay strong – so when magic was destroyed, so were the Riders. Thormir stared at red hand bleeding down the wood. The Pale Riders had sensed that magic had returned; they only had to find it – to find him.

Mary turned to him. "We must hurry!"

Casting another look at the bloody hand upon her door, she took his hand and hastened to the west gate, which led to the stables and out of Medani.

*　*　*

The stables were warm at this time of day. It was dusk and all the animals in the huge barn created so much body heat that it was hard not to be hot. However, small flaps in the roof could be released to let the hot air escape whenever the heat annoyed the stable master, or when the animals became restless. But today the heat was a welcome relief. Thormir had left Mary outside – she had said something about wanting to talk to Tangar. Thormir had taken that opportunity to visit Shadow. He found her pawing the ground and eating some hay at the far end of the barn. Thormir smiled. She had been his companion for three years now, and he would not give her away if his life depended on it. She had saved his life more times than he could remember, including on his recent venture to The Red Hills. As he stroked Shadow's mane he felt where he had cut himself open, where the thorn's poison had spread. *And now I am crippled, my mind is forever forsaken.* Small bumps could be felt where the skin had overlapped. Pulling away part of his tunic, he stared at his shoulder. Like his other shoulder it, once again, was well-muscled, but for the white scars that shone in a cross, perpetually marking the spot where he had been mutilated. He fingered the pale cross and lamented the fact that he would carry these marks for the rest of his life.

Opening his mind, he felt for Shadow. Soon he could feel her mind within his. He flashed a series of happy and sad emotions across the link so she would understand that they would be leaving soon and might not come back. She tossed her head, snorted, and looked at him. Her huge amber eyes blinked once and he severed the link; she had understood.

Bir trudged out from behind a pile of logs stacked at the edge of the barn. "So, you're leaving again." It was not a question. He did not look angry or sad, there was simply acceptance in his eyes. "Arrr well, the animal must leave the barn sometime." It was a profound thing for Bir to have said; it was not often that wisdom spilled from the mouth of Bir, more often it was an excess of mead.

"How did you know?" said Thormir, taken aback.

The corners of Bir's mouth twitched. "I have a sixth sense about these things," he said, tapping his nose, and leaving a black grease smudge there. "Also, you're carrying a bow and strapping three weeks' worth of food onto Shadow." Bir turned his massive back upon Thormir and walked down the row between the animals, the dry hay snapping under his weight. Nearly at the barn doors, he called back, "I was never here!" As he turned and walked out the doors, Thormir heard him begin a low chant, a few of the verses floating back to him.

"The mighty smithy stands tall,
sit upon his forge.
His bellows be wide, his hands be tough
hammer in hand, his face so rough,
so the smithy stands.

Morn 'til night the village hears his blow.
Slow to the beat be many a strike,
yet never does his hammer slow,
snub-nosed and blackened of face, he carries his task,
so the smithy stands.

Upon steel stork does his hammer land,
then to the water does metal burn,
only to come out bright in hand . . ."

As Bir's voice faded and he began another verse of song, Thormir realised he was still stroking Shadow, his hand following the smooth brush of her hair. Clicking his tongue, he urged Shadow to follow him out of the stables. As he left, he ran his hand over the carved horseshoe, tracing the shape for good luck.

Emerging from the barn, Shadow trotting at his heals, Thormir was surprised to see Mary already seated comfortably upon a white mare. Mary gazed down at him imperially and said, "This here is Essendar, and one of the finest you will ever find." Thormir did not disagree; the sheer purity of the horse seemed to hold it above any other. Essendar tossed her head at a snow fly and a sheet of white hair passed over her neck like a blanket of silk. Mary patted the horse's neck and Essendar stilled, calming herself. As Mary shifted her grey saddlebags and rucksack, Thormir noticed another horse behind Mary, a majestic stallion, on top of which was a figure he recognised – Tangar. Tangar's horse did not match the purity and elegance of Essendar, but it was easy to tell that the stallion would run to the ends of the earth to serve his master. The horse bowed its head as Tangar muttered his name and one could tell the extent or depth of the affection the stallion had towards his master. The horse held his head high and gazed at the emerging stars that glimmered through the overcast sky. The stallion was a patchy grey and white, like fallen snow upon a cobbled road. Tangar sat, sentinel-like, looking to the heavens. He looked at the flickering stars, but his stare was unfocused, as if he was so deep in thought that he couldn't see them. Across Tangar's back were two sheathed swords that crossed in the middle and ended at each hip. Over the swords was an unstrung bow and a large quiver of arrows. Tangar was indeed heavily armed, which seemed at odds with his calm demeanour. Thormir let his eyes wander to the saddle. Like Mary he carried the necessities – food, water, potions, and shelter – the weight of which had been carefully distributed across the saddle and back of the horse. In addition, strapped to the neck of the horse, was a leather cloth that held in place eight small throwing knives, also sheathed.

Before Thormir could ask, Mary answered his question, "The horses of the Tangri people can carry a lot more than normal horses and still run at great speed. Funnily enough, the only one who does not have a Tangri horse is me. Shadow and Lothruin here were both born into the Tangri people. How Shadow came to be here I do not know."

Thormir took a step back as if he had been struck. He whirled around and looked at Shadow. She winked at him, opening and shutting one great eye. He had always known she was special, but he had never suspected that she belonged to the horses of the burning north. He wished he could examine her mind so he could see her home and what kind of place she came from. She nuzzled him in the crook of his neck and he scratched her behind her ear, marvelling at her beauty and mystery.

Mary continued, "Although, I'll say one thing, I have ne'er seen I horse like yours before, Thormir – all the horses of the Tangri people are usually grey and reddish brown. A black Tangri horse is truly special, you should take good care of her."

"I know," Thormir whispered, still looking at Shadow, "and I will."

With that, Tangar and Mary rode towards the gate, kicking their steeds into a light canter. Swinging one leg over Shadow, Thormir reached for her with his mind and urged her to follow the others. Settling into the saddle as Shadow ran, Thormir set his thoughts towards Fern and his news.

* * *

Shadow, Essendar, and Lothruin galloped up the slopes of the tundra. The three horses passed glassy lakes, grazing deer and elk, and small farming estates set within small villages on the outskirts of Medani. After half a day's ride, they came across what looked like a tower that had been valiantly battling the ravages of time.

Drawing closer, they saw a small windmill standing at the top of a hill. From the top of the mill, one could look out over The Red Hills and even see the curve of Old Man's Hillock in the distance. The windmill's sail creaked in the ice-cold winds sweeping the snow-ridden landscape. The wood groaned in protest at the bite and push of the elements. The tower was made out of huge, rounded blocks of stone that fitted perfectly together – no room for a nail to slide in-between. It had been made with the finest craftsmanship; it was wonderful to behold, a beacon to all passing over the plains. Like the tower, the house was made of stone, faultless in craftsmanship. It had sat beside the mill for many a year and all anyone knew of the place was that it had always been there, and someone had lived within its walls. Passed down through the generations, the windmill had always stood there, listening to the whispers of the wind, its history all but hearsay.

Standing next to the house was a boy. He was completely nude except for a loincloth tied around his waist. As a shifter, from dog and to human, Fern never seemed to need a coat or any type of fur; indeed he never seemed to want it. People had laughed at him, but soon became jealous as the long nights descended, and the bitterness of the Carathron winter set in. Now, he stood, grinning at Shadow's rider. Fern eyed the other two horses warily as all three raced towards the top of the hill.

Thormir stirred from troubled sleep as he felt Shadow slow to a gentle canter, then a trot. He opened his eyes and stared at a majestic windmill that seemed so old that it was a wonder it hadn't fallen apart. How long had they been riding before they had reached this mill? Rubbing sleep from his eyes with his knuckles like a bawling baby, he looked around. Essendar and Lothruin were both grazing on lush grass, damp with melted snow. Lothruin nuzzled the soft brush of a starflower and, as a seed came free, and floated upward, he sneezed. Thormir couldn't help but giggle at the absurdity of the situation.

He looked around to find Mary and Tangar. Touching Shadow's mind, he urged her to stay, and leapt off the horse's back. As he hit the ground, he felt something rattle and remembered that he was still wearing his bow and quiver. He drew the bow and notched an arrow, noticing again how at one he was with his bow – it fit his hand so perfectly.

Thormir walked up the hill a few paces, rounding the corner of the windmill. He stiffened. Something moved in the shadow of the mill. He heard the soft crunch of snow. Thormir pulled the bowstring back further, his muscles tense. A rabbit hopped out into the sunlight, blinking and twitching its ears. Thormir straightened as he let go of the worry that a large, furious beast might be poised to ambush him. He looked at the rabbit, nibbling on a blade of grass pushing through the snow and spilled grain. He cursed – he hated being wrong. Only hours ago he had told Tangar that as they travelled north he would not need the heavy fur that clung uncomfortably around his neck; now he shivered into it, remembering the laughs that Mary and Tangar had shared, taking obvious enjoyment in his ignorance.

"It is many a day until we reach The Tongue of Hurst, and only there does the temperature change its mind." Tangar had said. "Treasure your furs; they can be used for many things – not just the warmth of your body."

Thormir sniffed, and his nose immediately objected at the cold air. He looked at the rabbit again, which was now digging for seed. Grinning foolishly, he thought anything that innocent should be able to live.

Noticing the rabbit stiffen, Thormir looked around. Nothing moved. Then, suddenly, with a blur of red and grey, a fox sprung out of the shadow of the mill. It pounced on the rabbit, its jaws closing around the creature's neck. Thormir heard the small crack that extinguished the rabbit's life. Bile rose in the back of his throat. He continued to stare. The fox paid no attention and, with the dead rabbit hanging limp between its jaws, it stalked passed him.

Disgusted with what he had just seen, Thormir turned and continued to explore the mill. The sound of frost crunching under his leather boots was loud in the morning air. He walked down the side of the mill, brushing his hand against the flowing grain of the stone walls.

Soon enough, he heard voices nearby. Thormir could tell it was a heated discussion between two people and as he rounded the corner, leading to the back of the house next to the mill, he saw Fern run up to him, extricating himself from the arguing Mary and Tangar. Thormir glanced around Fern to see Mary pounding her staff into the ground, clearly frustrated by Tangar's stubborn nature.

"Hey, I heard what happened!" said Fern, stopping in front of Thormir.

"Yes," Thormir said. "One of my more memorable experiences."

"Well, I just talked to Mary; it looks like we're staying here. I had a look around while I was waiting for you to arrive. It's no palace but it seems safe enough. Mary thinks it will be better if we travel at night – she mentioned something about a red hand. The woman who lives here has agreed to help us."

"So, what is Tangar arguing about?"

"Oh, he wants to keep on riding. He wants to get as far away as possible from open ground. He seems to think something has picked up our trail and is hunting us."

Thormir followed Fern indoors. After further conversation with Fern, in which Fern gave an account of the events with the traders and how they were attacked, both of them fell silent and looked out of the window. The miller's house was not spectacular, nor was it something to be admired. From the roof hung oddments: tools, and dead animals hung up to dry before cooking. A few herbs hung there too, giving the place a warm, homely feel. The only light in the room was a small candle. Mary, Fern, Tangar, and Thormir all clustered together inside. Dusk had fallen fast, and this seemed the safest place to stay for the night, far away from prying eyes and wagging tongues.

*   *   *

Midnight, the hour of the wolf, was merciless, the frost from outside crept under the gate. Despite the hour, the sky outside was steel grey. Frosty winds sliced the tundra, laying paths of ice and thin snow. The grey and black ice flattened the small pebbles and crumbled the hopeful grass of winter. It was cold, very cold. Some of the roof tiles had broken and their shattered remains lay on the floor, their gaps taken up by the bitter winds. Even the horses, which had been led inside for fear of the tundra's bite, were restless, shuffling this way and that, as if a sudden presence were making them uneasy.

Only hours earlier the small room had been home to a bright flame and warm bowls of soup, but now the claws of darkness and chill had tightened, sinking into what was once homely, draining every bit of comfort and warmth. The frost gathered upon the fabric of the hanging tapestry and turned the otherwise warm picture into a sinister scene of ice and snow.

In the darkness within the small room, small fingers of ice glowed as they crawled under the door and across the crusty carpet like tiny white centipedes. But the cold did not just walk on the ground, it flew in the air, catching in throats, and snuffing out the warmth of a single candle. Fern had changed into his wolfish dog form and was sitting quietly by the stony, fireless hearth. The chill had got to that too. That was the worst thing about the cold, it was that it formed an alliance with the pitch dark of the night.

The cups were now so cold around the edges that Thormir's lips stuck to the vessel when he tried to take a sip of his mead. He was doing so out of habit, trying to keep himself moving, and his mind from the knives of the winter chill.

Fern had growled once or twice at Mary. Her decision to stay the night in this place was not a welcome one, now especially, when the winds had set in during the early hours of the wolf. Sometimes called the 'wolf hours' these were the hours when dark dawn spread throughout the land and The Darkness spread its feelings of dread and the terror of tomorrow upon the mind. Thormir bit his lip as another gust of wind drew icily across his face. Outside, monsters scampered quickly through the night. Thormir could feel them, although he did not know who or what they were. He just knew that they were creatures that would tear flesh from bone, or maybe even devour limbs whole, like the ancient black serpents that crawled from the deep places. They were also fast-approaching, their whole will bending to one objective: finding him. Mary also seemed restless and Thormir wondered whether she too was recalling the old stories that spoke of dark things born of death and malcontent – things that bent to the will of evil. He shivered. How long would they have to wait out this night? The drapes covering the window billowed at his thought, and again he shivered with discomfort.

Eventually the owner of the small house bustled into the room. Until a few hours ago Thormir had thought that he had been in an abandoned home, but soon enough he had found out that the residence was keepership of the small, kind lady, Eyda, who had taken them in for the night. Smiling at him, she came to the table holding a small stub of a lit candle. Carefully, she placed it upon the hard wood and removed a loaf of soft bread from under her arm. Thormir joined the lady at the table and began to eat. He savoured the warmth of the flame and the dough of the fluffy loaf. But Thormir still felt that sense of fear that had been stalking around his mind all night. In the candlelight, Thormir saw Eyda's rosy cheeks shining red like two softened cherries, but the wolf hours brought darker thoughts and soon his mind was busily imagining that the soft red of her cheeks could bleed and the smile lines around her mouth could stretch and gape wide in terror. These are just thoughts and figments, he thought, and shook his head trying to rid himself of the night's terrors. And yet they clung to him like the silvery spider webs he saw woven into the corner of the room.

The three horses stirred at the back of the room. Before Tangar or one of the others could calm them, they tossed their heads this way and that, seemingly looking for a way out. Abruptly, Shadow made a noise unlike anything Thormir had ever heard before; a low, whining sound. She was scared, terrified by some unseen will. The other two were also making harsh noises that grated upon the ear, adding to Shadow's distress, which tore at Thormir's heart like a rusty knife scraping raw flesh.

Thormir saw Tangar rushing to the horses, trying to calm them, and Eyda's expression of benevolence transformed into the face of terror. *Where's Fern?* Thormir swivelled, heart racing, searching for his brother. He found Fern in a corner, but rather than his normal, confident self, Fern was backing away under a table, his hackles raised. Trying to contact Fern via mind-touch, all he felt was fear, utter fear, and then Thormir's mind was rebuffed and he had no choice but to sever the link. Something was coming. There was no doubting that now; and it had brought the terrors of tomorrow and the unnatural cold with it.

There was a stable nextdoor that Tangar had previously thought too risky to house the horses, given that they would be easy prey to horse-thieves. However, seeing their distress, he led them through one at a time, all the while keeping careful watch. He saw to it that Essendar, Shadow and Lothruin had sufficient hay then bolted the door. He returned and nodded to Thormir in acknowledgement and the two tried once more to sleep through the cold.

Screeching suddenly filled the air. Three piercing cries, followed by the sound of wings. These were not wings of an eagle but of something bigger, and the sounds of the screeches were piercingly sinister, and could only herald death. The living world had forgotten that sound, only the old stones were able to remember the cries of death that issued from those terrible beasts. The cries rose again, and were joined by more voices, coming ever closer. By now, they were circling.

Eyda, summoning all the bravery she could, told them to hide in the basement. Pulling back the crusty carpet, she showed them the way through a trapdoor that was wedged between rough flagstones. She stayed above ground, saying that the absence of a homeowner would warrant suspicion. Just as they heard the stilling of monstrous wings and the tread of three pairs of metal-shod boots outside, the last of the small company made it through the trapdoor and shut it with a heavy thud. As soon as the carpet ruffled over the floor, leaving a slight crease over the hard wood, the lady left them in the dark and went over to the counter. Eyda began to bustle around the room and through a tiny crack in the trapdoor and the thin knit of the carpet, Thormir could see her hiding the bowls of soup and jugs of mead that they had abandoned.

Eyda turned from Thormir's view, so he was left to imagine the terrified expression upon her face. *She has done so much for us and we have returned only worry and fear.* A sense of guilt welled up within him, but was quashed by his overwhelming fear. Despite his fear, Thormir wanted to help her – he wanted to rush at whatever was to come through that door, but lies and secrets were the best way of staying safe. Their flickering hope was entrusted to stealth and deceit. Hearing the door smash open, he felt his gut churning over.

Unseen by Thormir, a figure in a black tattered hood stood in the doorway, leaning heavily on a knotted wooden staff. Eyda picked up the rasping sounds coming from beneath the hood and she stiffened. *I can't move! Help!* But her thoughts went unheard. There was no visible face beneath the cowl, only a swirling, shapeless shadow, yet it held her gaze, the unseen eyes forcing her to remain frozen where she was. Although she could not be sure, she thought this thing, whatever it was, had to be a man or male – for his stature was tall and broad and his presence filled the small room. He wore a grey, leather tunic, which was protected by sheets of dirty white cloth that hung from around his neck. The figure's demeanour was so crude and harsh that Eyda wanted to turn from the rancid image. Gradually the rasping breath slowed into a low marauding hiss. Hiss. The sound went on forever, tightening around her chest. Her eyes bulged as she caught a glimpse of a silver dagger tucked into his belt.

The tread of two pairs of boots sounded on the icy gravel path outside and two more figures entered. They were just as the first figure, dressed in grey with vile white cloth dashed with black: the pure image of evil. The first figure looked directly at Eyda, who was frightened, and he deemed her disgusting, expendable. She was repugnant, no one would miss her, she was nothing – something to be used then discarded. To him she was fat and ugly – it would be so easy for him to slip his blade into the vault of her stomach. He would love that kill, it would be like carving a plump pheasant. But the urge was withheld.

The black hood tilted slightly. "When a nessst is broken, do you know what happensss to the birdss that can't fly?" He did not give her the chance to answer. "Those repugnant mutationss fall from the tree. They fall from the place which they thought was . . . safe . . . pro-tect-ed." He watched the lady as his voice transformed to his hiss. "They fall, and when they hit the ground, featherss broken and gashess on their belly, they find an animal which is willing to take them in. Have you taken in those broken, battered birdsss?"

Thormir was still watching through the floorboards. *Surely she would break.* He saw the pale face of the plump lady who was standing rigid, struck with utter terror. He turned to Tangar, about to ask him for help, but Tangar was busy hitting his flint, trying to find a spark.

Above them, the three pale figures encircled Eyda, like gigantic, terrible bats. Their harsh flaps of dirty cloth had been parted and now rusty gauntlets shone in the light of the waning moon that pierced the holes in the window drapes.

"Where issss the boy?" The edge of the first man's dagger flashed as he lowered it and Thormir saw his gaze focus upon the place where the horses had lain. He was grateful that Tangar had moved them to the stable. Raising his head, the figure sniffed the air, then seizing upon a scent he swivelled and gazed directly at the trapdoor. "Of course, when a broken bird falls, it alwaysss . . . leaves a stain." Slowly, he marched to the crease in the carpet and bent down. With a powerful yank, he revealed the trapdoor. With one hit of his armoured fist, the lock broke. Thormir heard the clink of the broken lock being tossed aside. Hearing a scrape and seeing the door lifting, Thormir turned to find Tangar now holding a bent bow and a flaming arrow. Training it on the trapdoor, he waited. Fern whined in one corner and Mary crouched in the other, muttering unfamiliar words under coarse breath. The door lifted and a harsh, grating sound preceded what came next.

The pale figure appeared. No face could be seen under the cowl. It looked down at them and whispered one word. "Birdsss." Then it shrieked, high and piercing.

Tangar released the arrow, which instantly took to the tattered cloth that the figure wore. The shape turned and flew out of the doorway, followed by his kind. They heard the flap of massive wings and then silence fell over them, blanketing their fear and quieting their breathing.

"Who were those men?" Thormir asked gravely.

"Those were not men, Thormir, and they do not ride upon any creature of the air that has recently roamed the skies. They are The Roc Riders, The Pale Riders, The Sceleg."

"Rocs? Were not those the birds of legend turned sour by the darkness that spread from Ironholt so many years ago? And now they have riders?"

"Yes, even in the Great War they had riders. Always The Roc Riders, The Pale Riders, travelled in the shadows and night, for they cannot withstand the heat of fire or the touch of the sun. But now they travel close to the sun's rising, their will grows strong. They desperately seek your magic. They are driven by their desire to feed off you and drain you of all life and power, for only then will their own terrible power be fully restored. We have become the hunted. Our road has become more dangerous and perilous than before. From now on we must travel by day, but tonight we ride. I do not think they will attack again during these wolf hours. But remember, we are being hunted. Be on your guard, and be wary. It is two weeks, if the weather holds, until we reach The Tongue of Hurst – if we are lucky the Rocs will not come for us again."

Thormir shuddered. He felt the stirrings of a seizure. Soon he would have another one, one of those cursed fits, the result of the miraki thorn's wound that scarred his shoulder. Lowering his hand from his shoulder, he thought of The Roc Riders and what they would do to him if he were found again. And so the night endured, and fear was allowed to linger, sinking its claws into his heart.

*　　*　　*

Thormir, Tangar, Fern, and Mary crossed over the plains of Guldor; the only part of the tundra that had a name that was not human. It was said that in the Third Age an elf called Guldor, ruler of the first four high houses of elves, with his people, tended to his lands, and that under his rule, the plains hummed with life.

Birds of all shapes and sizes nested there and all that was good in nature dwelled in peace – untouched by any darkness or seed of evil. Guldor and his kin sung to the earth and through the power of Nolwin, the forests and the plains heard their words, and all things understood their language. The music of their language called upon powerful magic, which they used to weave palaces of silken grass, and create vast, wooded halls amongst the towering trees. But, as with everything, time devoured the elves, as it is the executioner of all things. The beauty of the elves, who were once so loved, was soon forgotten by the grass and the birds. Only the ancient lays passed down through bards long of years remember their sad story.

The tundra here was no longer as icy, and where there had been snow-melt, there was a long expanse of grass that reached endlessly towards Hurst and the horizon. As Thormir rode over the grass, he noticed that it was studded with dew, and he named it *the weeping grass*, a fitting name, for nature wept at the passing of the elves. As he rode he noticed how the frosty air that hung around the southern plains of Carathron had changed into a cool, refreshing breeze, but still he was grateful for the thick furs that he had brought with him. The night was becoming darker now and stars could be seen winking red and gold in the world's roof. He could only hope that a shadow of a Roc Rider did not pass before them. Thormir flicked his eyes to his right and saw Fern, his great, shaggy body running alongside them. He had been talking with Fern constantly about what had happened in the mill. He reached out with his mind to Fern and asked, *How long 'til morn, do you think?*

Aye, replied Fern, *I was just thinking that myself. My paws are hurting, although this soft grass is easier on my paws than the icy ground near the mill.*

Thormir blew his hair from his eyes and said, *Okay, let's make this interesting – I'll race you to the next hill!*

Okay, you're on, Fern looked up at Thormir and winked. *Go!*

As soon as Thormir touched her mind, Shadow put on a burst of speed. Her hooves powered over the wet grass. Wind blew into Thormir's eyes and hair. He bent lower over Shadow. He looked at Fern, who was right beside them. He had lowered his angled head so that he was perfectly streamlined. The muscles on Fern's forelegs bulged as he ran. Thormir laughed and tossed his head just as Shadow did. He and Fern were neck and neck, racing over the flat between the two hillocks. Thormir rose in his seat slightly and urged Shadow to speed up. She nodded her head in response and increased the beat of her hooves. As he and Fern neared the top of the hill, Thormir heard a soft booming sound, but he ignored it, putting it down to the racing of his own heart. They reached the top of the hill at the same time, both laughing, Thormir aloud and Fern within his mind.

A massive foot landed between them. The ground shuddered. The foot was the size of a small caravan. It was completely circular, with five toenails buried in the flesh. The leg that rose up into darkness was covered in a brownish red fur that grew on top of a thick hide of wrinkled, grey skin. As if in slow motion, the colossal beast moved again, bringing its other leg down, this time close enough to almost clip Thormir's boot in his stirrup. As it made to bring down its foot again, Thormir had just seconds to prevent himself from being crushed in two.

CHAPTER SIX

BLOOD AND STONE
Rola roa calx

THUMP

Shadow reared up, almost throwing Thormir clean off. Fern stopped with a yelp of surprise, his hackles raised. The leg passed over them and was replaced by another. The ground shook violently.

Thormir realised that the animal had not noticed them, as it showed no sign of alarm. They were directly under the creature's belly, and Thormir was able to look up at the great torso, barely discernible against the pitch-black night sky.

The sound of hooves drifted up the bank, preceding the two horses. "We ride," said Tangar. Lothruin seemed calm despite his pawing at the ground. Tangar tugged on the reins in his left hand warily, and, urging them to follow, rode into the darkness. The night swallowed him.

Thormir thought there must have been a herd of whatever type of animal it was, as half a mile had passed before the ground stopped shaking, and the footsteps of the colossal beasts formed a distant tremor.

Rays of dawn were breaking over the horizon, illuminating the landscape around the group of companions. They were completely exposed on the vast plains, and the only cover was a forest far off into the distance. As they drew closer to the forest, he saw a flock of birds burst into the sky, exploding out of the dark green slip on the horizon. It was as if they were fleeing the woods with terrified screams. Mary called out and, turning his head, Thormir saw her heading for a small manmade formation of great pillars of stone that had erupted from the ground long ago. As Shadow drew closer to the stone pillars he saw strange runes carved into the stone. Nature had reasserted its dominion over this place long ago, but the majesty of its former glory still lingered about the ruins. Fern saw the runes too and he padded up to the nearest column and touched one carving with his paw, tracing the complex shape. Looking around, Thormir thought that this place must have been an ancient watchtower. Attached to his hip was his small hunting knife and, on his guard, he instinctively fingered the hilt. He had not forgotten The Roc Riders and the sun had not yet fully risen from its slumber.

It was still reasonably dark, despite the faint rays of light desperately climbing over the horizon. To his surprise, a sudden wave of utter sadness engulfed him. Thormir felt a lump rise in his throat and tears form in his eyes. Wiping the tears from his eyes and cheeks, he looked at the others. They too wore similar expressions. A sadness of incredible power hung over this place, as if the whole world mourned the loss of a loved one.

Essendar trotted beside Shadow and Thormir heard Mary whisper in a choked voice, "This was the last outpost of one of the greatest kingdoms this world has ever known. The once great kingdom of Dwarvenhiem lost to the last Great War and the downfall of magic. It is a place of grief and sorrow. Arr Barukdithil, how you are missed. You once stood proud, but now you are alone, and you are crying out for your makers, are you not?" Tears spilled from her eyes. She did not wipe them away, but instead let them fall. Each teardrop honoured the dwarves. "Do not be afraid to cry for your tears are not of pain, but in honour and in memory of a lost kingdom."

Thormir looked at the watchtower and felt the lump in his throat tighten. The roof of what was once the stone tower lay shattered upon the ground. Gargantuan blocks of stone lay still, as grass and moss grew over them, letting their glory fall into memory and time. The base of the tower remained standing, its top exposed to the elements. Mary dismounted Essendar and, leaning heavily on her staff, walked over to the base of the tower, where she ran her fingers gently over the fallen stone. Then she walked over to the door of the ruined entrance. She searched the surface of it with her hand and then pushed on the decrepit wooden door. It swung open and Mary disappeared into the tower.

Thormir dismounted, and left Fern and Tangar with the horses, still feeling the tightness in his throat. He followed Mary into the watchtower. The entire wall of the circular tower was covered in books. Varying from small to large, each book was bound, covered, and identified with a name and numeral. Silently, Mary drew a book from one of the higher shelves, leaving a dark gap in the ragged volumes. She handed it to him. Thormir looked at the cover of the thick book. Gold leaves were woven into the heavy material, the stems underlining the title.

He read the title aloud, "The Codex of Radieth Alzar: Written in the 47th Year of Princess Ellichem the Fourteenth's Rule". Repeated underneath in the same runes that Thormir had seen spiralling up the stone columns outside was what he assumed was the title in Dwarvish. Opening the dusty cover of the book, Thormir found, to his relief, that the language was his own, although the hand in which it had been written was, at various points, difficult to read. The first lines, however, were easy enough to decipher.

This book and script is to be placed and read in the great watchtower of Barukdithil; what the elves name Baradamroth, and in human tongue, Shadowwatch. Between the pages of this book are the records of the many spells and commands used by those who wield The Gift, The Light, The White Shadow. This book is not to be used lightly, for many have died for the sake of keeping the secrets that lie within these pages. I, Radieth Alzar, dwarf of the Valmar clan and Ambassador to the Tangri people, do claim that this book is not complete without its brothers.

Thormir shut the book with a snap and turned. "You knew!" he shouted in surprise. "You knew this was here. But how?"

Mary smiled sadly and said, "I suspected the book might be here, I did not *know*."

Thormir looked down at the book and saw, within the open pages, many words of power. Turning to the contents of the book, he ran his finger over four of the largest chapters within it. One gave instruction on fire, one taught the manipulation of water, another tutored in stone and earth, and the subject of energy and air took up one of the final chapters. Under each line of writing was a translation into a different language. It seemed that apart from what he had read, the entire book was written in Nolwin, with some of it translated into Estarion. So this book must have survived the Great War, for it was only in the Fifth Age that men began to speak in that tongue, forsaking Nolwin as their language. How can it be that old and look not a day more than fifty years – especially when it has been left to the elements and the cruel winters of the Carathron? Thormir turned to chapter one, "Hellesar". Next to the title was written, "Flrr". Thormir recognised "Firr" being Estarion for "Fire" and marvelled at the fact that he was looking at writing that predated the coming of his house and the Sons of Artur. As he looked at the title page of the chapter, scanning the page of painted flames, he muttered "Hellesar". A small ball of flame leapt into existence and hovered in front of him. It illuminated the base of the tower with an orange light that showed no sign of changing colour. Mary, who had been running her hands over the spines of the books, spun on the spot, her eyes widening at the sight of the ball of dancing flames. Thormir noticed that the flames seemed to be getting bigger, and he allowed his mind to open and calm, which appeared to reduce the flow of energy he was giving them. As he did so the ball stopped growing and stayed the size of a large cabbage, warming the morning chill. Looking up the word for stop, he muttered "*Stova*", and the flames vanished, plunging the room back into the dark of dawn.

"That was impressive, youngling, but do not try any more commands until we find the other two books, for only then is proper instruction given. Nolwin is a powerful language and many things that were not meant to be shall come to pass if you speak wrongly. Magic does not forgive mistakes. It is a long journey and we best be off, The Tongue of Hurst awaits us."

With that, Mary turned and made her way towards the door and back to the waiting horses. As Thormir followed Mary out of Shadowwatch, he noticed a faint glow coming from around the huge stone pillars that rose out of the ground. Slowly walking towards one of the columns, he felt heat touch his check. Warm air seemed to emanate from the stone, which was bathed in a soft blue light. It kissed his face. He drew closer, reeled in by his curiosity. Rounding the wide girth of the stone, Thormir stood in the light of dawn, and found ten glowing plants that were swaying to and fro. At first he thought they were some sort of mushroom, as their rounded tops indicated a connection with the column. But as he looked at the blue lights, he observed their thinly-veined tops and the way small beads of light flashed within their jelly-like heads. Thormir took a step closer, marvelling at the beauty before him, and as he did so the lights spun ever faster until the ten plants seemed to pulse and flicker, causing an immense heat to fill the surrounding air. Water droplets formed on the pillar and ran down the stone, twisting and turning through smooth groves of the carved runes. In that moment the plants seemed to hover, and then, with a surge, all ten of the glowing orbs came free. They floated in the air, their light blue tentacles hanging below them. With a gasp, Thormir realised that they were not plants at all, but animals. He stared at the cluster of beautiful creatures and they seemed to stare back, their momentum varying as they saw him. The gaze of the creatures seemed to look right through him. He reddened. He felt exposed, naked to their unwavering gaze. Then, as they flew upwards, gently moving the tentacles to gather speed, it was over. Thormir looked on, feeling the sadness overwhelm him for a second time, though this time it was because his worries and wariness seemed to have been lifted from his back for as long as he was with the creatures, but now those feelings were back again, and darkness closed in upon him again, enveloping him in his own anxiety and disquiet.

*   *   *

Thormir opened his mind until he could feel the life force of every creature that surrounded him. From the unease of a tundra rat, which was hiding under a moss-covered stone, to the focused concentration of the wildcat that was stalking a hare through the tall grass, he could feel the life force of the world within his mind. Thormir focused his mind on the white hare eighty feet away. He felt the knotting of muscles and the hare's exertion. He sensed fear and hesitation within the hare's mind. The dark red emotion flickered as the hare felt the wildcat's run cycle increase, and heard the panting of the predator draw near. Thormir's heart raced, then he grimaced as he felt the hare's life force extinguished. He withdrew his mind and, as he did so, the exposure he always felt when doing this exercise faded and then ceased.

Thormir looked around at his three companions; Tangar, silent as ever; Fern, happily lopping beside the horses; and then to Mary, who was squinting at him, assessing his performance.

"You will rest now, youngling, but we will soon practice again. You have done well, but you are exposing your mind too much. You must reach without reaching, touch without feeling. You must shield yourself from the outside, for if you don't, anyone could control your thoughts, examine your mind, or even kill you. You must remain in shade while you bathe in sunlight; you will be a shadow in the night. For, if you are to be successful in the practice of mind-touching, then you must go unnoticed by others."

As the companions reached the top of the gentle slope, Tangar stood up quickly in his saddle. He was squinting, looking at a point about a half-mile north of their position. He shielded his eyes from the few bright rays of sunlight that licked the ground. Thormir followed his gaze and saw a couple of buzzards circling above a small cloud of disturbed snow powder and tumbled rock. Three figures could be discerned amongst the dust, two on horses and another who seemed to be lying on the ground. His hands were bound with thick rope and the men were dragging him in circles after the horses. Shrieks of pain and desperate agony accompanied the mocking tones of the jeering men, which floated back to the company who watched from the hillside.

Thormir twisted in his saddle as Fern let out small growl.

"We have to do something – we can't just leave him!" Thormir winced as his exclamation was punctuated with another scream of pain.

Tangar was already untying his bow from his saddle with one hand, while at the same time taking an arrow from the quiver upon his back. Unlike Thormir's bow, his was longer and arched in a single curve. As the knots tying the bow fell free, Tangar raised the string, pulling it to his cheek, and with inhuman speed, he loosed two arrows towards their targets. A second passed until the first of the horsemen fell, collapsing limp upon his horse's neck. The second man tilted and fell sideways, as the arrow was stained red, passing straight through the hollow of his neck. The laughing of the horsemen fell silent, but the agonised whining of the bound man continued.

The company rode down the ashen slope. The dawn's first light had covered the landscape in different shades of grey, giving the morning a stony look. As they neared the balled-up man, Thormir noticed that Mary turned her head slightly, as if locating the exact position of the tortured man's cries, listening to the intensity of his pain. He thought nothing of it, just another oddity that Mary so often displayed. Just the other day he had caught her building a rock pile and saying, "It's turtles all the way 'til the bottom." He'd left the statement unchallenged. He thought the rocks she was using did look a bit like the patterned shells of the green and yellow turtles he had seen during his natural history lessons.

The man shivered; he was cold and in pain. As Thormir looked at him, a wave of pity and revulsion broke over him. The horses that had belonged to his aggressors were no more; Tangar had shot both in the head, despite Thormir's furious objections. Tangar believed the horses should be killed so no trail would be left that might lead soldiers or a stray hunter to their tracks and Mary had agreed. Tangar retrieved the arrows, wiping the gore from their barbed tips and returned them to his quiver.

Thormir cast a sideways glance at the horses and the men piled on top of one another. Fern, who was in his human form, had helped Tangar shift the bodies, moving them away from the injured man. Mary cut his bindings, and set about applying an ample amount of what looked like green dust to the bleeding scrapes and wrapping some spare linen around his stomach. She asked for his name but he responded by shaking his head. Either he was so hurt that no words could part his lips or he did not understand their tongue. Thormir thought the latter – for many odd tattooed runes ran across his face. Mary seemed to be staring at them and from the glint in her eye Thormir gathered that she might know something of the matter. Apart from the wounds severing the skin of his chest and belly, he was a fine physical specimen. Thormir, who was proud on his own strength and form, recognised that this man could easily best him in a fight. His ripped tunic revealed that he was not overly muscular but the sinews upon his arms, chest and abdomen showed clear signs that he was extremely strong and possessed superior endurance. A tattoo of a red and black dragon ran the length of his right arm, with the tail of the crimson beast wrapping around his forefinger. Another tattoo was etched into the side of his face, the ink running across his eyes.

Removing a small metal clip so that her hair fell in dirty orange waves down her back, Mary inserted it into the cloth, fastening the end of the bandages.

"You shall ride with me," said Tangar. It was not a question, but a statement. Gently, he picked him up from the sodden ground and helped him onto Lothruin. As he did so, the click of a half-sheathed sword was heard and Thormir noticed a hand and a half sword buckled to the man's waist. That was the only item he carried, along with his olive leather belt and tan tunic.

Tangar hoisted himself onto his saddle, carefully moving his body, adjusting to the extra weight and shape of the injured man. Tangar grabbed the reins and kicked his heels. Thormir followed, watching the white bandages wrapped around the strange man absorb the beads of blood that were still leaking from his side.

*   *   *

After two weeks and however many days, the full majesty of Hurst Forest came into view. It was no longer a dark green line on the horizon, but a towering force of gigantic trees, ominous sentinels of the tundra. They stared out over Carathron, the watchers of the South. They seemed to rise up into the clouds, watching over the tundra, acting as gatekeepers to the people who lived in this corner of the realm. The trees were so huge, so immense, that only the canopy of the forest moved, swaying slowly in the bite of the frosty wind.

From the maps he had studied during his free time at the stables and between lessons, Thormir knew that this was known colloquially as The Tongue of Hurst Forest. It separated the tundra from the world beyond. At the opening of the forest lay a city – or was it a town – the name of which eluded Thormir. He knew that Brogin lay south east from the tip of The Tongue, but could not think of the name of the city that they were approaching. He felt Shadow breathing heavily under him, so he touched her mind to reassure her: *We are nearly there. I admire your grace and courage. Your hooves must be the strongest in all the land.* Thormir recalled Mary instructing him on how to use his mind to talk with Shadow, and he smiled as he remembered their first exchange of thoughts and feelings. That had been so long ago.

At that he felt her acknowledgement, through the bob of her head, her snort, and the soft, warm glow of her mind. He retreated back into himself and began the exercises of concentration and mental agility that Mary had taught him. As he sat reciting the names of plants and solving set riddles, he let the rhythm of Shadow's hooves relax his mind.

When he next opened his eyes, they had come to the outskirts of the vast forest. He let his train of thought float away, and beheld a sight unlike any other. While the watchtower they had passed brought with it the emotions of pain and sadness, it also had a terrible beauty about it, like the last petal on a starflower being blown away by the first of the winter winds. The grassy plains and the weeping grass had a certain beauty as well – the last reminder of an ancient race that was no more. However, the sight that Thormir now looked upon was different to the rest. Here he beheld a magnitude unlike anything he could have imagined; the size and majesty of the forest was overwhelming.

*   *   *

The light of the fire cast eerie shadows under the huge root that arched over them. Tangar was standing by the edge of the mossy hollow in which they had set up camp. He stood looking out over the vast plains as if searching for signs of life, or the slightest trace that they were being followed, but no shadow over the moon could be seen nor hoof beat upon the plain heard.

As the company had drawn closer to the forest, Thormir had overheard Tangar and Mary debating the location of the camp. Should they camp on the edge of the forest or further in and risk the night in Hurst, a dangerous place to be even in the day? The two leaders had decided to camp upon the outskirts of Hurst, as they would have a good vantage point and it would provide a comfortable place for the horses to rest and gather their strength. As they had not brought spare horses with them, their three horses had experienced an arduous journey in which every ounce of their strength and endurance had been pushed to the limits.

Stirring from his lookout, Tangar turned and silently walked over to Mary's saddlebags and took out the bundle of rags that Thormir had seen her buy from Dusthane back in The Eastern District. He unrolled the rags onto the forest floor with a small flick of his wrist. On the unfurled white linen were two beautiful curved swords. The beauty of the identical swords seemed to be diminished by the poor light. Nevertheless, they were unlike any sword that Thormir had ever seen. The swords had no cross guards, but rather each blade joined seamlessly with the leather of its hilt. Each hilt was a hand and a half, which seemed odd, for these swords were not like any hand and a half-sword that Thormir had seen at the smiths in Medani, nor those he had seen in the weapons market. The blade too was shaped in a strikingly unfamiliar way – the metal was folded on both sides of the blade, with a groove running down the middle. The line of the sword was straight, apart from a curve at the end – the tip pointed away from the swordsman. Tangar picked the two swords up by the hilt and signalled for Fern and Thormir to join him. Fern morphed into his normal form and joined Thormir in walking over to Tangar.

"What do you think?" said Fern, grinning in his usual manner.

Thormir blew his fringe out of his eyes and said, "Arr, I don't know what Tangar is doing, but check out those swords! Have you seen anything like that before?"

Before Fern could answer, Tangar had joined them and they both fell silent. "We will fight. I have noticed that you both are inexperienced with a sword. Thormir, you have the hands of an archer – now you must have the hands of a warrior. Fern, your paws will not always be there to aid you, so you to must learn how to wield a sword. For the first half of the lesson I will show you the form known as 'earth'. In this form you and your sword must be one." He continued, "You must *know* your sword and know the limitations that you find when you use it. The earth can both be soft and firm; you can sculpt it and carve within it. This is how you must be. In this form you must be as flexible as softened clay, but as immovable as a mountain. When fighting, this form is used as a defensive position."

Tangar demonstrated, moving back and forth, each stroke of his curved sword was a mixture of parry and counter-attack, which dealt deadly blows to an invisible enemy. His accuracy and precision were so impressive that Thormir wondered where and how he had learned his skill. Not for the first time, he wondered how old Tangar was, noting between his arcing strikes, his blackened face and naturally silver hair that revealed no signs of age. After ten minutes of Tangar performing the earth form, Thormir had the form memorised – every step and every motion. If they moved the sword one inch further than it was supposed to go, Tangar had the both of them repeat the process. Tangar kept them at it for nearly an hour, and even then he was not happy with their progress.

Then a voice they did not recognise spoke. "You are not moving your wrists enough."

The three of them looked around. The bandaged man walked towards the group, holding the hilt of his sword with his left hand. He looked Thormir over, slow and steady, and seemed to take in everything about him, from the callouses in the skin on his fingers from where he had held his bow string, to his overhanging fringe and the loose flap of leather that hung from his right boot.

"You are not moving your wrists enough. May I?" Looking at Tangar, the man said, "Would you care to spar with me?"

Tangar returned a wary nod and with incredible dexterity pulled out the two long knives attached to his back. He twirled them in a figure of eight motion and took up a stance directly opposite the bandaged man. Thormir hardly thought this was a fair fight; Tangar, who was a skilled swordsman, was about to challenge a poorly-armoured man with strappings around his torso, covering the ugly wounds that sliced across his ribcage and chest. Nevertheless, he took up position and held his larger sword completely vertical. From where Thormir was standing, he saw one of the man's tattooed eyes reflected in the flat blade that was just inches from his face.

"YAA!" Tangar attacked, swinging both his swords in a horizontal motion, blurring the colour of the steel with the rapidity of his blow. The bandaged man stood still until the very last moment, waiting until Tangar's blow was inches away from his cheekbone, then twirled and parried the swing, moving his larger sword in a swift arc. Tangar paid the man's parry no attention, performing a complex riposte. The opponent back-stepped and caught Tangar's first strike upon the slight guard of his sword, then twisting, he slid his blade out from the hold and blocked the second offensive aimed at his ribs. Pushing Tangar's attack back, the man feigned right and then performed a series of overhand blows; left, right, left, each strike ringing the air.

Performing a succession of steps Thormir recognised, Tangar relaxed his swords, lunged, slid below the overhand swing of the bandaged man, and came to rest lying in his back on the moss. With one movement, Tangar flipped himself back in the guard position and waited. Turning aside to ward off an oncoming blow to his back, the man stopped, twisted and smiled, as if nothing else in the world were more enjoyable than swapping blows with an assailant.

With a spraying of sparks, the two engaged again, their swords binding, both men pressing hard. Tangar had the advantage with two swords, but when they had engaged, the bandaged man had trapped Tangar's right sword with his left armpit. With a show of strength, he twirled to the left, forcing Tangar to let go of his trapped sword, while at the same time raising his hand and a half to Tangar's exposed neck. Unbeknownst to him, Tangar too had raised his own sword to rest on his collarbone. The two men looked at each other, panting. A line of fire seemed to link them together, burning within their eyes. Just when Thormir thought they might take up arms again and exchange blows meant to wound or even kill, the two men broke off, grinning at one another. It was the first time that Thormir had seen Tangar smile, and the transformation it wrought upon his features was astonishing. His stoic expression had grown familiar to Thormir, but this new happiness was so unexpected it shocked both Fern and Thormir.

Pulling the blade away from Tangar's neck, and sheathing his sword with a click, he shifted his bandages further up his ribs and said, "I am Lucian. I have never faced a swordsman such as yourself. Your style is unique, to say the least – you are wise to teach it." He turned to Thormir, brushing his long, matted hair from his furrowed brow. "Did you notice how I kept my wrists loose? Doing so allows you to move your sword quickly and into many different positions, as well as increasing accuracy and the strength of your blow. If you have a firm grip on your weapon and strike a shield or such like, your wrist will jar, thus you must keep your wrists loose." Lucian grinned a big toothy grin at Fern and Thormir, but despite the expression of joy on his face, Thormir saw a sadness in his grey eyes, and wondered what could have happened in his past that had filled him with such profound sorrow.

For half an hour more the small group practised sparring, first Lucian and Tangar, demonstrating and instructing, then Fern and Thormir repeating and following their guidance. They were forced to stop when Fern won a sharp rap upon Thormir's wrist, causing lines of pain to shoot up his arm, but he took pleasure in the pain and the sweat he had earned. He was becoming a warrior, not just a skilled archer. The more he practised the forms and ways of fighting, the more likely he would be able to succeed in protecting those who lay exposed to the sword of the emperor.

CHAPTER SEVEN

HERITAGE
Endanza

The intensity of the howl was what frightened Thormir the most. The figure he was watching was slumped over a small, dark mound in the grass, crying out with his mind and voice, begging the heavens to show mercy. His howls split the quiet night like the screech of an owl, echoing around the forest. Pale fingers of moonlight touched his face, and then, in the half-light, he collapsed, shaking, exhausted, his cries unanswered. Thormir sensed a shadow creeping over his mind and the man's sadness became anger, a fury that could go unmatched by any mortal. He continued to shake, the small shocks evident in the shadow of the moonlight. Other forms came forth, but Thormir could not see their faces, as their hoods shielded them from the light of the moon. They stood over the figure, and two of them touched him on the shoulder. He flinched but did not brush away the gesture. The man fell silent and the night seemed to engulf the group in darkness; the landscape and all there was to be seen fading away into the greys, purples, and blacks of night.

Thormir opened his eyes. The dream had seemed so real, so vivid. He was certain it was unlike any dream that he had ever had before. It felt every bit as real as memory, as if he had been there, and he had watched that man cry over the grassy mound. He even felt the tightness in his throat and the hot tears running down the side of his face, tracing a path upon the curve of his cheek. But that was not what scared him, what scared him was that the men of the South were known to have dreams that told of the future. If that was his future, he did not want it. The pain he had just felt . . . he did not ever want to experience it again. He slowly donned his riding tunic and leather coat, and tied his belt, securing the position of his small hunting knife. After debating for a second, he decided that he should take his bow – better to be safe. His knees clicked as he arched his back and stretched, arms lifted high, angled back towards the sky. Appreciating the brisk bite of the morning air, he crept out of the camp and made his way through the small lumps that were the slumbering forms of his companions.

As Thormir walked deeper into the forest, a pang of homesickness overcame him. He was entering a world of secrecy, where everything was whispered and no city of men was free from the emperor's influence. Bir, the stable master, was now a distant memory. The picture of his face faded in his mind. Even his father, whom he usually disliked being around, was lost to the depths of memory and time. Then he thought of his mother, resting in peace under a twenty-year-old oak that stood in the middle of the High Graves that lay outside the walls of Medani. He drew upon her face, the one he had never known; the short, dark hair, the kind, blue eyes, and the way her chin creased when she smiled. But she did not appear before him this time. *Has she too abandoned me to this hell?*

And then it was upon him. He was shaking all over, uncontrollable, gasping for breath. It seemed to last for hours.

All of the memories of his previous life whirled around within his head until he became confused and dizzy. What was he doing here? What was the point of running? Surely running from the last free city of men was a bad idea? Wouldn't the place where he would be safest be Medani? Then it was over; the seizure was gone as quickly as it had come, and the pain of it began to fade into cursed memory. But his thoughts remained with him. *I will go back to Medani and resume my old life, I am sick of running. If there is a fight, I will fight.*

Thormir looked up, ready to turn back to camp and share the news that he would no longer run and instead would return to his old life and let events take their course. He had been walking among the trees for half an hour, allowing his feet take him in any direction, and he seemed to have come into a clearing in the vast columns of trees. Sunlight was streaming upon the ground, bathing it in yellow light that shimmered over blades of waving grass. The sight was so beautiful, so unlikely, it was as if summer and winter had become friends who were sharing breakfast together, melding their two personalities; so that the chill of Hurst Forest became less apparent and warm sunlight melted the night's dew.

Thormir caught sight of a doe standing on the peak of the grassy knoll, something you would not see in the southern deepest parts of Hurst – for only dark things lingered there. He took a step forward, gingerly reaching for the bow and quiver he had slung over his back. Taking two arrows and fitting one onto the string, Thormir took another step. A twig snapped under his leather boot. The doe raised her head, swivelling her ears. Just as she was about to lower her head once more, Thormir stepped out from behind a tree. The doe stood, looking directly at him. He could see her neck muscles flex with nerves, but still she held her place, standing regal upon the hillock. Thormir pulled the bowstring back and was looking down its notched sights, when he saw that the doe was walking towards him. The animal walked with dignity, placing her hooves carefully upon the ground. It was halfway down the hill when Thormir decided to shoot – after all, he needed the food and he had not seen so much as a rabbit since he had arrived.

He fired, but his fingers slipped. The arrow whizzed off, and sped off over the hill. Still the doe approached, but Thormir did not take another arrow. He'd gained a level of respect for the creature. There was now an intimacy between them. The fact that he had just tried to kill the doe, and that it did not mind, was comforting to him. As it reached Thormir, its head brushed up against his hand, and he rubbed it behind the ears. Its fur was soft and warm and it hummed softly as his fingers scratched the pink skin.

The doe swivelled its head and stared up at him for a long moment, searching his eyes for what exactly, he couldn't tell. Then, without hesitation, it sprinted away from him – up and over the hillock.

"Wait!" Thormir shouted and ran after it. "Don't go!" He felt strangely drawn to the creature, and when he reached the peak of the hillock and found no sign of it, only a sense of emptiness. For a brief moment he had gained a friend who accepted him for who he was, not what he was. He trudged down the hill. At least he could find and retrieve the arrow that he had fired.

Looking up as a new ray of sun split the canopy, he saw two birds dancing around each other, flying with such energy that they seemed to glow. As the birds flew closer to him, Thormir could see that something beneath their feathers seemed to shine and glitter. Sun birds. He had heard of the creatures from the greybeards that sat on street corners telling tales to the young children, but never did he suspect that they actually existed. Thormir continued to stare at them until the two birds landed on a thin tree stump coated with jagged bark. The birds were chattering around each other, hopping this way and that. Just as they began to sing to the rising sun, they caught sight of him and took flight. Swift as any hawk, they flew upward and burst out of the treetops far above. But all was not lost, for the birds seemed to have lifted the heavy air of the forest, and new light was touching that which had previously gone unseen.

Thormir focused on the rough bark. He moved his hand towards the jagged edges. An explosion of tiny, vividly-blue wings erupted from the bark, and he saw that it had not been the bark of a strange tree, but the wings of thousands upon thousands of blue butterflies. He watched as they spiralled upwards in perfect helixes reaching for the sunlight.

Thormir found his arrow embedded into a tree not far from the hillock. To his disappointment, the head was slightly twisted. He took the arrow all the same – maybe later he could see if Tangar could mould it back into shape.

Thormir turned and started back along the greenish-blue forest path. In front of him he noticed a small stone pillar with moss covering the base of the column. Picking at the leather cuff he wore on his right wrist, Thormir cautiously approached the stone. Like the pillars at the watchtower, the column was engraved with heavy-set runes, interlocking circles, and patterns of weaving lines. They were so intricate that when Thormir tried to follow one groove, he soon became lost amongst the others. The very top of the small pillar was shaped in the likeness of a pyramid; the point, once sharp, was now blunt and mossy, but the moss did not fully obscure the surface of the stone. One side was clear – the side facing Thormir. He peered closely at the runes and lines carved into the stone. The lines seemed to swirl in the middle of the stone and whirlpool into larger, arcing grooves. Looking closely, he saw that within the swirl were four small holes drilled into the stone with obvious dexterity. Putting his eye to one of the holes, he saw that it ran all the way through and pointed at another smaller column in the distance, which he otherwise would never have noticed was there.

"What are you doing?"

Thormir shot upright and whirled about. The rest of his company was standing behind him, and staring at him with inquisitive expressions. It was Fern who had spoken, standing with a puzzled grin creasing his wolfish face.

"What are you doing?" he said again, looking down at the stone Thormir had been examining.

"I don't know," he said defensively, but not unkindly. "I was just looking at this pillar. It seemed out of place, so I thought I'd have a look at it. The runes surrounding the four holes in the middle of the column, they are the same as the ones we found at the watchtower."

Mary stepped forward, sliding her feet over the mossy ground. Where she was about to tread was a root, sticking out of the ground, forming the shape of an upturned horseshoe. Just as Thormir opened his mouth to tell Mary about it, she stepped over the obstacle, seeming not to notice it. Shutting his mouth, he and the rest of the group watched as Mary let her old hands explore the rough surface of the stone, as if searching for something. Finally, she found the holes in the middle of the runic swirl and inserted four of her figures. The holes twisted her hand into an awkward position, but she didn't seem to mind.

They watched as the swirl of stone moved clockwise with the movement of Mary's hand; the circles grinding and setting their teeth on edge. Finally, when Mary's arm and wrist were quite contorted, there was an audible "click". As if realising what this was, the group watched as the swirls stopped, the stone key now unlocked. Mary removed her fingers and stood up. She looked down intently and waited. Then, after a minute, the ground before the stone opened up like a gaping maw, and revealed a shallow, stone staircase. Each step was perfectly carved. The staircase looked like the jaw of some great, ancient stone beast, either ready to devour them or lure them into the underworld. However, despite the razor-like stone steps, a bright ray of light could be seen at the bottom of the stairs.

"I will go first," said Mary with a stare so intent that here was no point debating the issue. Thormir and his companions watched as Mary slid her foot onto the first step then the second, keeping her left hand pressed against the cool stone wall. The group followed, their footsteps echoing in the small passageway.

Sunlight. Bright sunlight streamed in from the outside world as they emerged from the tunnel. The walk had only taken five minutes, but they seemed to have misjudged how dark it was in the tunnel, as the intensity of the daylight dazzled them. Despite the short the time they had been in the passage, they were forced to wait until their eyes adjusted to the light. Mary seemed to have no trouble with it, however, and stepped forward, making her way down the steps until she arrived at the entrance of a great stone basin that stretched for miles into the distance and plunged downward into darkness.

"Welcome to the lost city of Immoreth," said Mary. "The outermost stronghold of the Dwarven realm. Hidden deep within the forest, only the dwarves and those who are learned in Dwarven lore know where it lies. As well as stretching many miles outward, the city plunges into stone for two miles and can hold over 2,000 dwarves at a time. The dwarves named it Az Osten du Baraklemen, which in common tongue translates to 'The Breathing City'."

"Why name it that?" asked Fern.

"Because the stone here is alive," said Mary. "You will see this if you touch the walls. Touch the stone and feel it breathe."

Going over to a beautifully-carved sculpture depicting a Dwarven hero wrestling a great bear, Thormir laid his hand on the breast of the animal. At first he just felt the cool stone beneath his outstretched palm, and then just as he began to remove his hand, he sensed something more. The rock had begun to slowly rise and fall. The movement was barely noticeable but it was definitely there; a measured breath of life. Thormir tried to reach out with his mind, aiming his thoughts towards the stone bear, but hit an iron wall of nothingness. The carving must have been alive in breath, but lifeless in mind and body.

"How did they do it?" said Fern, voicing Thormir's unasked question.

Smiling at Fern, Mary said, "Why don't you ask them yourselves? Your books and lessons in the fancy halls of Medani do not hold the answer to every secret and mystery in this world."

Dwarves? I thought they all died during the last great battle of the age, thought Thormir. He could feel his heart pounding with excitement. *On the other hand, they could not just have been wiped entirely from the realm in an instant.* He had read in his books and his lessons that dwarves were the oldest of all the races and that their god, Numak, great sculptor of the heavens, had made them from the fallen boulders of the greatest of all the sky mountains. Thormir reached into his mind for the name of the sky mountain but found nothing. Suddenly, Thormir remembered the name of the dwarven king who had led them to victory in the Great War. King Tyran, the greatest and last of the Dwarven kings, and as he said the name in his mind Thormir felt the name emanate power. *What I wouldn't give to meet a dwarf, the things they must have seen!*

Excitedly, Thormir asked Mary, "Did King Tyran live here?"

The question seemed to surprise Mary. Her eyebrows nearly disappeared into her bushy fringe. "No," she said, "I doubt it very much. Certainly he might have visited this place many times, but no, I do not think he lived here."

Why is it so quiet?

Lucian, who was further into the city basin, shrieked. It was an unusual sound from a man so large. "Bodies!" he shouted. "There are bodies in the city – dwarves, I think. All dead, their bodies are crushed and broken. Do not come too close; I think disease might have taken them in death. Some evil has befallen this place."

Tangar immediately drew his bow and notched an arrow. Mary leaned heavily on her staff and began muttering under her breath. Fern padded up to Thormir, nudging his leg and baring his long white teeth into the darkness. Thormir felt Fern's consciousness brush up against his and ask, *What shall we do?*

Answering Fern's question aloud, Mary said, "We shall go further down; the air here is heavy with death. We'll see if we can find something that will tell us what has happened here."

*   *   *

"Arrr, the greatest wonder of Az Osten du Baraklemen," said Mary. "This is the forge of Immoreth, the forge of the undying flame. You should be honoured, younglings, for you are standing where the great Dwarven smiths would watch over the hammer and anvil of old. But it seems that the evil that has befallen this place has taken much more than lives. Memories, I fear, they shall leave here. The great will be forgotten."

The group was silent as it beheld a great pit of glowing embers. Lucian walked over to a stone statue of a dwarf raising a hammer in preparation to strike his metal. It was a simple carving, roughly hewn from extra stone, but its nature was somewhat moving to them all.

Thormir walked away from the open forge and down into an abandoned side street. Silence enveloped him. His heart raced. The dwarves had been truly wiped from Vâryá. The relief and excitement that they had all felt at the discovery that the dwarves were still alive was so short-lived that it felt like an iron blow to the stomach.

Only the 'chirip, chirip' of a rat broke the silence. Thormir felt a strange peace in this place. He knew that the bodies of a dead race lay in and amongst their houses and streets, but still he felt peaceful here. *Maybe I could come back here,* he thought, *when all this is done I could convince some people from Medani to come and rebuild this place.* He entered a house on the corner of the street. He had to duck his head to make it through the entrance, but once inside he had no problem standing. Strangely, the houses here were actually much larger and higher than the ones in Medani. Thormir couldn't help wondering if the dwarves had built such large structures to compensate for their small stature; a slight smile crossed his lips as he amused himself with the thought.

"Hellesar," he whispered and a small flame flickered on his palm. While the flame was hot, it only tickled as he held it above him. It had been too dark to see normally, but with the conjured flame held aloft Thormir could clearly see his surroundings.

Looking around the spacious room, he saw that whoever had owned this house must have been someone of standing within the city; as the light danced around the room, it hit many gold and jewel-encrusted ornaments that stood on forgotten stone tables. The remnants of old and discarded food were strewn on the benches and scattered across the tiled floor – the last bites of a slain dwarf. There had obviously been a fight within this house – many of the owner's possessions were scattered haphazardly across the ground: a broken kettle, a silver candle stick, a brilliant shield carved with incredibly intricate, interwoven patterns, the hilt of a small dagger, the broken leg of a wooden table, and a gold necklace with purple lace flowing through the links like so many waterfalls cascading until they pooled around a circle of gold in the middle of the arc. Picking the necklace up, Thormir examined it. It was cool to the touch and heavier than he had expected it to be. To his amazement he saw that runes were engraved into each of the small links. As he ran his fingers over the gold oval at the end of the necklace, he felt an edge mar the smooth surface. He carefully prised the gold apart, to reveal a portrait of a lady who seemed to be in her mid-twenties. He could not be sure of her age, for he knew that dwarves could live extremely long lives. *For all I know she could have passed her first century.* She was very pretty with long, flowing hair that spilled down her side and out of the picture. Her eyes were chestnut brown, and she wore a gentle smile that lit up her face and complemented her sunflower yellow robes. Around her neck was what seemed to be a replica of the necklace that Thormir now held in his left hand. Thormir wondered whether this woman was the wife or daughter of the household. He turned right as he made his way back through the house, passing the shield and the broken kettle and the table of stone, which looked like it had been formed from the bedrock itself.

Thormir decided to keep the necklace because he felt he should not forget this place, and he felt that this small item had not yet played its part in the world. He emerged from the house, ducking his head and blinking as his eyes adjusted to the new light. He extinguished the small flames that danced in his palm by cutting off the feed of energy he had been providing. He looked back up the street, past the bodies of the dead dwarves that lay strewn upon stone steps, crumpled between doorways, and beneath blocks of rock and fallen beams. Only now did he notice that the dwarves were not alone. Men joined the dwarves in the sea of corpses that lined the streets; their bodies were twisted and bent with arrows and axes that had been buried in their flesh, their faces contorted, their eyes a milky-white, and their mouths sagged in a silent scream of demented terror. Most of the men wore black armour, but some had nothing more than a grey tunic. All were broken in death. This battle had not been of ages past, but one that had just happened; it was a massacre in which a race that had lived in secrecy, and had been presumed dead, had fallen for the final time. To Thormir, the dwarves had returned to his present for a single moment, only to be squashed by the emperor's fist of steel. His eyes fell upon the nearest body. The grotesque soldier had his unseeing eyes open, and the whites had turned a sickly pale. But in death the man had not given up the standard he bore. He held a great, wooden pole to which was attached a banner made of crow feathers, upon which was painted the sign of The Crow. *The emperor must have known of their existence, then.*

Thormir moved further up the street, wading through the sea of bodies. Already he felt the bile rise in his throat, threatening to spill into his mouth. He felt the sole of his boot land on the palm of a dead hand and he winced. *Arrrgh, I am sick of this! I have to find Fern and the others.* This city of dwarves was destroyed, its people slaughtered, and sickness poisoned the flesh of all who lingered in the place. It was time to leave.

When the group arrived back at the gaping door to the city, Thormir looked back, and anger took told of him. *Who would do such a thing to so many people?* Of course he knew the answer. Upon his heart he vowed that one day evil would leave this place and be brought upon the people who did this, and he would be the one to do it.

*   *   *

The thunder of hooves rumbled over the ground, making the trees on the outskirts along The Tongue of Hurst shudder – *Horses, twenty, perhaps more*, thought Tangar, *I must warn the others.* The wind, which was blowing in undecided gusts, had tossed the smell of horse and sweat-ridden men over the small

span of ground between the two companies; so when the fifty or
so men rounded the pinewoods that marked the outskirts of the
Hurst's forested Tongue, Thormir's company were armed with the
excuses and a fictional tale they had each made up that accounted
for their presence in such an isolated area. They were outsiders
after all.

Tangar had warned them not to panic and ride away, but
remain calm so as to not raise immediate suspicion. Heads
downcast, trying to appear inconspicuous, they were not noticed
at once, for it was only when twenty or so brutish-looking soldiers
had passed that the call went out to reign in the horses and make
for the travellers, who had previously gone unseen.

Thormir and the others had tied their weapons to their packs
and draped their night sheets and furs over them so that they
would not seem threatening, but rather an ordinary group of
riders on their way to a city in the North. Lucian, who did not
have a horse and was riding with Thormir, kept his hand and a
half on his lap, under the folds of his ripped tunic, ready to use at
a moment's notice.

It had been five wearisome days since they had emerged from
the forest and had begun the long and arduous journey of circling
The Tongue of Hurst. Constantly they watched the skies for any
sign of The Roc Riders but the riders had not returned. Sometimes
at night, when all was still, Thormir could hear an unearthly
scream far in the distance and knew that The Pale Riders had not
forgotten him. The group had become tired, irritated and angry
at their lack of progress, and now, when they could see the forest's
ending, they had to endure this unforeseen occurrence. *Why
couldn't those numb-knuckled, worm-bellied, dirt-faced soldiers
leave us be and just pass us by without interfering in other people's
business and affairs?* Thormir scowled, but kept his head down
as the soldiers approached, covering his brow with his hood,
shielding him from the wind and unwanted eyes. He could hear

the loud snorts of protesting horses. He guessed that the soldiers had formed a circle around the group. Chancing a glimpse, he saw that all of the soldiers were dressed in black leather, and that all bore the same sword of some foreign design and a short hunting bow made of what Thormir thought was ash. The soldiers' dress, however, was not what caught Thormir's attention; it was the fact that they were all bald. Thormir held back a cry of disgust and surprise as he beheld the glistening dome of each man. Of course, some of the men wore helms, but it was evident that they too were bald, for they had no hair down the sides of their face or above their eyes. In Medani a man's hair was his pride and showed his status in society. Indeed, the only people who did not have hair were the criminals and the sick that lived on the side of streets and in the dark of the warrens that ran underneath the city. Criminals were often punished by having their hair removed. The rest of society shunned them until their hair grew back. Even after this, they would be remembered for committing a crime. So Thormir wondered in disgust at the men who now surrounded them. *Are they criminals? Where did they come from?*

A shout came from between the men. "Move aside soldier – hasten or flesh shall be taken by lash."

A man emerged from the circle of horses riding upon his own stallion, which seemed larger and more powerfully built than the other horses. A second later, Thormir realised that the size of the horse was proportionate to its rider. The horseman slid down the vast stallion's back, and walked towards them. The only other person that Thormir knew who could compete with the size of this monster was Bir, the stable master back in Medani. However, even he could not match this man's sheer size. It was not that he was extremely tall, it was that every one of his limbs was like a tree trunk: thick and powerfully built. The only flaw in his almost perfect physique was his vast belly, which would have preceded him into any room. He stood and stretched as he surveyed them.

Thormir could see the rider's fists clench as if in anger, making the muscles in his forearms bunch and knot together. He was relatively handsome in appearance, boasting a straight nose and strong cheekbones to boot. His eyes were crystal blue in colour, which caught Thormir's attention, along with his hair. He was the only one among his companions that had hair, and lots of it. His huge mane of shaggy grey-blonde hair fell around his shoulders, singling him out. A sleek moustache covered the distance between his jawbones. It curled at each end, rippling but not falling, held up by some unknown grease. Thormir also noticed that the way he spoke was very unusual. It was a different dialect to his own and he seemed to organise his words differently to the people from Medani.

"What dealings do you have in these parts? Lend tongue to ear or sword will find throat." He looked at them, scrutinizing each person in turn. Just as Tangar began their story of how they were lonely characters journeying their way to safer places, due to the rumours of wargs roaming the tundra, the commander of the group said, "Arrrgh, stay tongue for interest is lost. You strike vision of normality, but eye is not deceived of such prospect. These years past, many things bear cloak of deceit, and truth hides from eye and ear. It saddens heart, but dark days carry evil burden. Your horses strike form well. Coin must have fallen greatly into lap to make such purchases? Never beheld such strong beasts; and the one which stands black, so majestic, she must be a creature from legend." The soldier, who was obviously the commander of the horsemen, looked over the bags tied to their horses and continued, "Question tugs at mind. What hides beneath cover, and within bags? Thompson, Corville, search the scum."

Two soldiers dismounted and approached. The one with the tan skin and overhanging brow walked towards Tangar, pulled him down, and began to search him. Pulling off Tangar's cloak and blankets with a flourish of unnecessary strength, he revealed the weapons and supplies that Tangar carried with him. At the same time the soldier who had approached Thormir and Mary yanked the robes and sheets that covered their weapons. The soldiers surrounded them.

"Sir! Commander Reddard, sir," each of the soldiers exclaimed almost simultaneously, their harsh voices overlapping in a croaking cry.

"Arr, weapons, and of a fine make too, very fine." His eyes glinted with evident glee at such a find. "Lend quick tongue and find words as to you carrying such burden. Arr," he exclaimed and waved his massive fist through the air; a movement Thormir was sure would have crushed a man if the blow were to connect. "Do not let tongue part words of fantasy from mouth; you will all be going to the wall anyway, that or the yard will claim your fate." Then in a more commanding voice that rang with authority, he said, "Thompson, Corville, take weapons, bind hands, and ride. We join with the rest of the company."

Then Reddard turned and, just when he was about to mount his horse, he caught sight of Fern, paused, then said, "And clamp their dog in irons, I will decide fate upon our arrival. Move out!"

One of the soldiers ran back to his horse, and rummaged around in his saddlebags for a minute. Then, with a clanging sound, he brought forth a huge iron brace. While one soldier adjusted the links and chain around Fern, the other moved around the rest of them, securing the knots he had made around their wrists to a long piece of rope, the end of which was tied to his saddle. Fern had lifted his lip in a growl, but other than that he remained still.

They were wrenched off their horses. Corville approached Shadow, trying to rein her in, but to no avail. Out of the corner of his eye, Thormir saw two soldiers dismount and come to his aid. With a crushing blow Thormir knew what he must do, and the thought of it tore at his heart. Closing his eyes he opened his mind until he could feel Shadow's swirling thoughts and feelings. Concentrating with all his might he pressed all his fear and anguish into one word. "*RUN!*"

Thormir opened his eyes to see Shadow rear up and toss her head. He could tell she did not want to leave him. Just as he was about to shout at her to flee – to dash over the land and never to return – she turned tail. She galloped passed the soldiers. Seeing her turn, the other two horses followed her. The three horses ran hard, flying over the land, swift as the god Nasir, Lord of all horses. Reaching the peak of a rolling hill far in the distance, Thormir saw Shadow stop and turn her beautiful head and he could tell that she saw him as well as he saw her. *Goodbye.*

*   *   *

It was only a few hundred metres until they rounded the corner of The Tongue and began the descent of a small hillock, at the bottom of which another group of fifty soldiers waited, guarding thirty-odd people that were bound by the wrists and tied to two long ropes. However, there were gaps in the lines. Thormir saw that two or three of these spaces had the remnants of cut rope still attached, as if the person who was once tied there had not been worth the burden, and been disposed of. Dread filled him at the sight.

At first he thought that their captors must be slave traders, but their uniforms and the way they had talked of this *Lord Bath* had seemed true to the fact that they were soldiers of Orien. Thormir had heard of this city in studies: Orien, the black city. It had once been a great city that had thrived in the golden age of Vâryá, when magic still filled the world. The city's coffers had been filled with gold and its streets lined with splendour. The city had acted as a trading hub between the three realms of man, dwarf, and elven kin. Under this role, the city had flourished and been bathed in the wealth that trading brought to its gates. Meetings of great kings of old had been held within its high halls, as it served as a meeting point for the old alliance. And so the three circles of Orien had prospered from its geographical convenience. The city was built in three rings: the outer; the middle; and the inner circle, which had been called 'The Royal District', and within which The Gilded Hall was built. The hall was built out of the largest hardwoods that could be found in The Tongue of Hurst. To match its beautiful exterior architecture, the inner roof and columns had been gilded with the finest gold that could be mined within the mountains of The Al'Durast. Then came the cursed years in which the Dark Lord, Vandr, the betrayer of magic, set his eyes on all the lands east of The Al'Durast, and shadow had fallen. By the time the battle at Celiton was fought, all links with Orien had been cut. The elves in their wooded halls had all but been cut down by the evil power that had spread from the north. The dwarves, or what was left of their kin, had retreated to their mountain dwellings where all that was left of that noble race had perished. However, their majesty and bravery in battle was never forgotten as it was woven into the songs and tales of the southern bards. And men? The kingdoms and realms of men had been left to rebuild out of shadow and ruin.

And so Orien had fallen into dust and shadow. Its shine of golden wealth and prosperity had been lost and replaced by desperation, anguish, and a longing for a new leader to guide its people through the darkened mist into the bright sunlight that would bring back some of the city's majesty. For a while, Orien had become a slave city filled with corruption, violence, thievery and unsavoury business of every kind. However, out of this chaos, members of the house Bathos had risen to power and taken control. For a time, Orien had lived in peace once more, but while the order and rule of the Bathos family had quelled the many riots and murders, the family did not put a complete end to the crime within the city. The family had encouraged acts of theft and smuggling to the extent that they controlled and benefited from its profits. And so, Lord Bath of the Bathos bloodline now ruled the city with his few trusted disciples. According to the spies that Thormir's father had sent to live in the city, Lord Bath had a son and together they ran many guilds, organised a drug ring, and ensured the success of the smuggling trade with Elbank and Durnsay. As well as this, Lord Bath controlled the entire city, from the heavy taxes to the militarisation of the city's defences, as well as maintaining Orien's guise as a trading city. Through these works Bath's influence and power over the lands surrounding the city had expanded.

As for the people, Thormir had heard that most suffered under Bath's rule, while the rest, few as they were, prospered only from crime or economic support from the outside, if they were lucky enough to obtain it.

And we are heading there, Thormir thought despairingly. The one thing that comforted him was that he had knowledge of where he was going and what he was up against. He looked at Fern, who swivelled his massive head towards him and he said with his mind, *Brother, should we make a break for it?*

No. There are too many of them and they might hurt the others.

Who? Mary and Tangar and . . .

No, Fern tossed his head and pointed his muzzle towards the thirty-odd tired-looking people who had stopped at the foot of the hill, *them.*

For a moment another mind joined with theirs and they heard Mary say, *You must not use your gift. Do not use your magic, or else we will all die or face a destiny much worse than we do now. Promise me that no matter what happens to me, or your friends, or anyone in the group that we travel with, you will not use your magic.*

Thormir nodded in agreement and quickly closed his mind as a soldier looked back at them. It was as if the soldier had felt the tendrils of thought that had passed between Mary, Fern and himself.

Thormir had forgotten all about his promise to himself that he would return to Medani. Now that he remembered it, he scowled, dismissed it, and violently pushed it aside into the depths of his mind. As his feet moved forward in a stumbling, laboured routine, he thought to himself that anyone with his gifts should not wallow and stew in self-pity, but rather try to help others. And so he decided there and then that no matter what it took, he would, someday, free those people who had been enslaved and oppressed by Lord Bath, starting with the group of slaves he was about to join as they began the journey to Orien.

He felt the first tug on the rope and as he stumbled forward, a vision of blood clouded his mind. This was just the beginning; the inauguration of something more evil than he had yet faced. He heard screams of torture from the back of the group, and was reminded that he was still being hunted by The Pale Riders, The Roc Riders; those terrible creatures that sought the dark of night – and night was coming. Thormir stared at the horizon. *This is the beginning of an end.*

CHAPTER EIGHT

ROPES AND BONDS
Orda roa bands

They itched and tore at his wrists. Ever since they had abandoned their horses for the long march eastward, Thormir had studied every fibre of his bonds to the point where he hated them with all his might. Instead of focusing on the pain of walking barefoot over flat, rough ground – their boots had been removed so they could better conform to the dress of the other prisoners – he focused on the pain of the ropes that bound him. He bent his whole being towards hating those ropes, and when they succeeded in breaking the skin around his wrists, he had gritted his teeth and studied how each strand of rope curled and wove around the others in an intricate but simple pattern.

But it was not working. They had marched for nearly a week, inching their way closer to Orien, which had not even appeared on the horizon, and his focus on the ropes was losing its effect. His body had begun to protest; every ache and pain banged at the back of his mind, hammering on his consciousness, as he lost his concentration. His mouth and lips had become a desert, a crackling barren wasteland void of sound or moisture. He tried to ask a soldier for a flask, but only hot air and dust issued from his mouth. It was becoming harder, and harder to speak. He opened his wasted mouth in the hope that his voice would come to him, but before he could ask a soldier for water, another voice cut in.

"They will not give you any." The voice came from next to him, and in his state, the sound of it was like music that echoed in the caverns of his mind. As he listened to its echoes, he felt that it held pain, loss, and beauty – a terrible beauty, worthy of legend. Thormir looked in the direction of the voice and saw his rope partner looking at him with concern. Immediately, he felt the tips of his ears turn red and felt himself blush under her gaze. Though it was unlikely that she would notice his change in colour under the grime and sweat that plastered his face, he reprimanded himself for showing that sort of weakness.

He studied the woman's face more closely and came to the conclusion that she was more or less his age. In Medani he had never really taken an interest in pursuing girls; both he and Fern used to stand from a distance and laugh and comment on which of Medani's women and girls would be a fine match. However, in all this time he had never seen a woman of such unfounded beauty as the one who now walked beside him.

"I'm fine," he croaked. Embarrassment blossomed with him and immediately he wanted to say more, but she had turned away, her eyes fixed on the golden horizon. Despite her lack of cloth and her tanned skin, she held herself like any royal. Thormir recognised the signs, as he'd been taught to do. "Back straight and chin up," his father used to say, before giving him a cuff over the head.

Still keeping her eyes forward and her head turned to the distant line of scarlet, the woman spoke again, although her voice lower and softer than before, "My name is Selena."

The statement, wasn't begging a response, but rather it was offering a hand in friendship.

What Thormir meant to say was *My name is Thormir* but all that he managed was, "Thormir."

Selena nodded in acknowledgement.

"Are you travelling with anyone?" said Thormir. He knew nothing about Selena, but already he was interested in who she was and where she had come from. He felt Fern touch his mind and feel his mix of emotions, which were a dancing yellow-red colour. As Fern spoke with his mind, Thormir felt Fern's humour trickle into himself.

You like her, don't you? Fern's voice rang with suppressed merriment.

What? No, ssshhh. Again Thormir felt a flush creep up his face and around his cheeks.

What, do you think she can hear us? His tone teased Thormir's mind, but Fern quickly withdrew into himself, leaving Thormir to himself, to think on this new development.

Selena turned towards Thormir, a slight frown lining her brow. "Why do you want to know?" Her quick response did not take Thormir aback, but he heard a slight hint of steel creep into her tone, which gave away the answer to his question.

"I just . . ." Thormir faltered as no proper response came to him. He shrugged with what he hoped was careless curiosity.

The river that had formed upon her forehead now resolved into a tanned landscape that held no blemish upon its surface apart from the grit that accompanied the rough march to Orien.

"My grandmother walks behind me. We had travelled for many days with the group you walk with now before these animals set upon us. Many of our men perished in the fight that ensued. We were fleeing from our home town, which now lies in ruin, a burnt mess at the hands of the emperor."

"Where were you travelling to?" Thormir asked, glad that her steel had been replaced by softened words.

"Medani." The answer was short, but it came as a blow to Thormir as a rush of images, sounds, smells, and memories flooded to the forefront of his mind.

"You are from there, are you not?" Once again Selena formed her question as more of a statement and her insight into his background unnerved him.

"Yes, but I wish not to speak of that so close to unfriendly ears."

Selena nodded and turned away, gazing at the now blood-red dusk of the horizon. Thormir guessed it was approaching the fall of the sun and, as he had so often done over the last week, he gazed at the horizon, looking with hope for the end of his journey, and dreading whatever might await them within the high walls of Orien. It was just as he had spotted a tiny speck that dotted the expanse, that he was pushed to the muck by a sudden jerk and fall of the rope he was tied to.

The side of his face smacked the cold hard ground. There was no cushioning grass to cover the uneven rocks. As he grunted in pain, and felt the skin on his upper cheekbone slice open, he heard similar cries of pain from the rest of the group, who had also been brought to the ground. Cursing the fall, he turned to see if Selena had seen his weakness. His guts clenched and in an instant he forgot about his embarrassment. As he took in the slight trickle of blood and the purple bruising forming around her left eye, anger like nothing he had ever known welled up within him. Thunder clouds of fury washed over him, which he found hard to control. *What did this to her? What had jerked us downward with such force? Why shouldn't I just use magic to free myself and get Selena and the others away from this place?* Of course he knew the answer to his unasked question, and he felt himself hating the rest of the group for it.

As Thormir raised his head and tried to talk to Selena to check if she was okay, he saw a horseman ride up to the guard who rode next to him and heard him say, "That damned woman up front, the one with child, yes, she releases babe from womb."

The horseman cursed and rode off with the first to check on the situation. Thormir heard screams issuing from the head of the column and turned away. The sound was unlike any Thormir had ever heard. Even the cries of dying men did not scare him as much as this did. It was otherworldly and not natural, despite its origin. He realised that this alien sound was the frightened call of new life.

"We make camp! Sit, eat and sleep – we leave upon the sun's rising," Commander Reddard's powerful voice boomed from the front of the 'pack of dogs', as he called the company.

Sighs of relief spread throughout the captured men and women, but these turned into whispers of concern when they heard about the woman giving birth upfront, for to the untrained ear her screams might have been of torture not labour.

"Can one of you dogs take infant from belly?"

By Thormir's reckoning he deduced that Reddard was asking for assistance in encouraging and caring for the birth of the infant. He turned to Selena and was surprised to see her arguing with the lady that Thormir had assumed was her grandmother. The woman was stubborn as any mule bred by Bir, and looked as much. He averted his eyes from the argument, but not his ears.

"You mustn't!" Selena was saying. "If you fail, they will hurt you and . . ."

"I will help and there is nothing more to it than that. That woman needs my help – if I don't she might die in this accursed place!" Selena's grandmother raised one boned and knobbly finger to Selena's mouth and said, "Be silent, my treasure".

*   *   *

Hours had passed since Selena's grandmother had volunteered herself for the job of nursing the young lady through the ordeal. The screaming had increased every five minutes until now, when the sound became a nonstop chant of anguish that pleaded to the gods to make the pain cease and for her child to be alive and healthy.

Selena had her knees pulled up against her chest, and Thormir suspected that it was more out of fear than anything else. She had created a shield to keep out thoughts of harm and evil. He had offered to clean the blood smeared on her face, but she had pushed him away, saying that she needed no help in tending to her affairs. Now they sat at a distance, but still bonded to the same rope.

The cries of anguish seemed to affect the soldiers as well. Some stayed upon their mounts, others walked in patrol, but all seemed unnerved by the unexpected events that the blood dusk had brought. Suddenly a soldier that Thormir had noticed cursing while rocking back and forth upon a chopped tree stump sharpening a short knife, stood up and marched over to the groaning lady.

"Shut mouth, you stupid bitch!" his yell was harsh and louder than the woman's screams, and for a moment the shock of it quieted her cries.

The grandmother, who was bending over her, muttered to herself then said to the soldier, "Quiet yourself, you thug! The head and shoulders have emerged."

"Tighten jaw or the old nurse gets it, do you understand? If sound parts your pretty lips the ancient bitch finds dagger between ribs."

The woman clamped her mouth shut, and bit her lip to keep from screaming. Thormir looked at Selena, whose stricken face matched his own feelings of horror at the predicament. A silence descended on the camp; the only sounds were the shuffling of hooves and the breathing of those who watched in terror at what they all knew would come next.

And so it did, and in seconds the camp erupted into cries of pain, horror, and new life. As she had given a final push, arching her back in a last effort, she had opened her mouth and shrieked in pain. The labouring woman had drawn blood by biting into the outside of her lip, which had formed a beard of crimson that ran down to her chin. In that moment of agonised pain the soldier who had been standing over Selena's grandmother, plunged his short knife into her throat. As it happened, a sound foreign to the camp until then joined the others: the trumpeting bawl of new life as the newborn fell out of the grandmother's now limp hands into a soft pile of robes. The babe was splashed with her blood, which cascaded from the gash in her neck.

"No!" Selena's eyes were fixed on her now dead grandmother. "No!" her cry came again, as if willing her grandmother back to life. The pain of her loss, the sound of it, made Thormir feel as if the dagger had been plunged and twisted into his own chest, so that every second became an unendurable suffering.

Thormir felt himself crying, and when soft fur rubbed up against him he sensed the rumble of Fern's fury and doleful quivering at what had just happened. *You did all you could do, without all being forsaken.*

"What?" Thormir heard Reddard's cry of shock before he saw the man himself stride into his line of sight. "Shit on the gods, what took mind upon hand?"

The soldier, still holding the bloody dagger, cowered under the fire of Reddard's stare. He did not move back in submission, but rather stood motionless as the tirade washed over him. After a few brutal minutes of Reddard spewing harsh curses and promises of further discipline, the man was sent to fetch more firewood. "Do not return until wood fuels the night. See yourself from my sight Merek!" Reddard shouted after him.

The wind howled through the darkness. The thunderclouds that had travelled far westward loomed overhead, threatening their burden of torrential rain. A lone wolf cried to the night sun, and cries of pain and chants of grief rose into the air at the loss of their number. But, neither the dusk nor the guards cared. The soldiers stood silent, not heeding the anguish of their prisoners.

Eventually silence fell over the camp. Even Selena, red-eyed and wracked with pain, fell quiet, her continuous pleading becoming a choked throb in the depths of her throat.

The soldier who had made the kill had not come back and, from what Tangar had taught him of the lands around the borders of Carathron, Thormir guessed he would not return; most likely he would be taken by some predator of the night. Many such roamed the plains on the outskirts of Hurst, *not to mention The Roc Riders.* Without realising it, he found his hand reaching for his shoulder, feeling for the marks that blemished his flesh and poisoned his mind.

Thormir turned his head, searching for Mary and Lucian. He had almost forgotten about them in all that had happened. He caught sight of them at the end of the line and reached for Mary's mind. As he felt the old, familiar touch of Mary's mind brush against his, he tried to reciprocate, and then recoiled. He felt a solid wall of thought so strong that no word of communication could pass. Then a mental shout echoed inside his head, so strong and powerful that Thormir jerked his hands up to cover ears, trying to ward off Mary's voice.

CLOSE YOUR MIND!

He felt foolish at the sudden movement, especially given it was in response to a mental shout that could not be stopped by any physical means. Selena frowned at him with annoyance and he realised the rope joining his hands with hers, which had been clasped around her knees, had been yanked harshly.

"Sorry."

Selena merely looked away, hiding what he knew to be a new flux of tears.

CHAPTER NINE

MIST AND SHADOW
Boa roa scellýsa

The morning dawned a rusty brown, heralded by the call of the newest member of their party. Thormir couldn't remember what time he had fallen asleep, but it seemed that waking was more difficult than the struggle for rest after the night's events. So much grief and anguish resided within him. He lifted his cheek off the gravel-patched grass and looked around at his party. Everyone had bloodshot eyes and was even more subdued than before. He'd had another two seizures during the night. They had ravaged his body and almost taken what sanity he had left, leaving him tired and exhausted. The marchers looked gaunt and haunted, more so than before. This troubled Thormir; he feared that some might not make the rest of the journey. Like so many before them, they would come to rest on harsh ground, and be left to the mercy of the wild.

The fire was doused, the horses fed and watered, prisoners untied as they went to relieve themselves and then re-tied. And so, upon the second hour of the dawn, orders were issued and the company resumed their passage towards Orien, which had now become a speck of black that polluted the curve of the horizon. It was half a day before they seemed to make any headway. No matter how far they marched, it seemed that their progress was tantalisingly small, and Orien never got any nearer. Or was he gradually losing his mind, giving in to the pain that racked his body? At half-day the flats that lay around the borders of Carathron changed into warm rolling hills that seemed beautiful despite the pain they brought as obstacles.

Still the ropes tore at their wrists and jerked them forward in a painful two-step march. The only relief they felt was when they ventured into the softer grass that cushioned the hills that rolled towards the growing city. The grass cuddled their skin, cleaning and soaking the blood that painted the sides of their feet.

Thormir paid no heed to the screams and protests of his body as the wet, cool grass brushed against his wounds. All day he had been thinking of ways to escape this place and this everlasting march. But nothing he thought of seemed possible without hurting the others. These soldiers were not the type to allow other slaves to have hope for themselves after letting one prisoner escape. They would all make it to Orien, or no one would. He might as well escape in flight upon the back of a winged horse and live among the stars, never to be seen again by the eyes of men for all the chance he had.

As he amused himself with that thought, he recalled what his father had told him about death and the afterlife. He had said that whenever a mortal passes from this life, he ascends to the heavens, Elcala, and becomes a star to watch over those whom he loves and offer comfort to those who still dwell amongst the living. Thormir had not believed him, however, the same story had been told in his novels and the fantastic tales written by mad bards; that when one dies they turn into stars, hovering in the skies, venturing within the sky mountains. As a descendant of the kings of old, Thormir wondered whether they would offer him advice on how to escape this prison of unrelenting bonds and the continuous march east. No such words descended from the heavens, so he gave up. There was nothing to be gained from seeking what did not exist.

It was late in the day when the black figures emerged from behind a small mound. These people, men and women, seemed not to *fit*. They were an oddity marking the landscape. Something about them seemed familiar, but Thormir couldn't quite place it. They came to a stop, halting with eerily-timed steps at the base of the mound. Many of them carried small lanterns, while others bore wreathes of flowers that varied in size, the stems of which twisted and folded over each other to form halos of blossoming white. Many of the men and women, from what Thormir could tell of their form, wore hoods that were drawn over their faces. The robed figures placed their garlands at the foot of the mound of dirt, which despite being freshly dug was already in the process of being reclaimed by nature. As the figures stood back again, Thormir realised he was witnessing a funeral. Feeling that he had intruded upon their privacy, he averted his gaze from the ceremony.

Soldiers were marching along beside the burial mounds that dotted the roll of the tundra leading up to the gates of Orien. Thormir could not tell how long they had been walking for, but it seemed close to two weeks. Now that the journey's end was clearly in sight, small waves of relief washed over him. In front and behind him people were moaning, not from weariness, but from what sounded like disgust.

He focused on one of the trees that stood beside the worn trail. The tree was dirty and misshapen – its arms were outstretched, and its red and pink leaves hung crudely from its limbs. But now that he looked closer, he could see it was not a tree at all. It was a human. The human had been nailed upon a post of wood stuck into the ground. The man hung there, massive iron nails protruding from his deep wounds. Thormir could not tell whether the man was dead or alive, but he saw dried blood caked around the man's mouth, and he could only imagine the pain he must have been in when those nails went in. As Thormir looked up he saw that what he had previously taken to be dead trees lining the way to Orien, were actually bodies nailed to posts, many dead, others dying.

He averted his gaze and saw they were approaching with surprising rapidity – so much so that Thormir could make out the colour and design of the city gates. The gates of the city drew closer. Unlike Medani, that shone a bright red in evening light, Orien appeared black and terrible against the horizon.

He hated himself for the feeling, but as they stumbled through the hanging bodies, he felt relieved that this long march was nearly at its end. He squinted at the gates, which formed part of a high wall made from what looked like massive stones. The wall seemed to expand out and circle the city in a wide arc. However, far to the left he saw that the wall had crumbled, and that large stone bricks were scattered and broken all over the ground. The breach sagged open like a gaping mouth that breathed in the outside world. Scaffolding attached itself to the sides of the hole and ant-like figures were busy around the stonework. The bells of industry sounded from within the city, and shouts and chants of timed laboured rang from the broken wall. The ringing cry of a drill sergeant's song came from Thormir's right, accompanied by the clash of weapons. Thormir guessed that it was the sound of the soldiers being trained to cleave head from shoulders and to become as cold, as merciless, and brutal as the men who rode beside them.

"The Shadow Gates," Selena's whisper reached his ears; the name chilled him to the bone. "I have only heard stories of them. They were erected by the Bathos when the city was rebuilt after the war. They are a symbol of the power of the family. They are evil."

Not for the first time, Thormir wondered where Selena was from and how much she knew of the world. Knowledge of the war was not shared freely in these parts, and was banned, by punishment of death, within the empire. Of course, both he and Fern knew of their history and origin because they lived in the palace and had been educated in the histories of the land.

*   *   *

The gates boomed shut behind them.

Reddard jumped off his warhorse and strode over to the guardhouse that sat to the right of the massive lever and chain mechanism that opened and shut The Shadow Gates. The group of prisoners huddled together. The mother and the infant were next to Tangar. They had all been untied and they had moved closer together in fear of what was to come. Tangar spoke in a low voice to the new mother, who was looking increasingly frightened. The fact that they had been untied might have comforted their wrists and ankles, but the soldiers' confidence that no security was needed darkened Thormir's hope of flight – a hope that had remained with him for the length of their journey.

He tried to feel for Mary's mind, but again felt a mental wall blocking communication with her. He stared at her. She stared back and slowly shook her head from side to side. He felt angry with her. *Why won't she talk with me, after all she got me into this mess!*

Reddard finished talking with one of the guards and turned to the group. The guard summoned two more, and then the three soldiers marched to the back of the group, where a soldier was rocking upon his knees, breathing heavily.

So Merek had returned. The terrors of the night and the harsh land had not taken the soldier who had sliced the old woman's throat. He would deserve what he got for disobeying orders.

As they approached, the soldier muttered under his breath, "Water, give me water."

The three soldiers laughed. "Hear plea, he calls for juice!"

The other two let out harsh barks of laughter.

The soldier who had killed the grandmother was still kneeling on the ground. "Water."

"Water?" the others mocked, making rude gestures and screwing up their faces, trying to imitate the grounded soldier's pain.

One of the soldiers, a particularly brutish man with a troll-like face, picked up a stick and hefted it in his hand. Smiling at the others, he went up to Merek and prodded him hard in the cheek. Quick as a flash, a movement that betrayed his exhaustion, Merek grabbed the stick and bent it back towards the man. With his hand bent backwards, the brute was forced to retreat. Continuing with the momentum, Merek got to his feet and threw the soldier backwards, sending him sprawling in the dust. The other two guards rushed him, taking his arms, and bringing them behind his back. Putting a hand on his shoulders, they forced him back into a kneeling position. As Merek's knees ground into the hard dirt, the brutish, troll-faced soldier raised himself and walked over to him, stick in hand. In one motion he brought it across Merek's cheek and left an untidy cut, peppered with splinters across his face.

"Fix wound, and bring him. The general will want words."

The two leering soldiers nodded dumbly, raised the battered and sliced soldier to his feet, and shouldered him out of sight.

Reddard, who had watched the whole thing with grim, silent pleasure, brought himself back to the present by saying, "You be separated into two groups. Half will find themselves in the company of the wall and the quarry, and the others shall breathe the blood and dust of the yard. You shall be trained as one of us, as soldiers should be. Wishes of your master will be obeyed. Bring infant to hand." Reddard looked at the child. He would not kill it as Lord Bath had done to his son; he would give it fortune under the guise of a harsh hand. "Take infant to the palace and hand babe to the Lord's sister. She wishes for child anyway, seeing as womb has not granted such fortune." He winced as he heard the scream of the mother but such things had to be done.

"No!" the mother of the child screamed as the soldiers wrapped their sweaty arms around the small bundle of blankets and took the infant away. Even the child seemed to know what was going on, as it started to scream and bawl, clenching its little fists in fury at the injustice being carried out.

Thormir felt magic rise within him; the hot energy flowing through his veins, ready to be unleashed. It was his turn to clench his fists now. He forced the magic down, and restrained his anger with surprising difficulty.

The mother began to scream, beg, and plead. She clawed at the soldiers, but to no avail. She tried to grab her screaming baby, but it was held out of reach. At the sound of her baby's torturous cries, the mother began to shake uncontrollably and the scabs where she had bitten into her flesh broke, so that beads of blood ran once more around her chin. The soldiers who had the baby left their horses with Reddard and, nodding to him as they passed, they began to make their way through the city towards the palace and The Gilded Hall – ignoring the protests of the group and the screaming mother.

As the group of captives was separated into two parties, they hurled curses and insults at the soldiers.

"What fate shall greet the beast?" asked one soldier pointing at Fern.

Reddard turned to stare at Fern. "Kill it." He stroked his moustache as if he was mulling over the taste of his words, enjoying their meaning and eventual impact. He seemed to swirl the words around in his mouth, as if tasting a fine wine. Meanwhile, Thormir's fear was growing by the second. His brother was in grave danger, in mortal peril, and there was nothing he could do about it. He was bound in chains of hopelessness, and powerless against the evil that inhabited this terrible city.

Still stroking his facial centrepiece, Reddard stopped grinding his teeth, and said in a voice lathered in merciless evil, "No! Stay hand. The general will *appreciate* company of a beast more than we were granted."

Thormir's relief was short-lived as he realised that servitude under this general must bring a fate even more wicked and terrible than death ever could. Thormir met Fern's eyes, and felt Fern brush a single thought towards him.

If something happens to me, do not mourn, but remember.

The touch of this thought released its hold on his consciousness, and Fern turned his head away. As soon as he did, he bared his teeth at the five soldiers who now surrounded him. Two of the soldiers inched forward and tugged on the chain of large iron links that was attached to the cuff around Fern's neck. He made a choking sound as the iron dug into his neck, pulling him forward.

Fern paused for a second, and Thormir thought he might actually attack the guards. However, all his hesitation won him was another brutal tug on the chain. He stumbled forward, each step a forced movement, as the soldiers led him off deeper into the city.

Thormir felt like he had been struck in the small of his back, as well as the depths of his stomach, as he realised that he had lost Fern and was now losing Mary, Tangar and Lucian. He saw them being led away with the other half of the group. This was too much.

He watched as the last of their group was led around the corner of one of the tall houses that cluttered Orien's streets. Thormir noticed that, unlike the houses in Medani, the homes that lined the streets in Orien had gable roofs. The roofs seemed to be made of dense, black tiles that were held together with some sort of mud. Thormir had never seen this type of thing before, as all the houses in Medani had chipped, red-tiled roofs. These houses craned inward, looming over the streets, whispering with menacing creaks in their floorboards, and groaning as the world changed to evil about them.

But now, nothing seemed to matter. Not the foreign nature of Orien's buildings, nor the fact he was in pain, nor even his sensation of tearing, ripping, hunger. All that mattered was that he had just lost everyone he knew: he was alone.

"The rest of you, prepare to give aid and assistance to Lady Bath, who should be riding through gate shortly. You all know her as the sister of the high Lord Bath, so you will not give annoyance, or else lash shall find back and metal soft flesh. She returns before the party from Durnsay so hasten to proper fashion," Reddard addressed his soldiers.

The soldiers at once began busying themselves, then marched off in single file towards the northern gate to the city.

Thormir swayed as a feeling of desertion overcame him. The world seemed to close in around him, and the darkness of isolation dimmed his vision. Or was he just weary? Or was the thorn's poison working its way further into him? He could not tell anymore. He was tired. He felt soft skin, and then an arm and shoulder support his weight, and then darkness slowly closing upon him as he was led on.

*   *   *

Thormir choked and gagged as he felt a chunk of bread drowned in hot liquid being shoved down his throat. Spitting the bread out of his mouth, he forced his eyes opened. He winced as hot sunlight slammed into his eyes. The morning had dawned. A greyish fog lay over the city, pierced here and there with occasional rays of sunlight. He was surprised that he hadn't woken earlier, for he heard the bells of industry tolling throughout the city. It became apparent that after he had passed out they had continued on until they reached the camp where half of Orien's prisoners were working on the wall. As he felt the weird clenching sensation of his pupils contracting, a distant landscape and movement came into focus.

The wall was larger than Thormir had first thought. It dominated the campsite, towering over those who were repairing its breach. The break in the stone was about a quarter of a mile from where he lay, but Thormir still appreciated that Lord Bath had undertaken a massive project in an attempt to repair the injury. Lines of people carried stones up ramps, broke boulders into small pieces, and did many other laborious, back-breaking tasks.

He shut his eyes and wished that he was somewhere else – anywhere but here. Opening his eyes again, he sat up. Immediately he felt his abdomen protest. He saw his bread lying tired and limp upon the dirt and reached out. He thought he might as well eat it; at least it would provide some sustenance. Inches from the bread a hand closed around his wrist. Thormir looked up and saw Selena. She looked worried and, despite everything, he felt happy that she showed some concern towards him. *How is it, after all this, she still looks so . . . beautiful?*

"Here, have mine." Her voice flickered like a candle in a soft breeze, but other than that she gave away no sign of her emotion at her recent loss.

119

He only managed a gracious smile before he took the bread from her bound hands. He felt that if he spoke he might say something stupid, or worse; in any case, he did not even know that he could speak. That liquid, whatever it was, still burned within his throat. However, it had given him some energy, as he could feel the strength returning to his limbs.

Thormir found it odd that no soldiers patrolled or bothered to guard their company. He supposed they thought that escape from the wall was impossible for prisoners who had just been captured and dragged across rough country for weeks. He seemed to be right; up until mid-morning no soldier stopped or paid notice. When Thormir supposed the sun was at its zenith, what looked like a courier stopped by and gave each of the party a loaf of bread, some cheese, and several mouthfuls of water, and then took them one by one to relieve themselves. After that, he disappeared. Once again Thormir could feel himself aching every minute with the pain. Those minutes folded into hours and those hours turned into a whole day. During this time they talked little, each left alone to their thoughts. During the late hours of the night, Thormir thought he heard Selena crying into the pillow she had made out of her long hair and an extra robe, but in the morning, he saw no sign of red eyes or weariness. It was late afternoon before they heard the sound of heavy, metal-clad boots approaching.

A man walked into their line of sight. Like Reddard, he was truly massive, but unlike Reddard, every muscle and every line in his body seemed to have been sculpted to perfection. Thormir found himself unable to look away as the soldier stood in front of them, his black eyes surveying them under his bushy brow. Thormir looked intently over the features of the man who he supposed to be the general – he surmised as much from the cloak he wore around his neck and shoulders. The fur and lining seemed odd and uneven, not as they should be. There were gaps in the fur and differing textures between the patches of hair. Thormir realised to his horror that it was human hair. The cloak was made up of the scalps of human heads. Once Thormir realised this, he could discern more clearly that the scalps had been sewn together by the skin beneath the hair. He felt bile rise at the back of his throat; a feeling that was not helped once he saw what the general wore on his hands. At first glance it seemed to be a pair of charcoal-coloured gloves, but as Thormir lingered on the make, he saw that the gloves were actually hollowed-out hands, which had been prepared and stretched to fit their wearer.

He gagged as the general flexed his fingers inside the gloves and cracked his knuckles by pushing his clenched fists against each other.

In the corner of his eye, Thormir saw Selena throw a filthy look towards the general. She had an expression of pure disgust upon her face.

With a wave of his massive hand, the general summoned two soldiers. They acknowledged him with a strange movement of their right hand, and then stood alert beside him. Turning to the two, the general said, in a voice that sounded like the rumble of distant thunder, "All right, clean them up. You know what you do." The general flashed another glance at Thormir then left, leaving the party in the hands of the two soldiers.

"Men to the side, women to the other." The soldiers advanced and led each group of men and women respectively behind a different wall. The ground was muddy here and snakes of water could be felt swimming across their toes as they walked. Buckets and rags were set to one side. A man was already there, washing his hands in a cloud of foaming water. Unlike the brutish expressions and the immense stature of the many military men that Thormir had encountered, this man possessed neither warrior qualities nor any of the qualities that the men of Orien had displayed so far. He approached, sniffed, and spat on the ground as if he hated the taste of the air.

"Strip down then, you filthy dogs." A soldier behind them spat the words out, as if the taste of addressing this crowd disgusted him.

Thormir had never stripped in front of so many people, and with his bonds retied he thought the task all the more embarrassing. *This isn't fair; by all the gods this isn't fair.* Many of his company seemed to think the same as a number of them hesitated before seeing the soldier reach for his sword. Once the group were undressed, the first soldier blew a whistle and thirty slaves jogged towards them with buckets of water in hand. On the second blast of the soldier's whistle water crashed over the group. Thormir winced as the icy water hit him. Immediately his body began to shake; every inch of him screamed with pain, every blister was exposed and soaked so they became soft and fleshy.

The soldier then began forcing them to the ground, sending their knees thumping into the sodden dirt. As Thormir knelt in submission he noticed a small knife shoved into the belt of the soldier's surcoat. *If only I could reach it, I could cut us free and . . .* But it was a fantasy. *How could I escape anyway? I wouldn't even make it past the gate, let alone the fact I don't even know a way out of this hellhole.*

A hand, small by touch, but firm, wrapped around a clump of Thormir's hair and pulled. He yelled. Then, as the scream died in his throat, he heard another sound replace it.

"Snip . . . Snip."

He yelled again as he saw great clumps of his hair falling by his side. In his culture, a person's head of hair was his honour – a sign of wealth and nobility. And now his hair was being torn, wrenched, and stripped from his head. Similar screams were coming for behind the wall and Thormir assumed that it was not just his culture that held such customs. Running his hands over his newly-cut hair he was helped to his feet by a slave. His head felt weird, an unexplored territory of his body, foreign to his touch.

"Here," The guard handed him a small leather tag with a number engraved into the surface. "From now on you will wear this around your neck until told otherwise. Think not to remove it from your person for such consequences will be dire. From now on you are your tag. You have no name. You are just a number." The guard grabbed the back of Thormir's neck and forced his head down. "Now you bear no name, for you are numbered 134." Still forcing his neck down, he placed the tag around Thormir's throat and let it fall. The hardened leather bounced off Thormir's exposed chest as the tag came to rest just above his sternum.

Then came the heat. Thormir felt it behind him, before he saw what it was. He turned his head and soon the origin of the searing heat came into view. A man who had deep twisted burn marks all down his face held a long metal pole. Dreading what he would see next, he let his eyes wander to the end of the metal rod. The tip glowed red and orange, culminating in a white hot point; except there was no point, instead there were two letters, "B.O." indicating Bath and Orien. Before he could think, before he could swallow in anticipation, the metal pole was launched onto his left forearm. He screamed. The pain was extreme and brutal. It knifed his brain and cut into his very soul. Clenching his teeth, he looked down and saw his skin bubbling, red and swollen. *Once again I am marked.*

"Now, see yourself clothed and returned to the mess." The thirty slaves hurried up to each of the party and placed new clothes in front of them. The cloth was of a brownish hue and came with a small leather belt. It was obviously meant to be worn like a riding tunic. The sight was a little disconcerting; all of them short-haired, similarly clothed, and each reduced to just the number around their necks.

As they met the women, who had already emerged from behind the wall, Thormir saw that they too had been garbed, shaved, and numbered like the men. However, he had no difficulty finding Selena, as the soldiers had left her hair alone, as if she had changed their minds, *But how?*

As the slaves accompanied the party back to the mess, Thormir did not have a chance to speak with her. Instead he found himself next to the woman who had given birth what seemed a lifetime ago. She was quite a bit taller than he was, which struck him as odd as he had reached his full height and not one of the women he had seen in Medani outstripped him like she did. She must have been twenty-eight years of age, but the corded muscles in her jaw, the constant frown creasing her forehead, and the soft, velvet bags under her eyes gave the impression of someone much older. She, like him, had endured a hard time of it on the journey to Orien. The birth of her baby, the loss of a caring nurse, and then to have further hopes strangled by unexpected hands at the gates of Orien; it must have driven her to the very edge of madness. *No person should have to live with that pain.* He looked up at the profile of the woman's face. *I will seek vengeance on the people who did this; after this story has been sung, I shall take the lives of those who stole the blood-marked infant. First the dwarves, then the many slaves, and now the child – how many more must suffer? As for the woman who stands beside me, her mind should not be taken from this world – she is still relatively young and has a chance at happiness. For where hope is kindled, so too is happiness. And surely I am that hope. I will learn to use my gift, if only to set free the minds that are cursed with torment.*

She turned to him; the lines of her face clearly showed her anguish. Thormir could still see the self-inflicted bite marks etched into her skin – the deep cuts forming a sick mockery of a smile.

"Why?" Her tormented voice was cracked with suppressed sorrow.

Her question took Thormir aback. He had not been expecting it, and now that he realised he was supposed to provide an answer he found himself unable to form one.

"I . . ." he faulted on the brink of saying something to console her pain, but thought it best to leave it and leave the woman on her own, to grieve by herself. After a pause he said, "What is your name?"

A flash of anger crossed her face. "Names and words are powerful things and I do not so freely give mine away, especially to a boy such as yourself."

"I am no boy." This time it was Thormir who was stifling his anger, as the words so often muttered by his father echoed in his ears. "I do not appreciate being told what I am by those who barely know me."

The gravel crunched beneath their bare feet. The smell of smoke permeated the air around them. The crackle and spit of small campfires could be heard, coming from the lines of tents that Thormir knew were concealed by the wooden walls that were erected to divide the citizens of Orien from the slaves and the non-worthy.

Thormir turned from the woman's haughty profile. He did not resent her for berating him, but he did not feel like talking to her again. He felt that she would only want counsel with her own thoughts considering all that had happened.

Finally, but only after five to ten minutes of walking, they arrived at the tents and the mess. The smells of smoke, sweat, shit, and animal meat overwhelmed Thormir. As they turned the corner into the mess, the soldiers left without parting words. The group began to mill around the few tents that had been set up to house them, not knowing what to do. Thormir was full of nervous energy.

Then, a horn blew close at hand. It did not sound like a war horn or even an aggressive signal. The suddenness of the sound shook the group and mutterings and whispers ran through the crowd.

Mid-step, a man significantly older than Thormir leaned over him and whispered in a soft voice completely unsuited to the situation they were in. "They are coming for us." The whisper was so comically conspiratorial that Thormir almost laughed, despite his state of mind. The gentle voice repeated and continued, "They are coming for us. They will come in the though the swirling dust and take you to the hall of wounded dogs."

"All right, greybeard, all right. You keep thinking that." Thormir smiled reassuringly, trying to pry himself free from the man's mad gaze.

Like an iron vice, his left hand closed over Thormir's wrist, and he screamed, "THEY ARE COMING!"

CHAPTER TEN

"BECAUSE YOU AMUSE ME."
Teu skemta mi

That night the old greybeard's words haunted him. Sleep did not bless him until early dawn, and even then he was only granted two hours before he was roused by shouts and horns. However, when he did raise his cheek from the hard surface where he had been resting, what the old man had said had travelled to back of his mind. The group had been given their orders to move to the quarry, several miles away on the far east side of the city. There they were to join the slaves already breaking and shaping the stone.

It took almost half the morning to reach the quarry. On their arrival, the group could barely believe its depth – it went down for half a mile. The sides were jagged by the breaks and carved stone. Powder from the broken stone, and the stamping of feet from the countless slaves, swirled in small eddies while billowing dust clouded some sections of the paths that sloped up towards the surface. The tinkle and ring of small chisels and hammers echoed off the rounded walls of the quarry. A timed chant, the words of which were lost to Thormir, winged its way to the party, issuing from the nearest wooden scaffold, itself one of many that covered the walls and small caverns within the quarry.

The shape of the stone pit reminded Thormir of the beautiful dwarf city deep within the dark of Hurst Forest. But this seemed to be a mockery of the Dwarven city's power and magnificence. Unlike the dark grey stone of Az Osten du Baraklemen, here the stone walls were light brown and in some places the colour of coal.

It was then that it occurred to Thormir that he had never asked anyone how the breach in the wall had come to be. *But who would tell me? Not the people I am with. They would have no more of an idea about it than I have. And forget about the soldiers, they would just whip me or send me off to The Pound.* He had heard the soldiers talk and threaten to take slaves and members of their party to The Pound if they did not behave, keep in line, or do as they were instructed. When one of the soldiers had threatened the tall woman who had lost her child, she had said, "I do not fear death, for I have already died." The statement had taken the soldier aback and he had turned from her and walked back to his position in line.

Still, thought Thormir, *I need to know more about what has happened here if I am to escape this place. What is The Pound? And what could have caused such damage to such a strong wall?* All this and more he pondered as he and his party were led towards their designated place of labour within the pit.

By the time they reached their places within the quarry, the cold had left the morning and had been replaced by a merciless sun. However, despite the heat beating on the backs of their necks as they collected their hammers and took up positions amongst the stone, Thormir noticed a cloud to the north west. It was like no other cloud in the sky because it didn't move; instead it merely hung in place – a vast expanse of dark purples and blacks. Unlike the fog that had hung over Orien at the break of dawn, it seemed impenetrable by the sun. With a plunging feeling, he felt old worries return anew. Even the pounding of his hammer on the cracked rocks could not quell the feeling of dread that swirled inside the deep of his stomach.

Magic.

He was sure of it, and it seemed to have appeared overnight. This was why Orien was building its walls. Fear – fear of the unknown. This was why so many slaves had been put to work: some trained as soldiers, some sent to endure the high scaffolds, and others sent to work in the quarry – cutting stone for the wall. Now he had a weapon. Words could be just as deadly as the point of a sword if applied at the right moment. He just had to wait for the right time.

It was late in the afternoon when Thormir and the rest of his group heard the cry of pain. All of them turned to find the tall woman upon the ground writhing in agony. Her build did not fit the swing of a hammer, not to mention how she must have felt about the loss of her child. As he saw her squirming with pain, sorrow and a familiar dread returned. Thormir could see the break in her shoulder and the misplacement of bone from its socket. He was already running to help when he felt Selena streak passed him. She knelt beside her and cradled her in her arms. Selena passed a hand over the woman's eyes and whispered something in her ear. She nodded and seemed to brace herself. Taking her wrist and elbow, Selena positioned them straight, and then she took the woman by her upper arm and pushed.

She screamed, harsh and piercing, but even above the noise Thormir heard the bones click back into place. The woman heaved, her breast rising and falling with the relief. Finally, she stopped and turned wearily to Selena. Thormir suspected that she was about to thank her, but he saw her look of gratitude turn to fear. Thormir had frozen just ten steps away from both of them.

Three soldiers were now behind Selena, with hungry looks upon their faces.

No, not now, not again.

One of the soldiers bent down and with a sick tenderness whispered something in Selena's ear. Quick as a snake, she spun and in one swift movement, she chopped at the man's neck with her right hand. To Thormir's and the other soldier's surprise, the soldiers' dropped limp, but not dead. One of the two started forward and slapped Selena with the back of his hand. This time it was Selena who dropped to the ground.

The sight of Selena limp upon the dusty gravel enraged Thormir beyond all reason. He summoned every ounce of strength he possessed. Like an enraged bull, he charged at the soldier.

The soldier dodged his tackle and reached out to seize the back of Thormir's tunic. He felt the man's hand close upon the fabric and hold him in place.

"I think some time in The Pound will do you good. Maybe you will have learnt your lesson by the time you get out, if you get out. Oh, and your pretty, little friend will be going with you."

* * *

The day after he and Selena had attacked the soldiers, they had found themselves strapped to separate whipping posts. Despite the words of comfort whispered between them, the pain of being whipped in front of the entire camp, was not quelled.

After they had bled, the medic, who had stitched and covered their wounds in a thick, clumpy, yellow paste, had healed them the best he could. The paste had burned, but offered some relief from the pain. The next day they both woke to find that their wounds no longer hurt and had all but gone, but for the white, puffy lines that covered their backs.

Late that afternoon, soldiers had come and put them in the back of a carriage. Peering through the iron bars, Thormir could tell from the position of the sun that they had begun travelling in a south-westerly direction, closer to the centre of the city. It was half a day more until they arrived at what the soldiers called The Pound. The noise was the first thing that hit Thormir – it was deafening, and rang in his ears. It was the sound of fighting, jeering spectators, merchants haggling over coins, and screams of pain.

He had arrived at The Pound.

Pushed from the carriage, he and Selena had been clamped in irons and marched off, down into a cell beneath the ground. With horror, Thormir realised the water sinking into the mud was not water but blood, which seeped through wooden boards that formed the roof of the tunnel through which they were being led. What had he done to land himself in this place?

Finally they had arrived at his cell. Others like it stood opposite and beside it. They were filled with slaves who were either paranoid and scared, or who had already condemned themselves to the afterlife. All seemed to have fight left in them, for they snarled like savage dogs, willing themselves to win their freedom from this place.

From the bruises and cuts upon the men in the cages and the large medical area at the end of the dirty, blood-soaked hall, Thormir thought that this place must be a fight club, where a slave wins freedom or dies in the effort, and all for the sport of others.

*　　*　　*

By the third day in The Pound, his face was a crosshatch of cuts and half-healed gashes. He had tried to reach out with his mind – to find Fern, to find Mary, Tangar, or even Lucian, but he could not find them. Every time he had tried, thousands of voices opened up inside his head creating such a confused buzzing that Thormir's head throbbed and pounded for hours afterward.

Thormir felt hot blood trickle into his eyes from the most recent injury that had sliced his brow. He fingered the leather tag around his neck, passing a bloodied thumb over the grooves. He looked down at the figures that had been carved into it. Only blood covered the surface. *Who am I? What have I become?* It seemed to Thormir that he was being thrown from one bloody situation into another. It was as if someone had rearranged the chapters in his life story so all of the horrific experiences in his life occurred one after the other in one big waking nightmare.

Thormir brought himself back to the present, and his third day in this hell-hole; the noise of jeering crowds and bleeding men assaulted his ears. Selena was slumped in the corner of the cell. Thormir watched her with concern. Her breathing had become short and irregular. Selena's strength was fading, giving in to the evil of this place. But as he saw her strength ebb, he felt his own increase, as if Selena had given him a reason to fight, to seek a way out. He was fighting for her, he was fighting for all he had known and lost, and most importantly he was fighting to escape. *I will not die in here.*

Click. Clang.

The sounds came from the end of the hallway, from the door to the stairs that led up into the small, wooden arena in which the prisoners and condemned men would fight.

Thud, thunk. Thud, thunk.

The odd sound of the cell master's footsteps echoed down the hall. Thormir strained against his iron manacles. If only he could work the chain so that the rung at the back would soften and bend the iron. The u-bend that anchored him to the wall paid his efforts no heed.

Thud, thunk. Thud, thunk.

The condemned were screaming insults at the man who walked so calmly among them.

"Go eat horse shit, you dung-ridden belly slapper!" said a skinny slave in the cage two down from Thormir's, hoping his insults would yield a response from the cell master, better still that he be chosen to fight. He had a wild and frenzied face that bore all the scars of insanity. Thormir admired his courage. It was no small thing to laugh in the face of death, and this man had done exactly that.

The cell master stopped for a moment to glower at the skinny, wild-eyed slave, but then continued down the row of cells until he reached Thormir's. Placing his left hand upon a rusty iron bar and unlocking the gate, he pulled it open and entered.

He cast a quick gaze towards Thormir and then walked over to the corner where Selena lay still, asleep, wandering with the dream gods.

Slap.

The backhand could be heard above all the insults still being hurled at the master. Selena's eyes flew opened, and her hand jumped to her cheek. Gasping from the pain, she struggled to stay upright.

"Let's see how you fare against the next of our champions. Come on my lovely, it's your turn fight now."

"No!" Thormir moved to strike him, but he was too slow. The man caught his wrist mid-swing and twisted, bending his arm backwards.

"Well then, let us make this a little more interesting. You *both* will face the finest of our champions – you will face The Surgeon!" With a maniacal laugh and a high-pitched squeal, he threw his arms up into the air before subsiding into excited giggles. "Do you know why we call him The Surgeon? I will tell you. It's because he never kills with one hit, but slowly takes apart his opponent."

Thormir grunted. "Surely a surgeon heals and fixes wounds rather than taking this apart?"

The master let out a gruesome giggle, "Yes, yes. But you see he does put you back together again once he beats you senseless, ONLY TO TAKE YOU APART AGAIN! Piece by piece."

Bending down towards Selena, he uncuffed her. When he had done the same with Thormir, he grabbed them both by the upper arm and led them down the corridor.

Thormir squinted into the gloom and began reciting one of the poems that Tangar had taught him to use when he needed to calm himself before a fight.

> "When the seas rise and fall,
> and the mountains touch the sky,
> trees of Hurst will heed the call,
> reaching winds shall heed the cry.
>
> Change will come to Vâryá,
> and stars all shall seek.
> We shall come to proud Elcala,
> no more evil shall speak.
>
> Doriel will heal our heart,
> and the nightshade will die today.
> All shadow shall depart,
> leaving white light and crystal bay.
>
> The powers of Yana will return,
> and ancient Nolwin will voice the way.
> Songs of the elves, all shall yearn,
> yet I will forever wander, wander in the depths of day."

"BECAUSE YOU AMUSE ME."

The brightness of the flames flickering from wall-mounted brackets flashed and caused a momentary lapse in his concentration. The sounds of the arena and his cellmates cheering and jeering bombarded him as he was marched to his fate.

*   *   *

Thormir beheld the wooden arena. Thick beams of mountain pine formed a peaked roof that closed off the arena to the sky. The walls behind the top level of seats that surrounded the arena in rows were made of light, wooden slats that let in the sunlight or the glow of the moon. Torches held in metal brackets lit the faces of the 100 or so people that crowded the tiers of the small stadium. They laughed as a butchered slave was dragged from where he had fallen upon the sand. Their thirst for blood was evident in their expressions. Thormir watched as two slaves lugged the bloodied limp body through a small dark rectangular door. *Will we be next?*

Standing still, with his back to Thormir, was a man who was almost certainly the one they called The Surgeon. He had a full body tribal tattoo that covered his entire left side and reached all the way up to the dome of his bald head. His ears were pierced with metal rings, and as he saw Thormir staring at him, he bared his yellow teeth. A clear, frothing, red-tinged liquid fell in slow drops to the sandy floor.

To Thormir's relief The Surgeon, being slightly shorter in stature, did not have the advantage of height. Tangar had taught Thormir to always look for an opponent's disadvantage as well as their advantages.

"The key to defeating your opponent is to know them. Know their strategy, know their strengths and weaknesses, and most importantly of all things, know their heart." Tangar had said that any fighting technique could be defended if one used the routines that he had taught Thormir and Fern as they had travelled along The Tongue of Hurst.

As the master led him and Selena into the centre of the ring, Thormir studied their opponent. Thormir saw a deep cut just above his left kneecap. *Has he already had a fight a won, or is that just an old wound resurfacing? That might come in useful. If only I could bring him to his knees, then I could try to ground him or knock him out.*

When they reached the centre of the ring, the cell master pulled them to a halt. As Thormir continued to study the man in front of him, Selena nudged him and nodded to the left. There was a wooden crate on top of which lay a small bowl filled with odd implements and objects; things that no one would ever need.

"This fight be to the death!" the master yelled to the crowd. They fell silent. "This fight be to the death!" the master said again, louder and clearer than before. "No mercy shall be shown, no pity shall be given." The crowd exploded with bloodthirsty glee. It was clear that this was supposed to be a main event. Thormir had not expected to fight to the death. He had never killed without just cause; indeed he had never killed a man. The thought sickened him, but if there was a time to do it, it was now. *I will fight.*

The master continued in his clear, high-pitched voice, "It appears that we are joined tonight by a royal visitor. Ladies, gentlemen, dogs of the arena – I give you Lord Bath of House Bathos."

The master was not lying. Lounging lazily on one of the recliners in the only booth in the arena was Lord Bath. The lord's smug demeanour disgusted Thormir. He showed no proper signs of royal dignity. He had sandy blonde hair that fell and curled at his fat jawline. With a thickset neck and a general roundness of appearance, Thormir thought the man plump – no form for any member of royalty. Lying over his long purple and gold robes was a slave girl. She was dressed in a long, silver, silk dress that slid off her porcelain legs and trailed out of sight. Lord Bath was playing with her vivid red hair, curling it around a long, silver knife. Thormir watched as Bath took his knife and skewered a grape from a bunch next to him. Taking the knife, still with the grape stuck upon it, he carefully inserted it into the girl's mouth. She was forced to eat it. As if agreeing with his delight, his many gold rings flashed around his fat fingers. Bath took the knife and flicked it at her. A nick opened up across her cheek and Bath laid the flat of the knife against it. As he held the slave girl down, he put the knife to his lips and tasted her blood. He smiled – a crooked smile, and began wiping the silver blade over the girl's mouth and chin. Bath took a goblet from the side and raised it and saluted the crowd with a grin. At that moment his other hand slipped and instead of continuing to wipe his blade, he slit the girl's throat. His smile turned into a grimace of disgust and he tossed her from his lap. Immediately, he waved behind him and two young boys came and took her body away. He yelled something to someone and a minute later, another younger slave girl lay half-naked across his lap. He skewered a grape.

The master waited for the crowd to acknowledge the presence of Bath then waited for the sound to die down before continuing. "On one side we have two newcomers. He is the man who loves blood and gore – it is one-three-four!" At that simple rhyme the crowd went wild, waving their hands and shaking their fists, jeering and laughing. Thormir shifted uneasily as he heard the number engraved on the tags around his neck.

"And here," the master put a filthy hand on the side of Selena's face. She turned away slightly but the man continued, licking his lips as he did so, "we have a newcomer. She has never fought before but we will see where credit is due, it's one-three-two!" Again the crowd roared hungrily.

"And now the person you have all been waiting for. He slices, he dices, it's . . . The Surgeon!" This time the roar of the crowd was deafening.

"Fighters, pick your instrument of pain." The master brought out the bowl and blindfolded each of them in turn. Then each of them put a hand into the bowl and pulled out a small object."

With the removal of the black cloth from his eyes, Thormir saw what he had picked up: a writing quill. Selena had chosen a small disc or a tray of some sort. Glancing over at The Surgeon, Thormir saw a rusty iron razor resting in his palm. A crooked smile twisted The Surgeon's face, contorting his already broken nose.

"Behold, to The Surgeon I give a mace." The master opened the massive chest. Many deadly weapons lay inside, but Thormir had eyes only for the horrid black mace the master was shouldering. Giving it to The Surgeon, he turned to Selena and Thormir. "And for you, sir, I give a sword." His condescending tone only angered Thormir, but the master continued licking his lips, "And for you, my lady, I give a shield to protect your pretty, little face." The master's tongue darted from his mouth as he considered Selena. He licked his lips, showing off his pale yellow teeth.

The master clapped his hands and the same two slaves who had dragged the dead body from the sand hurried forward and carried the chest out of the ring, through the same black door. *Am I going to be the next body to go through that door?* Thormir's thoughts seemed to be mirrored by Selena's looks. Thormir knew that she was stronger than most women he had met, even cold at times, but now her face betrayed her fear.

He brushed a thumb over the edge of the sword. *Not even sharp. Of course it wouldn't be. This means the only way to kill is with a thrust, which is the easiest way to let yourself become exposed to an attack. Even if I get The Surgeon's mace, I wouldn't even be able to lift that thing.*

"Begin!"

As soon as the master gave his signal, The Surgeon started circling Thormir and Selena, who were standing next to each other – she with the shield, and he with the sword.

Remember your lessons Thormir, he thought, *remember what Tangar taught you. Calm yourself, think, and study your enemy, know him.* And so he did. Once again Thormir studied how he moved, how he was thinking, the slight limp of his left leg, the way he held his mace with two hands instead of one, and his attitude.

Thormir reached out with his mind, but before he could try anything, The Surgeon took the first swing. The mace whistled over Thormir's head as he ducked. Selena remained standing and positioned her shield so that the mace bounced off in an awkward direction. Her ploy did not work. As soon as the mace hit, the shield splintered up the side. Seeing the weakness of her defence, The Surgeon launched another attack at Selena, this time swinging the mace in an arc towards the other side. Thormir rolled forward and slashed his shin. He howled in pain, and turned to Thormir. Releasing one hand from his mace, he swung a massive fist towards Thormir. Thormir blocked it. The Surgeon swung the mace at him. Thormir dodged, blocked, and then swung his own sword, sending the rusty blade into the side of his cheek. Catching the one sharp area on the blade, a jagged cut opened, but The Surgeon seemed not to notice. He launched a massive kick at Thormir's torso. As the kick landed, it sent Thormir flying across the ring. His chest felt like it had been hammered a thousand times by the blacksmiths of Medani.

With a crash, Thormir smashed into the side of the wall, and fell to the ground, heaving in pain. Out of the corner of his eye, he saw the muscled wall of tattoos approaching; but then he caught another figure behind him, running then jumping. Selena brought the rest of her shield down upon The Surgeon's head. The wood splintered and The Surgeon stumbled and fell on his left knee. He was obviously not up to form, as the crowd seemed disappointed at the showing. Some even went as far as to boo him.

Still kneeling upon the ground, and leaning on one hand, which was firmly planted in the sand, The Surgeon raised his head and looked directly at Thormir. *Get up, don't be a fool, he will kill you, get up!* Again and again Thormir urged himself to his feet but with no success. He thought he might have broken some bones, maybe ribs, as he was slammed into the fencing. He looked over at The Surgeon to see him land a heavy blow on the side of Selena's cheek.

A surge of energy rushed into Thormir. Like hot fire it burned in his veins, and with it he bounded to his feet. He could feel a slight itch in his side, but other than that he felt stronger than he had when entering the ring; he felt the strongest he had ever felt. Revelling in his new strength, Thormir looked towards Selena to see if she was okay. She was lying motionless on the sand. The Surgeon was standing over her. He stared at Thormir. His sneer contorted his face into broken angles.

Thormir ran towards The Surgeon. Halfway to him, Thormir bent, picked up a sharp splinter of wood from the broken shield, and changed direction, heading for the fencing slightly to the right of where The Surgeon was standing over Selena's limp form. As he reached the wall he jumped onto the side, and then launched himself towards his opponent, pushing out with his right foot. In the timeless moment that marked the space between jump and impact, Thormir noticed that many of the men and women in the front row were white-faced and heavily exhausted, each leaning over as if to catch their breath. Even Lord Bath, who sat high in his box, was shaking his head, pale-faced and confused.

Then the impact. Thormir wrapped his legs himself around The Surgeon's neck and torso squeezing as hard as he could. At the same time, he brought the wooden piece down, plunging it into the soft of the man's neck. Blood spurted in small shoots around the wood, painting Thormir's face. Letting go as The Surgeon fell to his knees, Thormir hurried over to Selena. Only the whites of her eyes were showing, but she was still breathing. Thormir saw the slow rise and fall of her chest and thanked Doriel All-Father for sparing her life.

A heavy silence dropped over the arena. People were checking their tickets and wages in silent outrage. Some lad and girl that had been brought from the quarry had defeated their favourite killer.

"Kill him!" The master's high-piercing voice echoed above the silence. Thormir now realised that the crowd had gone quiet at the demise of their favourite hero, the bringer of death, The Surgeon.

"No!" It was the first time Lord Bath had spoken and Thormir recoiled in disgust as he heard words full of oily deceit seep through the slight slit between Bath's fat lips. "I will have words with The Pound's new alpha. I wish to purchase you. What say you to that, boy?"

The question was clearly directed at Thormir, something the master did not approve of, as was quite obvious from the expression on his face.

Looking straight into the sandy-haired, fat-necked, plump face of Lord Bath, Thormir said, "I will not go anywhere unless she comes with me! If you do not like that, come down here and I will fight and kill you like I did your precious Surgeon." Thormir pointed at the tattooed body being dragged through the black door, and glared at Bath.

The silence in the arena was deafening, only broken by the dialogue between Lord Bath and himself.

"Why raise voice? Certainly she will come." The oiled words seemed to soothe Thormir, easing out his worries and pains, brushing them away carelessly from his shoulders. However, the lathered words did not fool Thormir into thinking he and Selena were safe.

"Why do you want us?" The Surgeon's kick must have damaged his ribs, because he was having trouble speaking and his question turned to a cracked yell.

Smiling as he observed Thormir's weakness, Lord Bath said, "Because you amuse me."

"No!"

"No?" Lord Bath raised one eyebrow. The crowd stood in silence.

Thormir, still in pain, looked at the sneering face of Bath. *I will not become the plaything of lesser men. I will not let Selena come to further harm.* "I will not serve you. I will not become one of you."

A flash of anger passed over Lord Bath's face. "You will come with me, and you will serve me and my palace. And as for who you are, that is not for you to decide." Releasing the eyebrow that had remained poised in the same lofty position throughout the dialogue, Bath continued, "Ringmaster, hand these two victors to my guards. We await you outside. As for deal struck," Bath looked at Thormir and bared his obscenely white teeth, "the girl will join, but she will be absent from sight. Say your goodbyes boy, and you best have gratitude that I have not left her here with these foul dogs."

"No!" As Thormir screamed at Bath, arms seized his shoulders and pulled him to his feet. With that same strength as before, he turned and elbowed a soldier across the jaw. He heard a crack like splitting bone. He turned to see a fist arcing towards his face, and darkness enveloped him.

142

CHAPTER ELEVEN

THE DREAM
Drêyma

The wind ruffled Thormir's clothes and hair as he stood on the hilltop. Somehow he recognised this place; it was as if he had been here before. The night was cold and the wind that tossed its way across the plains carried sounds upon its back. Thormir thought he heard hoof beats and the whistle of arrows, but he could not be sure. The moonlight shone pale, lighting the backs of the rolling hills so that they seemed to sway back and forth.

Thormir took a step forward. He could see Hurst Forest in the distance. It formed a dark horizon. The dense forest blotted out all light like ink spilt on new parchment. But no matter, the night seemed calm and nothing but the hoot of an owl stirred the peace. He took another step forward. It seemed hard for him to move, as if he were under a great weight. His footsteps seemed to stick to the ground. It was then that he noticed he was wearing finely-made sandals, but not so fine that they would draw attention in a crowd full of nobles. Where did he get them? *They are not of the make of Medani.* He would try to solve that small mystery some other time. He felt that urge to press on, the same feeling he had

had ever since he had come to the hilltop. Something was driving him, wanting him to be near.

Just as he scaled the hill in front of him and came to its crest, he heard the cry. It was as if a soul was being ripped from someone, as if a heart was being torn from a living body. Only one thing could have caused a person to scream like that – death.

Thormir was scared. He had heard screams like that before, and this was far too similar for his liking. He made to turn back the way he had come, but then he saw them.

Dark outlines, not far from the forest. He could not count their number. They were gathered in a circle around a crouched form, which seemed to be guarding something. One of them drew closer. It appeared that he or she was a humpback, for as they bent down their back was illuminated in the pale moonlight.

The crouching figure howled again. Its power seemed to turn the night and the world around Thormir into a swirling velvet then pitch black. Thormir stared at the inside of his eyelids. He was shaking with cold and sweat. He knew he had been crying, for he felt hot tears run down the curve of his cheek.

"It was the dream again, wasn't it?"

Selena was staring at him. "I dared not wake you; you were thrashing about. I . . ." she swallowed. Thormir was ashamed to see that she was being hesitant with him, "I could not get close to you."

"It was worse this time," he said, "more real. It was as if I was really there."

"How did you see it?"

He shook his head – reluctant to answer. He hated this new weakness. His nights were now filled with that same dream, or else a violent seizure; either way he would always wake up drenched in sweat with his hands bawled into fists. He had already told her what the dream was about, so her question confused him.

"I mean," she paused as if gathering her thoughts, "how did the scene appear to you? Were you looking through your eyes or looking from above?"

"No, it's like I'm really there, like everything is taking place as real as I see you now." Thormir looked Selena over as she crossed her arms. She appeared fine, and her bruises seemed to have faded into small patches of green, blue, and purple. "Where are we?"

Selena looked up, and he could tell that the answer to his question would give neither solace nor comfort. "In another cell. You were out for quite some time. We are in the palace now. The guards will be moving me soon, to where to women are kept."

Moonlight shone through the bars of a high window. The shadows cast fingers of darkness across the cell floor, but other than that haunting image, the pale light seemed to calm both of them. For a while they sat together, looking at the shapes of the clouds cast across the midnight sun. Thormir was not shackled anymore so he stood up, stretching his aching muscles. *At least that's something to be grateful for*, he thought. He rubbed his wrists and looked out the window, with one knee resting on a small bench that had been pushed against the cell wall. The moon illuminated a large courtyard with a pool in the centre. The light cast a glaze over the surface of the water, turning it to a white sheet of glass. The courtyard that surrounded the large pool was tiled with large stone slabs; each tile had been laid with careful hands, the work of an expert mason. Lines of pillars formed a walkway around the outer edge of the square. These pillars supported a slight overhang of roof tiles that formed a cover bordering the courtyard's outer edge. Thormir supposed this was where the nobles would take rest and calm their troubled minds. Thormir knew it must be beautiful, but in his circumstances the glassy water seemed to pierce his soul and reflect his fear: fear of this place, and of the cage he was in. The pillars that surrounded the pool were stone guardians, watching and trapping the prisoners who wished to escape this place.

Thormir was determined not to let his fear defeat him, so he turned from the window. "How long do you think we will stay in this place?"

"Forever."

Selena's answer shocked Thormir. He never suspected that she would give up; he had not pegged her as a quitter. However, as she looked up at him, he saw a fire in her eyes, an inferno of determination that told him that she would not stay here. She would work tirelessly, in secret, until she had found a way to escape this place. With that realisation, Thormir sat down on the bench, leaning on the cold, hard cell wall.

He was tired, the kind of tired that drags the eyelids down with an invisible weight, making staying awake an endless struggle. Stretching in a vertical arc, he felt for his bruised and damaged ribs. He pressed against his third and fourth ribs. No pain. Pressing again, he searched for the pain. Nothing. Selena looked up as he pulled off the top half of his riding tunic. Looking down, he saw no purple-black-blue marks, but just unblemished skin, smooth and unsullied. He wondered at his lack of injury after the belting he had suffered in The Pound.

Before he could comment to Selena about the mystery, they both heard a soft padding coming up the hallway. Familiar beats and intakes of breath reached Thormir's ears, and he rushed to the edge of the cell. His knuckles turned white with anticipation. *Could it be? Is it really him?*

The shaggy head of Fern rounded the end of the corridor. He was not walking at his full height, but rather was crouched down, as if he was stalking prey. He turned his head quickly, picking up the familiar scent of his friend. Fern growled and bared his teeth. The pale white of his sabre-like fangs caught in the moonlight and his eyes flashed like two shards of flint.

"Fern!" Thormir strained his whisper. The padding turned into a quick run and then Fern stood in front of the iron bars. They looked into each other's eyes, and an understanding passed between them. It was an understanding of the hurt and pain they had suffered, and their relief that they had found each other. If the worst had happened to Fern, Thormir felt he might have become a wraith, filled with sorrow and pain at the loss of his brother.

He looked closely at Fern, and was surprised to see a change in appearance. Rather than the shaggy-haired dog, Fern looked more like a wolf – all of the friendliness of his dog form was gone, replaced by a menacing stealth. However, upon seeing Thormir, Fern had wagged his tail with joy, a feeling Thormir was sure he had not felt in a long time, not since Hurst.

Thormir too was overjoyed to see his best friend. A niggling worry had been creeping the dark depths of his mind, that his friend had been tortured or worse. Now that Fern stood in front of Thormir, he noticed that he looked healthier than ever. It seemed that this harsh city had changed them all – moulded each of them to its own fit. *Instead of the revered archer prince of Carathron, I have become a killer, lost in this foul city of scum. But Fern?*

Despite his confidence that it was indeed Fern standing in front of him, Thormir extended a tendril of thought.

Fern? Is that you?

Yes. His answer came full of excitement, followed by a low growl.

"Not many people can do what you are doing." Selena's comment came from the corner. She seemed calm but the music in her voice induced a kind of hidden excitement. She moved closer to Thormir.

"What do you mean?" said Thormir, knowing perfectly what she meant. He still did not know Selena that well, and was not keen to share the knowledge that he could communicate with others with his mind.

147

"You are talking to the dog, are you not?"

The question left Thormir trapped. If he said he could not communicate with Fern his long absences in speech would raise suspicion; if he admitted he could indeed communicate with his mind, more questions would be asked.

Before he could answer, another unfamiliar mind joined with his. The strength of the mental hit was enormous and Thormir struggled to repel the attack. He used all the techniques his tutor and Mary had taught him, so long ago. He concentrated on one single image, on a crack in the cell floor, so that he could erect a mental wall that no thought could breach. But this new mind smashed it to pieces. Thormir tried reciting poetry and scripture, mentally speaking the words that formed the epic that lamented the green lands of Guldor. His mental scripture was torn to shreds as the attack on his mind continued. Then, as suddenly as a startled bird taking flight, the other consciousness passed into his own – and like the waters of a new, bubbling spring the thoughts flowed into the river of his own mind. But like with any river, the water can be paddled both ways.

Music and song, filled with sorrow and beauty, echoed in the caverns of his mind. The music seemed ancient and powerful, a timeless echo of ages past, of a beauty lost and forgotten by mortal men. The world was dark now, filled with greys and blacks; no memory remained of the light that once filled every hall and corner of Vâryá. And yet, there was something about the song that spoke of youth, new beauty and a shining grace; a flame of hope burned brightest of all, and all seemed to dance around that glow in a measured beat.

Selena? Tentatively, Thormir melded his mind and extended the question to the new presence. Thormir looked at Selena, who had her knees pulled up to her chin. She was smiling at him, an expression that he had rarely seen. Her smile transformed her quiet, bold beauty into a glowing radiance. Despite her home being destroyed, and all their men being cut down and left to die, she still was a light, a bright glimmer of beauty shining through the greys of the world.

Yes.

As soon as her answer came, a wave of relief washed over him. He was not alone. *This here is Fern, my best friend.* Separating his thoughts from Selena's, he said to Fern, *Do not morph. I think there are some things that should remain secret, at least for now; otherwise we might do more harm than good.*

Fern growled in approval of the thought. *I have to go soon, so I will have to be quick.*

Smiling at the reunion with his brother, and melding his mind back with Selena's, Thormir said, *Go on, tell us everything – we haven't got much time to spare either.*

PART 2

"Memories are but ripples in the river of eternity."

CHAPTER TWELVE

FERN II
Fern II

Fern did not like this weather. He had always enjoyed the cold, harsh winter winds that generally blew all year round in the South and the tundra around Medani. Here it seemed too . . . uncomfortable. While it was not hot in Orien, the city did have those days when it sweltered due to a random heatwave blown in from Durnsay, or the plains of the northern tribes. Anyway, he felt that it wasn't just his neck brace that made his paws itch, but the shift in weather and normality. Plus, he missed Thormir.

The iron tugged at his neck.

He walked forward, continuing his path towards the man the soldiers called the general. For some reason, Fern felt calm. Maybe it was the fact that his height against the five soldiers unnerved them. In any case, he was not concerned for his fate, just for his friends, and Thormir, whom he considered his brother by blood. *If they hurt him, I will rip out their throats.* He could almost taste the blood of the soldiers upon his lips as he dwelled on the thought. *How I would love to seize them by their necks, and toss them from side to side until their bones shattered into a thousand tiny pieces.*

So their necks became a pincushion for the crushed bone splinters that punctured their flesh. But no, I must not, at least not now. I must wait. When there is opportune moment, then I will strike.

Fern watched small dust tornadoes circle up the street between the dancing children and the legs of frightened cats. *Cats are so distasteful. I don't see why all the humans like them so much. All they do is judge and point*, Fern thought. He watched as a street cat stopped and looked at him. Its red fur was dotted with the comings of snow, and Fern was sure that it knew he was no dog. He lifted the corner of his lip and growled. The cat took off down a corridor between the tall houses, streaking past a short man selling vegetables from a small, wooden cart, and disappeared from sight.

There was another tug on the chain.

He growled as the metal cut into him, sinking through his fur, and reaching his skin. He felt the rusty iron brace grind against the skin behind his head, and winced as small cuts opened up. He dug his paws into the gravel and tried to ignore this new sensation. The noise of laughter and merriment permeated the air: the sighs of tired parents, and the excited giggles of children as they played around a crackling fire. Fern suspected it was further off than the sound indicated, as there was no sign of smoke or the colours of a party. Instead the street was as it normally was – filled with shops yearning for customers, beggars looking for coin, and nobles spitting on the homeless. Fern noticed that small fights would often break out between men haggling over prices, only to be resolved seconds later with a shrug and a nod. Fuses ran short. The bitter winds and hard oppression of Lord Bath seemed to have whittled all the good and happiness out of the men and women here, leaving hard exteriors, fragile tempers, and a deadened look in every eye. Yet Fern noticed that within that deadened look was a spark of fire; a fire and a will to survive despite all measures.

These people would make good warriors, Fern thought. He could smell it in their blood. Thormir and Fern had been brought up amongst warriors, but unlike the people here, they would fight differently. *I think the men and women in this place would fight with more fire and less skill than the warriors in Medani. Medani's warriors would fight with less fire but more skill.* Fern turned his head to watch a half-naked slave pass him. The man's right side was covered in vivid burn marks. Four hard-faced soldiers, who held spears to his throat as he walked, marched resolute and wary. He turned to Fern and smiled – a demented expression contorted his face. He took pleasure in the fact that he had this effect on this beastly dog. The soldier who guarded the rear gave the man a nudge with his spear, drawing a small amount of blood. The scarred beast didn't even flinch, but flexed his muscles so the metal head of the spear cut deeper into his flesh. The soldier holding the spear pushed again and this time the prisoner walked, leaving the clanging of his iron manacles loud in Fern's ears.

The cuff around Fern's neck jerked again. This time he lost his temper. The red-hot anger that had been boiling inside of him ever since he had split with Thormir erupted like a swarm of bees from a beaten hive. Fern took in the situation. Five men: two in front, and three behind. His advantages were the element of surprise and his strength; their advantages were numbers and weapons. First: pull neck back, unbalancing the front two soldiers. Second: attack, snap necks, and twist to defend against on-comers. Third: kill the ugly, red-haired one, who has advantage of distance, with the spear. Fern's disadvantage was his own size as a target. The other two soldiers he would deal with when he reached them. Fern tensed his muscles.

"A-ha, there you are."

Fern was on the point of jumping and wrenching back his neck when a voice came. It fell harsh upon his ears, and Fern looked around for its source. A man stood about 100 yards away, waving a massive hand. Fern could taste the blood of the soldiers he was going to attack, but also he could smell the stench of the man hailing the soldiers down.

Why does this human smell of so many? thought Fern and he squinted as the soldiers turned abruptly to march towards his voice. He was massive for a human, and well-built. In fact, he was bigger than any man Fern had ever seen, including the chieftain of the Dacarrus that he had fought on the road to Medani. This human, however, did not have a single scent. Instead the scent of many humans was wrapped around him, yet none stood by his side. The man turned and leant over a table as if considering war strategy from maps and charts, his back facing them. Fern saw what he wore on his back. A cloak of hair, but the hair of many; scalps of murdered men, women, and children were sewn together so their hair fell in a patched mockery of a seamless fur cloak. This must be the general.

Fern flicked his yellow-green eyes and consented to being led up the stairs, and then into a great red tent where the general was now waiting. He was not alone. A fatter man lounged upon a pile of red cushions. Food including grapes, bread, and cheese had been arranged in a giant arc around his couch. Upon his belly, which was so vast it acted as a table, were three or four sausages and exotic fruits from which he was picking. Before Fern's arrival he had obviously been throwing grapes into his mouth while listening to some speech from the general, as a number of them were caught in his curly, blond hair.

He has enough fat in his belly to feed a family of bears throughout a summer, with spare for a cold winter, thought Fern, eyeing the expanse of the royal's belly. Fern established the man must be a royal, even though he was wearing purple, rather than red cloak lined with gold thread that was custom in Medani. *So this must be Lord Bath? Well*, thought Fern, *he is certainly royally fed.*

Naked girls stood on either side of Lord Bath waving fans, their bodies painted in intricate blue and gold patterns. Another woman lay with him. She too was naked but this one, Fern thought, had a bored, beaten look in her eyes; she seemed resigned to her fate of lying with fat men and pleasuring their every desire. She was just a plaything and she knew it. Bath was now running one of the sausages up and down her arm, leaving a trail of grease that caught in the light like the sticky, silvery-white slime left by night snails.

Lord Bath spoke. His oily voice slicked over Fern's ears and fur. "It seems I must take leave. Your whores and hospitality were well-received, your expense shall be covered. As for situation concerning the wall, send scouts to see how far The Crow's army sees us. When the time befalls us, archers must swell in number around the main gate. I shall not risk a battle on open plain for outcome of such a move would indeed be dire." Bath paused and licked his lips, "Arr I think that tomorrow or the day after I shall visit The Pound – I have a thirst for blood, then that ragtag mutt from Durnsay arrives for the feast. General, I wish you to be there. That's an order from your –" Bath hiccupped then finished, " – Lord Bath. Yes, Lord Bath."

All of the soldiers and the general bowed as the couch that Fern now realised was a bed was lifted and carried away by six slaves that were adorned in the palace garb. The air cleared and the smells of liquor and pungent gases left the tent with Bath.

The general turned to the troops, saying, "The fool does not know anything of warfare and yet he has the audacity to tell me what is right for the survival of my army. He is nothing but a drunk, a scoundrel, and the mind behind the scum, violence, and crime in the city." Carved wooden pieces, which had been resting in strategic positions on a map, flew in every direction as the general hammered his fist into the table. The three women left the tent immediately. It was as if they knew, or had experienced before, the storm that was the general's anger. The soldiers shifted their feet but none dared leave their post. Fern looked up and could see a thick vein pulsing in the neck of one of the soldiers holding the chain.

How I would love to rip into that, he thought. He could almost taste it – the blood, the warmth of another life force. But he stayed himself. He would wait. Then he would kill them all.

The general was breathing hard, his back rising and falling, leaning on his hands, staring at the maps and faded charts that littered every inch of the wooden table. As if in routine, he reached out for a wooden bowl that held a small bunch of vivid purple berries. Taking one and popping it in his mouth, he crushed it with his tongue, and sucked on its supple juice. There was a wrenching sound and Fern saw one of the whores lean forward, about to throw up. Fern knew why. She too had noticed the berries, and she too knew what they were. They were Body-berries. Grown within the general's estate outside the city, the berries had to be brought in by his own host of slaves. The general owned no adult slaves, but preferred children; so when the berries were delivered, it was by hands that had rarely seen more than eight winters. While the general reigned supreme control over all his slaves, the whispers of children can never be held back, and it was through these whispers that the slaves of Orien came to know what the Body-berries were; and how the general grew them. Through the children's hushed tones, they had learned that when the general was displeased with one of his slaves, he would lead them into his gardens and kill them. He would not kill by any blow or crimson stab. He would kill by suffocating the children; forcing their mouths open and filling them with dirt from his garden bed. The slave who had recounted this vulgar routine had told them that with each kill, the general would whisper the same thing, "You shall continue to provide". The slave had said through tears, "He loves them, he tends to them". In a choked voice he had told them that the general would hang and skewer the corpses on the branches of a single, white skeletal tree. Stripped down, they hung there, giant leaves of fading pinks and bloody reds. The planting of the seeds followed this; so that from the dirt that filled mouths of the rotting bodies, berries would emerge; erupting and growing out of the silent screams of suffocated children. Body-berries. Without turning to look at the five soldiers still standing within the arced entrance to the tent, he said, "What have you brought me?"

"Captain Reddard sends his regards." The soldier gave Fern a kick in the rear, and Fern snarled as the iron-shod boot connected.

"Reddard!" the general exploded and raised himself to his full and considerable height as he spun to the soldiers. "Reddard! Ha, that son of a stable house whore would lick every inch of my boots if I asked him to."

"Aye, sir." The soldier who stood to the left of Fern obviously thought that this comment about Reddard would please the general.

"What did you just say, boy?"

"I . . ."

"Reddard be your commander and you will not cast foul words upon him under my watch."

With that the general turned, stalked towards him, and whipped his hand across the soldier's cheek in a backhanded slap. The soldier's neck reared, and his eyes rolled up in his head as he stumbled backward.

"Take yourself to the mess, and see work done. Clean every shit and foul thing left by undesired hand. Do not think to drop duty for word shall find ear, and lash will find blood."

The red outline of the general's backhand was imprinted upon the soldier's face as he turned, opened the flap to the tent, and disappeared, nursing his pride and honour.

"So, what breed greets eyes?"

The soldiers hesitated to answer, then one soldier who had a dumb-slackened face said, "A dog, sir."

Another cut in, "It looks like a hunting dog, although the breed eludes mind."

Fern nearly reached the man's armpit; his neck and upper body both wider than the soldier. The general looked down at Fern and raised an eyebrow, obviously impressed with Fern's height. "He is indeed of a fine form." The general reached down, placed two hands around Fern's throat muscle, and lifted him onto his hind legs. Fern snapped his jaws and bared his teeth in protest, but otherwise made no move.

"He smells of mud and horse. Clean him, then cut off all this shaggy hair. This one will make a good war and hunting dog, of that there is no doubt."

*   *   *

Fern heard it clearly though the darkness, a single howl into the night, then more of them. There was no mistaking the voices of the wargs; their cries echoed out of Hurst Forest. He could not see them. He felt them. In his bones, he felt their voices. They called to him. Again and again they called to him. He smelled meat through the darkness.

The swirling darkness turned purple and the sounds of three musical howls turned to the clanging of iron as the general banged on Fern's cage.

"Dog! Wake up."

Thump.

A huge shank of meat was dropped into his cage. Blood was still oozing from the place where the butchers had been a little too brutal. But that was how Fern liked it. Even when he was in his human form, he always liked his meat bloody. Biting into the

160

flesh he felt the muscle against his teeth. Some blood trickled into his mouth – a bonus. Fern raised his eyes to look at the general; to his surprise he saw a large set of keys, unlocking Fern's cage.

Obviously the general thought he had successfully trained and tamed Fern to the point that Fern would return if he were let free. And Fern was willing to let the deception continue. He only had to wait until all was safe, once his friends were safe – then he would kill the general and all of his men. Taking another mouthful of meat, Fern stood up and warily padded out of the cage. The general turned, apparently satisfied with Fern's discipline.

Maybe, Fern reflected, the general did have reason to be trusting of his new pet. Over the past week, at the general's instruction, Fern had accompanied the men on their scouting trips out of the city. Each time they had ventured north west over the plains of Carabeorn, the scouts and he had seen the darkening shadow of the emperor's army approaching, marching towards Orien. Fern had protected the men and the general from raiding bandits or the savage mountain men that were descending from The Al'Durast. He had given the appearance of obedience, a trait clearly not unnoticed by the general.

Fern nosed the flap to the tent and slid out into Orien. A few small red tents surrounded the general's, and the few men lingering outside were warming their hands over a crackling fire. Two of the soldiers looked up at Fern as he walked passed. He growled and flicked his tail in annoyance. Averting their eyes, the two went back to their fire and spoke in hushed tones.

Fern stopped and took in his surroundings. Darkness had come early, for it had been a hot day, and Fern noticed the sunlight dimming and icy winds picking up, signalling the dawn of dusk. The thatched houses had already been touched with a sprinkling of snow and the speckled roofs reminded Fern of the red cat that he had scared when he was being led through Orien a week's past.

The people that walked the streets seemed to be moving to and fro undecidedly, like ants before a rainstorm.

Fern knew the way to the main street from where he was, but he decided to explore a random back street that veered to his left. He followed a short man who was carrying a basket of bread that was partially covered by a dirty white rag. The rag reminded Fern of the blankets that had covered the infant human before it had been torn from its mother's breast. A ripple of discomfort snaked down Fern's back all the way to his tail.

The short man seemed to have noticed Fern following him, because he picked up his pace. Fern thought it was almost comical as the man sped up, his short, chubby legs waddling along while the top half of his body remained still, trying to give off a relaxed vibe.

Arriving at a door some way down, he tried to hurry inside. On the threshold of the door one of the loaves of bread fell and tumbled to the cobblestones paving the streets. The short man seemed to think for a moment, decided he would rather live, then shut the door with a snap. Fern laughed, but in this form it sounded like a bark. A mouse seized the opportunity for food at the arrival of the bread upon its home turf then turned tail and, seeing Fern's huge form, launched itself into a small hole in the stone wall of one of the houses.

Deeper in, Fern had noticed that not all of the houses were thatched; some had wooden slats and looked, to Fern, like scales on the hide of some giant beast. As he padded down the street he began testing himself as to how quiet be could be. He placed one paw in front of another. He avoided the small twigs and dry leaves that would give him away to enemies. He smelled the air. He still tasted the dirty stink of the mouse, but new and more inviting tastes and smells wafted towards him. Still silent, he made his way down the alley. He stuck to the shadows, so that no one could see him approaching. Three people had passed already, and none of them had seen or sensed his presence. He felt proud that he could hide himself so well. The fourth person who passed stopped, peered into the dark, then walked on, oblivious to the fact that a massive dog lurked not six feet away.

The alley was widening now and the smells of ale, mead, wine, and all the other treats that a bar offered filled his nostrils. He saw the glow of the open tavern door. He made out the name engraved on a small wooden sign that swung back and forth, 'The Giant's Grotto'. The name of the tavern seemed inappropriate in almost every way. Surely a giant's grotto would be large and expansive, but this place just had its squeaky sign and a small, narrow doorway to announce its presence to the people of Orien. Nevertheless, Fern had the feeling that this was not a bar where anyone would be welcome. Instead, Fern suspected this was where thieves, criminals, and the ill-begotten bastards of Orien would come to gamble, drink, and throw knives.

He approached with caution.

"You took longer than I expected, you know."

Fern whirled around. Previously unnoticed by him, there was a narrow break in the alley where another road funnelled outwards. Sitting on the footpath amongst some rags, half-eaten food, and a number of odd possessions, was a beaten and weathered greybeard. He did not seem a threat and, as Fern saw light fall into the alley, freed from a heavy cloud, the man's face was clear to see. He did not look at Fern directly – his gaze veered to the side, staring at Fern's left shoulder muscle.

Fern lowered his head and growled.

Unperturbed, he arched his back and continued talking. "It is often said that destiny does not exist, that all manner of fate and set paths were lost with the passing of the last age. However, those who say this are wrong. I put it to you, dog – and believe me, I know you are no dog!" He cackled then hiccupped in surprised as Fern cut his laugh short with a deep-throated growl.

How can he know? He is just a poor man, a beggar. Maybe he is a threat. Fern tensed as the man continued speaking.

"I put it to you that you and everyone around you does have a destiny. Everyone is born with a destiny and a fate, and choices as to which path to take." This time his voice sounded a little annoyed. "We live in an age that has forgotten the old gods. All belief has fallen from the mind. In the South, people have forgotten the wargs and believe them vanished."

Fern tensed. The idea of the wargs carried fear into the hearts of every southerner and had become a taboo topic. Despite their absence for over 300 years. Fern had always felt that the wargs still dwelt within Hurst – waiting, watching.

Fern remembered reciting the stories of ages past with Thormir in their history lessons back in Medani. They had learnt about how the wargs of the South had rebelled against the southerners and the great battle that had ensued. The people who lived in and around Medani had defended their homes and lives against the wargs that lived in and around the outskirts of Hurst. As the humans had become greedy, and had begun to take their game and food from the forest, the wargs' way of life came under threat. They could no longer roam freely. The humans had built closer and closer to Hurst, until the wargs had attacked, taking back their land. During the great battle that took place on the plains before the walls of Medani, one female wolf was taken alive and presented to the king.

Until that time, the men had been losing. Rivers ran crimson, and all that was green had turned to mud and dust. The wargs had superior strength; their massive size and thick hides allowed them to evade arrows and spears. However, when one was captured, the men studied it and found their foe's weakness – fire and flame. The king released the she-warg back to her pack as a gesture of goodwill. As soon as she reached her kin, the king's men covered their arrows in pitch and set the wargs' dens ablaze.

It was said that the wolf-kin that survived turned grey, the colour of ash, and howled for forty days at the loss of their kin. Those wargs returned to the forest, disappearing into Hurst, never to be seen again. But the men and women of Carathron never forgot the power and beauty of the wargs. The memories of the slashed and broken faces of men, the burnt villages, the spilt blood; all passed into written word, into tale and bard-song, and into the stories that parents passed onto their children.

"Arr, name that falls upon ear is not unheard – the fearless ones, the shadow stalkers. Yes, it takes many names – the massive wolf that walks the trees at the edge of the forest. The beast has burning eyes and claws like silver daggers. The warg rips its prey with huge sabre teeth and . . ."

Fern growled a warning to the greybeard. The beggar had been sitting, describing the wargs as if they were something to be talked of with a light heart. Wargs would kill without mercy and would often make sport of those who ventured into their territory. These animals were not some desert rats, but powerful and feared creatures, not to be made fun of by a beggar. Fern turned to leave.

"These eyes are old and many sights have befallen them, and many come to me to see what they cannot. But in all my time that I have walked this earth, I have never come across one so lost from his path. Dog, you should not be here, you do not *belong with us*. How can you not see?"

Fern tilted his head. He could not get the measure of this man. Did he truly know that Fern was not a dog but a nineteen year old boy from Medani? *How can he?* But still Fern could not help suspecting that the man saw right through him.

Fern moved, his shadow flickering in the alley light. Fern stared at him, and watched the man as he bent over a piece of parchment and began to draw. As the sketch progressed, Fern recognised himself, but he was different. In the picture he was bigger, his back reached, neighbouring a man's shoulder height.

165

The shape of his head seemed to have changed to a more elongated form; it was sleek and deadly. As the picture came together, Fern saw Hurst Forest in the background. Again he watched as the ink whizzed over the canvas, leaving recognisable shapes looking out from between the trees. Next to him the beggar drew a human holding a banner that, even without its red and gold colours, Fern knew to be the banner of Medani.

The beggar stopped and Fern was surprised to see him heaving over the canvas trying to catch his breath. "I . . ." But he was shaking so badly that he couldn't finish the end of his sentence. He was jolting back and forth and rocking on his knees, until, with a final jerk that bent his body sideways, he fell gasping onto the ground.

Fern drew closer. The greybeard whispered something and Fern caught the sentence as the words slithered out from between the beggar's rotting, yellow teeth.

"The gift I possess is clear to you, is it not?"

Fern growled. He did not know what he meant, but an image of an answer seemed to take place behind a haze of impossibility deep within his mind.

"I draw the past, present, and the future. All of my drawings have come true – some for good, some for ill – but always they come true. It is you who will stand by this man with the flag. You cannot run from it. Find out who you are, and only then can you accept your rightful destiny – otherwise you will find that the journey to this time," he held out the drawing, propping himself on one elbow, "will be hard indeed."

The beggar shook the piece of paper in front of Fern's nose. "Take it, take it!" He did not stop until Fern carefully clasped his jaws around the piece of paper, making sure not to get the drawing wet. He hated the sensation of having something constantly in his mouth, and thought he might gag at the taste of parchment. However, he had tasted much worse in his time. He twitched his tail in amusement at the memories of life in Medani, and the pranks he used to play with Thormir. The taste of rat came back to him as the thought of one of Thormir's tricks returned. He growled. But Thormir was gone now and they were a team divided, lost to this cold, cruel world. Fern had wasted enough time on the man. When he turned to leave the beggar did not object, but let his voice drift away, saying, "Remember who you are – only then shall you find peace within your heart".

Who is he? Why am I even here? Wasting my time on a helpless vagabond. Fern, annoyed at himself for being lazy and weak with his curiosity, turned his head, spat out the drawing, then loped off. He headed left, past the open tavern door and its inviting scents, and made off towards the main road that was two streets away – or at least that's what his heart told him.

As he ran down the street, feeling the cold of the stone under each of his paws, he thought of that phrase; "Remember who you are."

He considered how it could be possible that his heart could know something his brain was unable to tell him. It did not make sense, but many of the things that humans did made no sense to him.

Fern sniffed the air as he ran past the dark houses set aside and apart by their dark alleys and side passages. He wondered whether the houses were always like this or whether it was just the dark clouds gathering overhead, shutting out the sun's blessing and covering the world in grey and shades of black.

CHAPTER THIRTEEN

THE SOUND OF DRUMS
Láta ocus panam

Padding down the main street, Fern noticed there weren't as many people as there should have been. He felt something soft under his paws and looked down, only then noticing that snow had begun to fall. The flakes dotted the street, covering the usually shiny grey cobbled stones with a thin dusting of snow. The sprinkling was so fine that it could barely be called snowfall at all, but the fact remained that most of the people of Orien were deserting the streets. Fern looked around; even the shopkeepers were in a hurry to get inside.

Only a few people still remained: men carrying buckets of food and water, men wheeling barrows, women in furs, shielding themselves against the cold, and two rebellious boys playing with tiny, wooden swords. Fern listened to the clatter of wood on wood before he picked up the sound of something else. It was a voice, gruff and gravelly, but a voice that could have once wielded tones of kindness. The man brandishing the voice was behind a wooden stall. Along with his muttering, he swung a butcher's cleaver. Fern could see scores of tools hanging from the wooden sides and the weathered crossbeam of his booth. At least twenty knives, polished and gleaming in the rare light, hung from the large nails that were secured to the top beam. Hanging there too were a few scented plants. He did not recognise the odd but pleasant smell, nor did he recognise the purple flower that grew at the end of the picked stem. With his superior eyesight, Fern made out that it was comprised of tiny petals shaped like arrowheads. As he realised that these purple flowers were there to stave off the smell of rotten meat, he saw the butcher sweep his unused bits into a small wooden bucket, over which flies zoomed and whizzed in interlocking circles.

The butcher must have noticed him looking into the bucket, for he said, "Go on, have it if you want – I don't care, won't be usin' it anyway. A hanging is always bad for business, never get any customers – all too busy making good with the sight of live meat swinging." The butcher twirled the knife in his hands then brought it down upon the lifeless head of a fowl as if he always did this at the end of a sentence.

Well, at least I know where all the people have gone. They must all be at the hanging. But then . . . where are Mary and Tangar and Lucian? They can't be dead. Well, from the gates they were taken to the right side of the city. If I am in the middle, that suggests . . ." Fern knew what that must mean. From the general's red tent, Fern had been able to see the vast encampment of soldiers that were training and camping on the right side of the city. Bath was obviously mustering a great host of soldiers, slaves, and captives, all forced to fight for his cause. The reason was clear: to defend his city against the empire. The Black Army was far over the Carabeorn, however they were not getting any closer. It was this very fact that Fern had heard discussed and debated in the general's tent on many a night, but only now did those debates makes sense to him. "Why" had been the most popular word in those long discussions that often stretched off into the early hours of the morn. None of the military heads could understand why The Black Army remained camped and made no move to attack. More than once, the table that held all the maps and documents had been violently kicked over by the general. When these rages came, the entire tent shook with the thunder of his voice, and his wrath spilt in a wildfire that would scorch any man within reach. Fern had seen many a man perish within the fire of the general's anger, but he had noticed that the general owned a whore whom he favoured, and she seemed to be the only one who could calm the storm that played upon his mind. *She* was a weakness.

Fern shook his head, trying to concentrate. *Where should I go? Should I find and recover our lost possessions? Or should I find Mary and Lucian?* He knew Tangar would take care of them, so what was the point? *At least for the time being. Surely they would want me to rescue Thormir and Selena? Damn!* Fern remembered that all of their possessions had been taken during their capture and were surely hidden in a secure place deep within the camp. If any attempt to escape were to be made, then it would be necessary to be properly armed.

First the book, then our weapons. Thormir will need that book that we found in Shadowwatch if he is to understand his powers. If the emperor found that book, he would possess one of the three books that held the knowledge and the ways to bring back magic into the world. *Magic controlled by the Emperor of the North!* With it, none would be able to resist the emperor's authority. The thought chilled Fern, and he remembered the broken and battered bodies lying still in the stony depths of Immoreth.

Second, I will find Thormir and tell him the news and . . . Fern's train of thought was brutally cut off as a small child ran past and pushed against his shoulder. The child looked back at him and instead of the kindly, inquisitive look he would have gotten as a shaggy dog, the child looked scared and horrified as he saw Fern's sleek, black fur and bared teeth – the look of a wolf.

"I suppose you want to go as well?" The butcher laughed. "Ha, a dog like you turning away from a bucket of fresh meat – don't suppose I'll see that again in my sorry, old life. Go on then." He waved his cleaver and pointed down the street, in the direction of the main square.

*   *   *

There was a great crash – a booming of drums. The echoes ricocheted off the houses, louder and louder as Fern drew closer to the main square; so did the people's screams.

As Fern rounded a corner that led into the main square, he saw the source of the noise. Screaming and waving their hands, the crowds of Orien were yelling at the top of their voices; some of them mocking, others in sympathy.

Fern, cautious to remain unseen as he drew closer, jumped on top of a crate. Standing on top of the wooden boards, Fern was safely hidden from the keen gaze of adventurous children and the other spectators by the shadow of an overhang. However, for a moment he heard the wooden slates of the crate groan under pressure, and he thought that three burly workmen standing close by might have heard the plea of wood even above the myriad of voices.

The crowd roared and Fern saw the focus of their excitement. Something or someone was standing on a wooden platform raised six feet above the ground. The platform rose off the ground, with a heavy crossbeam held up by two sturdy posts, and ropes hung, swinging side to side in a teasing dance of approaching death.

Five figures were being led to a corresponding set of dangling nooses. Looking from left to right, Fern looked at each in turn. On the far right of the platform another man wearing black robes stood straight-backed and authoritative. The event was so theatrical that it was more suited to a stage at the centre of a village fête than a utilitarian wooden scaffold. The master of ceremonies, a magistrate of some description, held a terribly long scroll between his hands and read the crimes of the first accused, emphasising and re-enacting wherever possible the gory details of the supposed crimes, to the ecstatic shouts of the crowd, and to the slender man who seemed to sway with nervous anticipation. As Fern focused on the man who was about to hang, he noticed his black, beady eyes swivelling rapidly under his large brow. Fern shivered as he looked into his sunken eye sockets. His pale skin, clearly unused to being outdoors, trembled against the backdrop of the thin snow, making him look almost translucent; he was more ghost than man.

"Move aside, move aside. Let me through. I am the son of your lord, move aside, I say. Are your ears absent head? Move, I say."

Carried on an open-sided purple litter was a large boy with curly, blonde hair who looked entirely too pleased to be present at a hanging. Only the affluent of society sat in these chairs and from them they could look over the scum of Orien and prey on those they deemed unworthy. In any case, Bath's son sat, beady-eyed, upon the couch, waiting, watching.

As he ordered the crowd to part, he had eyes only for the gallows. He played with something in his arms. Fern saw it to be a doll, made by a skilled craftsman as no stitching could be seen. Somehow Fern thought he knew this doll, but how could he? He had never seen the boy or the doll before. The boy picked up a thin, wooden stick that lay beside him and slashed one of the slaves who was carrying him.

"Well, carry on then. I don't have all day."

At the little lord's request, the magistrate, whom Fern had deduced was the orator and chief keeper of peace, read aloud.

"Randell, son of none, you are this day to answer for your crimes against the City of Orien and the House of Bathos. All of your crimes were sinister and wrongful in nature and they will be cited as such in the eyes of the law. Said felonies include pilfering, kidnapping, and the rape and murder of three innocent girls. All of these acts have been proven to have been carried out with great malice of forethought, and for these crimes you have been sentenced. On this day you will be hung by the neck until you are dead. May the gods have mercy on your soul. Do you have any last words?"

The orator stepped back as the accused, Randell, addressed the crowd. "Many of you think me a monster, and you are right!" He bared his yellowing teeth, "I may go, but ever the memory of me will haunt you." At his statement his eyes came alive, and darted around the crowd. Randell spoke up in a rasping voice that betrayed no fear. "I wish you to bear witness to a man who regrets nothing. I do not fear what comes next."

Randell spat at the crowd.

Before Randell could say any more, the magistrate nodded at the executioner to the right of the stage. Randell's body dropped and was left swinging from side to side. The crack of his broken neck was inaudible against the roar of the crowd. The ravens wheeled and the clamour of the wind swirled against the noise of the crowd.

Fern looked at the boy, still lying on the couch. He was clapping and laughing at the man swinging from the gallows. "Next! Come on then, next. Give me another!" he shouted over the top of the crowd.

The magistrate spoke again, this time directing his charge at a willowy boy who stood swaying to and fro in the centre of the stage. He wore nothing but a small, white tunic, which was slowly becoming stained with yellow as he wet himself. The crowd jeered and mocked him. The frost of death was coming, and it grasped at the boy's heart.

"Ronan, son of Arabella, you are this day to answer for your crimes against the City of Orien and the House of Bathos. Your crimes are cited as such in the eyes of the law. Said crimes be thievery of three loaves of bread. For this crime the punishment is death. On this day you will be hung by the neck until you are dead. May the gods have mercy on your soul. Do you have any last words?"

The boy, who couldn't have been more than eight years old, opened his mouth to speak. At that moment the lord's son yelled out, "Hang him!"

Not wanting to disobey a direct order from the son of Bath, the magistrate nodded at the executioner, and with a thud and a crack, the boy hung limp. He swung like a pendulum as he was locked in the intimate embrace of death. The wind that had been blowing every which way that day tossed the boy's hair with a playful flick. Bath's son screamed with laughter.

Fern heard another scream and cry come from the direction of the young lord. Bath's son stopped laughing and picked up his doll. Fern narrowed his eyes to focus on the doll. He saw that it was moving. The little arms and legs, the whole body, clearly alive. Fern tasted the air, the scent of the lord and the thing that he held between his pudgy hands.

Shock. Pure shock, then disgust, then anger, coursed through Fern as he realised what the doll actually was. What the lord had been holding and playing with was a baby. As if that was not enough, the familiar feeling that had troubled Fern earlier was justified. The baby that the lord held within his grasp was the baby that had been born during their trek to Orien, and torn from its mother at the Shadow Gates.

And now here is it, being toyed with by that disgusting lord, thought Fern as he saw Bath's son push a chubby finger into the infant's belly. Feeling for the scent of the infant again, he checked

174

on the child's health. The baby seemed to be healthy and well-fed and, fortunately, free of disease.

He had seen enough. The man who was to hang next stood on the stage, but Fern could not allow himself to be distracted by the routine execution of the next criminal. He had to find the group's possessions, and return to camp without arousing suspicion. Out of the corner of his eye, he spotted more scrolls that the magistrate had yet to unravel on a nearby wagon. Then it came to him: *Of course . . . the library*. It seemed the most logical place to hide a book. If you wanted something hidden, the most secret place is often the place where you most expect to see it. Although he had heard talk of the library during his time with the general in Orien, he was unable to glean its location. All that he had ever heard in reference to its whereabouts was, "Under Orien's spire be the place where books go to die".

Although clearly some sort of landmark, Orien's spire could as easily refer to one of the city's many defence towers as it could a temple, or a monument occluded by Orien's countless sprawling backstreets and inky-dark passageways. Fern turned from the square, where people were still screaming, the lord was still laughing and teasing the infant, and the dead man and boy were twisting limply.

Fern made his way down a side street that ran from the square, past the fletcher's store. The sign of a bow and arrow was engraved into the dark wood that framed the door into the shop. The recent snow had collected on top of the architrave, making the entrance to the shop look as though it was wearing an absurd, white hat. The sight amused Fern greatly, and he gave a bark of laughter. The sound bounced off the wooden slats that walled the houses, and made its way down the empty street.

He passed the signs of the hammer and anvil, mortar and pestle, a fish in water, and many others, as he padded over the stone cobbles with no specific direction in mind but aiming broadly for the northernmost quarter where he knew the buildings were tallest.

Like a new chapter in a book, the sky opened, briefly allowing the leaving sunlight to stray upon the crawling scaffolds of the towers under construction across the city; the contrast of the light from seconds earlier made Fern squint. Between his clenched eyelids, he saw a shady area just left of three barrels that had the insignia of the traders stamped on the wood. He waited there until his eyes adjusted to the new light. At that moment, he discerned that the shadow he was standing in was triangular in shape.

Fern tilted head against the sun and squinted towards where he thought the shadow was coming from. At first he saw nothing except the descending snow, the drips from the roofs of houses that lined the streets, but following the trace of the shadow, he spied the shape of a great, stone tower that was far larger in proportion than those surrounded it. On top of the tower was a tall, stone spire. The buildings that he had seen so far in Orien seemed to be reasonably new, the oldest being around twenty years' standing, but looking at the design and shape of the stones, Fern thought, *This must be one of the ancient buildings that still remain in Orien. Well, it doesn't seem that big a deal to me, it's just a pile of stones.*

However, Fern could see that this building had a nobility about it that the other buildings did not. An ornate carving of a falcon was perched upon the spire and, for a moment, he imagined how it would feel to soar across the city like the dragons of old.

The spire did not seem far away from where he had first found himself in its shadow, but as he drew closer, he realised that this notion was completely false. He was becoming anxious. People had begun to trickle from the main square to return to work. It slowed him down, but he was determined not to make his way back to the general's tent until he had the book. The trouble was, it was already getting dark. *I have to return to that imbecile before nightfall.* Fern glanced towards of the wall of Orien, which had come into view; he could see the sun making a sure descent towards the flat of the land. He watched the sun for a second more, tracing the silhouetted line of geese that flew along the horizon. He simply had to find the book for Thormir so they could escape this infernal place.

Looking around for the fading shadow that would mark the distance to the spire, Fern saw that it had disappeared. Puzzled and worried that he had taken a wrong turn, or gone completely the wrong way, he searched for the dimming lines that marked the shadowy triangle.

Nothing. No sign of his guide. That spire was his only hope, and now it had vanished.

A pigeon, a rat of the sky, flew close overhead, its wings beating hard against the cold, harrowing wind. Annoyed, Fern barked at the bird. His deep bark provided a distraction and the bird tilted and looked at him. The loss of the bird's concentration resulted in it being tossed into the nearest building. The wind roared and the pigeon fell to the ground, mere feet from where Fern stood wagging his tail. Fern looked to where the bird had hit the building and saw that it had struck not just any tall house, but one made of huge blocks of stone that sat next to, and on top, of each other. The stones were so large and so carefully crafted that there was no discernible gap or space between – only a faint line, weathered by countless seasons.

The building rose up until, upon the roof, a spire erupted, jutting towards the overcast sunset. No bird was perched upon the peak of the spire, but instead the black metal that held the top was a menacing spear pointed towards the heavens. Fern turned and rounded corners until he found the huge, wooden doors that barred the entrance to the building. Two gargoyles watched from atop intricately carved stone. They were sinister creatures the likes of which Fern had never seen. Their stone eyes glared down from their rocky perches. Fern felt them boring into him, twisting their malice and malcontent deep within him. It took almost all his strength to look away from them, and when he did it felt as if a great weight had been lifted from his shoulders.

Breathing hard, he leaned on the cool, wooden doors. Large iron braces pressed against his shoulder. Shaking his ringing head and curling his lip in concentration, he reared onto his hind legs and pushed. With a creaky groan that sounded like the swaying of firs in a winter storm, the two doors slowly inched open. From the dim beams of light that shone in from the setting sun, Fern could see rows and rows of wooden benches facing the front of the building, where Fern suspected there was some distant altar. As he entered the building he heard rats squeaking and running between the benches. They must have been sticking to the shadows, so as not to be seen by any eyes but their own. Unlike the cold that blew in from the outside, Fern felt a hot dampness press against his fur as he made his way up the central aisle.

With an almighty boom, the heavy doors swung shut. The outside world was barred from entering the hall. A brownish glow hovered between the pews and in and around the massive, square stone columns that rose from the thin dust, holding the arched, wooden ceiling in place. Fern twisted as he heard a metallic scratching noise. He readied himself to face some unknown attacker, but no enemy showed its face. Not even the rats seemed to be moving; the tower was still, quiet, empty.

Fern drew deep within himself and then, as he had been taught, breached the barrier that held his mind, and reached out with his consciousness, trying to touch any sign of life. He felt nothing except the tickle of the rats that occupied the pipes that ran under the building.

Under the building . . .

Fern remembered the man saying that the library or "the place where books go to die" lay beneath the spire of Orien. So that meant . . .

I have to go down. The library must be underneath the building. What a weird place to have books, deep beneath a city. He looked around, squinting with concentration. *There must be some sign . . .*

A man, or at least a statue of a man, was sitting on a stone stool in an alcove in the wall. Like the gargoyles outside, Fern thought that the stone figure seemed to be alive and watching him, even though his head was cast down and his eyes were fixed on the pages of a stone book. The carved man was a spectacular piece of masonry. As Fern approached it, he could make out the hairs on a balding scalp, the chiselled lines of two small scars that ran from his upper lip to the top of his nose, and even the cords of his jaw muscles as he held some train of stony thought. Approaching the figure, Fern lowered his head to look at the inscription engraved into the stone pages of the book that the man held between fragile hands. He read.

If you seek forgiveness and redemption, turn right.
If you seek knowledge and the answers to life's questions, turn left.
If you have come to this place to escape some peril, you may stay,
But know this: no one is ever free from themselves.

Fern felt a shiver snake its way down his tail as he read the last line; somehow he felt the statue had this effect on everyone. He shook himself and read the lines again, picking up the second in particular, because it seemed to apply most to what he was doing.

Seek knowledge and answers. Books, it must be. Turn left. Fern growled with weariness; he was angry with himself for taking so long to find the tower.

Through the yellow-brown glow he could make out the cut of two doors. They were demented and ugly, made entirely of metal with cords of twisted iron. Again he felt that someone was watching him. Hackles raised, he slowly approached the door. Placing a paw on the cold metal, he pushed. It swung inward. The oiled hinges were silent as if honouring what lay below. As soon as the door moved forward, a tormented wind rushed from deep within the chambers below. Dust blew a fierce storm into Fern's face as the small particles hurled themselves into his eyes. He winced in pain as his eyes stung. At the same time, a tiny light, a torch, appeared at the bottom of a long flight of boot-worn stairs. As it flickered into life Fern could make out the side of a hooded face.

As Fern made towards the face, a blanket of shadow enveloped him. The darkness pressed upon him, but he was not worried as he could see perfectly well in the dark – in fact that was how he liked it. As he descended the cobwebbed stairs, he thought he heard whispering – softer then louder – but every time he tried to catch the sound, it would slip away like a stray thought lost to the recesses of the mind. Deeper and deeper he descended until he stood at the very bottom.

CHAPTER FOURTEEN

WHISPERS OF THE PAST
Umous suro

The dark of night passed over the city of Orien. It clung to the houses, forming depths to the shadows where there should be none, slithered on the bitter wind, and seeped under the windows and down the smokeless chimneys. The Darkness fought against the lit lanterns and tried to put out the glow of the streets; sometimes it succeeded and an inky and almost palpable veil of shadows smothered the cheery glow.

Only the solitary hooting of a dusk owl could be heard, calling to its mate from somewhere deep in the blackness. No child played with their toys, or ran errands for thieves in the street; no cat stalked the cobbled streets; and no night vendor called for customers. As the dark of night clung to the sides of streets and slithered around every corner, whispers of treachery and the slip of black cloaks and hoods could be heard, only interrupted by the sound of a dagger finding flesh.

Down the market street, where the light snow remained unmelted, left past a barber's shop and a few paces down a side street, a chanting and muttering issued from a small, metal grate that had long been forgotten by the street sweepers and passers-by.

Beneath a few fallen leaves and under the sticky cobwebs that hung between the metal rungs, there was a small but deep, stone shaft that led far below the city of Orien. It was here that an ancient and largely disused passageway led to the catacombs of Orien's great library. Few knew of its existence and fewer still went to visit its dusty, stale, worded halls. The library itself was built during the last Great War to hide and store books of knowledge and the scrolls and records that gave meaning to the way things were. Once the war was over, and magic gone from the world, the library was forgotten, its treasured knowledge all but lost. The need to survive had taken precedent over scholarly learning. With the arrival of the Bathos family, the already duplicitous citizens of Orien had been encouraged to believe that the best form of survival was self-made success. History had been cast aside in pursuit of profit, itself re-moulded as a means to avoid being press-ganged into military service or enslaved. No honour remained in this place. Bettering your life was now a trade – one that dealt in plundering, and gold taken from the wrong hands. Knowledge was something gained at knifepoint, not something to be studied, compiled and stowed for future reference. And so today, buried deep beneath the city, lay a library filled with books that had stood the test of time. No one but the royals and a few significant figures even knew it existed. Thus, even if a passer-by had heard the muffled noise issuing from the grate, the sound would have not been recognised for what it really was – a meeting of the Daughters of Sa'bil, and the welcoming of a visitor.

*　　*　　*

Three women, each of them tall, each of them dressed in black, were standing before Fern. Among the three was the hooded figure he had seen at the bottom of the stairs. He felt a little disconcerted as they stared down at him, accusingly. It was the same expression they had worn when they ushered him into the library.

"Welcome," they said. Their joined voices unnerved him and he growled in return. The three smiled, but only their lips moved; the warmth did not reach their cold, continuous stare.

"Welcome," they said again, their voices a mixture of intertwined thought and emotion. "Welcome to our sanctuary. We are the Daughters of Sa'bil, but you may call us the Robed Sisters."

A fitting name, considering they are wearing robes. Why they don't just get on with it? he thought. Fern curled his lip.

"We are an ancient order and we serve only to protect, so we mean you no harm, dog son of none."

Their proclamation had startled Fern. *How could they know?*

"Why hide what is not hidden?" All three women smiled at him. Their fierce, piercing, unified gaze, and eerily, untied voices forced him to look away. He growled in annoyance. *How do they know about me?* It was almost as if they were expecting him, waiting for him. *But they do not seem dangerous, just . . . unnerving.*

A few more moments passed before the three said, "Morph."

Why not? He felt the usual tingling sensation and stood up, now naked apart from the cloth tied about his waist, which was fastened with a small, jade green clip with silver lining that was fashioned into the shape of a small fern leaf.

Now he stood cold, looking into icy faces, trying to see past the set smiles and condescending eyebrows.

"I am here for . . ."

"A book? You are in a library, after all."

Fern pushed back his mane of curly, black hair in annoyance and answered curtly, "Yes. It would have been brought here recently, probably by a soldier or a courier for the royals."

All three increased the width of their thin smiles and said, "We come by many things, and these halls hold many books brought in from foreign lands, but we did intercept a courier carrying a heavily-bound book. It had set runes and golden thread woven into the cover."

As their voices died, Fern's excitement overflowed. "Where is it?"

"But why is it important to you?"

Fern watched as one of the Robed Sisters disappeared. He pondered whether to answer the question. "It belongs to someone close to me. The people and soldiers that serve this city robbed him. Now I have come to retrieve it."

"Why has he not come himself?"

Fern could see that he had aroused the attention and curiosity of the women before him. In this case Fern thought the truth might lend him good fortune. If these women, who did not seem unwelcoming to him, could help him, he might just be able to aid Thormir and Selena. "My friend has been captured, and taken to the quarry."

Voices apart this time, one of the women said, "I saw Lord Bathos taking a youngish boy from The Pound. Apparently he had been in the quarry, then transferred to The Pound as punishment with another of his group – a young girl, if I recall correctly."

The second Robed Sister, the one whose black, shiny hair almost reached her waist, spoke. Her voice was husky yet smooth. Every note was filled with a seductive tone. "It appears that your friend is being held within the walls of the palace. There is no way in or out of that palace that is not watched by eyes that would be unwelcome to a spy indeed. Your friend is gone – it is the way."

"It is the way," repeated the other black figures. The woman shifted as she beheld the anger that Fern knew to be burning within his eyes.

He would not let this be the end of it. *I will not let it.*

"I have your book," said another voice behind him.

The long-haired, hard-faced, husky-voiced woman spoke with a finality that put a stop to the proceedings. "Fern."

He started at the reference to his name. *How could they know?*

She repeated, "Fern, my sisters will allow you to walk these halls on one condition. That you never return here. Your kind have already done too much damage to humanity – the least you could do is honour those who died in the Great War, honour the histories. Now take your book from my sister, walk these halls, then never return."

There was a flash of crimson in the sisters' eyes but then it was gone, replaced by the glow of torchlight, a reflection of the many torches set in brackets around the walls of the massive library. Fern had been so focused on the dialogue and the suppressed hostility passing between them that he had not noticed that the torches had been lit. They highlighted the prominence and expansiveness of the hall. Towers of books and scrolls lined wooden shelves that were set into the carved, wooden bookcases.

"You must take your book. Leave this place."

After ramming the heavy book into his chest, the sister stalked off like a cat in the night, leaving him alone amongst the towering rows of books.

CHAPTER FIFTEEN

FEAST AND FLESH
Taxi coméda roa caro

It was the first time all of the slaves had been together at the same time. They stood in three rows of ten in the courtyard. The song of winter had subsided, heeding the call of the sun. Lord Bath was especially pleased with the weather. He strode up and down the courtyard, seemingly deep in thought. Thormir thought it most likely that Bath was still enjoying the memory of last night's dinner, and had forgotten about the address he was to give to his slaves.

Since Thormir and Selena had arrived at the palace, days were pages in an uneventful book. Those pages soon gathered into chapters, and Thormir realised that it had been two whole months since they had been shoved into that wooden carriage and carted off to the palace. Following the fight with The Surgeon and his subsequent separation from Selena, every day had been the same. Bath had taken a liking to him, and kept Thormir by his side as his personal servant. To Thormir's great surprise, Bath had begun to pay him. It was only a small amount, but with nearly two months having passed, he had received a decent sum. But life was not easy in the palace; one step out of line, one broken wine flask, was enough to earn you eighty lashes on the pole, to which you would then remain tied for a length of time subject to the whims of the lord.

The pole stood in the middle of an empty courtyard at the back of the palace, where the sun could find it, so that open wounds would burn, and the crust of their scabs would splinter, scattering drops of fresh blood. It was that or the frost of The Darkness would find you. It was in those times that the frost stuck to your raw flesh like pieces of shrapnel, and insects would crawl into and eat your exposed muscles just to keep warm.

Nevertheless, the endless boredom was just as torturous as the pole. They had tried to find ways of escaping the palace, but so far had had no such luck. All of the stone walls were too high to scale, the palace wagons were too small to be used as a passage out, and the guards were too wary of people to be fooled by a donned disguise. He and Selena had both asked the other prisoners and house slaves of possible ways of escape, but the glint of hope had all but faded in their eyes and no useful answers left their lips.

After Fern's first visit to their cell, Selena had been moved to different quarters, and Thormir had not seen her lately. They had been allowed to meet again when Lord Bath travelled down into the city to oversee and further instruct the goings on at the wall. Bath had ordered that five bodyguards and several slaves follow him. This had afforded Thormir the opportunity to be in Selena's company once more, however they had not been allowed to talk openly. Instead they opened their minds to each other and shared their news of days past, and as much information as they had been able to gather. Apparently most of the women were new to the palace, and some were just there to keep the nobles and palace men and women company at night. Selena said that many of the women had come from Orien. They were rounded up for their beauty, and taken to the palace, where they were forced to become the slaves of Lord Bath. Some of the women had volunteered to work at the palace. Selena said that these women had joined the palace years ago when times were harder in Orien. The trade routes had been subject to frequent raids by bandits, who made the most of the inclement weather when no produce could be found. Winter had lasted a long time those years, and it was then that they had decided to join the palace. Slavery at least promised regular meals, and a roof, even if the price was a lifetime of service to the Lord of Orien.

Meanwhile, in Thormir's wing of the slave quarters, the men had accepted him without question, treating him as one of their own. The slaves received no free time – the slave masters, the soldiers who were in charge of disciplining the groups, took them to task from dawn to dusk. From cleaning the wine glasses, to feeding the bloodhounds in one of the palace basements, all of the slaves were driven by the fear of a striped back, or time on the pole if they disobeyed.

And so, those days of boredom and torture stretched into weeks, and the weeks into months, until they found themselves standing in front of Lord Bath, who was striding up and down the courtyard thinking about food and other delights.

Bath stopped mid-step, straightened, turned towards them, and then began to speak in his oily voice. "As you all know," he paused, gathering himself, "an army is soon to upon our doorstep. My mind is clouded as to their intent, but the armour of the city is in disrepair. Our walls lie shattered and our number pales in comparison to the force that, with its fingers burned, threatens to return in far greater numbers. Nevertheless, we must prepare our arms. From our greybeards to the youngest farmhand, all shall take up sword and shield for our cause. But, concern still plays upon mind, for we need to swell our number. Tonight we shall host a great banquet in honour of Duke Chevaux, who rules Durnsay and a few smaller towns to the north of our great city. I will attempt to convince him to give aid. Tonight, if any man asks something of you, you will comply. If they ask you to lend eye as they take your best friend, you will watch. Am I clear?"

The three rows of slaves shuffled but nodded in agreement. Thormir felt disgust, anger and hopelessness rise within him.

"Good. Begin preparation."

* * *

Thormir stood naked. He was in the palace courtyard with the rest of the slaves. Duke Chevaux and his followers were walking slowly between each slave, commenting on their physical attributes and moving on to the next.

Duke Chevaux looked at Thormir then turned to Lord Bath and said, "This one is of a form, is he not?"

"Yes, I found that one in The Pound, fighting against our best dog."

"Really? Call for demonstration."

"What host would I be if such request were not met by eager hands?" Bath smiled then ordered for swords to be brought forth from the armoury.

When the slave who had been sent to fetch the swords returned, she said, "There ain't much in the armoury m'lord. I did best I could."

Bath flashed a look of annoyance her way and she scuttled off and returned to serve wine and water among the visitors. Thormir, who had been listening carefully, pricked up his ears at the mention of a weapons room in the palace. The idea that there was one, and that it could be accessed, burned like a red ember within him. Squinting forward he could just see into The Gilded Hall where a vast feast was being prepared – he thought he saw Selena filling cups of glistening red wine, but could not be sure.

If they had any luck, those weapons could be made to serve a purpose far from the hands of Orien.

Bath thrust a sword into Thormir's hand. Unlike the weapons in The Pound, this was shiny, precise, and deadly sharp. Torchlight nicked its edge and the faces of the slaves standing behind him were reflected in the flat of the blade.

"And who faces our champion, m'lord?" Chevaux turned to one of his lackeys and conversed in a whisper. Then he laughed a big, booming laugh that seemed to affront even Lord Bath. The men behind Chevaux shifted nervously from one foot to another. But Thormir realised that their nervousness was not born of fear, but due to eager anticipation of the fight to come.

Chevaux spun his head, shaking his mane of golden-brown hair from his eyes. Smiling, and as if he knew perfectly the pain he would cause by issuing the order, he said, "Make him fight this one." Chevaux pointed to a man who stood two along from Thormir.

Thormir saw where the duke was pointing. His heart sank, as a snake of anger coiled in his stomach. His opponent was a greybeard whom Thormir had befriended during his weekly trips to the wine cellar. Every Wednesday they had lengthy conversations about whatever took their fancy. To Thormir, the talks were a relief, as the time that the slaves had to talk amongst themselves was limited at best. Wednesday had helped him somewhat with getting used to being a slave. When Thormir's nights were wracked with the nightmares and violent seizures that his wound had inflicted, the old man was always there to comfort him. His contact with Selena was all but gone, lost to the many chores that burdened their time together. So when Bath ordered Thormir to fetch new selections of wine from the palace cellar, it came as a blessing that he found a new friend in the keeper of the wine. The man was ancient; he did not seem to remember his own name when Thormir asked, so Thormir had named him Mr

Wednesday. Over time Thormir had shortened his name to Wed and, with his new name, Wed had become more animated and forthcoming with information about the world as he knew it and the workings of Orien. These conversations had lasted for half an hour or until the moment felt right to return to Lord Bath without raising suspicion of the friendship they had formed.

And now Thormir was supposed to fight the only friend with whom he had regular contact. He watched as the short sword was jerked into Mr Wednesday's naked arm. Despite his mixed emotions at fighting the wine keeper, Thormir noticed that Wed seemed no stranger to a sword. Muscled cords bulged as his wizened fingers closed around the hilt. At that moment his naked body seemed to stiffen, showing the form of an ancient warrior. Thormir looked into Wed's eyes as he turned to face him, and found himself staring into the soul of a man who would do anything to survive. Suddenly a phrase that Wed had spoken when they had first met was whispered back to him, "Never get close to anyone in Orien, not even if you consider them your best friend".

"Fight!"

As Chevaux's arm motioned for them to begin, Wed lunged forward, the point of his sword shooting towards Thormir's bare chest. Thormir knocked it aside at the last minute but still he felt the tip of Wed's sword draw a line of blood across his belly.

It was obvious that Wednesday had received military training, as his swordsmanship was not that of an inexperienced man but of a soldier – accurate and firm. But he was old and the fire of youth seemed to have left him, replaced by the winter chill of old age. Thus, the swing of his sword and the movement of his body were slow and unpractised – hardly a fair fight for Thormir, who had practised the forms of earth, wind, and fire every morning and night in the dark of his cell.

Wednesday's next blow arced towards Thormir's neck, but was given away by the slight twitch of his shoulder a split second before the action. Thormir knocked it aside, stepped left, and wondered at what he saw. He was fighting a changed man.

Deflecting a blow once again, Thormir flicked his gaze over his surroundings. The Gilded Hall stood as it had for ages past. Torch firelight danced off the large spots of flaking gold that patched the walls and columns of the hall. The torch smoke trailed in an upward spiral, whisked towards the small, wooden grill that aired the hall, through which the velvet night could be seen darkening the twinkling stars.

The distraction cost him. Thormir felt steel slice through the outside of his arm, cutting through the first layers of skin, but not deep enough to hit muscle. *I do not want to hurt him. By the gods, I have just spent the last two months with the man. We are friends. But then why is he attacking me?* Thormir was driven forward by this thought. *I will not kill him, I will just best him in the fight, make a show of it, and maybe the duke will be pleased and spare Wednesday's life.*

Thormir blocked Wed's next blow with an elegant slide of his sword, then parried and tapped Wed's left leg with the flat of his blade. Wed collapsed onto the tiled floor. He leant on his left leg, his grey-white beard touching the marble as he grunted in pain.

Thormir, who had expected this, twirled and with a totally unnecessary "A-ha" brought the point of his sword up towards Wed's throat and, with the flat, lifted Wed's chin so that he stared into his eyes. The former fire was gone from them, and a peace ran through the small shoots of green that flecked the brown rim around the black of his pupil.

"Very, very impressive. I might have a mind to make purchase of your stock, Bath."

"By all means, but let us discuss matters of business and coin at proper time. Tonight is for you. You must drink our wine, enjoy our women, or men if that is your wish, and feast on our food. Come, your seat awaits you." Lord Bath put a chubby hand on the small of Chevaux's sculpted back and guided him away from the slaves and to the banquet that was awaiting them further down the golden hall. Bath's long, painted fingernails clinked slightly on the chain mail that Chevaux had donned for the occasion.

So what do we do now? In answer to Thormir's unasked question, the slavemaster stepped forward and told the slaves in a harsh whisper to stay still and not make a sound.

Thormir, who was not really paying attention to the tall, gangly man, searched for Selena among the women and girls who were circling the hall table, holding plates of wine goblets, fresh fruit, and other comforts that the nobles could feast upon. He was disgusted when one of the men, a guard from Durnsay, grabbed a slave girl and pushed her onto his lap and began to kiss and touch her in a wild frenzy. With one hand he held her by the hair, while the other crawled over and explored her body. Then, to Thormir's surprise, the man took a goblet of wine from another passing slave and poured it over the girl's body and began to lick the taste off her glistening neck and breasts, which swayed with the motion of the hand that gripped her. For a moment the girl made eye contact with Thormir and he could see the terror she felt behind the guise of joy that she showed to please Bath and his guests. Back in line with the other slaves, those that were not tending to the guests, Thormir continued to search for Selena. His heart was pounding; he could not let Selena fall prey to the same fate as the other slave girls.

He still had not seen Selena, but he was sure she was down there, and that she was waiting on the guests and the royals of Orien. Bath slurped and burped, and vulgar obscenities waded through the scented hall.

The night pressed on. Time was becoming blurred. *How many hours have I been standing here?* Thormir noticed that the candles in the hall had drooped, their wicks curling, their waxy skin falling upon silvery trays. As he searched the faces of the serving women he noticed that dinner seemed to be at a close. The men had devoured the last of the food, and were now looking for the all joys and exotic wonders that a woman could bring. To his horror he saw Selena being taken into one of the side rooms that they had prepared earlier for private entertainment and the privacy of the guests. It was Chevaux who took her and Chevaux who pushed her out of sight into the red-curtained room that Thormir knew to be scattered with cushions that arced around a large bed.

"Because you amuse me . . ." The phrase uttered by Lord Bath and long since lost to memory, whispered in his mind, and the single strand of thought chilled Thormir, evoking images of a dark and sinister nature. "Because you amuse me . . ."

CHAPTER SIXTEEN

SELENA
Selena

The wine glistened like fresh blood within the neck of the sculpted iron jug that she was trying to hold completely still. She was finding the task harder than she expected, as she had just seen Thormir fighting an old man for the sickly pleasure of the guests. They had laughed and jeered as the greybeard tried to best Thormir, but to no avail. Thormir had done his best to make it into a show, allowing himself to be cut more than once. It seemed to have worked for he was now standing back in line seemingly searching for someone amongst the crowd before him.

Steadying the wine, she noticed the small pockets of air rise to the top and as they released, she thought it a celebration – those who had been trapped within the dark of a cellar, now set free, each pop a victory for freedom. It had become habitual for her to notice the small things, for that was her light in her darkness, the beam of focus that led her through her misery. The loss of her elder and her capture had left her weakened, but just as the tiny pocket of air had, she would escape this place.

After she had left Thormir's cell and had been moved to her quarters, she found that her contact with Thormir had become limited so their conversations had to be stolen in dark passages when no one else was around. Nevertheless, they had shared what little they knew of potential escape routes from the palace. They had learnt the timetable and routine of the guards, the nobles, and royals, but still no flaw could be found. She had smiled when she saw Thormir had lost hope for himself but kept on fighting for her sake. Both of them struggled to find fault in the routine operation of the palace.

She was aware of his timid advances but she paid no heed; it was not that she could not see a future for them, but that she spared no time for the trivialities of romance. Furthermore, she had taken Thormir to be a threat as soon as she had learnt of his ability to break minds. However, she was not sure what he knew of the art. From the quick touch of his mind, it seemed that he only knew how to communicate words, and knew little of the art beyond that point. She was sure that he was unaware of the fact that one could read, alter, and create thoughts for another if one was skilled enough.

"Girl! Pour more wine." Bath's hairy hand reached towards her holding a polished, golden goblet, which she recognised as one she had polished hours earlier.

The elegantly-painted neck of the jug spilled its blood-red liquid and she watched as the level of wine in the man's goblet rose. Once she had finished pouring, Bath's hand retreated behind the expansive mane of his long, curly, blond hair. The banquet, she thought, was surely one of Bath's best. As she walked, offering wine here and there, she observed the art that the chefs had created. Wild oxen were very hard to kill; their hides were tough as boulders, and covered with a lot of matted hair to keep out the cold. To make matters more difficult, they usually travelled in small herds across the tundra and the northern plains but rarely came close to the cities. It was exceptional that one man could kill one with a spear or a bow, as the ox's hide was so protective and its long curved horns were so deadly in close combat. A goring from such a pair of horns could slice open the belly of any man who dared get too close for comfort. It was rumoured that for some of the wandering tribes that travelled along the trade routes and plains between Orien and Silverhaven, the killing of one of these beasts was a rite of passage. So when a head was served, it was a delicacy in honour of a distinguished guest.

Two heads were displayed on great, silver platters, surrounded by six dips and sauces of varying colours. A huge salad rested in between the two meaty heads, surrounded by a vast wildness of leaves and fruit berries. Beside them were several roasted chickens, their skin still brown and crusted, and the hungry guests quickly tore off their legs and sides.

Chevaux and Bath seemed to be toasting and both laughed at the same time, and called for more wine to fuel the occasion. Selena thought she could do with some wine as well. She had just seen Thormir fight and nearly kill the only friend he had made in the palace – not that she had many herself. It troubled her to see him so timid with his blade. On the way to Orien, he had spent hours telling her excitedly about the forms and ways of the sword that he had learned from his friend. She had not denied him this opportunity to open up to her. Talking seemed to take his mind off the troubling matters that shadowed his swirling thoughts. Anyway, she had enjoyed it, and listened with interest to how one could sweep a man's legs and pin him to the ground in one motion. Thormir had mentioned something about the forms being called something like earth, wind and fire. Anyway, it seemed that Thormir had lost his will to get out of this palace. That troubled Selena. *I am not sure I can do this alone. I need him and Fern – that dog of his – to help me. That dog seemed to be far smarter than Thormir was willing to let on – it could be of use.*

197

"Wine girl!" Chevaux shouted again and hammered his considerable fist on the table.

As she approached, she heard Bath say to Chevaux, "My Lord, why don't you consider taking advantage of our more ... exquisite cuisine – this one, perhaps?" Bath motioned towards Selena with a slight nod of his head.

As she saw Chevaux catch Bath's meaning, she heard, "Yes ... yes indeed. The road has been long, and long-awaited desire has escaped me."

"You may choose any woman you wish."

"Lord Bath, you do indeed indulge me; the hospitality of your house shall not be soon forgotten." He paused, "I will take this one."

Selena froze as the duke pointed a greedy finger at her. He flashed her a toothy smile then turned to Bath.

Bath smiled too. "You do indeed have excellent taste. First the boy, now the girl."

There was a scraping sound as Chevaux's dinner chair slid backwards over the diamond-tiled floor. A dusky reflection of Chevaux could be seen in the tiles as he stood up and made for Selena. She glanced towards Thormir, but he wasn't looking in her direction; he seemed to be searching for something or someone in the crowd.

As he reached her, Chevaux's firm grip closed around her upper arm, putting his face close to hers. He whispered into her left ear, "Tonight you will fulfil my every wish."

She recoiled.

Chevaux grinned and tossed his brownish hair out of his eyes, then combed it back into place with his hand. Unlike any of the guards, Selena noticed that the duke had well-kept fingernails, and bore no sign of the journey that he had made from Durnsay, except for the purple bags of weariness below his eyes. He remained one of the most handsome men she had ever seen, but the purple eyes and slightly sunken look of a man after a long journey gave the duke a more angular and threatening face. As she stared, he bared his teeth at Bath and said something in a triumphant voice, but all Selena could hear was the thumping in her ears. She knew what he was going to do to her and she had no way out. She was helpless. Alone.

Pushing on the small of her back, he led her to one of the many side rooms curtained off from the rest of the hall. Selena felt the five pads of Chevaux finger's quivering with excitement. She noticed a slight dampness at the back of her tunic and was disgusted when she realised that the duke was sweating as well.

Pushing aside the red curtain that covered the entrance, Selena preceded Chevaux into the chamber. The lighting in the room was dim and it flickered with the slight movement of the flames issuing from the few candles artfully scattered upon corner tables.

Chevaux placed a hand upon her left shoulder.

She stopped.

The duke's warm breath fell heavy upon her neck. The waves of warmth crashed over her nervous body and fell down her tunic past her breasts. Selena could feel goose pimples forming, triggering a tingling sensation that ran down her arms.

"You are new to this, are you not?" Chevaux pressed his hand against her arm and turned her to face him.

She nodded. There was no point in lying.

"Arr, so the petals have not fallen from the rose." Chevaux looked deep into her eyes as if measuring her worth, but all she saw was a greedy hunger. Running a finger up her left arm, he said, "Well then, I am honoured."

Reaching the top of her shoulder, he plucked at the clasp that held her tunic. She could only watch as the silver brooch clattered to the ground. Her tunic crumpled to the floor in a heap that seemed to mock the tidiness of the room.

How can I escape him?

199

She felt muscular arms embrace her and lift her off her feet.

Maybe . . . but no, I have never tried it. Selena thought of the lessons her elder had given her in the ways of entering a person's consciousness and controlling their actions.

The duke's arms tightened around her naked body and she was forced to arch her back. She tossed her head back and her curtain of black hair flew before her eyes. As she felt a single tear escape the corner of her eye, she felt the brush of lips against her breasts.

Help! Somebody help!

No answer came as she was thrown onto the soft cushions that lined the bed. Selena drew on every memory that she had of her lessons with her elder and threw herself at Chevaux's mind. First she had to find his consciousness. It was not hard. The energy of his mind was as a beacon, red and throbbing with conquest and lust. Selena formed a mental spear and pushed into his mind. A rush of thoughts, sounds and images overcame her for a moment. As her mind sorted through the images and sounds in seconds, she found herself looking *at herself* squirming upon the bed. She saw and felt as Chevaux pinned her arms down, spread, facing the ceiling.

Selena turned from this and delved deeper into his mind and as she did she saw flashes of thought pass over her eyes; a golden feather, a huge army gathered on the sunrise, villages filled with charred bodies, flames still licking at corner beams of houses now turned to rubble. Then the thoughts passed and were replaced by an image of a letter, the stamp of Orien, Bath asking for more men . . . a war was coming.

Outside of her exploration into his mind, Selena felt Chevaux's naked body press against hers. Sweaty hands were beginning to rub over her back and torso.

Come on! She was panicking now.

Selena was searching Chevaux's mind for the place in his consciousness that would indicate the entrance to the part of his brain that controlled movement. *There!* she thought, as she found the small lump. Pushing her mental spear deeper into his mind, she took control.

Sleep!

Chevaux's body fell limp, the heavy, energetic panting now replaced by deep breathing as the duke fell unconscious.

Selena pushed the slab of muscle off her chest. She had not realised it until that point but she was crying, or at least tears were falling from her eyes, just as her breathing was harsh and shallow. She bent and picked up her tunic, running the fabric through her hands, wincing as she saw the bruises forming on her wrists.

The room seemed dimmer than before, the wax forming a slow cascade that dripped down the side of the candles into the small blue bowls that were holding them in place. The soft material of her tunic now seemed harsh as she brushed it over her cheek, drying the wet trails that her tears had traced down the side of her face. Noise from the feast and celebration outside seemed dull, but Bath's oiled voice slithered under the curtain and door that led to the chamber.

"Check on Chevaux. See whether he has been pleased. Oh, and ask him what time he shall rise tomorrow, for I wish to talk with him and heed his counsel."

Selena looked at the duke again. He was face down and snoring amongst the cushions that covered the bed. Selena realised that any minute now another slave would enter the chamber and see to it that Selena was with Chevaux. She had no choice then but to climb back into bed with Chevaux and wait until her position passed inspection.

The red bed covers sent shivers up her spine as she pulled them over her body. She made sure that they seemed ruffled and had the appearance of being tossed around in frenzy. With her free hand she grabbed a handful of blanket and twisted it. She did this twice more to the effect that the sheets that covered her were haphazard and messy. To complete the image of exhaustion, she stuck her bare naked leg out from the sheets and let it hang over the side of the bed, while she raised her right arm over her head. The door to the chamber opened as she made the final touch to the image and a slave entered. Selena had not seen his face before, nor did she recognise the slouch in his shoulders or the slight hunch in his back. The slave was just a boy. She put his age around twelve or thirteen. While his mission was to come in and check on Chevaux and Selena, he averted his eyes when he saw Selena lying, partially-covered, and Chevaux snoring into the pillow.

"Tell My Lord that the duke's wishes have been fulfilled."

The boy nodded curtly, turned, and hurriedly left the chamber. As soon as he was gone she crept out of bed, fastened her tunic about her, and then left the room, closing the door with a soft thump.

* * *

"So, did you please him?"

"Yes, My Lord."

"Describe it to me."

"Lord Bath, I would prefer not to . . ."

"Do it, girl, or I'll have you sent to the post."

Selena had never had to make a fiction that involved such fantasies. She faltered. "I . . ."

"What did he make you do?" The crunch of a chicken bone and the slurp of wine followed Bath's words.

He was the only one still eating at the table. The guests from Durnsay had either retired to bedchambers or taken a slave for their own. Noises of forced celebration echoed from the far chambers and the red curtains that covered each entrance seemed to shudder in a non-existent wind. The nobles of Orien and the royals had not left the table, because Bath had not stood up and did not permit such things.

"What did he make you do?" Bath repeated his words and held out his goblet for some more wine. Selena poured him some more wine and this time the liquid splashed over the edge and trickled down Bath's hand. He didn't notice her mistake.

"I . . ." Selena began, but was cut off by Lady Bath.

Lady Bath was the sister of Lord Bath. All who lived within the walls of Orien knew this but an outsider could have figured it out in no time, for they shared the same mop of curled, golden hair. She too wore a thick, gold chain around her neck that blended well with the trailing, black garb she had donned for the occasion. Selena thought her the most beautiful at the table, but her familial tie to the Lord earned an instant dislike. Before the feast had begun, Selena remembered talking to two of the slave girls who had helped her clean the glasses and heavy goblets.

"I heard the Lady Bath lies with all the palace guards. She even takes to some of the women. It is said she doesn't even know who the father of the little lord is."

"Aye, I heard the same but I heard that Lady Bath had her son from the seed of a guard and then had him killed before he could speak of it."

"No! Did you hear what the little lord did a week's past?"

"No."

"Well, I heard he had a slave taken to the markets and ordered to build some sort of machine or structure of the like. By sundown the slave had found himself inside the structure he had built with no way out."

"No!"

"Aye, then he had soldiers pour pitch on the wooden box structure thing and set it alight. The little lord just watched and listened as the man burned alive. Some even say he ordered his attending to play a fiddle while he watched the man devoured by the flames."

The memory of the conversation flickered into the distance as Selena heard Lady Bath speak.

"Brother," Lord Bath fixed her with a beady gaze, "I will not have your son listen to such filth. Get your bitch to tell her whorish tales some other time, but her words will not fall upon the ears of your son tonight.

With that, Selena watched as Lady Bath rose and, taking Bath's son's hand, led him away from the table and up a flight of stone stairs that led to the royal chambers a floor above. Selena did not see the flash of anger that shot across Bath's face, as he began a tirade of abuse, the focus of which was the discipline of his house. He tried to stand but did not push his chair back and, as a result, his belly pushed against the table, taking him off-balance. His chair flew backwards, and crashed onto the floor. The carved, wooden bird that adorned the top right-hand corner of the backrest broke off, bouncing across the diamond tiles in a mocking attempt at flight.

Bath turned to Selena and saw her gaze flick between him and the chair. "What are you looking at, you stupid cow? Be off with you and go back to doing whatever it is you do around here; I have no need to be waited on like some mongrel pup." Bath seemed to think for a moment. Then, with a flick, his previous train of thought returned to him, as he began his next diatribe of insults and observations at the state of his house.

Faltering on his feet, he made his way up the three steps to the stone platform where several men stood waiting, trying to remain as still as possible; slaves to their statuesque form.

"You!" Bath shouted, "What be your name, man? Answer me, damn it! What be your name?"

"Atmund, mlord. Atmund, son of Toemund."

"Well Atmund, son of Toemund, have you forgotten your position?"

Bath ripped off the leather tags around Atmund's neck and threw them to the floor. Spitting at the slave man's feet, he said, "You're a bloody disgrace to his house!" With that astute observation, Bath drew back one of his fat fists and punched the slave full in the face. Selena saw him hit the ground with a 'thunk', blood oozing from a small cut above his right eye.

Bath threw back his head and laughed. "Ha ha, the man still knows how to throw a punch." He laughed again and then squinted and noticed Selena still watching. He spread his arms wide and shouted, "Arr, my favourite little whore. Did you see that punch? One punch and he was down! Ha ha!" Bath burped, recovered, burped again, and then grinned like a child playing with his first toy.

Selena thought it best not to point out that the slave had already been on his knees and that he would not have dared fight the Lord, so she decided to say, "Aye m'lord."

"Indeed." Bath raised one blond eyebrow and said, "Make yourself useful and fetch me some more wine, and be quick about it." He announced his last request with a giant burp that seemed to catch him by surprise and unbalance him again.

Selena forced a cough and raised her hand to her mouth to hide the round of giggles that the sight of Bath's drunken staggering had given her. Brushing her hair over her eyes, she turned and made off for the cellar with a smile still on her face. Biting her bottom lip to bury the temptation of laughter, she walked down the corridor that led to the kitchen and the wine cellars.

The stone hallway was impressive in its own way. It had been built completely straight – there were no curves or seams in the stones that lined the walls. One torch attached to the wall emitted faint light that drifted towards Selena, growing ever brighter as she approached the wooden door that was the entrance to the kitchen. No dust lined the floor of this corridor, so her footsteps were not muffled by a grey tread. Instead, they were louder than usual.

Turning the beak of the eagle-shaped door handle, Selena entered and the noise of the kitchen was joined with other senses. All the kitchen hands had departed for their quarters, aside from the dish wenches who were busily clattering dirty dishes that they were cleaning and shining along with the myriad of cups, and cutlery. In the corner of the room a group of men were hunched over a meal they had made for themselves and a pot that was still cooking.

The whiff of cooking sherry from a sister kitchen brought to mind a story that Thormir had shared with her when they had sat side by side during one of those stolen hours. It was a story of when he had been injured in a great and fierce fight with ten wild beasts all as tall as any man and twice as strong. This had landed him in the care of Mary, his elder, who had cared for him during times of fever.

The aroma of dried leaves, herbs and spices brought unwanted tears to her eyes and she brushed them away in annoyance. The dish wenches had not even looked up as she had entered, for which she was glad. She didn't want to attract any undue attention.

She continued walking past the many pots and pans that lined the walls, opposite the many tools, wooden skillets and ladles that hung there. She stood underneath a massive, stuffed ox head that hung over the closed door to the wine cellars. Selena stared into the massive, brown, lifeless eyes that looked down at her, and she felt for the beautiful creature that once had roamed vast plains, not bothered by the concerns of the world. The patches of grey fur that surrounded its tusks could have been as real as the day it had been condemned to the afterlife. She wondered if the rest of the animal had been given a proper burial, or if the butchers had just hurled the remains of the beast into a fire. But she knew what the answer would have been – this was Orien, a city without honour, drained of hope and happiness. All that remained of any human spirit was endurance, the will to survive, to keep living, even under the rule of a group as cruel, as ruthless, and unforgiving as the House of Bathos.

And then, not for the first time since she had come to Orien, or even since she had begun her journey to Orien, Selena longed for her home. She stood with her hand on the door to the wine cellar, longing for the touch of the red grass that grew in the fields around her village. She could see, in her mind's eye, the small trail of grey-black that the chimney smoke left against a red sunset. She remembered the feel of the small, yellow flowers that cushioned her back as she lay facing the sky on the slopes to her house and counted the birds that migrated east for the summer. With a pang of sadness, she remembered her brother running and shrieking with laughter as he bounced towards her through the long grass, and the face of her mother smiling gently behind him holding a wooden board that held bread, cheeses, and cups full of honeyed wine. That day all of them were excited for the end of summer celebration and the village offering to the gods of snow – to Jynsal, one of The Four and god of winter and night, but also to Nixi, daughter of Jynsal and tamer of the snows.

Selena smiled sadly as she remembered her elder telling her that when winter came early after summer it meant that the god of snow had let her children down from their mountain homes to play and be merry; when winter darkened and the snow fell so hard that it was hard to open your door, it was just Nixi coming for her children; and when ice tiled the paths and walking became slippery, it was the tears of the snow children because their fun was up and they had to go home.

When Selena had become too old to believe such tales, and she had learnt about the winds and tides of the moon and stars, she became aware that those winters were just the result of the sun, turning from them to shine on the South. Even though she had forsaken all belief in the gods, the stories, as told to her by her elder always stayed with her. They seemed a plausible explanation for winter, and she liked them. But her elder had never told her stories of the South, of the men of Orien, of any cruelty she might have suffered, nor about how to cope with the loss of her entire family.

As Selena looked though the glassy film of tears that covered her eyes, she realised she was gripping the door handle so tightly that she could feel the tips of splinters working to cut the soft of her palm. She loosened her grip and turned the handle, entering the darkness of the cellar.

CHAPTER SEVENTEEN

A CLOSE SHAVE
Flien

The lights had been dimmed in The Gilded Hall, the slaves had been herded to their cells, the royals had retired to quarters, and yet Thormir stood alert – patient, but exhausted. The feeling of weariness, the blissful temptation of sleep, tugged on the fabric of his mind. But he had to stay awake. Lord Bath, in his drunken haze, had chosen Thormir to guard, and wait on him during the hour of the wolf. Thormir would have to remain awake all night, until the rise of the lion.

Another night without sleep – this can't go on.

The thought of murder, of taking Bath's life as he slept, was something that had crossed his mind, but he knew that it would be too dangerous. The guards would catch him before he got far, and he had yet to find a way out of the palace. He smiled as he reflected on what Fern would probably do given the same situation.

"Just tear out their throats," was Fern's usual refrain when he regarded something, or usually someone, with distaste. In this case, Thormir believed that Fern would say a lot more and come up with an array of creative ways to inflict pain upon his captors.

"Boy, lend hand to robe!" Bath was struggling to get free of his many robes and golden chains, and was moving like an injured duck. Thormir walked over, trying not to let his eyelids close. He had to be careful while undoing the clasps that held the robes, because Bath was still moving from side to side, flailing about, the movement of his arms forming great, chubby windmills. Thormir chuckled slightly at the thought, and the sound brought Bath to a stop.

"What amuses you so, boy?"

When Thormir failed to answer, Bath opened his mouth, evidently for a follow-up question, burped, then stumbled, naked into his immense bed that lay in the centre of the room. "I must be rested, for much is to be done tomorrow. We shall leap from this state, and land in the depths of good fortune, only then . . ." He rolled over. Speaking into his pillow, he said, "Do not wake me unless the old gods have broken the Mists of Parthelion and are crossing the Reaching Sea to th . . ." The rest of his sentence trailed off as he fell sound asleep.

Thormir placed a gooseneck jug of cold water on the side table, and retreated to the far corner where he sat down, feeling powerless.

Looking for something to do, he saw a book resting on one of the many tables scattered artfully around the chamber. The cover had not been cleaned for some time, and small mounds of dust had settled on the leather. However, the title could still be seen. In flowing calligraphy, *The Tales of Arren and Nathalia* and underneath was written a single line in Estarion. Thormir recognised the names, especially that of Nathalia, as the women of Carathron revered her for she was thought to be a descendant of Isseannur – one of the first four gods created by Doriel. It was said that Nathalia held such beauty that light trailed from her dark hair, and when she sang, birds would rejoice and fields of brown would turn green. The book looked as old as the legend itself – its ancient pages foxed and spotted with age.

The sight brought back a memory of Mary presenting him with a book, ancient beyond living memory, its contents containing secrets of the most sacred order – magic. Thormir rubbed his right arm, where the blue coil of energy had left a scar. He could still feel the bumps and ridges that the burn had engraved into his skin, like some confused maze. The book – the book that was written in Nolwin, and held the key to understanding his power – was among the possessions that had been stripped from him. Where was it now? he wondered. The first thought that came to mind was the guardhouse and barracks that lined the right wing of the city. Surely they would store all stolen possessions in those guarded halls? The second place that occurred to him was more of a feeling – what if Orien had a library of its own? It was hard to imagine. He knew that Medani was home to a vast library, but in all the readings and scrolls found in it, he had never read anything on the history of Orien's buildings or the city's layout. Of course, he knew of the landmarks such as the Shadow Gate, but he knew very little of the city structural layout.

He closed his eyes and tried to remember the few words of power he had learnt during the journey to the forest and The Tongue. He whispered what he thought to be one of them, but nothing happened. Maybe he had the pronunciation wrong. He tried again. The sound of rushing wind filled the chamber, but the cup on the table that he was trying to move remained resolutely still. His scar itched as he muttered the word of power. He remembered Mary telling him that despite the magic being gone from the world, he possessed the sacred fire; he, and he alone had been touched by the phoenix. He was Flametouched.

Of old, the races of this world would use magic by drawing on the magic that surrounded them and then manipulating it.

Mary had said that magic was once a life force, just as real as earth, fire, air, wind, and rain. It had existed within the world as a power to be drawn upon when needed. The elves had called it, Eol Bellon, blessing of Doriel, for magic was so deeply ingrained in who they were; it was part of them, to the point where it would drain their own life force if it were not to exist. And so it had – the elves had made their last sacrifice in the Great War, uttering words that would remove the magic from the world, vanquishing the enemy's power, and in doing so their race perished. So the elves were the first to go, fading from the earth like dust in the wind. Then the dwarves and men had marched on Ironhalt, taken the city, and killed Vandr. Then, the dwarves too had faded from the world, their large kingdom decimated, their kind never seen again.

Bath stirred and muttered in his sleep.

Thormir could feel his eyes getting heavy and the fog of impending sleep clouding his mind. Forcing himself to stay awake, he opened the cover of *The Tales of Arren and Nathalia*. The pages were torn in some places, and were a brown-yellow colour in others; near the front, some of the pages bore a round tattoo, as if someone had used the opened book as a coaster. He squinted and tried to see the lettering, but the light was too faint. Moving one of the small chamber candles closer to the book, the letters became visible, legible. Ignoring Bath's audible snoring, he looked closer. Amongst the lettering and script of the book, certain letters were circled, and some underlined. It was as if someone had deciphered a code. Turning a page, he noticed a list of things that he could only presume meant . . .

The creek of floorboards and a flicker of light under the door interrupted him. Someone was outside.

Thormir's heartbeat hastened and he could feel a surge of panic. But perhaps he was overreacting; it could have been a slave sent to get wine or milk, or a stray mouse in the dark, lost on its way back to its hole in the wall.

Dimly, he saw the small, carved lion head revolve, as the door handle turned. A ray of yellow light split the dim bed chamber as the door was pushed ajar. The light from the hallway lit up a corner of the chamber, giving colour to the tapestry that hung from the wall. His heart pounding, Thormir watched, as the light lit the side of a sewn huntsman's face, and the curved, sleeping cheek of Bath came into view. Thormir thought he could see the rhythmic bump of a pulse in Bath's fat neck, but he couldn't be sure.

What appeared to be a small man entered the chamber. As the light from the open door sliced across this figure, Thormir saw thick, gnarled, corded muscles that bunched around the man's arms. As the light caught, he saw metal links that formed a small vest of chainmail worn underneath a thick, armoured tabard. Over the tabard two empty leather sheaths were strapped – one shaped for a small dagger, and the other, a buckle of some kind, perhaps for a larger weapon already left behind. The shadowy figure walked with no sense of innocence, rather it walked with the resolve of a trained killer. The man hadn't seen him, but Thormir didn't take his eyes off him as his own hands spidered across the table next to him, searching for something that would deal damage.

Just as the man pulled out a knife that glinted silver in the door light, Thormir's right hand closed around some sort of metal hilt. The weapon was cold, crude, menacing, and crafted for a single purpose.

Thormir tensed as he stood up carefully, ready to launch himself across the room. But the shadows in the room must have shifted because, quick as a flash, the man hurtled towards him. He made no sound as he crossed the chamber floor. Springing higher than Thormir had thought possible, he collided with Thormir.

This time there was a crash as an avalanche of ornamental, silver statues, books, and plates plummeted to the floor. He felt like he had been hit by small boulder. As Thormir winced in pain, he opened his eyes and felt a heavy pressure on his abdomen. A silver knife was pressed hard against his neck, just enough to draw beads of blood but not enough to truly slice the skin. The man was sitting on top of him, one hand holding the knife, the other hand pinning his left shoulder to the ground. Thormir felt the metal of an armoured knee press between his third and fourth ribs.

The man's face was turned, so it was hard to discern his features properly, but Thormir could see that he was looking cautiously at Thormir's right arm, at the burnt and scarred skin that coiled there. The whites of his eyes showed, and Thormir was sure that he wore an expression of shock. Suddenly he flipped the blade so that the blunt side pressed cold against Thormir's neck.

He shifted his gaze, looking intently at Thormir's face as if trying to imprint it into his memory. His eyes were beady, dark, and calculating. Drawing his head close to Thormir, he said, "Take the ways beneath the city, and head to the mountains. There, I will find you."

With that, he got off Thormir's chest. However, he did not release the pressure on Thormir's arm. In fact, he increased it as he took the silver knife and pressed it into the palm of Thormir's hand, and sliced the skin.

Thormir cried out in pain. His yell echoed around the chamber, yet still Bath slept.

CHAPTER EIGHTEEN

STRANGERS
Estran

Strange shadows danced across the arched stone roof of the cellar. Selena's hand shook as she held out the lantern before her. Her hand did not quiver because of nerves, but due to the weight of the lantern she held as she made her way between the aisles of bottles, vessels, and huge casks.

The flame danced upon the wick, and a shadow did a two-step across the cellar's stonework. For a brief moment, Selena could make out the cracked and faded fresco that covered the wall – a forgotten god holding a vessel of wine while talking to the merry crowd that gathered at his sandaled feet. The image was wiped from the wall as the shadows danced onward. Selena turned down aisle twenty-one, making for the aged bottles of Tyberian wine, imported and brought by trade routes now cut off by the empire to the north.

She tapped each bottle and muttered as she decided which one to choose. "No, no . . . no . . . no . . . yes." She rested her finger on the dusty surface and traced the engraved number sealed upon the stopper of the bottle. Grabbing the neck of the bottle and pulling it out of its hiding place, she tucked it under her arm as she picked up the lantern that she had placed carefully on the ground.

I really don't like coming in here. Why does it have to be so dark? For God's sake, didn't the people who built this place think to put torches on the walls, or at least some sort of light near the door? This lantern is not nearly bright enough for this stupid pitch-black cellar. Selena swore as she stubbed her toe on the end of the wooden shelves that held one row of bottles. She nearly dropped the wine, and she moved her arm slightly so that it was cradled more securely. As she shifted, she moved the lantern so she could look for the exit through the dark.

Selena screamed. A rat, eyes gleaming in the dark, looked into her eyes and squeaked. Normally Selena would not have jumped at such a thing, but, as always, the dark brought the terrors and fantasies that the mind conjures when left to itself. Startled, she let go of the lantern and wine at the same time. The lantern seemed to land first, the clanging of metal and a small shower of sparks illuminating the crash of the wine bottle that splintered and bled into the grooves between the stone tiles that paved the way between the rows of bottles, casks, and jars.

The rat scampered off down one of the aisles, leaving Selena holding her head in her hands. Through her fingers she glimpsed the blood-red wine, dark against the stone, flowing down the grooves. Selena noticed that the floor, which she had thought to be perfectly level, had a tilt to it, as the wine was picking up pace.

She could hear a trickling, like a series of coins being dropped into a well. She picked up the lantern and, on all fours, she followed the trace of her spilt wine. The dark liquid was flowing towards a line of barrels in one corner of the cellar. It was slipping down the grooves in the floor between the barrels of liquor, and she quickly wrestled with one, turning it on its edge, trying to keep up with the pace of the wine. Shifting the barrel one final time she discovered an iron grate wide enough to let a large man pass through. The teeth of the grate had partly rusted away, where wine, and presumably ale had, over many years, eroded the entrance to a large drain below.

An idea, quickly, excitedly, formed in her mind. She rolled the wooden liquor barrel back into position, trying not to make too much of a sound. It had not escaped her that Bath would soon send down another slave to see what was troubling Selena. *Not that he cares*, she thought. *The stupid oaf is probably just thinking about the contents of his belly and a good night's sleep. I must tell Thormir! Finally a way to escape!*

*   *   *

The following day, Thormir found the dim passages of the servants' quarters hard to adjust to after the orange rays of dusk that he had left just a few moments beforehand. Thormir could feel the familiar sensation of his eyes widening, reacting to the darkness. He blinked hard, trying to rid himself of the discomfort. This earned him a shove in the back from the heavy fist of the stoic guard that led him back to his quarters. As he was led down the hall, he reached a bank of torches secured in rusty, metal brackets, which flashed in the corners of his eyes like fireflies, illuminating the edges of cell doors, sharp in the dimness. As he was led, step by step, back to his cell, he thought of all he had discussed with Selena: their plans for later this night, where they would meet, and the escape. It had been hard to get a moment together, but they had finally found an hour where they could sit and devise plans to escape this wretched place – hope was kindled. One day had passed since whoever it was had failed in their attempt to kill Lord Bath and had nicked Thormir with their dagger, but his words continued to haunt Thormir. Thormir had pondered those words over and over again, trying to remember every little detail, stretching his memory for any clue as to who this man was. It was through this process that Thormir had deduced that it was only when the short man had seen the snake-like marking burnt into his arm that he had loosened his hold on Thormir and had assumed the expressions of joy, wonder, and shock upon his rough face. Thormir could only guess as to this and the circumstances following, but nevertheless it had pressed heavily on his mind, so that work and tasks were difficult to carry out.

Stoic, stony, and expressionless, the guard moved forward and took a large, iron circle from his belt, on which keys of different shapes and sizes swung back and forth.

There was a 'thunk' and the heavy door to Thormir's cell swung open. Stoic, Thormir's guard and keeper of the keys, used his baton to crack Thormir across the back, forcing him inside and behind bars. Rays of moonlight shone across the cell floor, coming from the small window that entertained the wall. The small bars across the window only served to make Thormir feel all the more caged, casting fingers of shadow that moved across the dusty floor as Thormir moved to his bed.

It was only then that he saw a shape of a female figure standing in the corner. She raised her head, shifted, and stepped forward into the moonlight. Thormir gasped. At first he thought it was Selena, but this girl was slightly shorter and, from what he could tell, had lighter skin than Selena. The rays of moonlight brushed against her body and Thormir saw that she was wearing a red, lace dress that emphasised the curves of her body. Feeling his face grow red, Thormir looked away.

"Why are you here?" His tone was not accusatory, but was strong enough to cover the nervousness he was feeling. Lord Bath had indicated that he would send a reward to Thormir, and judging by his vulgar nature, Thormir presumed that this *was* his reward. She was very beautiful. However, despite his feelings towards the girl before him, there were also his feelings towards Selena to think about.

"Pardon, but m'lord Bath sent me to please you."

Thormir distractedly straightened the blanket on his bed that he usually left tangled and disorganised, then turned to address the girl. He looked at her, and saw the sadness within her eyes. She was younger than he was, but nevertheless he felt that calling her a girl lessened what she was, who she was.

"What is your name?"

As he looked into her eyes, Thormir saw shock and surprise. She hesitated, and for an instant Thormir thought she had forgotten her name to the years she had been here, trapped in chains, caged by the bars that Lord Bath had set before her.

Meeting Thormir's gaze for the first time, she said, "Maria." As she did so, Thormir thought he saw a spark, or something, alight within the depths of her brown eyes; it was as if the utterance of her name gave her a new meaning, recognition of who she was before this, but still she seemed lost, as if wandering the grey between heaven and earth.

She moved towards Thormir, sliding one strap of her dress over her shoulder. It fell lazily against her arm. She took a step closer. The night kissed her hair, and for a moment she wore a diadem of white-gold moonlight. She moved her hand to the other strap that held her dress. Her fingers lightly touched the red lace, forming a wave as it fell over her fingers. She was inches away from him now. She reached the top of her dress and began to push the strap over the curve of her shoulder. Thormir reached out and stayed her hand. He fastened her dress in place. As he slid the fallen strap back over her shoulder, he let go of her hand. Her fingers slid out of his and the warmth left their gentle touch.

Thormir stepped back slowly, and as he did so, it was as though a rope that had linked them had been cut, leaving both free but alone. The moonlight was cold now, shutting out the warmth of but moments before.

"Do you not want me?"

Thormir looked deep into her eyes, and in her questioning gaze he saw the gratitude that she felt towards him. "I do not wish to lie with you. I do not wish to lie with a woman who does not wish as such."

Maria bent her head and stared at the ground. A tear skirted her cheek then fell to the stone tiles. Thormir, who thought he might have hurt her, stepped forward, not knowing the extent of gratitude she felt towards him; for what Thormir had done in that moment had been the first act of kindness that she had been shown in a long, long time.

Thormir put his hand on the side of her face and gently lifted her chin. Brushing away a tear with his thumb, he said, "You may stay the night. Return in the morning, that way Bath will think . . ." He smiled gently at her, and was glad to see her give him a small smile back. "Come", he put his hand on the small of her back and guided her to his bed. Taking the blanket from where it lay, he gave it to her, keeping her from the cold that bustled into the cell on the slow breeze that circled the palace courtyard. As he gave the blanket to her, he saw her shiver and tighten her grip around the furs.

"I have not seen you around the palace before."

Maria looked up at him with tired eyes. "I work in the kitchens."

"Then why . . ."

"Because Bath uses me as one of the palace whores." Thormir heard no anger or resentment in her voice, just weariness and resignation to the life that she had been given.

"How long have you been here?" he said. He did not want to scratch the surface of a healed wound, but his curiosity got the better of him.

Maria looked up at him and paused. "I came to the palace kitchens when I was of eight years," she paused again then said, "I have been . . . working for Bath since I was eleven."

Thormir clenched his fists. The injustice of this place was endless; everywhere you looked crime was taking hold of the city, tightening its dirty grip on the city's people. It seeped under doors, poisoned the water, and made the winter air feel unclean. But they would escape; he would escape this rotten place. He would ride west, where he would find he knew not what.

Thormir felt Maria's eyes upon him.

"You do not belong here."

Thormir turned. He noticed that her eyes were searching his with a hungry look, as if trying to memorise every little detail.

"You do not belong here," she repeated. "Your face, you do not belong here."

"What do you mean?" Thormir suspected she knew. Selena had picked up on it from the moment they had met.

Maria lowered her eyes and brushed away another tear forming on her lashes. "You are a noble, are you not? You are no ploughman, of that much I am certain."

Thormir fiddled with the tags that were hanging over his tunic. "I was a noble."

Maria backed away from him, using her hands to push herself further along the bed. She did not seem afraid, but looked at Thormir with a new respect. He turned away; he hated that she had turned from her initial view of who he was as a person and now looked upon him as someone who was of higher birth than she.

"So you are not so much a slave than a prisoner."

Thormir looked at Maria as she said this. He had not expected such an insight to come from her. She returned a smile. It was in that moment, in that second of a smile, that Thormir decided that Maria was going to join him and Selena when they escaped in just a few hours. Any minute now, Selena would be putting the poison in the guard's cup. He thought he could hear the soft tread of feet making their way over to the guardhouse to where Stoic sat, smoking his short, fat pipe. A few minutes passed and he thought he heard the whisper of footsteps, but it must have been his imagination. Maria put a hand on his knee and he was brought back to the cell with a brutal finality, to the bars, the cold slices of moonlight and the chill of the night. He shivered.

"We are all slaves to our fate," he said.

Maria drew closer and offered one side of the fur blanket to him. He reached out with his left hand to take the warm cloth. Suddenly he winced and clenched his teeth hard. Pain shot through his shoulder. It was a ripping pain that seemed to tear his flesh. He looked down and saw that the cut, where Wed had sliced him, had opened up and was leaking. Even though the cut was clean, he saw that it had become infected. Maria drew close and bent to inspect the wound.

"Wait here," she said and putting her thumb and her index fingers together, she whistled for the guard.

"Well, it's not like I'm going anywhere," Thormir said.

Maria flashed him a quick smile then turned as she heard the guard's footsteps. The man that appeared was not Stoic, but some other dog sent to do Bath's bidding. He was a short, dumpy man whose helmet – for he wore one that covered the top half of his face – was too big for him and moved side to side as he waddled towards the cell door.

"What?" His rumbling, slurred speech suggested he had been drinking liquor, and was disappointed when the bottom of the bottle had presented itself.

Maria said, in what she thought was her most dignified and imperious tone, "The servant needs herbs and water from the kitchen."

The guard's beady eyes flicked back and forth. He brushed his whiskered face as if in deep thought. "Fine, but be quick about it." He rattled around with the keys at the lock until the bolts were drawn back and the door to the cell swung open.

*   *   *

Maria returned within the half hour. The smell of herbs signalled her presence along with the hollowed swish of water within a shallow jug. The guard who had let her out had stood waiting, swaying to some unknown beat. *Probably the throb of yearning for more wine,* thought Thormir. He had ignored the guard completely during their wait, which had seemed to annoy the man even further, as now he had no wine and no hold of fear over his captive. Instead, Thormir had laid on his back, and traced a curved line written upon the ceiling, his eyes following the graceful pattern.

Thormir looked up as the smell of herbs drew closer. It comforted him that as soon as Maria, whom he hardly knew, had seen his wound she had wanted to help him. It was comforting that he was so cared for by a person who, two hours ago, would have been a stranger. The sound of her sandals on the stone floor neared, and he saw the guard too look up from where his double chin had been resting on his neck. A clatter of keys and bolts, then the swish of the cell door, and Maria was inside. She was holding a wooden board covered with leaves, all the same elongated oval, and some red and blue berries. Coming over to the bed, she laid the berries and leaves on the blanket.

"You got all this from the kitchen?"

"Yes."

"But how did you know what to find?"

Maria looked up and once again he saw the sadness that resided within her eyes. "My mother," she paused as if deciding how much of herself to give away. "My mother showed me how to find the berries and leaves in the wilderness. She showed me to how fix and make the leaves into a paste for healing small wounds and cuts, to cure headaches, and clear infection. As for where to find them . . ." She shrugged. "I work in the kitchen."

Straightening the board on the bed, she knelt on the floor. Taking the jug, she poured a splash of water on the wood. The water barely touched the sides. Indeed it seemed to slide and settle back into the middle. Organising the berries and leaves into a laced, intricate pattern, she then crushed them into the water. She did this three times, each time pushing the leaves and berries together. Maria seemed to be waiting for something to happen. On the fourth twist and push of her fist, the berries burst apart, and instead of a red-blue liquid, which Thormir assumed would come from the berries, a powder exploded and puffed out in a comical cloud. The powder settled over the moist leaves. By the fifth go, a red paste had formed on the broken leaves.

Looking at the result, Maria smiled. She wiped some paste on two of her fingers then said, "Show me your shoulder."

Thormir hesitantly agreed and pulled up the sleeve of his tunic.

He shuddered as Maria wiped the paste over his cut. At first an agonising pain coursed through his shoulder. Then it seemed to pass and was replaced by a feeling of alternating hot and cold that soothed the wound.

"Don't check on the wound for a few days now, give it time to heal."

Thormir nodded. "Thank you."

Maria wiped her wet hands upon her dress, and then came to sit by Thormir's side.

"Maria, we should get some rest – there is much ahead of us." What he did not tell her was that at that very moment a hatch door was being opened within the cellar beneath the palace halls.

Maria picked up the fur blanket. She moved up to the corner of the bed, and laid her head to rest against the wall without further question.

Thormir waited for the soft, steady breathing of her sleep then got up from the bed. He arched his back and flexed his muscles. Unconsciously, he touched the marking around his right arm. The squeak of a dormouse was the only other sound to be heard. All the other prisoners and slaves had fallen quiet, either out of tiredness or exhaustion from the pains of inflicted wounds. He went over the plan in his head. First there was Fern's part in all this. Securing the book, weapons, and supplies was all his job. They had decided to leave Tangar, Mary, and Lucian. Tangar would take care of them, plus Thormir had a mind to return to this place and free all those who were slaves to the injustice of this city. Thormir then saw in his mind's eye the role Selena was playing, poisoning the guard and holding the entrance to the sewers. Now all he had to do was wait. He looked to the window and was pleased to see that the moon was blanketed in grey cloud, a perfect choice for an escaping shadow.

CHAPTER NINETEEN

"ARCHITECTS OF DEATH"
Aedium môrs

Thormir had been pacing up and down, sometimes exercising, sometimes relaxing, but always his worries came back to him like sprites in the dark. He tried to brush them away, as if they were just small children, but they always returned in the dark of night. *Would they escape? Would their plan work? Where would they go? And how many men would Bath send after them?* But the question that really bugged Thormir was: *What am I?* He would find answers. But not here.

Thormir's thoughts switched again, but not out of nerves. Something was in the corridor. It was not some figment of his dreams, or sprite conjured by darkness, but something else. It seemed to be darker than that pitch corridor. Eyes shone at him as the shape moved closer. A deep growl emanated from a powerful chest. Fern. Fern nuzzled a sack through the bars. Inside were fur cloaks, two daggers, arrows, Thormir's bow, and food for three weeks. He could also make out the shape of the book Mary had given him. Thormir's trepidation at being apprehended by a guard or some new attacker fell away. Thormir slotted the two daggers into his belt.

Selena's in the cellar, waiting for us.

Thormir nodded as he felt Fern's mind press against his. It had been a long time since he had talked to his best friend. They were both glad to see each other, but they wasted no words of comfort. Tonight, time was not their friend.

Thormir looked directly into Fern's eyes. *There is no way of saving Lucian, Mary, or Tangar, is there?*

No – but I think they are strong enough to defy the city's will. Already there are stirrings of rebellion within the camp. Whispers are heard here and there – but remember it is very hard to kill an idea, and that idea is spreading. There is still hope for them.

Thormir clenched his fists. The idea of a foolish rescue was hard to push away, but they had to stick to the plan. *Where are the keys?*

Fern growled. *The guard didn't have them on him.*

"Damn!" Thormir swore aloud and heard Maria stir behind him. "Be quick about it, then," said Thormir, knowing only too well what Fern was about to do. He turned and saw Maria waking in a daze.

"What is it?" she asked, looking around.

"Do not ask questions and you will be fine." he said. "We are escaping, and you," Thormir whispered, and glancing back at Fern, "are coming with us."

Fern agreed with a swift nod. *Thormir, remember our food is scarce.*

Fine, she will have mine – just break the door.

No, you keep yours, I will hunt.

Fine, just break it!

Fern punched the lock with his front paw. One of the hinges snapped. With another firm shove, the second came loose and split from the wall. Fern did not wait. He took up the bag and padded onward. Thormir and Maria followed close behind. Thormir drew one of the daggers although it was not exactly sharp. He could tell it had not seen the likes of a whetstone for a while, as there were a few dents in the blade. Nevertheless, it would serve its purpose.

The wind whispered and flicked their hair as Fern, Thormir, and Maria crossed the courtyard. They passed a stone fountain in the middle of the tiled square. Its waters were dry, but still it watched the three figures hurrying silently across the court. The three reached the furthest corner and passed under one of the lining archways. They were in shadow.

Clink! Swish! Clink!

The sound came from behind them. The three turned, ready to face whoever, or whatever it might be. Thormir saw who was making the noise. A guard wore a vicious pair of iron-heeled and capped boots. He held a spear that he leant on as he walked across the stone courtyard. Clink, swish, clink. The sound had become a routine for the guard. First the pain in his right foot, the swish of his left foot as it moved forward in a sideways arch, then the effort of moving forward with his right. Clink, swish, clink. When he had taken the wound the pain had been unbearable, and he had suffered from a terrible fever that had held him for days. When the muscles and skin had finally healed, the general had told him that he could not re-join the Royal Guard, as he was no longer fit for duty. Instead he had been assigned to the palace guard, which involved an endless trek of dusty corridors and palace chambers. Indeed, he thought that the only use for his spear was to support him as he moved forward in his monotonous routine. He licked his front two teeth, sliding his tongue over their sharp points. He thought he had heard something in the slave's quarters.

Thormir gave the signal to move on. The guard was clearly unaware that they were there. Now, only time was their enemy. They picked up their pace. Finding The Gilded Hall was not as easy as he and Selena had foreseen. When Fern, Maria, and Thormir arrived at the rear entrance to the hall, they had only just managed to escape the puzzled look of a guard who was peering in their direction as if trying to make out a shape in the darkness.

The three of them entered the immense hall. As expected, a fire was still roaring in the enormous stone hearth set in the middle of the hall. The only other light was coming from four torches that were burning in the four corners of the room. All was quiet. The banners that hung from the ceiling didn't stir as the three of them crossed the wooden floor. Stone statues appeared to wink at them as the torchlight brushed over their faces. The corridor to the cellar was close, only a body length away, when they heard something. Thormir turned and moved in front of Maria, gripping his dagger tightly. There was nowhere to hide. He calmed himself, breathing in through his nose, and out through his mouth.

He would strike at the neck first – that way he could stop the scream of surprise. Let them try to scream when their chest was filling with blood. Anger gave him strength. He remembered all the things *they* had done to Selena and to him. He twirled his dagger so that the blade faced downward – an easier blow. The soft footsteps came closer, and a boy, not eight years old, appeared holding a jug. His mouth opened as he saw the three of them. Instantly Thormir rushed towards him and pressed his blade against the young boy's neck. Thormir couldn't do it. *It's so easy, just push in two inches, and finish it*. But he couldn't do it. The boy dropped the jug of water he held and screamed and yelled for help. Thormir heard the clatter of armour and the ring of drawn weapons as guards approached. The first through the door was a tall man who drew, strung, and fired an arrow from his bow with unnatural speed and accuracy.

Thormir twisted around the boy so that he was protected. A second later he felt the impact – the tip of the arrow nicked his shirt. The arrow, he knew, had passed right through the boy – now dead, lifeless. *Another dead by my hand; I hate what I have become. Death follows me.*

Fern smashed the wooden door down and bounded into the next room then down the stone stairs to the cellar. Thormir pushed Maria through after him, stuck his dagger in his belt then pelted after the others. The next room was a blur, the herbs and spices just colours as they hurled themselves forward. Selena was waiting for them at the bottom, holding open a metal grill that usually covered a hole that led straight to the sewers of Orien, a way out.

The guards were close.

Each of them launched themselves into the hole. Selena, Maria and Thormir slid onto their knees, then twisted and dropped down feet first. Fern came last as he guarded the door. Too big to come through in dog form, he took on regular human form, shifting with the usual blur of black and white, at the same time banging the grill shut. Landing on two feet, he stood up and grinned.

"Come on," he said, and he and Thormir ran forward and down the arched stone passage that was becoming a blur as all of them picked up speed. Thormir thought of the boy's lifeless body lying dead on the bleak, raw tiles of the palace hall. *Did he have a name? Who were his family?* He tried not to think about it.

Left, right, left, the stone passage turned at odd angles and spilt in certain sections, but Fern never lost his sense of direction; his nose led the way as he ran. Since he had shifted back from human to dog form, he now relied on Thormir to communicate. Fern barked to signal Thormir and the girls to stop.

The soldiers must have found a shortcut through the passages!

Before they could decide to whether to continue, the four of them had unknown hands put over their mouths and were being dragged backwards through a small doorway that they had missed within the bend of a corner. Thormir could just see the chin of the man who was dragging him, but nothing else. It was pointless to struggle against the mass of muscle, and in any case he did not think he had the energy to do so – he had the feeling that drawing his daggers would make no difference. These did not seem like people who favoured the palace ways, but still there were worse things than six palace guards that haunted the passages and halls of Orien. He tried to move but the man holding him was too strong; even Fern had been pinned and was being dragged backwards after Thormir. They were thrown down into the middle of the group of men that were now encircling them, guiding them into a stone chamber. Thormir picked himself up and twisted to see if the others were okay. For a moment Selena's eyes met his as they both pulled themselves to their feet, then they flicked away and the spell was broken. Maria was already standing, open-mouthed, taking in the chamber.

Free from the grip of his attacker, Thormir took the small dagger from his belt. Not knowing what his plan was, he charged at one of the men who had pinned Fern. *I will not lose my brother again! Whoever they are, they will pay!* A wall of muscle moved in front of Fern and blocked his way. As he looked up into the face of the muscled wall, he saw that it was smiling at him. *Reminds me of The Surgeon, back in The Pound. That was such a long time ago.*

The man in front of him sported a short, black beard that matched his hair. His face and hands were dirty – the sort of dirty that could pass for skin tone, but the matching grime on his ragged armour gave away his filth.

The huge man cracked a broad smile that was not unkind. "My name is Hector."

Thormir recognised the giving of the name as a peace offering, and as was custom, he gave his back with a curt nod, "Thormir."

Hector tilted his head and considered him for a full ten seconds. Finally he said, "What are you?"

This question stumped Thormir, so he repeated, "Thormir." He watched the man's smile widen. *Is he some kind of dimwit?*

"I said what are you, not who are you. For example, you *are* my captive. From what it appears, you *are* one of three companions and a dog who have escaped from the palace, and you *are* a friend of mine, for any enemy of Lord Bath and the slack-jawed guards of Orien is my friend."

Well, haven't you got me just figured out? He was, however, relieved to find that Hector was a friend, and one who might be able to help them escape beyond the walls of the city. Hector turned from him now and was directing his men to let Fern go. His men were reluctant and hesitantly obeyed the order. Fern stood. His whole body was shaking with anger. His upper lip was curled, revealing the whites of his teeth.

"Well then, *what* are *you*?" The question was directed at Hector and Thormir added a challenging inflection into its delivery.

Hector boomed with laughter and arched his back. His armour squeaked as his great chest heaved up and down. "What am I, you say?" *Yes, you stupid fool. Just answer the question.* "They call us . . ." He gestured across the room to his five men who had now stepped back to either side of a small pool into which a greenish stream leaked. All of the men were well-muscled and wore haphazard arrangements of armour. Weaponry of all types was strapped across their chests and backs – knives, swords, axes, and many other instruments of death. These were men not to be messed with. "They call us gladiators. We are fighters of the arena."

"Then you must know of our fight with The Surgeon."

"I do indeed Thormir, you were most favoured by Bath."

A phrase taught to Thormir by his teacher echoed back to him: "The world is an unsavoury place, best not to step in the shadows." He was, now, truly, in the shadows. He looked around again. *These men like killing.* "So, Hector, tell me, do you like killing men for entertainment?"

Like darkening clouds before a storm, Hector looked at Thormir, and there was written anger. He placed a giant hand around Thormir's neck, and, with one arm, lifted him entirely of the ground. "Listen here, and listen well." Thormir kicked at Hector's waist wildly but to no effect. "You may think of us as you will. But know this: we, none of us, *like* killing, either in the past, when we were forced to kill, or now, when it is for our own survival. We were *trained* for the *entertainment* of others, with the promise that victory would bring us freedom – it did not. So it would seem we are the same, you and I. We were both slaves. Now we are outlaws and we will escape this place together; both our companies, we shall be free." As he finished his sentence he dropped Thormir to his knees.

Maria rushed over to him. She put an arm around his shoulders. Her look of concern gave away all of her feelings towards Thormir. *I hate seeing him hurt. He saved my life, and this is how the gods repay him. Surely they should give love and mercy, not more pain?* Maria wrapped her arms closer around him, her heart pounding with a feeling she had never had before. "Are you okay?" Her tone was full of concern, but fear was written all over her face.

"Fine," he grumbled. Thormir realised that these men must be the escapees that Lord Bath and Chevaux were discussing before they debated over their land, trade and the men that would aid Bath in a time of war. *There were only six of them; Bath said there had been twelve.* The night he was forced to fight he was told he must remain where he was afterwards – and while he did so, his eyes and ears still remained active – and as he stood there he had learned much. He had learnt that Bath commanded a pitiful force of willing soldiers; the others that marched in his ranks were either slaves or forced farmhands. He needed aid from his allies.

He knew the King Darkin of Carathron would not come, so he turned to Durnsay – the coastal lands to the north. It was here from where Duke Chevaux hailed, and this was the subject for the meet. Bath called for aid in this dire hour. Orien's arrows were numbered, its sword's scared with fifty notches, and the city's horses prized as a treasure above any gold or jewel. Orien quailed at the call to war.

Thormir stood up and drew himself up to his full height. He was still not a match for the tower of armoured muscle before him. "You escaped four days ago, did you not?" He did not wait for a response. "That means you and your men have been lurking around in the sewers beneath the city for three days at least, unable to find an exit. If you come with us, you will be out of the city before the sun rises." Thormir was glad to see the effect that his newfound authority was having on Hector and his gladiators. Some put their hands on the shafts of their weapons while others played with the dirt that had gathered between the grooves in their armour.

Raising his voice a touch, so that it echoed around the chamber, he moved forward. Fern moved beside him, hackles raised. "You," Thormir addressed Hector directly. "You and your gladiators have put a stick between the spokes of our cartwheel, but if we hurry we can still make it before the change of guard." He paused for effect; *they just need one more push*. "Follow us, and we can be free of this place . . . forever."

One big brute of a gladiator stepped forward and nodded. He crossed the floor, avoiding the moving puddle of green liquid, and stood next to Thormir. Once again Thormir noticed how big the men were compared to him; it also didn't help that his new follower wore two swords, and bore armour that was adorned with three small knives. Nevertheless, his company was appreciated, as it seemed to convince the other gladiators to follow Thormir through the sewers and out of the city; that this path, his path, was the right one.

His mind melding with Thormir's, Fern said, *We can't trust them. They don't smell right.*

We will have to trust them if we are to be free of this place.

Thormir shut his mind. He heard movement in the hallway from which they had come. Thormir turned as he heard a swish of a spear and instinctively ducked. Too late. The barbed head of the spear cut into his face and he fell to the ground. Crimson blood splashed onto the stone floor. Clenching his eyes shut with pain, he felt the blood from his face sticky between his fingers. Upon hitting the ground his vision blurred for a few seconds, and he felt the oncoming of a seizure. *Not again. We were so close. Not again.*

CHAPTER TWENTY

LET THE PURPLE FLOWERS GROW
Sin pa méllo laûriel harnaea

Fern had protected the two girls by launching himself at them and pushing them to the wall. As for the others, Hector and his ilk were standing around as if nothing had happened. On his knees, Thormir shook his head, trying to get rid of the massive headache that was pounding at his skull like so many hammers. His seizure had only lasted a few seconds, and yet it had wracked him of all his energy, draining his strength until he was utterly spent. He looked around for the guard who had thrown the spear. Nothing. *If he has escaped more will be coming . . .* He squinted at the pool in the middle of the chamber; lying in it was the limp, dead body of the guard. Three knives were embedded in his chest.

"We thought he needed a bath." Hector lowered a giant hand and effortlessly pulled Thormir to his feet. Thormir grunted as Hector slammed his hand into his back and said, "So where to now?"

Thormir tried to return Hector's toothy grin but winced as he felt the pain in his knee, in his leg, up his arm, and across his cheek. The closest he had ever come to this agonising, throbbing pain was when he had fallen off Shadow while riding in Medani, and slid twenty yards across icy gravel. Despite this, Thormir realised that he had been thrust into the position of leading the group to safety and if he did not carry out this entrusted task, he might not get another chance, ever. *Ignore it. Ignore the fact that no one has mentioned my fit. Ignore the whispers and stolen glances being hurled in my direction. Rise above it.* "Aaargh." He shook himself, mainly to brush the dirt from his shirt, but also hoping that the movement might rid him of his aches and pains. It did not. *I have to lead them; we are so close.*

* * *

Fern was ahead of the group as they kept up a strong pace through the sewers. The warm green-yellow liquid splashed around their ankles as they overtook its current. At first Thormir had led the party, but seeing that he did not have Fern's sense of direction and acute sense of smell, he had again let Fern overtake. Fern sought the path of the cleanest air – a way out.

The sewers were not straight as Thormir and Selena had planned, and sometimes a lonely ray of sunlight would leak in through a grate above them, lighting up the dim, dusty-brown colour of the walls. Occasionally the air was so thick with hot vapours that it became hard to see where they were. But all these things, all these annoyances, mostly went unnoticed by the massive dog, Thormir, the six gladiators, and the two young women that trailed behind, tired but hard-faced, determined.

After what seemed like forever, Fern began to slow. He turned a corner, and the rest slowly followed. The air here was noticeably cleaner and the temperature had dropped from the lingering warmth to a cold draft that Thormir could tell led to the exit. Following Fern, he rounded the corner and saw the outlet that would leave them outside the walls of Orien. The only problem was the metal grill that barred their exit. The green-yellow liquid swirled around the bars, its freedom taunting Thormir.

"What's the hold up?" It was Hector, speaking from behind Thormir.

"Bars."

Even though his answer was simple, Hector knew exactly what he was talking about as he caught sight of them.

"Move aside there." Pushing Thormir out of his way and positioning himself side-on to the barred grill, Hector moved forward, cursing as he splashed around in the brown and yellow liquid. He had not tried this way through the sewers over the last few days and, with escape so close, he was not going to be robbed of victory by a few metal bars. With a mighty effort he drew himself back then launched a kick sideways at the bars. The rusty metal grill shuddered then fell down into the mud. *Hardly a stealthy escape.*

* * *

The morning had not yet broken, nor had rooster woken from slumber, as the ten companions raced out of the sewers and around the walls, heading for the stables. As they wiped their boots of slime in the grass, Thormir thought it was odd that no scream or laugh came from the city. But it was after all still early; no one should be up. The guards had yet to change their posts. The stables came into sight as Thormir passed a hare dashing away from the corner of his eye. He could hear the others behind him keeping pace. They were so close. The horses were of little concern, there would be enough; it was the noise they would make when they mounted and rode off that worried him. Thormir squinted. Like so many other things, uncertainty gnawed at him. A boy was moving among the horses, brushing them down.

Are you seeing this? Thormir opened his mind to Fern's.

Of course I am – I'm not blind. He paused. *What are we going to do?*

I don't know, let's just wait and see.

See what? The kid will call for help.

I just . . . I don't want to kill him. Thormir could tell from the colour of Fern's thoughts that he did not approve. *He doesn't deserve it.*

Do you want us to escape or not?

Of course . . .

Well then, take him out.

Fine, I'll do it. I'll knock him out if he screams. But I will warn him first.

The sound of crashing interrupted them. The boy was using a piece of metal, some sort of bar, to hit the troughs. Thormir recognised the noise; he had hit the troughs that had iced over in the night many a time himself. The group were now around fifteen feet away from the stable. The boy looked like he had only seen about seven winters, and starved through all of them. As Thormir approached, he thought that seven was a bit young to send children to work at daybreak in the stables, but then Orien was not the most forgiving of places.

Thormir placed a hand around the boy's mouth just as he turned to tend to the ice on the third trough. "Don't move, don't call for help, and we will not harm you." Under his hand he felt the boy nod and Thormir could tell he was scared. He nodded to the others. Each of them found a horse for themselves. Thormir was glad to see that both Maria and Selena could ride, unlike the many young women of Medani. The nine horses trotted out of the stable, a mixture of grey, brown and black. Thormir could see his horse waiting for him at the end. The next few seconds were a blur; in a single motion Thormir pushed the boy away and sprinted to his horse. In a single bound he mounted his horse and kicked it into a gallop. The others joined him as they heard the boy's cry of alarm go up. Seconds passed then the blare of the hunting horn cracked the silence. As if the horn had summoned the day, the few orange rays of dawn split the purple black of morning. They rode.

Hooves could be heard in the distance and there was nowhere to hide – only the waves of green, then the long flats, until they crashed into the first leaves of The Tongue of Hurst. Thormir knew for a fact that The Tongue was a week, maybe two week's ride away. Without rest, the horses would tire, slow, and eventually die. Before long they would have to fight. But for now they rode hard into the wind. Thormir had forgotten how cold The Darkness had made the winds across Carathron and its borders and he drew his furs a little closer. Before long, the piercing headwind became refreshing. It reminded him of home, of hunting in The Red Forest, playing with Fern, and riding around the countryside. How could it have gone so wrong? And with that he found himself wondering, not for the first time, what that phoenix had done to him.

*   *   *

Two weeks had passed and it was still hard to believe that they were being hunted, but every hour they could hear the horn in the distance, never farther, never closer, just there. Hurst had come into view at half-day, and judging by the lay of the hills and the height of the distant trees, Thormir thought that they would be under cover by morn.

So far their desperate ride westward had consisted of eight fires, twelve meals, and one storm, during which they had been forced to hide under stick shelters and endure the cold. They had already run out of supplies, and their system of rations had failed badly. Still Thormir had forced the others to ride. Once they reached the forest they would be safe; at least from the soldiers. As for the many eyes that roamed and crawled the forest, he was not so sure. His daggers were cutting into him but still he rode on, persevering. None of the others objected to the ride; they all knew what was at stake, and it seemed that the horses too sensed their urgency and the chance at their own freedom from the tether of Orien's stables. But that was not the only reason they fled towards the cover of Hurst. A day ago they had noticed the slim shapes of The Roc Riders circling high in the sky under the deepening shadow of a cloud far in the distance. *Evil surrounds us.* Thormir craned his neck towards the sky and saw a single eagle circling high above, catching the currents of warm air that didn't favour the wasteland below.

Hector turned to bark over the noise of the wind at the others. "It's going to rain. The horses are restless and exhausted; they cannot keep this up for much longer. We must make camp."

Thormir approached Hector's left flank. "No, we will make it to the trees if we ride through the night. We can rest then."

Even though Thormir wanted more than anything to rest, to lie down and close his eyes, even if it was just for a minute, he was determined to lead the group to safety.

He fiddled with a latch in his saddlebag and drew out a thick piece of meat. He tossed it to his left and watched as Fern leapt up, caught it, and then swallowed it in one motion. Thormir laughed, the first laugh he had had in what seemed an age. And soon he was laughing, bent double in his saddle, tears flowing freely from his eyes. Fern leapt up again and opened his mind to Thormir's, and too, began to laugh, both in mind and body. Hector too resumed his usual grin and paid the wind no attention. The horses too seemed to sense the change in spirits among the group, and started shaking their heads, galloping towards the dark of the forest.

*   *   *

A purple mist covered and clung to the land in great blankets as the nine horses arrived at the edge of the forest. The trees stood smaller than he remembered, but perhaps that was because Thormir had been on the opposite side of The Tongue. Here the trees were shorter, darker, and more menacing. He yawned. His weariness was getting the better of him now, pushing aside the clawing of his hunger and making his eyes droop so that he could barely see through his lashes. Indeed, he was slumped so low on his horse that he might fall aside and crash into the purple mist.

"Strike up a fire!" Hector jumped off his horse and was already giving orders to his men. *Well, it is his right; they are his men,* thought Thormir.

The man who had first come to stand next to Thormir back in that stone chamber, who Thormir now knew to be Rake, was walking over to a small patch of dirt they had found. Carrying what looked like a tree under each arm, Rake dropped them in a pile and came over to help Thormir down from his horse. Knowing that Rake would catch him, Thormir slumped off the horse and felt powerful arms beneath him. With the sense of a man who knew how to carry a deer more than a man, Thormir was tossed over Rake's shoulder and slid to the ground near the firewood. Opening his eyes a touch, he saw Maria and Selena, both with their knees pulled to their chests, looking as tired as Thormir felt; only Fern padded around them, wagging his tail with evident pride that he had not succumbed to weariness.

Slow poke. I saw you riding that last mile. You looked ridiculous, sprawled all over your horse. Thormir felt Fern's teasing amusement as their minds touched.

How can you be happy at a time like this?

Easy. Just don't be sad.

Thormir thought that he would not trade Fern's company for anything. The term "best friend" was thrown around a lot in Medani. Your barber was your best friend, your friend of a friend was your best friend, but Thormir thought that amongst the verbal chaos, Fern was, without doubt, *his* best friend, and he wouldn't swap what they had together for anything.

Fern nosed him in the ribs.

Aaargh . . . What did you do that for?

Don't you want to impress Selena, or is it Maria?

What? Shut up . . . No.

Fine, whatever, just get up, we have work to do; we'll freeze to death if we don't get this fire started.

There was an all-too-knowing look in Fern's eyes as he padded around with a doggish smile playing around his lips.

Before long, a small fire was crackling, sending up whiffs of smoke into the overcast sky. Thormir followed the smoke upwards, looking towards the heavens, and once again saw that same eagle high above them. *Doesn't it have an eyrie to return to?* His temper at having had no sleep had not abated in the short time he had been sitting on the log heating his hands and face. The only upside to this was that, for the first time in a long time, he was sitting, free, next to a fire. Maria was next to him, huddled into the furs that Thormir had lent her. Selena was sitting next to her, her long hair crashing over her shoulders, her eyes reflecting the dancing fire. Five of the six gladiators were gathered across the other side of fire, talking in their own ways. Rake sat silent, massive, and brooding. Thormir had found that ever since he had taken his place by his side back in the stone chamber, Rake had remained close to him, as if he thought that it was his duty to protect him. While this annoyed Thormir a little – he was no infant babe who was to be cared for, it did comfort him that this warrior would ride as well as sit next to him. It was Hector, however, who had told him Rake's name and not Rake himself. The absence of the ritual of names concerned Thormir and while Rake did not seem his enemy, Thormir thought it better to sleep with one eye open. Rake had not said anything since they had left or even in the chamber; he had just watched, silent, massive, and brooding. Nevertheless, Thormir could not stop himself from liking the character, silent though he was.

Thormir pulled his knees in and shut his eyes. Then came the soft padding of Fern's feet. They were joining their minds, conversing and making plans for the future, although this was often hindered by them teasing each and laughing at crude jokes. Fern had gone hunting in the forest for food while the others had set up. Thormir looked up from his makeshift bed. He had to chuckle. Fern was carrying a buck between his jaws, and looking very pleased with himself. Eyes wide and tail wagging, Fern dropped the buck near the fire. He came over and looked Thormir straight in the eyes.

Ha! I won.

Fern told Thormir that he had come across a small herd of deer on the outskirts of the forest. Thormir had bet Fern that he could not catch a fully-grown buck and bring it to camp. Thormir smiled, *Fine, you are the better hunter, but I can still fire a bow better than you.*

Why use arrows when you have these? Fern held up a paw and Thormir gleaned the shine of licked claws.

Let's just eat the thing.

Thormir got up and strode over to the deer that was already being prepared by the gladiators. With no more than two strides, he tripped and fell face first into the dirt. With a startled cough, he spat dirt out of his mouth. He had landed right on the tender spot where the spear had cut through his skin.

Fern, in human form, had tripped him up. Thormir swivelled on his knee. Fern was coming at him. Thormir laughed as he launched himself at Fern. The two collided. *Dodge, step and jump – that should work.* Fern skidded in the grass as they tackled and threw each other. They rounded and circled. Thormir ran at Fern, laughing, stretching muscles in his face that he had rarely used those last few months. As they both jumped, bracing for impact, Fern shifted in mid-air and tackled Thormir around the midriff. They crashed to the ground, spinning around and on top of one another. Thormir ended up on top, pinning Fern's paws to the ground.

"I win!" said Thormir, as much with his mind as out loud. As he said it he saw the girls laughing and clapping. He smiled, pleased with his victory. Looking at Selena laughing was truly something. The firelight seemed to play around her face, making her more beautiful than ever. Maria too was laughing at the performance and . . .

Thormir felt an odd sensation under him. There was a shift of black and white then he was flipped on his back as Fern became his human self again. Standing over him, Fern was growling and showing his teeth, just as he did when he was in dog form, but Thormir just laughed and soon Fern joined in, both of them doubled over. They were all laughing hard now, and his stomach to hurt with the effort. The six gladiators watched the display with bemused expressions on their faces as they finished preparing their portion of the buck and pushed the rest over the fire to Thormir. Choking with laughter, he accepted the meat and, with his dagger, sliced off a couple of raw pieces for Fern who caught them in his mouth and wolfed them down, imitating his doggish behaviour. As he did so, Thormir noticed that Fern's jawline had changed; it had become slightly longer and more defined. Fern looked up and they stared at each other, and Thormir felt a warmth like none other spread throughout him. They were together again, brothers, best friends reunited. Together they could face anything. Calming himself, he went over to where his horse was resting and nestled against the slow warm breathing of the mare.

*　　*　　*

Fear rushed through Thormir as he woke from his dreams. He felt exhausted, and angry with himself as he realised he must have had another torturous seizure during the night. Overcast clouds blocked out most of the sun, so it was hard to tell what time it was, but he felt that it must have been around mid-morning. His horse obviously felt so, because it was already busy grazing further off. They had slept long enough, too long. But what had scared him so? As he pushed himself up, he felt it. Vibrations – vibrations in the ground. There was no mistaking the staggered thumping of hooves, loud and closing in.

"Damn it!"

The others were stirring now, brushing away the damp, purple mist that seemed to swirl above the ground. They listened as two horns blared nearby, roaring over the hills.

Thormir looked at the others, "Into the trees!"

The group dampened and kicked dirt over the fire and rushed towards the trees. The gladiators drew their weapons and Thormir his bow. He notched an arrow, and waited. It wasn't long before the men appeared, riding fast over the far hillock then looking over the place where the group had been camping. *Our horses!* The horses were objecting violently to the sudden excitement and in an instant one of the mares yanked at her reigns and bolted from the trees. *Get it!* But it was too late – they had been spotted.

Rake stood beside Thormir, holding two swords with such a menacing stance that Thormir was quietly thankful that he did not have to face him in battle. Their pursuers were no more than fifty paces away when Thormir released his first arrow. It missed his target rider, but plunged into the armpit of the rider following. *Good enough.* Thormir drew and loosed; this time he shot into empty space, hoping that his target would ride into it. He did. The arrow hit the soldier full in the chest, but his armour stopped it from going any further, and he broke it off at the head. Thormir's target pointed two fingers at the forest, and two of his riders broke from the pack, drew longbows from their backs, and strung. Two shafts whizzed by Thormir's cheek. He breathed deeply. *Stay calm; know your enemy. What do they want? Why are they after us?* He concentrated and reached out with his mind.

"They want us alive! Use that, press that to our advantage." He passed on the message to Rake and Hector, who was standing, scratching his arm, completely unfazed that nine men had been sent to capture them, and perhaps even kill them. As Thormir looked between the trees, he saw one of the burly gladiators suddenly shudder from the impact of an arrow. He twisted from the force of the shaft, but only as if he were brushing aside a small annoyance, before righting himself. He snapped off the arrow, and glared at the oncoming soldiers.

Thormir stuck his head around the trunk of the tree behind which he was hiding. Three shafts whizzed past him, two missing him and the other grazing his arm. *Another scar.* He drew his bow, rounded the tree and – one, two, three. His hands were a blur as he fired each arrow. *So much death.* The first arrow pierced the eye socket of one archer; the second took him in the pit, where the armour was weak; and the third thrust through the soft of the soldier's throat. The soldier's hands snapped up from the reins and clutched at his neck, pulling the arrow clean out. The mistake could not have been more evident. A shower of blood and matted sinew instantly littered the muddy grass.

The soldier hit the ground hard. Thormir looked upon the dying woman whose helm had fallen from her head. Two soldiers on horseback paused as they saw her go down: *Our advantage.* Thormir gave the command. "Attack! Attack!" Rushing forward beside Rake, he kept firing arrows but he couldn't manage to hit the last archer, who was firing from a safe distance and barely visible through the purple mist. Thormir's gaze flicked forward again and he saw, to his horror, a horse charging towards him. The soldier upon its back had a gloved hand outstretched, ready to seize its first captive. Thormir dropped his bow. He barely had time to reach for his dagger when the horse was upon him. Now it was his turn for a blood shower. A gush of blood erupted from the horse's chest and drenched him in red. He heard a scream. *Was that me?* He saw a hand flop onto the ground. It twitched, then was still.

Thormir looked back to the horse's chest. A sword was buried deep in flesh, but it wasn't his own. He turned as he saw the weapon being drawn from the quivering stallion. Rake gave him a quick smile. The other gladiators had taken down two more soldiers, who lay bloodied on the grass, but now three more riders advanced on their position. Fern was by their side and Thormir knew from their connection that bloodlust was on his mind. He heard a rumble and looked towards the heavens to see a storm brewing, dark clouds rolling in to completely obscure the sun. *Perfect, this is all we need.* They advanced. The soldiers kicked their horses, which reared into the air, trying to scare or block the defenders. The gladiators didn't care. Thormir saw Rake reach up to one of the soldiers, evading his sword, and pull him clean off his horse. To Thormir's horror, he saw that a grounded soldier had risen and was behind Rake. Thormir raised his bow and counted. He breathed in and then slowly exhaled.

The arrow shot through the air and lodged in a muscle near the man's neck. In one motion, Rake swivelled and despatched him of both life and head. Rake nodded a "thank you" to Thormir and joined the others.

Fern launched himself at the soldier closest to him.

Thormir stumbled as he felt pain, so much pain. But it was not coming from him, it was coming from Fern. Thormir saw Fern twist unnaturally and fall to the ground in slow motion. An arrow was wedged deep under his foreleg.

No. NO!

Thormir ran to Fern and skidded in the mud as he fell to his knees. He was shaking as he felt for the wound. Fern growled and, taking his meaning, Thormir looked behind him to see the archer approaching and raising his bow.

NO!

Thormir raised his right arm and felt a surge of energy rush through him as he looked at the soldier. A blue light shot from his hand, and he felt his scar burn. *Arrr!* Thormir shuddered from surprise as he saw his snaking scar rise up and burn red hot. But the surprise of the instant pain was nothing compared to his shock at seeing a brilliant blue light and a ball of energy shoot towards the archer. A power he had never used before was coursing through him: magic.

There was a snapping sound. The sight was ugly and not one soon forgotten. The soldier had been broken. Every bone in his body had been shattered: his spine snapped, his skull collapsed, and his limbs all spent and torn asunder. He was twisted in his own skin. In some places the soldier's bones stuck out of his body piercing the flesh with ease, but Thormir didn't care. He turned back to Fern, who was quivering. Thormir felt the connection between their minds becoming as feeble as a single thread of a rope. Thormir put his arm under Fern's head and lifted it, feeling the warm fur rub softly against his skin.

"Maria! Make that paste!"

He didn't even know she was there, but the next second he heard her say, "I don't have the plant and berries . . ."

"Then find them!" He felt a tear whisked away from his face as he snapped his head around and glared at Maria. Understanding his want and urgency, she hurried into the dark forest.

Fern, we have to move you into the forest.

I'll . . . I'll be fine, just leave me here.

NO! No, I will never leave you. You are my brother, he choked. *My brother, I will not leave you.*

"Rake," Rake bounded towards him, "Rake, carry Fern to the edge of the forest."

Rake did as he was told, and bent, gently scooping up the massive dog in his arms.

Thormir turned to the others, "Start a fire! Bring some water and rags. And your heat your sword, we must seal the wound." Hector's flint cracked and soon a fire was blazing. It had no warmth about it, but looked like a deadly beast brought to life just to burn and hurt.

Maria had not returned and the resentment towards her was growing in him every second that passed. *I will not let Fern . . .* But he could not think that, *Not now, not today, not ever.* Fern was shivering now, and Thormir remembered the time so long ago when Fern had come to his aid as he lay, bleeding before the gates of Medani. *Not today.*

Fern's mind touched his own with a slow pace, one full of weakness and peace. *Do you remember that time we nearly got squashed by those huge beasts in the fields on the way here?*

Yes. I do.

You know that I won that race, right?

Thormir smiled, and Fern raised his lips around his teeth in return.

An idea came to Thormir and hope was rekindled in his heart. *Shift . . . shift!*

Fern blinked once. *No, I am stronger like this. And, besides . . . I can't shift.*

What?

Thormir, I can't shift.

Thormir recoiled at the sound of his name. Fern rarely used it but rather substituted it with some crude phrase. *Don't give up. Please, don't give up.* Thormir would not lose him again.

I have not the strength to fight this. Fern's whole body was screaming with pain. *I feel the arrow itching my heart, and my paws have gone cold.*

Maria had not returned.

I . . . we will heal you. I cannot go . . .

You can weather this storm alone, brother, you do not need me.

The mist was rising, and as it did he saw that it was not the mist that coloured the ground purple, but that small, beautiful, flowers had released clouds of purple pollen that was catching and hanging in the cold air. The flowers had vivid, purple petals that swayed and bent theirs heads in sadness. Fern drooped his head and Thormir let it fall as he saw the flowers surrounding them. Looking at Thormir, his best friend and brother, Fern closed his eyes. The link between them was very faint now. *Let the purple flowers grow over me – I think they are nice, don't you?*

Thormir stared at his brother and, as he held him he knew he was losing him. When Fern spoke he sounded tired, *Ava letha du lysá bronus.* And Thormir heard the phrase they had repeated together, both in sadness and in joy, *"Let the stars be with you, brother."* Tears ran down Thormir's face and he felt his heartbeat quicken. *There has to be something . . . something I can do . . . anything!*

Ava letha du lysá bronus, Fern repeated. Thormir knew he was waiting for a response that would mean he would let Fern be at peace – free to rise to Elcala. *Let me go.*

Thormir was shaking so hard he thought he might break. *No.* "No!"

Let . . . me . . . go, Fern blinked at him.

Ava letha du lysá bronus. Tears ran down Thormir's face as he said the words.

Do not mourn me. Remember me. Fern's breath became a rasping sound, until he was still, silent.

Thormir held him. His heart was dead, numb. Then realisation hit him: Fern was gone forever. He let out a scream of pain and loss that echoed throughout the hills and into the murky forest. Fern was gone, and there was no bringing him back. *I will never see him . . .* He screamed until his throat couldn't take it, until his lungs had had enough. It was only then that he sank over Fern's body, feeling his dying warmth and yet not feeling. He took great heaving breaths. He could not feel anymore.

He heard the rest of the group gather around him. Some of them were silently wiping away tears while others just put a hand on his shoulder. But he felt none of it.

I am alone.

CHAPTER TWENTY ONE

SORROW
Dôlon

The next morning cracked through the clouds like shattered ice on a frozen lake. The storm had dissolved in the middle of the night, leaving a clear sky. The purple flowers that had once been beautiful now bowed from weariness, drooping their tips in mourning. The grass around them had been battered by the gale and swayed in the sleepy swish of the morning breeze. No sun cut through the trees. No colour gleamed on the hills. The world was now made of greys and blacks – a lonely and desolate place full of sorrow and loss. The feeling that he had lost a part himself had haunted Thormir all night, leaving a space filled only by torrid anger, and torment at the loss of his best friend – his brother. As he had sat under the dense foliage of the forest that night, dark thoughts crept into his mind: thoughts of anger, power, and vengeance upon those who had taken his brother from his side forever.

He looked over to the base of a large fir and saw the huddle of blankets that covered . . . Now *he* was gone, Thormir was finding it hard to say, or even think, *his* name. He choked and looked away, staring out through the trees. Every time Thormir tried to remember the events of the battle from the previous day, he could barely recall anything after . . . it was all blank.

The group had had to pull Thormir off Fern's body – that, he could remember. Hector had filled him in later that night as the storm roared over their heads. They had not travelled for the rest of the day or night – none could summon the energy – and if they had any it would have been spent on tears. Thormir shifted his weight, moving a twig from under where he was sitting, and considered his feelings.

The gladiators, apart from Rake, who had remained with Thormir, had stripped the bodies of the fallen, and taken their weapons, food, and clothes. Each fallen soldier now lay dead and naked, soaked and splattered with mud, an insult to the flowers that surrounded them. Hector had said that shortly after Fern's death he had seen two soldiers escaping, one being the scar-faced leader of the group, whose hand still remained lifeless upon the grass.

Thormir flicked his gaze towards the roof of the shelter of branches they had made for themselves. He saw through to what lay on top – the cloaks from the dead soldiers. It had been a good idea to use them as an extra layer of protection from the rain that had managed to make it through the protection already provided by the first.

But he didn't care. He cared for none of it: neither for the twisted scar on his arm, nor the drizzle still finding him, nor the company of others, nor the loaf of bread he held in his hands. All food tasted stale, all liquid of dust – he was numb to the world. *I wish I were dead.*

A phrase that his teacher had taught him came to him and he recited it out loud, 'If death should come while I am in the company of friends, let it come to me first.' *I wish it had. And what now? Where do I go?* The answer was clear. *West. Surely not home. What is the point? Anyway, Mary said that danger and darkness would fall upon the city if I stayed in Medani. It might already have.* He touched his shoulder and remembered his wound. Had he been right? Had the wargs risen again? There was nothing he could do now. From the bag that lay crumpled beside him, he took the large leather-bound book and began to work his way down a list of words that he could use to command his powers. *"Arek – To break . . ."*

*   *   *

It was midday. They stuck to the edge of the forest, each leading their horse behind them. The going was slow and more than once there was a slip on rocky moss or a fall due to the potholes covered by fallen leaves, branches, coppice, and heath. Thormir was tired of being wet. The weather had soaked everything. Despite the furs and the extra cloak that covered his back, sides and shoulders, the rain still seemed to find every piece of exposed skin and thin clothing. The drizzle had become a beating rain that cut in from the north, driving into him as they led their horses under the cover of the trees.

The group had decided on this route as they thought it would be more sheltered from the rain as well as being hidden from roaming eyes – Thormir had not forgotten about The Pale Riders and Tangar's warning of them. Weeks had passed since they had first set camp in Hurst, and where once the forest had been a dry place that shut out the elements. Now it was a place of discomfort and Thormir bit his lip in frustration with every step he took. He tipped forward for a second and secured his pack, lifting it higher on his shoulders.

At two weeks, since their arrival at The Tongue, Selena had roused the group by spotting The Al'Durast in the distance, rising high into the sky, but day after day had passed and the only progress shown was the size of the mountains. Thormir had guessed that the mountains were large, but he had not truly appreciated just how big the range of peaks was. Forming the spine of the South, The Al'Durast rose higher than he could have even imagined. These were truly wonders of nature. Most of the time he couldn't even see the top half of the range, as clouds circled the peaks like a nest of giant, white snakes, always moving, never revealing their secret. But even this wonder could not wash away the sorrow and pain that Thormir felt. Only the trudging of his footsteps could clear his thoughts. Sometimes he opened his mind to feel the energy and life around him. Once he felt a lone elk wandering not far from them, and in another instance he found himself following the thoughts and energy of a mole as it burrowed through the dirt, annoyed that its worm had escaped capture. *At least we are the same, mole, you and I. I have lost my friend; you have lost your dinner.*

Hector's deep voice came from behind. "Maybe we should ride from here. The mountain's villages shouldn't be too far – Norhill, did you say it was called?"

Thormir agreed, but before he had a chance to answer, a voice came from between the trees.

"Oh, I wouldn't do that if I were you. But . . ." the voice paused and then chuckled, "I am not you, so you go ahead." The voice paused as if its owner were looking around. "Oh, put those weapons down. Those useless pieces of metal and wood are no match for an old hermit with a cane. However, I was once told to never offer advice unasked, so maybe you should continue, but if I was you, which I am not, I would raise your thinking hoods and shelter beneath wisdom." A chuckle bounced through the twisted forest. His beard seemed to precede the old man out of a space between the trees. The long beard was mostly white, until it deepened into a dark green-brown where it trailed along the forest floor. The group lowered their weapons as they saw the sarcasm take its meaning.

"Who leads this group?" Thormir didn't answer, so Hector took his place.

"I do." Hector's answer seemed to startle the hermit, an expression that then turned to amusement.

"What are you doing here?"

"We are travelling west to the mountain villages, most likely Norhill."

"Aye, I heard that, but you still haven't answered *my* question. What are you doing here?"

"We are travelling . . ."

"No." The hermit's voice sounded like a whip over the rain.

To Thormir's surprise, Hector said, "We are fleeing the city of Orien, where we were kept captive."

The hermit's eyes brightened. "Excit'n times. 'Tis good. Well, I suppose you'd be likin' a place to stay? Come with me." The hermit turned and began to hobble his way back through the trees, still talking, whether to himself or to them Thormir couldn't tell. With a jerk of his wrist Thormir reined in his horse and turned to follow the hermit. If he could just lie down on a bed, or even sit on a stupid bloody chair, it would make this trip altogether worth it. *I swear, if this hermit does not have a proper chair and a bed . . .*

"And stop."

Thormir almost bumped into the man as the hermit came to a stop. "Welcome to my humble stump – 'tis good, no?"

"You live in a tree stump?" Maria sounded both amused and disgusted at the same time. She had changed during the trip through the forest. She had become hard and silent. Thormir felt she thought he blamed her for the death of his brother, but he didn't. She had not found anything that day in the forest, and Thormir had accepted that *he* might not have survived even if she had applied the paste. Thormir had overheard Selena comforting Maria saying that, "There was nothing you could have done, the wound was too grave, and even with your skill it would not have healed. He understands."

"This isn't just any old tree stump, my young lady. This . . ." The hermit paused for effect, "This is the last of the great musk trees. They were here before the oldest firs were no more than a seed in the ground. So you, young lady, might have some respect. 'Tis good."

Maria looked taken aback by the hermit's words, and even more so when he began to hum a cheerful tune, completely at odds with the weather that sliced into the forest. Thormir raised his eyebrows as he saw a small door being opened, then even higher as the hermit disappeared inside. Not returning was evidently his way of saying "Come in." So Thormir and Hector nodded to the group and they tied their horses and entered the stump.

It was like nothing any of them had expected. The floor and the roof were wooden and in some places separated by five massive roots that dived downwards. The large, open area expanded outwards in every direction. The hermit's clutter littered the space, but more than anything Thormir was surprised to see hundreds of books lining countless shelves. Scrolls too were crammed there, their contents were likely secret and known only to the hermit. Thormir went over to a shelf and opened one the books entitled *Codex of Law in the South*. The pages were all blank. Randomly Thormir tried another book and the same thing happened – only blank pages. He whirled around staring at the hermit, who was looking straight at him in turn. "Why are your books filled with nothing?"

The hermit smiled. "Firstly, one cannot fill a book with nothing, because nothing doesn't exist, however, you can fill a book with something even if that something doesn't exist. For example, these books are filled with something, yet to you they are nothing. Nothing doesn't exist, so there must be something in them. The clue is whether you can see it as absence or something. What should be there, or is there, or is not there is all rather like making up your mind, wouldn't you say?"

The hermit turned to the others, leaving Thormir's mind working hard to try and make sense of what he had just heard. "As for the others, you may find your beds down the hall to the left. Please care not to abuse my books." Leaning on his side, the hermit turned again and said to himself, "A cup of tea, I think." The hermit tapped the table with his cane as he passed, as if it had done him some wrong. The table did not object.

Putting down the books, sliding his pack off his back and leaning it against the door, Thormir followed the hermit into what looked like a kitchen space. The hermit was busying himself around a small fire that he had going, over which a small metal pot hung by the handle. "So, why did you warn us from riding out, towards the mountains?" Thormir's question seemed to beg of the hermit an obvious answer, as the hermit's response was simply a long roll of the eyes. *This man is very . . . odd.*

"Well, for one you must be tired, wet, and starved. Secondly, not two nights past I heard a large group of people, of the unsavoury kind if you get my meaning, pass this way. They were on horses too. And, by the look of them, well-armed; for I went I did, and peeked through the trees. I think one of them might have seen me, for they stopped a minute, but he thought nothing of it, the big, ugly brute. 'Tis bad, no? Third, it's a-raining and a-blowing a gale out there." The man pointed a nobbled finger at the door. "If you want to drag yourself back into the rain, be my guest, but you will not ask those," another point of the finger, this time in the direction of the hallway, "to join you."

"Are these men you speak of from the highlands? Surely we should ride for help, or at least ride away before they return."

"From the mountains? 'Tis being said that the villages on the slopes of The Al'Durast are crawling with shadow and plague. 'Tis possible that these men venture from there." The hermit paused and scratched his chin, "No, no, you should not ride this night. More than one thing will hunt you if you venture forth – for three shadows pass over the skies above. Remember, in hiding do not light a fire. You will ride in the morn I think, for in night there is counsel."

"Why are you helping us?" Said Thormir.

The hermit lowered his arm and gave Thormir what he thought to be a sad smile. "When you get to be as old as I am, something I would not wish on you, you see things how they should be, and you try to guide people upon the path that would most aid them." He chuckled and turned to prepare the tea.

It wasn't long before the others came to join them. Thormir felt alone again, lost in the grey void where he found sanctuary as well as the painful memory of the terrible loss of his brother. Soon the babble of the others filled the wooden halls, and only then did Thormir slip off, grab his pack, and settle into his quarters. Rather than nine puffed and warm beds waiting for them, there was a mixture of cushions and blankets, but at the sight, exhaustion overcame him. In the corner of the room was a chair. *Simple, wooden, perfect. A bed and a chair – my wishes granted, at least for the time being.*

Thormir lay down on his back, propping his head up against a soft place in his pack, and stared at the roof. He noticed that the ceiling had been made of a single, curving root that had buried itself deep in the ground below. Trying to drive away more thoughts of loss and darkness, he began to trace the lines on the root as he had done in Mary's cabin so, so long ago. He was just at a curve in the trunk when a piece of something hit him in the jaw. He cried out in pain. He looked around quickly for his mortal enemy; a loaf of bread sat innocently where it had just fallen.

"You know, a man I met once who said that, 'A loaf is deadlier than any sword or spear,' but here it is offered as a meal for a hungry traveller." The hermit shifted in the corner chair and somehow Thormir knew that he was smiling. Not amused, Thormir picked up the bread and sank his teeth into its doughy depths. After a month and however many weeks, the bread tasted wonderful, and a welcome change from the stale loaf and meats they had been picking away at.

"I have just been tending to your horses. They are fine beasts indeed. They seem pleased to be riding with new company. I have been talking with one, and he told me all there was to know about your journey so far." The hermit paused, "I am sorry for your loss. I am sure he will be missed by those who loved him."

Thormir stared at him – lean, bent – and wondered how the hermit could have known about them, about him. *As if! This old fool cannot talk to a horse.* Assuming that the hermit must have followed them through the woods, he continued to eat. "Where are the others?"

"Kitchen," the hermit grumbled into his beard. "Tell me why you lead them west towards the ranges? Surely further north would be safer? You could have travelled to the islands, or Durnsay, or further north. 'Tis better."

"When I was held captive," Thormir began, "a man came to the chambers where I was keeping guard and told me that I had friends to the west that they would keep me safe. At least that's what I thought his meaning to be."

"I see. Well then, you must do it. If there is one thing I have learned in life, it is to never miss a chance to give your feet a purpose. You must get some sleep, and so must the others, as tomorrow you ride to The Al'Durast and to Norhill, for the rain will have gone and I suspect the bandits stuck, wallowing in mud, their cloaks drenched and their spirits dampened."

Thormir closed his eyes as he heard the hermit leave, and the others settle in. He heard the thump of a massive body lie on its back and assumed it was Rake. He was comforted. On his other side he heard no sound at all. He imagined Selena would be lying there soon, concerned for him. For all the companionship, he still felt alone.

CHAPTER TWENTY TWO

A DOUBLE TAKE AT
A DEAD END
Till qualt

The hermit sat on one of his carved stools turning the pages, running his hands over them before continuing to the next. His great, white beard swept past the book and curled onto the floor like a sleeping dog. Thormir had to admit that at that point the man did look very wizard-like, or at least what he thought a wizard might look like – magic in one hand and staff in the other. No, despite the appearance and the fact he was apparently reading an empty book, he seemed ordinary enough, or as ordinary as any hermit should be in these times.

"The rain has passed you know, 'tis good." The hermit began to speak as he looked down at his book. "So you best be riding as soon as possible. It should take two or three days but you must reach Norhill before the gates shut, otherwise you might have to bribe the guards with what little coin you have – or else I suspect the men you have with you will willingly kill them for you. Not a good welcome to the town, I think. Once there, I advise you to head for Goat Horn Tavern. There, you will find the inn keeper, Amelia Pope, a truly wonderful woman . . ."

The hermit trailed off with his advice as he remembered the curve of her beautiful smile, the wave of her hair, and her eyes, dark brown with lashes like curled combs. In the months he had stayed in Norhill he had fallen for Amelia, but had done nothing about it. He cleared his throat. "There you will find her, and if her house is not full, it rarely is, she will fit you with rooms. As for getting to Norhill, it lies at the base of Calx Mons, the largest of the mountains in The Al'Durast – do not stop until you get there. If you stop, there is a chance you will find yourself heading in the wrong direction and pass Norhill completely."

Finally the hermit looked up and stared at Thormir. His eyes shifted, resting on the scar that screwed around his arm. "You should cover that up, you know. People more unkind than myself might have something more to say about it."

This time Thormir saw the hermit stare directly at him while at the same time feeling a brush on his mind. He recoiled then felt the fingers of thought let go. Thormir wondered what he had just felt. Apart from the mind touching his, he felt that he was joined with one far more powerful than he had ever felt – one that was old, old beyond measure.

Who is this man?

The hermit smiled sadly at him. "You must let go of your memories of him if you are to move on."

As if something had cracked within Thormir, he began to shake and his voice croaked when he spoke. "This is hell. Living without Fern is becoming unbearable. Every night I cry until I am screaming into my furs; the pain of it, it tears at me."

The hermit nodded and still with his sad smile he said, "Hell? Hell indeed, for hell is for the living, in death is where one finds peace. Take comfort in that your friend is at peace." Raising an eyebrow, the hermit said, "By chance, where did you leave him?"

Thormir thought it was an odd question but answered all the same. "We left him lying in the crook of an old oak on the edge of the forest near the beginning of The Tongue. He was broken, He –"

"Broken?" The hermit interrupted him with consummate rudeness.

Thormir barely noticed and continued, "Yes. He could not shift forms anymore, he just . . ." Thormir paused at looked directly at the hermit. "What comes after death? What have I left him to?" He felt a tear curve his cheek but he let it fall.

The hermit looked at him and smiled, "Death is another one of life's great mysteries; but if you really want an answer . . . I believe death is when the shadow of this world is pulled back to reveal sunlight as you have never known it. And then you see . . ." The hermit paused and his eyes glazed over before speaking again, "A stone arch and a far green country that pales the most beautiful of things yet living in this world. A horse waits for you beside the arch, and it shines white in the newly-born light. Then you ride through the purest grass and into a sunset of shining crystal."

Thormir caught his breath and found himself longing to be with Fern.

Getting to his feet, taking up his cane, and hitting the corner of the table with it, he proceeded to his books, where his knobbly hands spidered across the volumes until he felt the spine of one in particular. Opening it and feeling for the page, it took him all of two minutes to nod thoughtfully and sit back down on his stool. "You want vengeance on the soldiers who did this, do you not?"

"Yes."

"Indeed – vengeance is sweet but remember, taking the lives of those men will not bring back your brother."

Thormir had not decided what he would do with those two soldiers if they ever met again; all he knew was that death would be too good a punishment for them. The man with a scarred face, the one with one hand, it was he who had escaped – the leader of their pack. "Tell me, before we leave, why do you read from a blank page?"

The hermit laughed. "Like I said before, there is a something to your nothing. Come here and I will show you. Feel the pages."

Thormir approached the hermit and laid his hand on the ageing pages of the opened book. As soon as he did so he felt small ridges and bumps in the paper. "What are they?"

"Writing. A language I designed myself."

"But why use that? Why not ink?"

"I lost my sight many years ago, more than I care to mention. Now all I see is eternal nothingness. These days it is my mind that keeps me sane. Books are fuel for the intelligent mind, and with all the humbleness I have to offer I do admit that I am an extremely clever man indeed . . . And so I need my books. I read and I learn."

"But you walk, and seem as if you were with vision!"

"You are very kind – I am glad to have come across you and your party . . ."

The rest of the group, the gladiators and Selena and Maria, were all sitting down at the table and helping themselves to the wine and cheeses that had been set out by the hermit.

". . . it is not often you find such interesting characters, apart from between the pages of a book, wandering the forest paths these days . . ."

Thormir decided not to remind him that they had not so much been wandering, but struggling onward through the endless tangle of Hurst.

"These past years have been filled with violence and death. The stench of it sweeps over the landscape, a foul breath on the wind. The Darkness coming over The Al'Durast crosses the daylight as easily as a hand through the flame of a candle. The grass wilts in the spring and the winters are long; few things still remain beautiful and untouched by the breath of dried blood. This land is dying. Men have turned from reason to violence; they rape women and children for sport, seek food from others, and innocents are hanged. Trade, once a friendly matter between brothers, has turned to secrets and lies, deals cut between allies and to be shared with none but the most criminal of minds. It is a sad thing indeed when the stars watch over a dying land, and the people ask the heavens, where are you, my gods? They get no answer, and yet they still believe . . ."

Thormir thought it odd that an old man, and a hermit, could know so much about the goings on of the world. But he did not ask, not for lack of curiosity, but for the fact they had to ride.

*   *   *

Thormir and the others looked northward, staring out from the edge of the forest. In his mind's eye Thormir saw a map of the land and knew that they were staring across the beginnings of the Carabeorn, The Great Plains, far to the north of Carathron and Medani.

"Arr, yes, the Carabeorn," said the hermit. "One of the few places in the world to have kept its original name. For some reason men never took the trouble to name it in Estarion." The hermit tilted his head slightly, as if listening to the gentle breeze. "Your path lies in that direction." Raising his arm he pointed a north west. "Flats and rolling greens lie ahead. After that and land becomes rockier, until you reach the foothills of The Al'Durast."

Thormir smiled to himself as he thought of what Fern would say at taking directions from a blind hermit.

The hermit stepped out and turned. His beard tossed playfully in the breeze, dancing happily in the swaying grass. He looked at each of them in turn, his beady, all-knowing eyes flicking between them. With a sudden jerk, the hermit nodded to them as if giving his approval. They were all about to mount when they saw the hermit was, or seemed to be, staring at the horses with a ferocious intensity. Then with a gentility that betrayed his stare he began to sing:

> *"Lysá na pa ceneth ocus eythá fir,*
> *En, qualneth na pa vindir eythá áfir*
> *Lycaro, renná! Filis ocus Nasir, renná!"*

The effect of the hermit's song was instantaneous upon the horses. They all tossed their heads and it was clear that they had understood his words. Every one of them was raring to run – to feel their hooves beat upon wild ground, to chase the roaming wind, and to carry their riders across the great plains and into the shadows of the fierce mountains.

Thormir gaped at the hermit. At the hermit's words the wind had picked up and a wildness that was not there before had formed within the air. It was as if the world had listened to him sing. Apart from Mary, Thormir had never heard anyone sing in Nolwin before. Unlike Mary, however, the hermit had sung with such experience and beauty that the language had struck them dumb, and left them open-mouthed and wanting to hear more. Even Rake who was usually impervious to any charm stood, still silent, but this time in awe of the first and oldest language. It was as if the wandering power of Nolwin had been re-awoken, and a new star had been born unto the world to shine upon them, even at this hour.

The hermit closed his eyes and when he opened them, they looked glazed, as if he was remembering a vision of ages past. He looked in Thormir's direction and in a softer tone than before, said, "Go now, and remember, even the smallest candle can light the greatest darkness."

THE SHADOW OF FIRE

*   *   *

So they rode, flying across the landscape, the nine of them forming one line as they galloped towards the mountains and Norhill. The horses seemed to enjoy being out of the dark green of Hurst and back in the open.

All of the gladiators rode their horses differently to Thormir: they rode standing, crouched in their stirrups. Selena and Maria, who had both changed into leathers in the hermit's house, rode the same as most of the men, if not a little higher. Thormir rode with his head down next to his horse, the wind flowing over his back. Rake, who rode next to Thormir, seemed very interested in this technique. Thormir saw him try it out of the corner of his eye, then saw a shake of simultaneous admiration and disapproval that Thormir was so able to do something that Rake could not. Thormir grinned.

For the next two days, Selena led the group. The land was becoming rockier so the group rode in a line – the first finding an easy route so that the rest could follow. She seemed to know what she was doing as she guided her horse though the terrain, tugging on the reins, never slowing down. Small brooks and the occasional heather forced their way, but always they rode in the straight line, never varying their course. They did not even stop for lunch; instead the meat and bread given to them by the hermit was eaten on the hoof. They only rested when they felt the horses tire. Otherwise they would press on, maintaining the same course north west.

Like on their previous journey, no milestones were to be seen written upon the land. The only signs that marked their progress were the passing of the broken things. The watchtower of Tarn Noldur sat far on the horizon, fighting a battle against time. At half-day they passed the skeletons of what looked like a family of three and their horse – their scattered bones still bore the remnants of torn flesh. No sign of The Roc Riders had been seen, but on the nights that seizures did not come, he thought he heard the shrill cries closer then farther away, ever-pursuant, ever-seeking the power he carried within him. Thormir had told the others about what he had heard in the deep, dark hours of the previous nights, so now at least three of them carried a torch when they rode at night. Fire was their ally.

Weapons, spoiled and rusted by harsh weather, were dotted here and there; the survivors of long-lost owners – the road through the plains had become treacherous. Where their path dipped into the path of falling streams, rugged shelves would frown upon them until they emerged, forging their path over the Carabeorn.

Still they rode onwards, the promise of a bed and ale driving them forward. Just when their horses had started to slow, Thormir saw Norhill over the crest of the furthest hill, pressed up against the first cliffs of The Al'Durast. The horses too must have sensed they were not far from hay, water, and stables, for they put on a burst of speed, pounding up the hill until they reached the gates. As they dismounted, rather than the picturesque village that he had expected from the hermit's descriptions, Thormir saw high, daunting, wooden gates tower over them. Huge, iron bars held them upright. *We are not welcome here.*

Thunk! Thunk! Thunk!

Hector knocked with his massive fist. A small door embedded in the gates sharply snapped open. A fierce face appeared in the rectangular opening. "Show us your teeth!"

The yell was so unexpected, and the statement was so peculiar that Thormir took a step back.

"Show us your teeth!"

Each of them raised their hands to their mouths and pulled open their lips. Nine pairs of teeth were shown to the guard. Once he had seen their teeth and gums, he relaxed into a soft slump, though his eyes remained hard. They heard the sound of four latches being unlocked, then the slide of two metal bars being drawn back, and finally the moan of the heavy, wooden doors as they swung inward.

As soon as all of them were in inside the gates, five guards accosted them, looked them over, and scowled as if to say, "A bunch of ill-begotten scumbags." It was raining again. It was only a light drizzle, but still enough for the guard's hair to be plastered over his forehead and his eyes.

Since their escape from Orien, the group had acquired a weathered, harsh look about them. To top that off, their fur coats had begun to droop sorrowfully, bowing to the rain.

"Why did you want to see our teeth?"

Hector's question seemed to take the guard by surprise and the others stirred, uncomfortable at broaching the topic.

"I ask for our own safety. Men, bandits, and outlaws, whatever you like, they have been travelling around the countryside. Something drives them from their homes. Starving and violent, they have raided many of our wagons in search of food and weapons. When they do not find the food, the driver becomes their prey. They eat men, stripping them to the bone. No man should be found or buried that way. There have been reports from the towns scattered across the plains that the savages have developed a taste for man flesh; they say it drives them into a craze that they can't stop. They say savages have travelled as far as Harroforde and that one sign of the savage is their teeth, which they have sharpened and are stained brown. Their gums are a bloody red."

Thormir thought he was going to be sick. *How did it come to this?* Maria gagged as the soldier continued; Selena too seemed to go pale at the mention of the savages. The gladiators who stood beside him, who were usually unfazed by anything that would jolt the wits of any man, shifted from side to side.

"So that is why I ask. I would be a fool not to."

The increased tinkle of rain on armour was the unannounced sign that they should be moving further into the town.

Hector and Thormir had asked for directions to Goat Horn Tavern and the soldiers let them go about their business. It was not hard to find. About five minutes from the gates they saw the sign hanging from a metal bar that stuck out from the side of the house like a lonely outcrop from a sheer cliff. The squeak of the rusty chains that blew in the wind was only surpassed by the sound of hard rain on metal. From the orange light that shone from the inn, Thormir could see, engraved and painted, a man drinking from a giant goat's horn. He smiled. He was exhausted, and relief washed over him at the thought of a warm bed. He would get a full night's sleep.

*   *   *

Amelia Pope's brown eyes stared into his. "Well? What will it be? How many rooms? Eight, with the ladies sharing?"

Thormir's mouth would not work, so she turned towards Hector and addressed him. Thormir watched as Hector and Amelia made all the arrangements, from where they were to store their packs, where the nearest stables were, and most importantly, where the nearest whore house was. The question seemed familiar to Amelia and she swiftly gave him directions to The Sinful Strumpet. With a booming laugh he turned back to the group. "All is in order – horses, packs, and our rooms for the night. Now . . ." He turned to his fellow gladiators and said, "Who is up for a little fun? Let's see what the women of this town can do." His men laughed in approval and headed out the door. "Are you coming, Thormir?"

"No, I'll stay. I need a drink." Thormir noticed that Selena was paying close attention to his words.

"A drink more than a woman to lie at your side? Suit yourself. Our rooms are upstairs to the left." With that Hector and his men left the tavern, evidently hungry for something more.

You would think a tavern would have better lighting than this. Torches in brackets were oddly placed around the room, causing the lighting to be patchy so that some places were in shadow – almost darkness – and the only sign of company was the whiff and spiral of grey smoke coming from a shadowed pipe.

Across the room, a gale of laughter erupted from a far table. Looking over, Thormir saw a greybeard with long, white hair telling a tale to some of the town's children, who sat in a circle around his chair. Two of the children tugged on his cane, each pulling with all their might, their faces screwed up with concentration. The old man wore pure robes of white. He seemed to shine from within as he spun his tale for the children. He paused, obviously for the effect of suspense, and as he looked up his eyes darted slightly left of where Thormir stood. Maria shifted behind him as the wizened man's stare ended, and the suspense of the tale took its full and considerable effect on the children, who responded with joy at the story's end.

At the bar the lighting was a warm orange. Only Amelia Pope and another, short, shadowy figure were at the bar. The man who was drenched in shadow, was hunched and sitting close to his drink, taking the odd sip. The hood he was wearing fell all the way over his face, making it hard – even impossible – to see what was beneath the heavy cloth.

Maria and Selena both sat down. Thormir followed and mused, *It is the little things that make life worth living – the simple things in life that reward us at the end of the day.* The stool he sat on was heaven compared with the saddle. Amelia must have seen the change in all of them, as she said, "Hard day?"

"You have no idea." Thormir thought it best to spare the details, while still giving a friendly answer.

"Well, these are on me." She handed each of them ale, which burned in their throats, but thoroughly warmed them up.

"This stuff is amazing," said Selena as Thormir and Maria nodded in affirmation.

"Think of it as a welcome to the village."

The hooded man beside them, stirred. As he lifted his mug and took a sip of ale, his sleeve slid back to reveal a heavy metal gauntlet. Thormir tensed. He had seen the like before. Thormir had to admire the craftsmanship that had gone into it. Curving snakes of interwoven metal adorned the steel, forming an intricate grid that curled around his arm.

"Come with me." He did not turn but there was no doubt that he was addressing Thormir. "Leave the girls."

The figure dropped off his stool. He was not as tall as Thormir expected. He walked away, down the corridor that led to the stairs up to the quarters above.

"Ale?" The hooded man held out his armoured forearm, offering a goblet.

Thormir shook his head. "You know . . . where I come from, a friend will introduce him or herself before continuing the conversation."

"Is that so?"

"Yes, so if you state your name I will consider you friend. If not, I will consider you my enemy."

"You better mind yourself with that philosophy. What if you know and trust the name of someone and then they turn on you – will they then become your enemy? Or will they remain friend gone foul? Relationships are like your crops – if you do not tend to them, they will grow foul and they will cease to exist. My name is Baldur; I am a bad crop in your harvest? You see, knowing my name does not change anything. I might as easily stab you in the dark as ride alongside you as a brother in the fields of the afterlife."

Thormir was unmoved. "What are you? Why do you seek me?"

"We have met before. Do you not remember?"

In an instant, the sensation of being choked in the royal bed chambers came back to him. *Has he come to finish what he started?* "Assassin." The word came from Thormir's lips as a hiss.

"You make it sound as if I have done something wrong." He pushed his hood off his head revealing a beard, brown hair, fierce, deep-sunken eyes, a strong nose, and a furrowed brow. He was short, and strong.

"What kind of man are you?" The question might have seemed rude, but he didn't really care.

"I am not man, you imbecile, I am a dwarf of the Valmar clan."

"No you're not, that's impossible. The dwarves faded from this world after the last Great War." For some reason Thormir did not mention Immoreth and what they had discovered within the stone city.

"Oh really? So what am I doing here? Riddle me that!"

"That proves nothing!"

"Umm . . . do you see how short I am?"

"Yes, but still . . ."

"Well, I can't exactly prove it. But I know the way into the city under the mountains, the Heart of The Al'Durast."

Not for the first time, Thormir doubted his judgement. There was only one way to be sure. "Fine, then you will lead me there . . ." *At least we will find sanctuary. Orien and Bath will never think to look under the mountains, let alone think that dwarves even exist.* "But I will not go without my friends."

"Of course, we will wait until the morning when your friends will have exhausted their . . . appetites."

"Fine. Now, leave me, I need to sleep."

"This is my room."

"Oh." Feeling foolish, Thormir left the room and headed downstairs to tell the girls what had just happened, after which they all headed to their separate rooms, the girls bunking with each other, and Thormir to a bed of his own. Thormir smiled, considering for a moment what could have happened if he had followed Selena.

The room was simple: a bed, two chairs, a table, drawers and a carpet were the only decor. He liked it. After the harsh wilderness this was anything but the bare necessities – this was luxury, and with that thought, he fell asleep.

He was roused in the middle of the night when the creak of the door, soft footsteps, and soft tap of a hand announced Selena's presence. He stood up, wary but excited. She moved back a bit. She was very close to him. He could see every eyelash, every drop of moisture on her lips. She raised a hand and touched him on the side of his face. He responded in kind. Despite what they had been through, her beauty had remained unblemished, and her skin remained dark, tanned, and beautiful. He curled a lock of her hair behind her ear and looked into her eyes. He felt as if his heart were pounding in his throat as he moved towards her. She seemed unflustered. He felt her lips touch his. The touch was soft at first, but it was too much to hold back the frenzy of fire that flew between them. For a moment they stopped and stared into each other's eyes. An inferno of passion was burning within them – a burning feeling that they would never let each other go, no matter what. They fell onto the bed and he began kissing her on her lips and down her neck. They smiled at each other, both feeling, at that moment, the same longing for one another.

Selena smiled at him and, with a whisper, she said, "Wake up, we must go. Wake up, you oaf, you sleep like a stone under a mountain."

The fierce eyes of a dwarf stared into his. In that moment, Thormir could not have been more annoyed; the fact that his dream was not reality and that a dwarf's face was staring down at him had him so angry, he thought he might take up his hunting knife and stab Baldur just for waking him. Instead, he hurled the dwarf off him with all the early-morning strength he could muster.

"The girls are saying their goodbyes to the horses. I told them of our plans. I do not think we will be needing the horses anymore."

Oh, great – so not only do I have a dwarf ruining my dreams, but I find out that Selena is comforting a horse. Well, good morning to you too, world. Heaving his cloak of furs over his shoulders, he stood up, stretched, took up his pack, and followed the dwarf down the stairs and out of the tavern, nodding to Amelia on the way out.

She gave him a seductive smile and went back to cleaning the bar. The bard was sitting in the corner where, except for his long, white beard, he was covered by shadow.

It must be very early if it's still this dark. Indeed it was very early; early enough to slip out of Norhill unnoticed by those whose tongues were too easily seduced by plying wine or honeyed words. With a soft tread, the party reconvened and quietly headed out of the town. They moved over the patchy grass and wet gravel before slipping through back gate into the heath beyond.

Unlike in the Hurst forest, the trees here were clad in a grey, smooth bark that was cold to touch. This was common among trees that grew so close to The Al'Durast. Before long, Thormir could see the cliff through the steely trees, which were spaced wide apart in a distinguishable pattern. They were getting close to the cliffs at the base of Calx Mons. He cursed as he stepped over a puddle and felt his fur cloak collect the rest as he continued walking. *This place is deserted. I've never seen anything like it. If a bard were to describe this place, they would see it as a wasteland – trees that look dead and bare, but somehow alive and watching.* He thought he heard an owl scream, then he saw a flicker of a shadow, heard a twig break, and then nothing. Thormir felt around, trying to detect any life in the area, friend or foe. He could sense nothing apart from themselves. Then, without warning, Thormir thought he could hear music. He knew it was Selena. She spoke to him across his mind.

Why so nervous?

He saw her walking in front of him, her hips moving from side to side. He replied, *I don't entirely trust the dwarf.*

He didn't want to show her that this place had him unsettled; even the leaves that moved in the wind looked like giant spiders scuttling along the ground.

He seems fine to me.

I was once told by a wise man that trust is earned . . . I think we should be wary.

Do you trust me?

He smiled. *Do you trust me?* He knew what her answer would be.

Not really.

So how can I trust you, if you do not trust me in return?

Well, I suppose someone has to start first.

Thormir felt her mind close to him and he smiled. He didn't tell her that the wise man had been talking about how to mount a horse.

"Stop." The slow grumble of the dwarf's voice flew back to the group, carried by a gust of wind. The wind was picking up, snaking its way through the trees, sweeping the wasted ground, and carrying the withering leaves into frosty graves that lay between the cracks in the dew-covered earth.

The dwarf crouched and felt the ground; he muttered something under his breath. The earth shifted and a breeze that seemed to come from beneath the ground lifted the leaves away, revealing a small slab of stone. *Small enough to remain hidden or disguised as part of the earth. Big enough for any man or dwarf to pass through, or down. Smart.*

The dwarf brushed his hand over the slab of stone, seeming to whisper as he did so. A grinding sound, a jolt in the earth, a draught of wind, and the door was open. Baldur turned and smiled. Rake grunted in disapproval from behind Thormir, and the dwarf disappeared into the stone passage that led down, down under the cliffs of The Al'Durast.

PART 3

"The doors of freedom never close on the brave."

CHAPTER TWENTY THREE

THE DEMANDS OF A KING
Péto Enran

A group of five dwarves filed into the stone hall. Thormir's own party had not been waiting long, but long enough to appreciate their surroundings, and long enough to be stunned by the sight which greeted them. Even the gladiators were speechless, and stood open-mouthed at what they saw.

The roof of the hall was made of great, stone limbs that arched the distance between the towering walls. The walls themselves were masterpieces; they stood as sheets of pure, shining stone. In some places they were engraved with stories of ancient heroes and decisive battles. In four places this was so. Four stories, two on either side, were told in the room. In between the smooth stone and the half-faced stories, were arches, embedded into the sides, so that small hollows were carved into the wall. In each of them stood a different stone figure, standing on a raised, stone platform. The stone hero closest to Thormir held a double-bladed war axe to his chest, over his beard. He wore heavy, stone armour, with each of the metal links visible to Thormir. The hero looked upon him, and he cowered as he realised that he was in the presence of a great king of old, immortalised in stone.

While many of the kings and heroes wore much the same armour, each carried different weapons from axe to halberd. Thormir felt a different sensation as he stared into the eyes of each of them; they stared back in turn, and their stone eyes seemed to stare right through him. He looked away from the last hero he had locked eyes with. As he flicked his gaze away, he caught the name Velorgrim written in stone underneath. Something stirred within him, a sadness conjured from memory lost, but it was faint so he paid it no attention.

Suddenly, as if he had just realised something obvious, he remembered a question that had been nagging at him from the moment he had entered this great hall. Where was the light coming from? The room was illuminated, but not by the orange-red glow of a bracketed torch or the flickering light of a lit brazier; no, this light was white, it was as if the sun had travelled beneath The Al'Durast as a favour for the dwarves. Thormir looked around the room, searching for an explanation, unsure he would find anything at all. Then, he saw what he was looking for. A series of mirrors had been placed in the top corners of the room, such that the sunlight that entered from a small hole in the wall was magnified and reflected. One mirror was angled slightly differently to the others and, following its ray of light, Thormir found himself looking directly at one of the dwarves standing in front of him.

The mirror's light sparkled upon a gold cuff, which bunched together at the bottom of the dwarf's beard. The red gems on the gold on the beard-brace were not the only signs that this dwarf was of high status – the dwarf also wore a navy, golden-lined cloak over his thick furs. The king was sitting on the only stone throne built in the hall. He leaned on one arm, revealing elegant leather armour.

A dwarf next to the king wore no armour, but robes of pure black over which gold chains hung from around his neck. This dwarf had a sneering smirk on his face, and it couldn't be clearer that he disapproved of their presence.

"Baldur," the deep voice of the dwarf filled the hall, "you have summoned me for counsel to what you hold. Before you explain the presence of these humans in the Hall of Kings, you will give a full account of your mission in Orien."

"Your Majesty, my king, father, if I may, my report of my mission to Orien and return to The Al'Durast includes the story of how I came be with the humans."

"Very well, you may start, son. I will not stop you, but be sure not to leave anything out."

"Yes, father."

The realisation that he had been and was in the company of Dwarven royalty had surprised Thormir, but he tried to keep his face expressionless as Baldur gave his account of all that had happened to him.

"Father, as instructed, I left our capital Baraklemen many months ago. I had been sent to gain intelligence on the svay, and the empire to the north, and to assassinate Lord Bath, keeper of Orien. In this I have done two of the tasks. I would have succeeded in the last if Thormir here had not stopped me in my attempt to kill Bath. However, the meeting between us that night in the royal chambers must have been fate, for he has a weapon that will change everything, but that piece of the tale is not ready to be told – first the svay.

"The humans that live in the town called Norhill know nothing of the svay that trouble us to the north; all except one. They call him The Red Eagle. He is a great bard and master of lore. He has great honour and wisdom, for his eyes have seen many years and his beard is long and thick." The king nodded in obvious approval of this last attribute and Baldur went on. "He knew many things, including the whereabouts of a small group of svay who have ventured south and plan to attack a town just north of Norhill and south of the Farthing pools. When I ventured to ask more, the bard simply said that they would attack two days from now in the deep dark of dawn.

"Gathering information on the empire was easier than I had anticipated. As I travelled to Orien, I passed some nomads and small villages, as well as a group of refugees, who told me of the corruption and torture happening in the north. The emperor does not venture from Ironholt but sends his servant 'The Crow' to do his bidding. They say that he recruits his soldiers through convincing them of 'The Cause', or what he claims to be 'The True Religion'. In every town and city he takes, he has ordered The Crow to burn and pillage every temple, and build a new one honouring and worshipping The True Religion. Any who do not pay homage or do not respect the religion are burned outside the city walls. The Crow is currently taking his army to capture Silverhaven; it is said that the army numbers over 40,000. I am told that they have weapons that we have not seen before, and that they can hurl flaming balls of fire and rock over city walls. It is also said they have bows that have a further reach. If they have truly taken Silverhaven, Your Majesty, they will have an army well over 40,000. He has already sent a force over the Carabeorn with orders to wait for the rest of the army to arrive once Silverhaven has fallen. I fear their next stop be the southern lands and Orien, and once that is taken, it is only a matter of time before Medani will fall under the rule of the emperor. He will rule the all lands east of The Al'Durast, and I fear that he is one who will not stop with one war. He will search for another, he will search for us, and we do not have the strength to fight the army that he will wield. I hold no lie within my words."

Baldur paused and rubbed his forehead with his forefinger and thumb, "I continued to Orien. It was not difficult to find work. As

I took up the role of barber, I learnt that Orien is rebuilding much of its defences, especially its great outer walls. To do this Lord Bath has given orders to capture many of the refugees travelling on the southern roads – he either turns them into soldiers or slaves. Often the slaves will be taken to labour on the wall or work the quarry, where they will cut and shape the stone. That fate be the worst, for their tools and method are completely wrong. I have even seen a woman torn from her newborn and given to the quarry, where she was beaten. If any slave misbehaves they are either flogged with a barbed whip or sent to a place called The Pound, where they are forced to fight against an unbeatable man.

"I let a few more months pass before I made an attempt on Lord Bath's life. This was unsuccessful; however, in the attempt I met Thormir here."

The king raised his bushy eyebrows. "And the weapon?"

Baldur took Thormir's right arm, pulled up the sleeve, wrenched him closer to the king, and traced the coiled scar. "He is Flametouched; he has The Gift."

A dwarf dressed in a long, golden, bearskin cloak that indicated his position as the treasurer, recoiled at the sight of Thormir's arm, stepping backwards and almost tripping. The king's reaction was not what Thormir was expecting at all. The king's face was expressionless as he addressed Thormir, "Show me."

Thormir was lost. Perhaps the king wanted him to prove that he could wield the power, as he had done during most of the fights he had been in, but even then he had done it unintentionally. "I, I can't really do it on the spot. It comes to me if I am under pressure. My teacher, Mary, was also captured in Orien, but did not escape with us."

The king nodded, and just as had Baldur had done, rubbed his lined forehead with his thumb and forefinger. "You will travel with your brothers to defend the town that Baldur mentioned in his account. He will witness you fight and will report to me what you have done. It is against our laws and impossible for us to lie to our fathers, so I know he will speak the truth."

The black-robed dwarf leant over to the king and whispered something. It must have been of great importance, as the king immediately said, "You must be a great warrior, to escape the high walls of Orien, and to defeat Lord Bath's many men in battle. Go, and prove your worth."

Thormir was shaking wearily, and was about to tell the dwarf king that victory can be a double-edged sword, when he saw two dwarves swiftly approach Maria and Selena from behind. Before he could warn them, before he could think, he saw the dwarves circle the girls and each hold up a cup of liquid that seemed to be smoking and giving off a foul scent. Thormir watched as, at the same time, both girls swooned, coming to rest to the cold, stone floor. Two more dwarves entered and the four of them carried both girls out of sight. Thormir wheeled around.

"So," His voice was trembling with suppressed anger, "You spill honeyed words so you can create a distraction."

The king's deep-set eyes burrowed into Thormir. "I never speak with a forked tongue, nor do I guise my speech in a cloak of deception. However, your women will not enter Dwarvenhiem again until you have proved that you have The Gift. Only then will they join you." The king paused as if considering something else, and weighed up the odds of his important choice, "If . . . you do have The Gift, there is one who will be able to help you understand your ability – but guarded secrets shall not be divulged so easily. I will wait until you have shown your power."

Thormir nodded curtly and forced a plastered smile across his face. "I also have a request of you, oh mighty king under the ranges."

His flattering turn of phrase must have caught the king's attention, as he raised an eyebrow and stared down at Thormir. "Make it."

"I wish you to go to war."

"Is that so? Why should I? Why should I risk the safety of a nation, of my nation, just to support your war? No, I think not. I do not see the shadow of your enemies cast upon the horizon marching towards The Al'Durast. Indeed, it seems that men are fleeing the forests and mountains and heading east. So, tell me, why should I go to war? I know that the men serving the empire are marching south to your homelands, but we dwarves are safe, safe in our stone halls. The boulder that is your enemy shall shatter against the mountains if they decide to attack us, if they even find us. No, I think we will not aid you – I will not put our people at further risk. We already face the svay in open war, and must defend our lands from those creatures that would settle amongst the northern peaks. The svay desire territory on the northern slopes of The Al'Durast. They spoil everything they touch, so we either kill or drive them back west from whence they came – but the war over the northern summits continues. My army only numbers 9,000 strong – these numbers cannot forge an army strong enough to compete with the number of men that march towards Orien. I cannot help you in this."

Thormir took out from his pack the small locket that he had pocketed when in the dead city of Immoreth, or as the dwarves named it, Az Osten du Baraklemen. "Perhaps this might change your mind, Your Majesty?" Thormir tossed the locket towards the king so that the gold circle arced and fell into his robed lap.

The dwarf king caught it in his tough hand that wore three rings of different sizes, each adorned with a sparkling gem. The king stared at the locket for a full minute, examining the detail of the metal, the picture within, and the hinge of the locket. "Where did you get this? Why have you the picture of the Khan of Az Osten du Baraklemen? What has happened?"

"My friends found it in the dead city."

"Dead city?"

"Yes, it was made entirely of stone – beautiful too – and it rose up and dropped down into the earth for miles. All we found there were dead dwarves – some tortured, many with limbs cut or missing, but all dead. There too, we found the banners of the enemy and they bore the symbol of the emperor and his puppet "The Crow". It is my belief that the dwarves killed the majority of those who attacked but they themselves died in the effort. All the women and children were cut down – Your Majesty, it was a horrible sight, one that I will never forget."

The king bowed his head and muttered something under his breath. Beside him, Thormir saw Baldur solemnly bow his head too and close his eyes as if he were praying to his gods. Raising his head, the king's expression was as hard as the stone throne he sat upon. He turned and looked directly at the treasurer, and then at another dwarf. In a voice Thormir *could* hear, he said, "Call the banners."

The two other dwarves bowed and exited the room. "It will take a few days for the khans to gather, but you will have my vote in the matter. The Khan of Az Osten du Baraklemen was a close friend – this crime shall not go unpunished. However, the choice to avenge our fallen shieldmates does not fall to me alone. The banners of the nine Khans of Dwarvenhiem shall gather, and then we shall decide whether to go to war."

CHAPTER TWENTY FOUR

THE THORMIRIAN KNIGHTS
Pa Thormirian Ens

The shadows and greys of morning brushed through the forest. The trees here were not like the firs of Hurst, but were tall, wooden skeletons that stood still, not bothered by the troubles of the world. They offered little colour to the forest other than tones of grey, which added to the shadows and mist that swirled in and around the deadened grass. No birdsong rang at the break of sun. Shimmering through the mist, sunlight was almost reluctant to enter this lifeless forest. Sound had abandoned its seat here for a more cheerful corner, perhaps a bubbling brook or a lush, green meadow, but never this bleak domain. This was not a place for life but death. It was almost a cemetery of nature.

Thormir opened his mind, searching through the forest. No animal lurked, twitched or breathed. It was as if everything that could be hunted had either been slain or had fled. A chill travelled through his body at the thought. He flexed his bow. He did not expect to find any animals, except for a few grubs eating the carcass of a bird that was unlucky enough to fly into this part of the world. The night before, Baldur had said they were close to Stockhud, only a day's ride from the town, which was to be attacked by these so-called svay. Thormir was scared – the coming battle would be no Medani street brawl – but he did not admit it to the others, who seemed perfectly calm. No, this time he was walking into a fight against an unknown enemy, substantial in number, and who were clearly inhumane to the point of being thirsty for slaughter. He remembered Mary telling him that what man fears the most is the unknown. The thought offered Thormir little solace. He tightened his grip around his bow and notched his arrow again.

He moved his hand down the shaft, feeling the fletching before his three fingers came to rest on the bowstring. He leaned a little to his right and spied another tree directly behind the first, which was standing in front of him. He drew his hand back to rest near his cheekbone and took aim. *Waste of an arrow, but I feel like shooting something.* There was a reason that he was known as a great archer in Medani. He had long since learnt the ability to curve the path of an arrow, and to hit concealed targets. It would not work with a tree behind something as tall and wide as a stable or a cart – that was just ridiculous – but one tree behind another tree was hardly a challenge. He could feel his fingers on the bowstring, one above the arrow, two below. Slowly he drew his thumb up above his top finger and pushed the string slightly inward. He drew in his breath then slowly exhaled. He released. With a dim satisfaction, he watched the arrow sail past the first tree, scraping the grey bark, then hit the tree behind, finally burying itself into the splitting bark.

Thormir felt a hard hand upon his shoulder and he turned, whipping out another arrow ready to release it into the chest of his attacker. He looked up. Rake was standing in front him with a puzzled expression on his face. An arrowhead was being pointed directly at his heart. Thormir lowered his bow and nodded back. Rake tilted his head signalling that that they should head back to camp. He shouldered his bow and arrow and walked beside Rake until they reached the small camp that the group had set up the night before.

It was not long after they put out the fire, packed the burnt sausages, and moved out that they broke through the treeline. Thormir was hoping that the grey of the forest would cease once they reached the edge, but the dull, silver tones continued over the small plain that led to the gates of Stockhud. Smoke rose in great, swirling pillars over the distant town. They were too late.

As they crossed the plain and came closer to Stockhud's walls, they saw that the wooden pikes and outer defences of the town were completely shredded, as if splintered by claws or teeth. *What creature could have done this?* Only the Wargs of Hurst came to mind, but they were far from the forest and the hermit had said that no wolfkin came close to his home, which was near Norhill itself. He felt the bite marks in the wood. They were deep. *Fangs, surely.*

Silently, the group proceeded through the gates and into Stockhud. They too were broken; half of a door hung pathetically, the other half had been brutally thrown to the floor. Stepping over the broken rubble of the gates, they quietly walked into what had been the main street that ran through Stockhud. It was destroyed, and covered in bits of wood and chunks of collapsed walls. Torches, fallen from brackets, lay burning themselves out in between planks of shredded houses – signs of violence and bloodshed.

The door of the closest house creaked open. Thormir heard some of the gladiators draw their weapons. To Thormir's right, Rake drew his two swords and lavishly spun them in a figure of eight motion. Thormir looked left and saw Jord, the only gladiator who had long, blond hair that fell in thick braids across his back, notch an arrow.

"Have you ever seen anything like this?" asked Thormir, still watching the arrow fixed in Jord's hand.

Jord's usually hard eyes softened and the gladiator responded, "No, not marks like these." Jord ran his hand over another bite mark, sunk into a wooden pillar that held a balcony corner. "Nor have I seen so much ruin."

Thormir flicked his hand, gesturing to the bodies that surrounded them. "Look at these wounds . . ."

Jord peered over Thormir's shoulder. "No blood."

This time it was Thormir who notched an arrow.

The group recoiled as the cry of an infant echoed out of the broken framework of a house. Baldur immediately drew his two axes and looked at the house with obvious trepidation. The only one who did not recoil was Rake. He stepped out of line and made his way towards the house. Thormir turned and followed. A large crossbeam had fallen, blocking the doorway. Placing himself under the beam, Rake grunted as he bore the full weight of the wood. Stepping back and twisting, Rake tossed the crossbeam into the splintered rumble of a smashed cart. Thormir, to one side of Rake, covered his back, training his sights on the doorway as Rake entered. The infant's crying increased, the pauses between each sob decreasing until it sounded like a single cry of fear and pain. *What is this? Make it stop.* Thormir had heard the cries of a dying deer and gurgles of wounded men, but the helpless cry of the infant was something else. Its cry seemed to cut straight to the core, clutching desperately to the hearts of those who were able to help.

Rake stumbled then regained his footing as he made his way through the door. Thormir lowered his bow. There was no enemy for him to shoot at. Stepping over the shards of wood, they both entered the front room, leaving the others waiting anxiously outside.

The cries came again, louder this time.

As the group made their way through the house they saw broken tankards, picture frames with their paintings ripped apart, tables overturned, and then a corpse. Splayed out on the floor, the man lay positioned in a great cross, marking his own death. He looked at peace, despite his broken body. He seemed to be protecting a thin, wooden door that muffled the sound of the infant. Thormir opened the door, swinging it outward, and saw what crouched and lay behind it: a mother and her baby.

The mother looked as terrified as the child sounded. She was rocking and nursing the child as only a mother could. She was singing a soft tune to it, desperately trying to calm her baby. Thormir reached out with his mind and, as he had been taught, he mingled his consciousness as best he could with that of the baby. He felt no thoughts within the infant's mind, rather he sensed a swirling of colours. A mixture of blues, reds, and yellows, circled the consciousness of the baby – there were feelings of terror, confusion, and an odd sense of defiance. The child stopped crying as it felt Thormir's presence within his mind. It looked at Thormir with round, innocent eyes as Thormir increased pressure on the baby's mind and pushed calming thoughts between them. Thormir thought of the things that he loved to do, things that calmed him when he was angry or frightened, and pushed those thoughts and feelings into the consciousness of the baby. He saw the infant's heaving chest slow and grow calm and heard the cries turn to small gurgles of tiredness. The baby blinked at them with his round, blue eyes, and to Thormir's great surprise, Rake blinked back, that same slow measured blink. The edges of the babe's mouth curled upwards then he opened his small mouth in a perfect O, popped his thumb in, and began to suck away, happy at the new company.

Thormir felt that the grey shadows and absence of colour they had travelled through those days past had disappeared when they had heard the cries of the infant; he was a beacon of colour, hope, happiness, and innocence. Innocent to how cruel the world had become, unaware of his father's death, or the fact that his mother was dying. As the mother sat holding the baby in her arms, rocking back and forth, she fought what she knew must come. Both Rake and Thormir saw it in her as she turned to them. She herself felt it – the darkening of her eyes, the slowing rhythm of her heart, and knowledge that, like her beloved husband, her body was broken, and her mind bent. She looked up at the strangers but they did not seem to want to hurt her. Thormir watched as the mother held out the small bundle of robes and towels that covered and warmed her treasure.

"Take him. Look after him." She collapsed, palms holding her shoulders from the floor, as Rake took from her baby boy. She looked at Rake and Thormir. "RUN!"

"Run?" Thormir only questioned her because there seemed to be nothing to run from.

"RUN! THEY ARE COMING!"

Thormir and Rake needed no further instruction and turned to leave, but as Thormir reached the door he turned and ran back to the infant's mother, who was now slumped against a wall.

"Come with us! I can save you."

"No."

"I will not leave you here." With that Thormir hoisted her to her feet and wrapped one of her arms over his shoulder. He felt her shallow breathing but he was not going to let her die in this wretched place. *I will not let these floorboards become her final resting place.*

Suddenly the woman screamed and Thormir felt her breasts rising and falling with the jolting beat of grief, for they had just passed the man lying, splayed, across the floor. She looked upon her dead husband and both fear and sorrow rose up within her. She felt weak – so weak. *Soon I shall join him in the afterlife.*

The group made their way up onto a balcony that looked over the street's decrepit houses, whereupon Thormir realised how much the house they had just been in had muffled the sound of the wind. As they made for the steps Thormir saw the others waiting. They too seemed to have noticed the wind pick up. It flew in their faces and whistled like . . .

"Arrows!"

"Everyone, get to the edges of the street now! Hide behind anything!"

An arrow whizzed past Thormir and nicked the brand on his left arm. Beads of blood spattered across the letters B.O. Cursing, Thormir was forced to let go of the woman. "Stay with her!" Rake nodded at Thormir and came over to where Thormir had left the lady resting against the outer wall of her house. She was panting from the effort of walking, but as she looked at Rake, she saw her baby wrapped in blankets and the weariness melted from her face, only to be replaced by a look of concern. She held out her arms for her little boy. The baby squirmed in his warm blankets but did not object as Rake gently placed him in his mother's care. Thumb still in mouth, he was oblivious to the fight that was going on in the main street. Rake nodded again as Thormir took his bow from his shoulder and felt for an arrow. *Finally, let's see what these things really are.* "Stay with them, Rake. Do not let anything happen to them." Another nod from Rake and Thormir was off down the steps.

The gladiator closest to him peered between the planks of an overturned food cart, scoping out the enemy. Thormir looked closer at the man's attire and recognised Aiden – not one of the biggest gladiators, but as good at killing as the rest. He wore a long, curved, thin sword at his waist that was sheathed beside another sword; the latter shorter and wider than the first. A shield that was painted black with gold flames erupting from the centre was slung across his back. Aiden turned to Thormir as he approached.

"A good day to die. There are about fifty of them – three archers are positioned on the rooftops and are firing arrows like mad."

Thormir felt his heart pumping a hard rhythm through his veins as he too waited for their attackers. "Seriously? Eight against fifty?"

"I'm thinking these are the vile creatures we were looking for. Maybe that dwarf king of yours doesn't want us to come back at all. Oh, and by the way – don't forget to use those powers of yours so we can get out of here alive."

"Fifty shouldn't be too hard, should it? I think I can get at least five, and you and your brothers are trained killers."

"Look at you! A few fights and suddenly the fledgling thinks it can fly."

Hector, who was crouching with Baldur behind a cart in the middle of road, turned to them grinning and said, "If they fight as well as they shoot then we are in for an easy workout." Hector stood and let out a mighty yell. Twirling his sword, he jumped over the upturned cart and ran at the svay, bloodlust written across his face. He made it two strides. On the third, an arrow shot from a rooftop sliced his thick cloak and smacked into his armour, cutting through the metal. The shaft stuck there, poking out from the middle of his chest. Looking at the shaft, Hector smiled, just as another hit him, this time slightly lower and to the left. Hector fell back and collapsed into the dust just as another arrow found its mark.

"NO!" Thormir made for his body, but Aiden held him back. His eyes were hard, filled with a fire that only a gladiator could possess. The other gladiators began to roar like five wounded beasts, their howls of pain and fury crashing over the ears of the svay. Thormir looked at the three gladiators hiding across the road and saw Jord, bow out, arrow at the ready. They locked eyes and nodded at each other, then the six of them, with Baldur at the rear, charged at the enemy – fifty svay not forty metres away. The charge was not the wild madness of a wounded bull, but the calculated strike of a pack of wolves closing in for the kill. As Thormir shouted his orders, the men obeyed without hesitation. Three of the gladiators stuck to the edges of the road, running between wooden beams and making difficult targets for the archers. Jord, the fourth gladiator, climbed upon the nearest rooftop and began firing his own arrows at the attackers. The three archers on the far away roofs immediately loosed a hail of arrows at Jord, one of which bore deep into his thigh. Jord gasped and bent to one knee, snapping off the arrow. Back on his feet again, Jord drew and fired one more, which hit a svay right between the eyes. As the two archers on the roofs paused, Thormir used the opportunity to stand, draw, and fire.

His two arrows flew towards the second rooftop archer. Quick as the arrows were, the svay archer was quicker. It darted off the roof with inhuman ability and landed lightly on its feet. Looking around for either cover or its kin, Thormir could not tell, the svay spirited towards a fallen beam. Using the still-attached sign of the smithy's shop as a jump, the svay launched into the air, its silver sword arcing towards Aiden's exposed neck. Thormir did not have time to fire another arrow before the shining sword finished its flight. Aiden turned out of instinct, and sliced open the belly of the svay. Ignoring the guts and intestines spilling over his head, he turned again and plunged his sword into another. Not having time to withdraw his weapon from the twitching body, he whipped out his dagger and threw it at the throat of a third svay running towards him, who fell back, dropping its spear. Aiden wrapped himself around the svay's fallen spear, broke it in two, and took the sharp end. Leaving his other weapons, he ran onward, roaring at the approaching warriors.

On the other side of the street the battle was going the same way. Hot blood sprayed over the houses, staining the thatched roofs with crimson. Flesh was being torn from limbs, blades of silver flashed and steel clashed, but still the gladiators fought on, leaving a bloody trail of bodies behind them.

Shooting the last of his arrows, Thormir watched as the brothers in blood and arms, Bors and Berin, dispatched three more of the svay. He could almost see the bones fracture in the svay's jaw as Berin's hammer ploughed into the side of its face. Berin roared and belched in bloodthirsty glee. However, he was not quick enough to save his brother from the plank of wood that a svay smashed into the side of Bors' leg. Bors fell to his knees. Blood spattered the splinters of wood. The svay stood over him. It raised a sword high in the air. In desperation, Bors grabbed a large splinter of wood, stood up with a jerk, and shoved it into the svay's neck and jaw. Even from where Thormir was fighting, he could see the look of shock on the svay's dying face. But not for long. The warrior's choking expression was suddenly disfigured as the tip of Berin's dagger emerged from one of the svay's bloodshot eyes.

Thormir looked around for Jord, forcing his gaze away from the blood bath ahead of him. Jord was nearly out of arrows and was on his knees, grimacing as the broken arrow poking out of his thigh worked its way inward, diving through his muscle.

"Retreat!" Thormir swivelled as he heard Baldur's inherited booming voice echo down the street, bouncing between the fallen shops and crumbling houses. Thormir counted around twenty svay chasing after them, some jumping over roofs the others on foot, hot the heels of the three gladiators. *We are going to be beaten to the ground.*

Searching for something to turn the tide in their favour, Thormir spotted two piles of netted barrels and crates roped to the roof of two separate shops, one on either side of the street. Thormir focused on his target. He felt the power of the bow; it was part of him, an extension of his arm. He brushed the fletching of the arrow – no excuse for a bent feather. He inhaled, counted to four, and drew back the bowstring to its full extent. He slowly exhaled then held the empty breath.

The arrow sliced through the netting and sent the crates and barrels tumbling over the roof and crashing to the street below. Doing the same on the other side of the street, he forced the group of pursuing warriors into a winding line of two. *Easy pickings.*

Seeing the success of Thormir's tactic, each gladiator turned. Taking up positions on either side of the opening between the crates, they began to butcher the oncoming warriors. Thormir watched as the svay fell under axe, sword, and spear.

Then there was a scream. A high-pitched shriek of fear. A mother's scream of love, protection, and terror. *Rake! The baby! The mother!* Thormir stumbled back, running past Baldur who, seeing his fear, followed suit.

Thormir reached the balcony where he had left the small party just in time to see the mother collapse to the ground. She had deep bite marks all around her neck. Rake was on the ground, knocked out, lying motionless on the wood. A svay lay beside him with what looked like scratches around its neck. Another svay warrior looked up at Thormir, searching him with evil, wicked eyes, then flicked her gaze away.

Prying the baby from its mother's arms, the svay gently picked it up, and began to rock the babe, almost nursing it, reassuring it that nothing was wrong. She stood over Rake, smiling at Thormir with sharp, pointed teeth. Thormir felt his arm, his scar, itch and then grow hot. The warrior licked the blood off her lips, and then drew back her head, ready to sink into warm flesh.

"*Arek!*" Thormir threw out his arm and felt the white-hot energy rush through him. In a flash, the warrior flew back, her head twisted sideways in shock. Thormir had used the word for "break" that he had read in the thick, leather-bound book, which he had left with his things in the Hall of Kings. As the warrior flew backwards, the baby fell down onto the vast expanse of

Rake's chest. Running to the balcony, Thormir reached down and scooped it into his arms. Under a single thick curl of brown hair, the baby blinked up at him, happily sucking on his own thumb.

"You're all right." Thormir brushed his forefinger against the chubby curve of the babe's cheek. "You're okay. You're going to be okay. You're all right." He looked at the svay lying unconscious, "Bind her hands!"

Closing his eyes, he heard nothing in the background; only the silence of a lost mother and a fallen companion. He heard Baldur's rough breathing beside him. He opened his eyes. The dwarf was looking down at the mother of the infant. "Sad, very sad. The child shall never know her face." Baldur stretched out his arm and pressed his fingers on her eyes, sliding her lids down. The residue of fallen tears carved their way through the dirt on her face. Picking up some fallen canvas from the ground, Baldur wrapped it around the mothers neck, covering up the deep and bloody scratch marks. No longer did she look scarred and mutilated, just asleep, walking the dream paths of the eternal night.

"We need to give her a proper burial," Thormir stated. He was speaking half in a daze. *He didn't even know his parents. He will have no mother to nurse him to sleep after nightmares, no father to teach him to hunt.* The infant twisted to its side and shut its eyes, at peace with the horror that surrounded him. Wiping his small, snotty nose against Thormir, he buried his face in his blankets and fell asleep, his small chest moving up and down.

Plumes of white clouds were greying at the edges and bulged outwards, suppressing the imminent rain. They were closing over Stockhud. The winds had died down. Without it the air felt dry. It caught in Thormir's throat, forming a lump that he could not move, however hard he tried. The feeling of death had returned. It tore at him and clawed at his heart. It scorned at his mourning and revelled in his loss.

The wooden floor creaked. Thormir watched the flicker of eyes, and the twitch of a grimy nose, as Rake came back to them. Rake stood up, looking furious that he had been knocked over and left to lie there. Brushing himself down, he noticed the body slumped against the wooden post. Letting out a howl like a wounded boar, he dropped to his knees. Placing a hand on her neck, he slid his fingers under the canvas, pressing against the mother's wound, and drew back as soon as he touched some of her blood. With a gentleness that did not fit his build, he wiped his middle and forefinger against the mother's brow, painting two lines of red. Although Thormir did not know for sure, he thought that Rake was blessing the women for safe passage to the afterlife.

Thormir looked behind him, sure that more of the svay were fast approaching. There was no sign of them. No sign except for the pile of bodies that bloodied the ground before the feet of the gladiators. Severed limbs and spilt innards created a mound of mutilated and disfigured corpses that blocked the small gap between the fallen barrels, which were now sticky with blood and gore.

"We have to get a move on," said Baldur impatiently, "more of those foul creatures might come back for us. And I think we should take the svay warrior with us – this is the first time we have captured one of them alive; now the fall of the hammer on the anvil of fate might strike a different beat. No longer are we fighting a veiled enemy."

"Baldur," Thormir snapped, his tone sharper than he would have liked, "I will not leave the mother and father of the baby to lie in the rubble. I will give them a proper burial."

"Aye, I should think you would have done the same thing for me as well, Thormir."

Thormir, Baldur, and the rest of the group turned to see Hector grinning and limping towards them. He looked white-faced but in good spirits. The party exploded with joy, and questions were instantly hurled at Hector.

"How did I survive? Ha! I was never dead. I think I just lost a lot of blood or was knocked out cold."

"But the arrows!"

"Arrows? Ha!" He grinned at all of them, his eyes resting on Thormir and the child, and then said, "Arrows cannot kill me! I am Hector, the killer of men, champion of whores – nothing can kill me." And with that proclamation he looked down and snapped the arrows from his armour, then pulled a third through his thigh and wrapped some torn cloth over the wound. "Arr, I see you suffer the same wounds as I, Jord, you maniac."

"Hector! Well, it is a pity none of us died to mark this victory over that scum." Jord said, limping as he led the horses. "I tell you it's bloody grim back there. Those – whatever they were – they have stacked the bodies of all the townspeople in a great pile near the stables. I tell you, it's one of the most disgusting things I've ever seen. Fathers, daughters, sons, mothers, and elders – all are tossed, dead into the mound. Some have been burned, their skin blackened by some inferno. The stench of their burnt flesh fills the place. It is no way for innocents to die."

Thormir pictured Jord's description in his mind and felt bile rise in his throat. *Why? Why would someone do that?* The death of a whole town at the expense of at battle lost. The svay had no victory in this, they had gained nothing, and yet they had disfigured a whole village, murdered all that opposed them. *What right did they have to kill these people? And yet I have killed, and for what? To commit murder for people I did not even know. They might not have even deserved to be saved. No! I mustn't think like that. No one deserves this fate – neither friend nor foe.*

Thormir looked towards the gates that led from Stockhud. He saw the forest in the distance, the skeletal trees piercing the mist that stuck to the lifeless ground. He looked above the grey forest and, through the clouds, saw the sun capping the mountains, its orange rays rising over a dip in the peaks.

Baldur's hand closed around Thormir's right arm, and he flipped it over. His scar was burning and every detail of the swirling ridges was showing in detail; a crude mark, red raw upon his skin.

"You used your power." Baldur's eyes were wide and his heavy eyebrows were raised high. He was in awe of what Thormir had done. "You spoke in Nolwin just then, did you not? You spoke the elder language and your power listened. Truly, you have The Gift."

Thormir remembered the word, "*Arek*", he had instinctively yelled at the svay to knock it out, to break its will. He also thought of the time when he had first read that word while sitting at the edge of Hurst, and what had happened days before. The cold air caught in Thormir's throat, and he looked back at his company.

"We are to bury the infant's parents outside the city. Make your things ready to ride out. Clean if you need to, but we ride after we pay our respects." The group nodded in solemn agreement. Some of the gladiators grumbled, muttering weary curses, but none raised a question of defiance. It would be wrong to leave the parents of the child to lie here, to be found with shattered skeletons amongst broken streets and collapsed houses.

Rake, who had disappeared inside the house, emerged carrying the father of the babe upon his back. As Baldur had done, Rake had closed the man's eyes, so it seemed that he had joined his wife in the dream paths where only the dead walk. *But they are not at peace yet; soon they will join each other. The earth will claim them, then they will rest.*

An old guilt had returned. Thormir was reminded of how they had left Fern without burying him. They had just left him, lying there in the forest, covered in blankets. Fern, his best friend, his brother, would never be at peace.

THE SHADOW OF FIRE

*   *   *

They had not used shovels to dig the graves, but sharpened planks picked from the wreckage of a destroyed house. It had not taken them too long to dig the graves as the ground was soft and the grass damp with dew. Now the two bodies were side by side, lying together in the earth. Thormir had placed an arrow on each of their chests, as was the Medani custom. Aiden had given a small token that he had worn around his right wrist, as a symbol of good luck. There too lay some other small trinkets that the other men had given out of respect for the two parents who had tried to protect their baby against the darkness that had entered their home. Thormir noticed a rare flock of birds circling in a halo above them, and it was as if they too were mourning the loss of the babe's parents.

As the company stood there, gathered in the silence of dusk, they said no words of mourning, no hollow utterance of respect and death; rather they just added to the silence. After some time, sleep and weariness caved in upon them, but none made an objection, for they were not just mourning the loss of the two who lay before them, but the sacrifice the parents had made for the baby that nestled against the cloth and armour that covered the expanse of Rake's chest. He would never know his mother or father. Finally, the heavy silence lifted and, as it started to rain, they covered the bodies of the parents. Placing headstones at the end of the graves, they turned and walked away.

It continued to rain as they rode from the gates. Thormir looked back and saw a flash of light in the distance, followed by a deep rumble of heavy thunder. They headed towards the grey forest, urging the horses forward, racing across the plain. Not yet ruffled by the storm, the grass swayed lazily as they flew towards the trees. Thormir felt for and then released his conscious self to explore the energies that surrounded him. He felt the ants in the ground preparing for battle, organising the walls of defence around their homes to protect themselves against torrents of water. The insects seemed to feel the will of the heavens, but the same could not be said for the lone fox that stalked the treeline, hungry for food. Even the birds took refuge from the heavens' fury by hiding in the bare protection and shelter of the trees, a place where they rarely ventured. All took cover except for an eagle, a master of the skies that cared not for the storm, but winged its way south towards Hurst all the same.

"Baraklemen and the Hall of Kings awaits us. My father will take great heart in the tidings of your power," said Baldur, yelling over the cry of the wind.

"Will he let Selena and Maria go?" Thormir matched Baldur's voice as he tried to make himself heard.

"That I cannot tell you Thormir, for I myself do not know his mind on this."

"Well I will remind your king that it is our choices that define us. Shall he use me as a tool for his own devices, or will he keep his promises and prove his title?"

Baldur leaned into his horse, urging it forward. "Time judges all things."

Despite its bare, grey-barked, skeletal trees, the forest did offer a little protection from the howling wind. Thormir could feel his horse getting more nervous. He placed a calming hand on the horse's warm neck and thought of Shadow and the other two horses they had lost when they were captured. In that moment of desperation, he had urged her to run away and given her the chance for freedom and escape, to live in the wild, forever to roam across the great realm of Carathron. *I will see her again.* As he patted his horse, it became calmer, tossing its head as they slid through the bleak forest. The company hurried through trees, paying no heed to the storm and wind that whipped around them.

It was only when they could not go on, and the horses tired, that they stopped. The bear and wolf hide furs that they had worn about them ever since they had travelled from the hills of Orien did not seem to have kept the cold from chilling their blood. They did not have the luxury of fire that night. Even though they had made one, the bitter cold and the icy dark had snuffed out the warmth of the flames. It was only through pulling their furs close about them and gathering together that they did not freeze. Still, when they woke early that next day it seemed that their blood had slowed and chilled, so that any movement – let alone riding – was almost impossible.

The horses were in no shape for riding the next morning. When dawn broke the group was greeted by the sluggish movement of their own limbs, the difficultly of rekindling the damp wood, and the ridges and hills of frost that had settled in the crests and valleys of their ruffled furs. Thormir tried to warm his hands under his cloak, but all he felt was his own icy touch. The group grumbled about their sore backs and cursed at the bitter cold that slapped their faces with obnoxious audacity.

Hector, who was good with flint, had a fire going in minutes; quite a feat considering the damp ground and dew-covered sticks that lay around the base of each grey, skeletal tree. A small spiral of smoke trailed into the sky, which had turned a clear, icy blue after the thunder and lightning that had ravaged the heavens the previous night. Jord approached the fire, leading the line of horses closer to the warmth. "Horses need to be warm as well." Jord shot Thormir a grin that turned into a grimace. Thormir didn't know whether the cold or his wound caused this, but he suspected the latter.

It seemed that Baldur was the only one unaffected by the cold. Not far off, he was practising his forms using his two short axes to slay a rush of invisible foes. His shining armour flicked shards of light onto the edges of his axes so that he moved in silver flashes, becoming a shimmering dance of death. Thormir watched from where he was sitting by the fire as Baldur finished a form by hurling his blades at the trunk of a tree with a 'thunk'. Baldur clapped his hands together and laughed, a strong, deliberate, grinding sound.

Rake looked up and frowned at Baldur, his heavy eyebrows closing to a V. It seemed a contradiction that such a large, powerful, menacing man had taken to caring for the infant. When the boy had soiled himself during the night it was Rake who cleaned him. When the baby started to cry in the deep hours of the morning, it was Rake who had quieted him. So when a careless fool of a dwarf started playing with little axes and made little to no effort to quiet himself in the presence of the baby, Rake was more than a little displeased. Thormir chuckled as he observed Rake's annoyance from across the fire.

The flames crackled as their heat reached the inside of the wood. Thormir watched a damp, mossy stick break in two to reveal the dryness within. The moss, which had folded like a soft, green carpet, began to smoke as the flames licked it. The smoky trail increased from a soft, grey spiral to a thick, dark, twisting coil of swirling ash. Thormir thought it looked almost poetic – evidence of lost life blown away by the cold south-easterly winds. He shivered. The south-easterly winds were not perturbed by the bleak, bare, desolate forest. Instead, they blew a gentle, icy breath between the trees, through the heaths, and over the ashen hillocks. Leaving his hands to hover over the fire, he felt his mind beginning to wander, wading through the memories of the months past. *Stop it.* But each in turn seemed to keep flooding back, filling his eyes with images, his nose with scents, and finally his mouth with the taste of bile, as the meaning and context of each took hold. *Stop it. I have to keep running. I can't give up now.* He knew that if he stopped, stilled himself, and dwelled on the past, he would break apart. He was sure that he would explode with the pain that he had kept buried and caged away in some lost corner. He would not let that happen; he would keep running from it.

Thormir looked up to the top of an old pike tree and saw a great crow cawing at him. His natural inclination was to ignore it, but he knew that they were extremely smart, and in the past crows and ravens had been used to send messages over great distances.

Thormir thought back to his years growing up in Medani, his home, and remembered visiting pigeon cages. He remembered the old man who looked after the pigeons. And he remembered the pigeon keeper telling him the reason why Medani used pigeons instead of the wise ravens. "Ravens be big and bulky, whereas a pigeon is smaller, faster, and be fly'n over further distances." Thormir had thought he would never miss his home, having escaped the pressure and expectations of royalty, but now he longed for it – for familiarity, comfort. He smiled at the memory. *Home. Home. Keep running. Time to go.*

Baldur was busy instructing the group to move out. The gladiators looked to Thormir for confirmation. He nodded. Thormir assumed that the men did not entirely trust the dwarf, even though they were now brothers-in-arms. *And why should they? Even I do not entirely believe it. Just look at the situation I am in. I have just killed many members of a race that I didn't even know existed. I fight alongside professional killers, and I am friends with a dwarf, a member of a race thought to be extinct.*

The group prepared to move out with a dousing of the fire, saddling of the horses, checking of supplies, and a quick sharpening of metal edges.

The road ahead – though one could hardly call it a road, more of a patchy trail through the grey – did not look remotely inviting; rather it was more of a reluctant calling back to Norhill. Thormir noticed how the leafless, craggy branches that were like sharp daggers of splintered wood, joined together in a menacing arc, which looked down on them as they passed under the malicious eye of the grey forest.

Thormir saddled third in line as the group left camp. In front of him rode Aiden, with Baldur sitting behind him. Thormir watched the armoured back of the dwarf as he shifted this way and that. He seemed thoroughly uncomfortable riding such a large horse. In front of Aiden and Baldur rode Jord. He used only his heels to guide the horse, as his hands were not on the reins. Instead, Jord held his bow at the ready. He peered through the mist and trees, trying to spot anything unusual. No enemy shifted in shadow, no twig broke under careless hoof; all was quiet. However, Thormir could tell that Jord was uneasy, and thinking on it, he also felt that this silence was too foreboding for his liking.

Thormir flicked the reins and urged his horse into a trot. His scar tingled as he thought about all the men and women lost for the sport of the svay, the men and women who had fought and sacrificed their lives so that others may live. Then he thought of the mother and father who lay at peace outside the walls of Stockhud. He drew his furs around him in an attempt to protect himself from the memories.

He traced his scar, the unknown mark of his power – the power that had been pushed upon him. This question of his powers had been nagging at Thormir ever since he had seen the svay buckle. *Mary told me that it was controlled by language, but how do I manage to speak Nolwin?* Thormir knew that the language and words that were used to hold and release this so-called magic were written in the leather book, *but is saying a word enough to use the energy? And how can I learn to use it without having to fight?*

The only person other than Mary who seemed to know about what was happening to him was the hermit, but he could not ask him for help; one, because he lived in Hurst, now far out of reach; and two, because the man seemed a little mad anyway and might provide nothing more than a nonsensical answer that would be no help at all. He needed to know what it was, what *he* was. He had tried to ignore the sideways glances and the paused conversations, but still he could not pretend that they were not there. The gladiators had done a good job in trying to disguise their looks of curiosity, but Thormir could still tell that they talked of his condition. He was infected, dirty, violated by this power. More than that, Thormir knew that they all whispered ill of his sickness, and the seizures that often left him sweating and exhausted when he woke each morning. *I do not want this, any of it.*

CHAPTER TWENTY FIVE

TRAPPED
Reîus

Upon arriving back in Norhill, Thormir had seen the townspeople moving in a frenzy, hurrying back and forth like ants before a storm. However, amongst the fray lay the inn that they had stayed in. Its framework still stood, but the tavern's insides had been gutted by a terrible fire. The poles and decks of the inn were now scorched black and in ruin, void of their former warmth. Two or three bodies lay at what had once been the entrance. It was obvious that they must have denied entry to whoever committed this atrocity. The group shifted warily. A sense of blame lay around the town. The people were searching for an answer as to why their houses had been laid bare. Baldur turned and told them that they had to make for the Dwarven capital immediately, to address the king, and find out what had happened. All Thormir thought about was whether the girls had got out alive.

Now he stood in the Hall of Kings listening to the king recount the events – the storming of Norhill, and the burning of the village. "And you did nothing to stop this! You sat within your stone halls and made no effort to go to the aid of a burning village?" Thormir felt dread and despair pulsing through him as he took in the king's words. "Two of my friends have been captured and I don't know who by or where they are going!"

The king darkened his gaze and continued. "The red cloaks came two days ago, riding in from the east on armoured war horses. Reports say that there were about thirty of them, all heavily armed. They seemed to know where the girls were staying. After establishing a perimeter, they went for the inn first . . ."

"And?" Thormir was becoming increasingly irritated at the king's aloofness.

"Boy, I am King of Dwarvenhiem, my words will not be questioned. I would have thought you would have improved your manners seeing as you were just travelling with my son."

"I am not from here, so I will not abide by unfamiliar terms. But you, King of Dwarves, will tell me how you found this out – how you knew where and how my friends were taken."

The Dwarven king looked upon Thormir, eyes blazing at the challenge. "Fine, Flametouched, you will hear the truth of it. The soldiers in red cloaks took your friends. They rode in from the east, as I have said, so we believe they are indeed from Orien. Other soldiers were heard calling the commander 'Reddard'. We do not know what this means – maybe a name, or a position? The attack upon Norhill was swift and ugly. Three were killed. The assault on the town did not last long, and from this we assumed they were only here for the girls. That means they want you. They too have figured out your power and potential, and they want to play you. If I am correct, if you follow them, you will ride head on into the jaws of a trap. If you stay here, you will be safe, and the girls will remain alive; for as long as they have them alive, they know that you will come for them."

"I do not care – they entrusted me with their lives! I have let too many people down. Too many have already died to protect the power I hold."

"Yes, there is the power. Baldur has shown me the truth of it. You are indeed Flametouched, and yet you seem to push away this honour. You have a tendency to do these things, do you not, Thormir Darkin, son of King Darkin, Lord and protector of the True South and latest in the long line of kings who serve the red city of Medani? Are you not the son who always rejects the truth about who he is, pushes away a royal life, choosing instead to play like a babe in the muck of horses and the shit of pigs? You chose farm life over your responsibility to the crown, your inheritance. Yes, we know of your life in Medani, and what you forsake. And now you hold true power, you choose not to help others, you choose to throw it away. You are a child not worthy of such an honour. You walk into your battles without knowing yourself, and thus not knowing your power."

"I do not have to suffer such impudence." Said Thormir. "You have done nothing to help us. You will have to fight me before I let you prevent me from protecting those that I hold dear."

"Tell me why it is, boy, I should go to war for the sake of your love?"

"Need I remind you of what we found within Az Osten du Baraklemen, within the forest of Hurst? Dwarves and men slain, the remnants of a brutal battle between the two. But those men who took the lives of so many of your own wore the insignia of the enemy in the North. The emperor already knows of your existence and, believe you me, he will send more men to fight you. There is only so long you can hold these stone halls. More men join his cause every day, believing in his True Religion. You will soon face an army numbering over 50,000. Do you really think you can hold out against that force? He will come at you with all he has. The emperor's wrath at your defiance will match that of Tiranus, the thunder god himself. You need more men. If you can take Orien, I believe the people will rise against their own and take down the corruption of Lord Bath's regime. Then those men will need help fighting off the army that is approaching from the north. If you join with Orien's soldiers, you will have a force close to 20,000 – still small compared to the emperor's force, but an army to be reckoned with all the same."

The king frowned, and for a moment his eyes were buried in a scrub of eyebrows. "I have already called the other seven khans to our capital, Baraklemen, so we will discuss it then. You will need to present your arguments to them – only with a unanimous vote shall the rest of my kin go to war. As for what you will do now, Baldur will take you to visit someone who might be able to help you with your condition. Thormir, I have seen what you did in Stockhud. You have driven the svay from taking refuge there. You and your so-called gladiators will be stripped of your titles and be given ones more deserving in light of your achievement. Gladiators, approach."

The gladiators and Baldur, who were tentatively hanging back, moved forward so that they were standing in line with Thormir.

Thormir was still shaking with fury. Once again he had let his group down. He had let the girls be captured. *It is all my fault.* Feeling weak at the knees, he was sure that he would slam into the cold ground at any minute, but he shut his eyes and began the endless struggle of keeping his weakness at bay. By the time he opened his eyes he was gasping for breath, and sucking in great lungfuls of air. Clutching his side he looked up.

"Kneel."

The gladiators did as the king instructed. "Gladiators, you have fought well, alongside Thormir and my son, so I rename you Knights of Dwarvenhiem, and protectors of the light."

Jord stepped forward and bowed. The king raised an eyebrow. "King of Dwarves, I believe and I think the rest will agree that our title should be, the Thormirian Knights."

"Aye!" the gladiators shouted, "We are the Thormirian Knights! We are Thormir!"

Thormir had not realised that he meant so much to the gladiators – or rather as they were now, knights.

"Thormir," said Hector, "you have helped us in our escape, you have rescued us and given our lives meaning. We are in your debt."

Then it occurred to him that the sideways looks he had been getting were not ones of exclusion and disapproval, but of appreciation and awe. For the first time since Hurst he felt that he was . . . liked. It felt good. But still he felt the emptiness, and the urge to *run*.

"Thormir, you and your knights will need new armour. Your knights look like they have paid a visit to the pit and roped together pieces of scrap metal – this is no armour for six knights of Dwarvenhiem. You will go to the smiths and ask for armour of your liking and fit. Knights, go make merry, fill your gut, wet your beards, and rest from the chaos you have been through. My clerks will take up your packs." The king stood up, heaving himself out of his chair. He held his palms out upwards towards the stone roof. As he did so Thormir and the knights followed.

*   *   *

Two days had passed since the verbal exchange between Thormir and the king. Two days since he and the knights had been given the Dwarven title. Two days since they had re-entered the vast expanse of the mountain city. Buildings crafted of stone towered from the ground under Calx Mons, these were gateways to the treasures and halls of stone that stuck out from the ribs of the mountain. Great Dwarven homes were all built into the stone, and paved roads ran between the buildings, forming highways running under The Al'Durast. Despite the massive expanse of the city, much of it lay bare and uninhabited. According to the king, only about 2,000 dwarves lived within the great, stone city. For this reason, only about one quarter of the city was used, and the other three lay in neglect, not having been occupied for many centuries. Baraklemen was the greatest of all cities under The Al'Durast, but now it was a shadow of what it had been during its golden years. Despite being past its prime, the city rang with the hammers of the Dwarven smiths, the bustle of markets, and the shouts of trades gone wrong. In the centre of the city was the great Dwarven palace, which in Dwarven tongue was named "Az dur du Erikluin". Baldur, who was acting as Thormir's guard and their guide through the city, told them that the palace was the only building in the mountain city that had no corners, as the creators felt that an entrance to the palace should be seen from every angle. Baldur also told them that, up close, the pillars within the palace were each carved with a different story. According to Baldur, there was one column in the western wing of the palace into which was carved the story of a great forest fire that took place on the slopes of The Al'Durast in the third age of Vâryá. He said that sometimes, if the light struck the column right, the stone would burst into flames only to cool seconds later.

"Those flames will never be forgotten. Blue they shone that day, and at night the sky above burnt red, a reminder of the terror of fire."

The first night they had arrived in Baraklemen, Thormir and the Knights were taken to where they were to stay, high in the ribs of the mountain. That had been the first time Thormir had truly had a good night's sleep since they had left Orien. As Thormir suspected, they did not stay in cold, stone caves or empty caverns, but were housed in large, heated rooms. The dwarves had obviously gone to some effort to make their guests comfortable. In one corner of his room was a massive tapestry depicting a hunting scene of five dwarves and two dogs, and in front of them, a fleeing snow fox. The dwarves rode a different kind of horse than anything Thormir had ever seen before. These horses seemed to be very powerful, but with a much shorter build, as opposed to the taller warhorses bred in the East and the South, in "man country". In the other corners of the room stood a large, carved wooden cabinet, an oak writing desk, and a large mounted ox's head. Over the beautiful, wooden bed hung a strange piece of art made from what looked like bone. According to Hector, a dwarf mother had taken the infant that Rake had been looking after to a nursery, so Rake was now alone. When speaking with the others, Thormir realised he was the only one who had a bone symbol hanging over his bed head. *Is that the symbol for those who had been Flametouched?*

News had come the next day that several of the dwarf khans had arrived in Baraklemen. Each khan and his clan host, the dwarves that travelled alongside their khan, were being housed on the western side of the mountain. According to the breathless messenger that had relayed the news, each khan had brought a small host of armed soldiers and advisors. When pressed, the messenger conceded that he thought that the khans of each clan must be expecting trouble, as there had not been a gathering like this for over 1,000 years.

"You, Thormir, are either the careless miner who breaks the scaffold, or the smith who fixes a blanket of broken mail; only coming events will tell. For all our sakes, I hope the hammer doesn't miss the anvil, or else you wield a sword unfinished, and your words fall as pebbles against a cliff."

Baldur had then told him that whenever a large group of dwarves got together, there was always the likelihood of trouble and disagreement within the ranks and clans. Thormir still did not know how the dwarves had sent the messages up and down The Al'Durast so quickly, nor how each clan had arrived within the space of more or less a week when the journey should have taken months, especially for the farthest clans. Despite his wondering,

317

he noticed that upon the arrival of all the clans, except that of Az Osten du Baraklemen, the mountain city seemed to vibrate with the energy of the dwarves. A constant arrangement of music could be heard throughout the city, including pieces played by the great orchestra of Dwarvenhiem, and majestic chords sung by the royal choir. No place in the city was untouched by its melody, a music that had not been heard in the great capital for years uncounted. Thormir thought that he could listen to it without ever getting tired of its sound. It helped to escape the pains of his life. Noticing Thormir's wonder at the haunting sound, Baldur had told him that the orchestra was not playing any composition written on sheet, but playing "the sound of stone" – the song of the mountain. "If you listen," Baldur had said, "when you are alone and apart from any other sound, if you listen, you can hear it – the sound of stone, for it does not come just from the mountains and stone in The Al'Durast, but from within you."

Thormir did try, while alone in his room that night, to listen to the world around him, taking in the notes of power that apparently resided beneath the earth. He heard nothing. The only sound of stone he could hear was the persistent buzzing of a fly. *How did a fly even get in here?*

* * *

When Thormir rose again the following morning, Baldur showed him around Baraklemen. When Thormir asked where the knights were, Baldur said that they had been sent away to *take care* of a few stray, wild men who had ventured from the highland villages and had begun raiding a stockpile of weapons and armour that the dwarves kept at the ready, in case of invasion. In Thormir's absence, Hector had been put in charge; a change he would have expected, but that displeased Thormir all the same. He did not like being kept out of the loop. At that moment, Baldur seemed very smug as he lit up his pipe with a reddish plant. Thormir had seen Baldur breaking the plant from its original chunk into smaller pieces earlier, so this made sense, but the deep blue smoke that rose from Baldur's mouth did not.

When he explained the smoke's colour and the glow of the ash, it turned out that the reddish plant, when smoked by different people, gave off a different colour for each person. Thormir was fascinated by this odd phenomenon and, even though he had no desire to try it himself, he wondered what his colour would be.

For the rest of that day Baldur educated Thormir on the history of the dwarves and the realm of Dwarvenhiem. He claimed they were the first of the races to have offered an alliance, and the first race to form a peace treaty. When Thormir pointed out that it takes two sides to form an alliance, Baldur scowled with the same expression that his father had worn upon Thormir's second meeting with him. Asking a few questions to resume the conversation, Thormir established from Baldur that despite the exhaustive expanse of The Al'Durast and Dwarvenhiem, the entire populous of each clan was supported from the food grown within the mountains. When asked about the sunlight that would have to feed the plants, Baldur began a lengthy explanation as to the design and operation of sun mirrors. The size of the sun mirrors varied from the size of a thumbnail to the size of two horses. According to Baldur, the slant of each mirror could be adjusted and attuned to the slightest angle, as the mirrors had to follow the sun over the course of the day and the moon throughout the night.

"And what if it's cloudy?"

There was a pause, and then Baldur said simply, "Torches."

The use of torches as an alternative was so obvious that Thormir felt a fool asking, but Baldur continued to explain how the metal was crafted and shined, how the braces were made, and how the sun's rays lined up and followed the mirrors. In his explanation, Thormir learned of the sunroom, which was built high up, near the top of Calx Mons. Baldur said that this room was so hot during the day that it had to be cooled by the icy mountain winds that were funnelled through a series of small, stone tunnels. The sunroom was made entirely of mirrors that were set to different angles so that the room was not a rectangle but an oval, designed to mimic a giant crystal. Only the best engineers could alter the mirror dynamics in the room, and they had to wear special suits that were cooled and padded. But it was only entered once every ten years for adjustment, such was the strength of its design, and it had only been refurbished only once in its 700 years of existence.

The sunroom and the histories of Dwarven politics and lore were not the only subjects broached during that day. Baldur happily explained the design of the houses, and how the dwarves could craft stone with such skill that no blade could slide between the blocks. He also answered one of the questions that Thormir had been dying to ask: what was that stone statue that stood near the entrance to Az Osten du Baraklemen?

Although Baldur nodded, smiled, and gave a lengthy answer based on what he knew, Thormir came away from the conversation more perplexed. He did understand that it was very old and had been made by the Flametouched, who had sculpted the stone. They had, Baldur explained, pushed some sort of sleepy consciousness into the stone.

That night, in his room, high in the gigantic ribs of the mountain, Thormir wondered if some day he would have the power to make a stone breathe with life. He doubted it. He had been struggling to summon any sort of power since he had returned to Baraklemen from Stockhud. No sensation rushed through his body, nor did he feel more than a slight tingling in his arm. His power seemed to have left him; even his ability to expand his consciousness had been weakened. He felt broken. And before long, he would be on his way to meet the Dwarven mentor he'd been promised – a person that could help him understand who he was, what he was.

*   *   *

Thormir was wandering the corridors with his head in the clouds when a sharp, agonising pain shot through his right foot. Thormir yelped and grabbed at whatever it was, hopping on the spot. "Damn it!" he said, realising it was a dry, split edge of a pebble of some kind, "I thought dwarves were supposed to be good at carving stone!"

"We are," said Baldur, "but we are also better at seeing in the dark, unlike you clumsy humans. It always puzzles me that you do not have anything special about you. For example, you and the men of your city that were born in the South – why haven't you developed a fur coat to keep out the cold? Instead, you wear the furs of other animals as if they were your own. We dwarves need to see well in the dark, so we have eyes that can do so. Nightfall does come in the South doesn't it?"

Thormir grunted. Baldur chuckled. They moved on.

The walls of the passage were oddly damp. Thormir walked with one hand on the smooth wall. He let his fingers slide over the damp surface, causing small droplets to fall to the floor. He couldn't understand why the wall was wet, but nevertheless it did feel nice; the cool surface was a refreshing sensation after the dryness of the tunnel. He knew that they were somewhere deep inside the mountain and, judging from the slight slope, below the ground floor of the capital. It was a pity, he thought, that the dwarves couldn't have put any sun mirrors down here, or even a few more torches.

"Is there any reason that this place seems so . . . empty?"

Baldur stopped and turned to Thormir. Despite being a dwarf, he had a surprisingly large presence and sense of power. "This, Thormir, is not a place for dwelling, this is not a place for comfort. Dwarves do not often come this way; it is against the king's orders to venture into this passage."

"Why?"

"It is not my place to tell you. All I will say is that this . . . is a prison."

The passage suddenly seemed darker. The few torches that lit the way appeared to flicker at the change of mood. The already-dark tunnel seemed to change, and host many more shadows that should not have been there. It occurred to Thormir that the small droplets that he had been sliding from the wall with the tips of his fingers might not have been water.

"This place has not played host to more than one prisoner for a very long time, but with your capture of the svay warrior, this prison welcomes the new company."

"You're welcome," he said grudgingly. He did not like this place at all. A pair of eyes stared from out of the dark grey tint of cage bars.

"Help me." The voice was harsh but somehow Thormir could tell that there was kindness held within.

"Come on!" said Baldur, his voice harsh and slightly nervous.

Thormir turned away and, under the firm grip of Baldur, was marched off down the corridor.

Baldur said, "We are nearly there."

He was right, and before long the passage ended at a heavy, arched, wooden door. A warm light, which seemed at odds with the sinister mood of the hall, brushed under the door and spilled onto the ground in a puddle. Treading in the light so that his steel-caps shone, Baldur reached up and opened the door, twisting the head of a carved bear, which formed the handle.

They entered. At first impression, the room they entered was spacious, not like a cell at all; more the kind of room a philosopher or academic might have. Books lined the walls, adorning the room with spines that spoke of old knowledge. There were breaks in the wall, filled with small, carved animals: mice with five legs, birds with two heads, and what appeared to be a creature with the head and wings of an eagle and the body of a wolf. Thormir also saw a fox stalking between the volumes, and a carved squirrel bent double as if looking for nuts in the forest of books. On one of the highest ledges, between two thickly-bound books, he saw an image of the same breed of horse that was also pictured in the tapestry in his room, high in the ribs of Calx Mons. The animal was beautiful, it's mane flowing straight behind it as it galloped over the reaching fields.

Baldur nudged him and signalled for Thormir to look to the corner of the room. Thormir squinted into the smoke that swirled in the corner. The smoke was not unlike the smoke Baldur had enjoyed not a day past. However, unlike Baldur's, this smoke was a pure golden colour. The harder Thormir stared at the smoke, the more detail he saw: the way it sparkled, and the way it spiralled in perfect helixes towards the top of the room, where it mushroomed and made for a small hole in the high, stone roof. For some reason, the smoke filled him with the same feeling that he had felt when he had arrived at the watchtower near the fields of Guldor. Sadness and loss pulsed through him. It was as if it were testing him, waiting to see if he would break down or remain strong.

Out of the smoke walked a man. He was not a dwarf as Thormir had been expecting. He seemed neither young nor particularly old, but somehow ageless. Although his body was that of a man of fiftyor more, his eyes seemed far older – grey-blue, and ancient. Even though they were fcct away, Thormir could tell that they were boring into him, and examining every detail of his character.

As they lingered over Thormir's scar, Thormir thought he saw a twitch of a smile cross the man's clean-shaven face.

"Leave us. We have little time and much to explain."

Thormir remembered the harsh commanding words of Reddard, the oiled words of Bath, and the majestic oaken words of the dwarf king. This man spoke in a quiet voice, but every word was heard. It was ancient beyond measure and Thormir could tell that he knew things that even the wisest scholar in Medani, or the keepers of knowledge in the library under Orien, could not hope to know.

At his bidding, Baldur turned and left the room, closing the door behind him. Suddenly the room seemed very quiet and empty. The man continued to look at Thormir, forcing him to turn away. It was uncomfortable to have a complete stranger study him.

"I like your carvings," Thormir said. The man said nothing. He just blinked and walked over to a large wooden desk cluttered with many drawers, which Thormir imagined all had secret parts and hidden vaults to store oddities and treasures.

Ignoring Thormir's praise, he said, "You are Flametouched, are you not?"

"Yes, you knew from my scar, didn't you?"

"Yes." The man approached and held out his arms, his palms facing upwards. "Give me your arm."

Usually Thormir would have hesitated, but somehow he felt a sense of trust, even though he had only met him minutes earlier. As Thormir held out his right arm, he noticed that the curve of his arm had increased and the muscles had become more defined. Curling over his arm was the snaking burn, clearly visible, a scar that would never heal.

Thormir looked up not into scrutinising eyes, but kind ones, filled with pity and concern. Thormir placed his arm into the man's palms and waited. As the man closed his eyes and strained his face a little, only to the point that Thormir could see the clenched muscles around his jaw, Thormir felt an itching sensation in his arm. The itch became so powerful that Thormir would have taken a sword to his arm to stop it. But he could not move, he could only look down at the burning scar. Then, to his amazement, the scar began to fade until it was gone completely. However, strangely, Thormir could still feel it upon his arm.

The man opened his eyes and smiled. "There. Now your scar will only appear when you use your power . . ."

Thormir looked at him and was about to ask how he managed to do such a thing, when he was cut off.

". . . as does mine." Pulling aside the white hem of his robes to reveal his bare chest, he showed Thormir a scar directly over his heart that was shaped like a long willow leaf. Thormir only saw it for a moment, as it had already begun to fade.

"Are you Flametouched? Why are you imprisoned? Why aren't you fighting the emperor? Can you teach me to do that? Why has my power waned ever since I left Hurst?"

The man smiled. He turned and went over to a table in the corner of the room. With practised skill, he took a sharp knife and began to shape the body of what Thormir saw was turning out to be a small sparrow. Each flick of his knife cut away a small piece of wood, detailing a feather on the neck of the bird.

"I can tell from the manner of your questions that your mind is certainly ordered. This is good; it will help with your studies, I think." He tilted the neck of the sparrow and flicked some wood from the crook of the bird's wing. "I will answer your questions as you have put them. Yes, I am indeed the last of the Flametouched. That is what dwarves call me, or at least that is the literal translation from their tongue. I was amongst the last of the Flametouched to have been given the white fire – that is to be touched by the wing of the phoenix. It appears to all who wield The Gift. I remember when I first felt the energy pulse through my veins. I could feel every fibre of my being. Then, the phoenix touched me over my heart. From that moment on, I went from Solomon the Urchin to Solomon the Flametouched. That is my name. Like the others, I studied here, deep in The Al'Durast; all of us trained to be keepers of knowledge, protectors of the five realms, and keepers of the peace. That was our history. For a while The Flametouched did their job, but as with anything of power, time brought the stirrings of evil. A man was trained in the art of white fire, but he turned against us, and began using his gift against the world. He began to share his power. It had never been done, as it is an abomination, but he found followers who drank his blood, and uttered words of power that he had given them. Vandr was obsessed with changing the laws of nature so that magic could be harnessed and taken from other people. He became so strong that during the Great War it was decided that the only way to stop his madness was to rid the world of magic itself. So the dwarves, the men of the South and East, and the Elves of Elgaroth and the High Forest, joined their power as one and suppressed the power of magic. This was a sad day, for what the elves did not realise was that, because their life force is so deeply intertwined with magic, they would slowly die. It took just ten days for the last of the elves to leave this world. Some say they have not gone but live on in different forms; the spirits in trees, the souls of lost animals. With the Red Gate of Ironholt broken, and with Vandr finally killed, the world tried to rebuild itself, but the influence of magic had been underestimated. Nights endured into the day, and the winters lasted longer. Slowly shadow spread, draining Vâryá of all light. Crops struggled to grow, and the trade that had once flourished between all cities diminished. The world suffered. But I was not there to help. I had not been there in the Great War; I was a coward, and I had run, hoping the world would not catch me. But it did. One of the last acts of the dragons before sealing themselves in stone was to take away much of my power, leaving only enough for me to heal wounds and perform other small tasks. This was not all they did; they cursed me with eternal life, so that I would always remember my mistake and my cowardice. When the dwarves heard what I had done, they took me and imprisoned me here. I remained here, bound and shackled to the wall, before the new king, the one that rules today, decided to free me and let me have a dungeon to my liking. But always I am kept down here . . . reminded of what I have done."

Thormir struggled to comprehend the enormity of what he had heard. He was talking to a Flametouched but also a prisoner, a man who had run away from the Great War. But perhaps he would finally get some answers. *I thought I was the only one, but now, maybe . . .*

Solomon was adding the final touches to the tail feathers of the sparrow as he continued. "You ask why even now I do not fight the emperor. From what I can gather, this emperor is uniting many men under his banner through the cause of believing in this True Religion." Solomon smiled sadly. "Men are so easily swayed, but why shouldn't they be? For an age the world as they know it has been struggling, so blaming the gods must be easy for them. Maybe they believe that changing who they pray to at night or in the heat of battle will give the world some more hope, so that the fate of everyone in it will not fall into shadow, but instead will rise up and build a stronger empire for men to rule. But the emperor has another agenda. He wishes to raise the power of magic and control it for his personal use, so that he can crush anyone who opposes his rule. Hmm, yes – no, wait – yes, he wants to reunite the three books!"

"The three books?"

"Yes. Before the Flametouched died, the elves wrote down the phrase that could bring back the power of magic into this world, but they split the phrase up into three parts. Each section is written in the last page of a book. Here," Solomon walked over to the table Thormir had noticed and picked up a thick, heavily-bound book. "This is yours, no?"

"It was given to me by a friend."

"Yes, I suspected it was."

Flicking to the back pages, Solomon found what he was looking for and as he held the book up, Thormir saw a phrase, 'Nol Lysá', scrawled across the bottom of the page. He shivered as he read the words. Even though he did not understand them, he felt their power run through him.

"This is what the emperor truly wants."

"How do you know all of this if you are trapped down here?"

"A man is never trapped if he has his mind, and it is the mind which allows the freedom to explore."

"You know, you remind me of a friend I made in Hurst Forest."

"Really? Do tell."

"We met a hermit while we were travelling. He gave us shelter in a storm, as well as directions to Norhill. Like you, he was very . . . knowledgeable." Thormir thought it best not to say "odd" – that might seem rude, so he inflected his words so that his meaning was clear but not overt.

"I see. Can you describe him?" For some reason, Solomon's eyes were sparkling, each coloured fleck dancing.

But then a booming knock came from the door, followed by Baldur's voice. "I need Thormir to come with me, Ancient One, the clan meet is about to begin and the king has requested the presence of Thormir and his knights.

"Wait, dwarf! Let me finish before you start your grumblings!" Solomon turned to Thormir and said, "We will pick up this discussion tomorrow – a dwarf will not be kept waiting."

*   *   *

"So what did you think?" Baldur asked, looking up at Thormir.

"Why didn't you tell me he was Flametouched?"

"It was not my place. A prisoner has the right to tell his own story, even if he is behind bars."

"Oh, well, how very wise of –" but a mental spike drove into Thormir's consciousness. Suddenly his senses were gone and were replaced by someone else's. He saw darkness. She was cold, so cold. He felt the open cut above her eyebrow.

"Help me!" The voice cut into his mind, driving through his skull like 1,000 razors.

Thormir stumbled over, clutching his head in pain. He could feel sweat running down his back, carving torrents of worry and anxiety. But still he felt the consciousness press against his, even though it was fading.

"Help me . . ." Her voice repeated, but this time with more urgency.

CHAPTER TWENTY SIX

THE NINE KHANS
Pa néner ya enrans

Thormir had still not quite recovered from the pain of the mental probe by the time they reached the king's court, nor had he stopped wondering who had attacked him and asked for his help. He had an idea of who had done it but he wasn't going to form any sort of conclusions without further investigation. It had been such a foreign mind, each thought had been constructed so differently. However, Thormir guessed that it was the svay captive who had attacked him. He wished he had never let Baldur convince him to take the creature back with them. *What good has it done us anyway? Even now Maria and Selena could be sitting in a dark cell or worse, and we just do nothing!*

Baldur led Thormir into the king's court. The room was smaller than Thormir had expected. Seeing the size of the Hall of Kings, and noting the grandeur of Baraklemen, Thormir had expected the king's court to be somewhat larger. However, his impression of the room was not at all diminished by its size, as the room was a masterpiece of design. Under hurried whispers, Baldur proudly pointed out the features of the room, and proudly told Thormir where he had contributed to the design.

Baldur was particularly keen to explain the two main features. Firstly, the sun mirrors that were hidden in the stone in such a way that the rectangular marble table in the middle of the room was lit at all times. Secondly, there were a series of hidden gaps in the stone through which archers could shoot. Baldur told Thormir it had been designed this way during the Great War.

All nine clans were to gather to discuss and debate topics of higher importance than an increase in taxes, which were usually communicated through the sun mirrors or messengers that travelled the length of The Al'Durast. The khans could be hostile to one another, and it was more than likely that the meet would be awkward and very tense. In any case, the king had stationed Valmar archers around the room, monitoring the situation from between the subtle gaps.

The knights were already seated at the massive table, their imposing figures out of place within this elegant setting. Thormir sat down next to them with Baldur. As he did, the doors to the room ground open, and in came the treasurer and another dwarf; the latter wore a red cloak and was heavily armed. Both made their way to the head of the table, where they sat either side of a great throne that was obviously meant for the king. Next to enter the room were two dwarves, slimmer and shorter than those Thormir had seen so far. These dwarves made for the opposite two corners of the room. Thormir noticed them stiffen as the next dwarf entered the room. The dwarf who entered was dressed in heavy robes of black lined with gold. He wore a square-shaped hat that looked too proper to fit in with his bushy beard.

While this was going on, Baldur was giving him a flowing, whispered commentary as to the names of each dwarf and their position. Apparently this dwarf was the royal clerk and keeper of records. His name was too complicated so Thormir did not care to remember it. The clerk made his way to the throne, and placed a giant book on the table directly in front of it. Taking another smaller book from his pocket, he looked up and began. "So we commence the 642nd clan meet." His voice was squeaky and took Thormir aback, as he had been expecting more of a baritone. "All khans of Dwarvenhiem have gathered here today, and by sacred rights will be allowed to enter this room."

As the speaker continued, Thormir noticed that the two dwarves in the corners had taken out rolls of paper and had begun writing.

The clerk continued. "The council acknowledges the presence of the two High Proästs of Dwarvenhiem."

Two more dwarves walked in. They were dressed in pure white robes and had no beards. According to Baldur, each dwarf clan had a different way of dressing their beards. This way every dwarf could tell and show where they were from and which clan they belonged to.

Baldur had told him that the clan of Morildurak had no beards.

"Priests?" asked Thormir.

"Exactly." Baldur looked wary of the two dwarfs. They walked past the table imperially, with a fixed smirk upon their faces. "Morildurak is the most religious clan in Dwarvenhiem. Their clan laws mainly revolve around their moral and religious beliefs," said Baldur. "The High Proästs will often deal with the matters too trivial for the king to deal with, so they are always travelling up and down the length of The Al'Durast."

The high priests took their seats next to the dwarf in the red cloak, who Baldur explained was the Master of the Axe, and second to the king. He was a member of the Valmar clan, and was the king's right hand and advisor.

"The council acknowledges the presence of Khan Toshin of Arlib."

As the clerk finished, a shorter dwarf waddled into the room, and sat himself down in the furthest seat. He scowled as he began to stroke his short, black, square beard.

"The council acknowledges the presence of Khan Roland of Keleadgurdil."

Again, precisely as the clerk finished, another dwarf walked in. This man, or dwarf, had a devious way about him, which made Thormir uncomfortable. This feeling was not helped by Baldur telling him the Keleadgurdil trained their soldiers as assassins, who were used by the king when someone needed . . . removing.

The clerk straightened his slouching back, flicked the page of his book, and then continued, "The council acknowledges the presence of Khan Galian of Helmhetter."

Thormir took his eyes off Khan Roland, who had begun to curl his grey beard around a forefinger, and looked to the doorway. Through it walked the biggest and most powerful-looking dwarf Thormir had seen so far. He wore golden armour, and an insignia of a hammer and sword crossed above a single star was embossed upon his chest plate. He had his long, black beard bunched together in two gold braces. Thormir watched the other dwarves stiffen. This khan obviously wielded power and influence in clan politics. Thormir's suspicions were confirmed when Baldur said that Helmhetter, the clan obsessed with war and fighting, were also the Valmar clan's biggest ally.

"The council acknowledges the presence of Khan Stonebridge of Inzek."

"Skilled miners. See how he wears his beard as a throwover. It is a sign of respect to his clan. They all throw their beards, because they don't like their beards to touch the ground when they are mining." Baldur's eyes were glinting; he obviously liked the ceremony.

"The council acknowledges the presence of Khan Illan of Bin'zu'kum."

"Not much is known about this clan," said Baldur. "They have retreated from contact since the Great War. It is said that their losses in the war were many."

Khan Illan walked into the room and sat down in his designated chair, not looking at anyone else.

The clerk straightened his back again and continued. "The council acknowledges the presence of the High Proästs as representatives of clan Morildurak." The clerk turned and nodded to the high priests, who returned the sign of respect with smiles that did not reach their eyes. The clerk shuffled, obviously uncomfortable in their presence. "The council acknowledges the presence of Khan Jyrell of Thrinmark."

Baldur whispered that the Thrinmark were often called the bookkeepers, and that they lived at the very end of The Al'Durast, the closest clan to Medani. At the clerks words Khan Jyrell, their leader, walked in. Thormir could tell that she was very pretty, by dwarf standards, and he grinned as he saw the expression on Baldur's face, which earned him an under the table punch from the dwarf.

The seven khans were now seated, all of them idle, stroking their beards, or fidgeting with papers they had brought with them.

"Khans of Dwarvenhiem, you will now take the oath. Please stand."

All of the khans and members of the council rose to their feet and began to speak the oath of Dwarven court. "I swear by helm, hand, and hammer, that I will serve Dwarvenhiem and never let the stones of our great nation crumble."

The sound of the shared oath died down, and as it did so the clerk began again. "Remain standing. The council acknowledges the presence of Khan Viggon of clan Valmar, reigning King of Dwarvenhiem, lord and protector of the realm."

The king, followed by several other important-looking dwarves, entered the hall. Viggon had discarded his motley furs and now wore velvet robes that covered shining armour. He gave off more of an authoritarian feel; his image emanated his power and influence. All of the khans, apart from Galian of Helmhetter, shifted uncomfortably, obviously recognising the king in their presence.

He strode over to his throne, accompanied by his followers, and placing one hand on the stone chair, he lowered himself so that he sat at the head of the table, looking down at his subjects. He did not speak for some time, during which all those in the room remained standing. Thormir watched as the king looked over the massive book in front of him, turning its pages and taking note of certain lines in the text, signalled by a slight contraction of his eyebrows or dip of his head. Thormir wondered what he was doing. Just when he was about to bend to ask Baldur, the king raised his hand and waved for them to sit. Even the clerk had kept quiet in all this time, which was almost an impossible feat for him as it seemed that he was a dwarf who liked to talk.

"There is but one subject that we should be concerned about – it be the reason I went and called this clan meet. It has recently come to light that the enemy in the north, the empire, has become restless. Our spies tell us that the emperor has significant influence over the men. Instead of his subjects hating the control he has over their lives, they welcome him and his ideals into their homes." The king paused and pressed the tips of his index and little fingers together, forming a four-spire cathedral. "The emperor has a sly tongue, and has convinced his subjects that there is a higher calling. He wishes them to ditch the ways of the past, to forsake their gods and worship the one who will save them. He calls this The True Religion – what manner of truth we cannot say, but one thing is clear: he is using this belief, this foul religion, to sway the minds of men, to convince them to invade other cities and kingdoms. Many cities have already fallen to their knees and bow to his will. Only Silverhaven resisted the invasion, but when they were overrun and their city walls shattered, they learned of The True Religion and found solace in it. The whole city embraced the word and now they fight for the emperor."

While the king was speaking, Thormir noticed the treasurer look away from the council, as if bored, and nod to one of the guards standing beside the king.

"What's more, they now make for Orien and the passage to Medani. Once they take Medani, the emperor will have full control over all the lands east of The Al'Durast; and his quest for power is unlikely to stop there. It is my belief that he will keep going until every race and everything that is good and innocent in this world is gone or under his rule . . ."

The clerk began to speak, "The council will please acknowledge ─"

"Why should we go to war with another people?" said Khan Toshin. "Arlib clan can barely manage to hold off the svay in the North. We have the most to lose if we abandon the safety of the mountains to go fight a war that will barely affect us." He pushed himself up on the cushion he had procured and looked expectantly at the king.

The clerk looked put out that he had not finished his announcement and, not knowing what to do, he looked to the king. Thormir followed his gaze.

The king, head bowed, fingers still in spires, said in a quiet voice that nevertheless carried around the room. "Have you not noticed who is missing from this room? It is a sad day indeed when we are blind to the absence of one so important."

Whipping out the locket that Thormir had given him when they had arrived, the king slammed it on the table and slid it into the centre. The sun mirrors caught the gold lining so that the woven, metal thread borders of the locket glinted and sparkled white. "Khan Jaslin is dead, along with all of her clan. Erekamen is no more. One of our most significant and powerful clans has just been wiped from the face of this land. And do you know how this happened? No, I suppose you don't. A force of men overran Az Osten du Baraklemen. These men held the banner of the emperor. From this we can only assume that he knows we still exist and dwell in the halls under The Al'Durast. My sources tell me that upon entering the city, Az Osten du Baraklemen, the place was filled with a stony silence. Death lingers there. Not one was left alive – our women and our children all slain – some even as they slept in that place."

The court was silent. No one moved. The gravity of the matter suddenly occurred to Thormir; that this might influence the decision to go war, to fight against the emperor; not just in defiance but for vengeance.

The sly, blue-bearded dwarf Thormir had seen enter, leant on one elbow and looked at the king. "If we do fight, where will we go?"

"Yes, I should like to know that myself," said Inzek Khan Stonebridge, "as well as how we intend to defend our realm while we are away. Together, we number around 20,000 now, if I am not wrong." He looked at Khan Jyrell and when she nodded in confirmation Stonebridge continued, "However our army numbers only or nine or 10,000."

"Indeed, our numbers are low, our power is waning, but we still have fight. My council," the king's voice was picking up now as he glared at his subjects, as if urging them to understand his will just by looking at the burning rage kindling in his eyes. "This is the time to act; before the enemy has a chance to make the next move we must go to the people of Orien. We must go to the aid of those who have long needed us, for without our help, Orien, the whole city, will be taken over or destroyed. Should we go to Orien, we will march along the line of Hurst until we reach its end. We shall look upon Orien, and we shall see either a city crumbling in ruin or a city looking for hope – we shall be that hope. We have hidden under the mountains for our own protection for a long time, to make sure our knowledge and our race were guarded from harsh realities, but if we continue like this . . ."

"Erekamen is gone. This means that our wealth in trade has gone. Unless we do something, we are forsaken, no?" Illan had a quiet and heavily-accented voice. The council looked at him. Thormir remembered what Baldur had said about the Bin'zu'kum clan. *Not much is known. Their losses were great.* "We should go to war. Our realm will fall if we have no money to feed the people, no?"

Thormir turned towards the head of the table as the high priests responded to the question by looking at the king and saying in a synchronised voice, "Illan speaks true. There are rumours . . . that the treasury is running dry."

"Aye. Well that would explain the higher taxes," said Stonebridge.

"The bookkeepers of Thrinmark will go to war. Whether we will do so to fight for trade or to uphold old alliances – we will go to war." Jyrell said and smiled at the council, who for a moment seemed captured by her beauty. Even the knights seemed ruffled by her charm.

Her spell was broken as Toshin roared, "Ha, the bookkeepers! You are just a bunch of page-turners and ink-spillers, but I suppose you will need protecting in the heat of this battle; so clan Arlib will do this. We shall go to war, but on one condition. We are the northern-most clan in The Al'Durast and our lands are vulnerable to attack by the svay. We wish for each clan to select a few warriors to help protect our lands while we are gone."

"Aye, I'll agree to that," said Roland. He was twisting the end of his thick, blue beard into a curl and then straightening the twist repeatedly. "Aye, I'll agree to that. And I guess we shall join you on the field of battle as well."

It took a few more deliberations, half-hearted insults, two meals, and the thorough smoking of many pipes, but finally clans Inzek, Bin'zu'kum, and Morildurak joined the vote to go to war. The only clan left to join was Helmhetter and, because they were strong allies of the Valmar, Thormir assumed that Khan Galian would join, or if not, be won over by the others' persuasion. However, Thormir recognised that the powerful dwarf was the only thing preventing Dwarvenhiem from going to war. The council was silent as Galian took a hearty sip of his pipe stem and leaned back. He seemed totally oblivious to the gravity of the situation, but aware that he was the one that the decision rested upon. He blew red smoke from his pursed lips. The smoke spiralled to the roof, catching a crimson colour in the light from the sun mirrors.

"We will not go to war."

Those six words, spoken as if they were nothing, struck a heavy blow. Thormir's mind reeled. *Why? Just why?*

"We all understand that Helmhetter Kilcalia falls two weeks from now . . ."

"Kilcalia is a religious festival held by the Helmhetter celebrating the glories and sadness of war. The Kilcalia has never been cancelled apart from the years spanning the Great War," Baldur explained to Thormir in a whisper, which dampened Thormir's hope even more. *But surely there was some way to overcome this festival?* Despite feeling like a crackling fire suddenly doused in cold water, he still believed there was a chance of convincing the khan that they had an advantage.

Ignoring Baldur's desperate tug on his shirt to make sit him back down, Thormir stood. The king looked at Thormir and rather than seeing anger there, Thormir saw surprise. Responding to the king's nod, the clerk stepped forward, straightened his back, and announced, "The council recognises Thormir, son of

King Darkin, lord and protector of the South, and leader of the Thormirian Knights."

Thormir had never been given a title apart from the many profanities Fern had put his way in return of some of Thormir's. So when the clerk finished announcing him it took him a few seconds to realise that he now had the room's absolute and undivided attention. "I address this council both as a noble of Medani, and as one who has endured much since departing the borders of Carathron. But, I am not here to complain, I am here to ask Galian Khan of Helmhetter some questions: Have you ever lost someone with no way of bringing them back?"

The light caught on the braces of Galian's beard as he considered Thormir's question. Galian's eyes bored into Thormir as he answered. "No."

"Well, I lost my best friend and brother and, instead of following the killers, I continued to flee, which I now realise was the right thing to do, as now I can help others in escaping the corruption of Orien, and with your help, fight off the coming storm. The enemy will first demand retreat, and when Lord Bath says no, they will show no mercy. Remember that these men stand united in belief, and there is nothing more dangerous than that. I have seen what they can do. I have seen the bodies of your shieldmates, scattered and broken deep within Az Osten du Baraklemen. Even now they lie there, mouths gapping wide, in silent screams of death. No matter what you say, soon this storm will hit you head-on – better you deal with the threat now than run away and wait until the storm of the emperor's fury and the cunning of The Crow and his army crash down upon you. The emperor possesses one of the three books that have the power to bring magic back into this world. This would surely mean that he himself has The Gift. If he takes Orien, he will have free passage to the South. After Medani and the cities of the Carathron are destroyed and their people are enslaved, he will own the east. He will wield the greatest army that has ever existed since the fourth age. You will be no match for him. He has to be stopped. Would you offer no hope to those who need it the most? Would you leave them to darkness and ruin?"

He saw the knights and Baldur turn to him, obviously picking up on Thormir's not-so-subtle jibe in an attempt to rally the khan. But Galian was unmoved as he said, "I will not go to sack some village in the hope that it will drive away the enemy. Nor will I join with Orien's people to fight those scum who fight for beliefs based on lies."

Galian was standing now, and Thormir smashed an iron fist into the stone table. Galian still did not flinch. "And who, dare I say, are you to offer such wisdom and insight into the matters of war and the politics of Dwarvenhiem? You are a human; why don't you take your human followers and jump in a pit of mud so that you can bathe in your own stink? For you are pigs, are you not? The knights stood up and shouted in outrage, launching rebukes of their own at Khan Galian.

Galian's smile deflected their insults. "We will not break our oaths for any but the highest laws. This council must have a unanimous vote to go to war and I say no. The Helmhetter will not forsake the Kilcalia for a war that is not ours," said Galian.

This debate continued for quite some time – so long, in fact, that the sun mirrors dimmed and more dwarves came in to light the torches. Thormir was tired of this; he could feel his eyes drooping and his will and devotion to keeping them open was petering out. He just wanted to return to his quarters and sleep. He remembered that Solomon, the last of the Flametouched, had instructed Thormir to read one of his books, which he had said would help him understand what magic truly was and how it worked, rather than just saying words and hoping for a result.

His eyes jerked open and the images of Fern, Selena, Maria, Tangar, Lucian, and Mary vanished as he heard the clerk give an odd little cough. The clerk stepped forward, pushed his shoulders out, and straightened his back. He gave a decisive sniff and announced, "The meet is concluded for this day. The council will be held at the same time tomorrow. You all are advised to return to your companions and your quarters in Baraklemen." He sniffed again and began to announce the departure of each khan, in the reverse order to that in which they had entered the room. Robes trailing, armour clanking, and pipes twitching between pursed lips, the dwarves exited the stone room. Before long, the knights, Baldur, and Thormir were left alone; the only company were the dancing stories formed from the shadows cast by the torches.

*   *   *

The shadows and their stories were far from Thormir's mind as he sat at his desk. The plush, leather chair seemed almost too comfortable to be a chair. He had to keep pushing himself forward to lean on the desk to prevent himself falling back into tempting comfort, followed by inevitable sleep. His sleeping had been so often troubled with cheerless memories and painful seizures, he almost felt afraid to close his eyes. The book he was reading was not a guide to the language of magic, but a guide to its workings. As Thormir read on, and admired the intricate, pencilled drawings, he learnt that magic was more science than enigma. As chapter five, "*The Intricacies of Power and Intent*", stated, magic was more the manipulation of elements to achieve desired results. An example given was starting a fire from wet sticks in rain. As stated, there were two issues here; firstly the rain and secondly the sticks. Isolating the first issue, the book instructed that one would have to firstly stop the rain from falling and thus dousing the fire. This could be done through guiding the rain around the sticks and the fire; or throwing a cumulative heat so strong that other elements could not affect it; or stopping the rain altogether.

The chapter enlightened Thormir to the fact that magic was more about the energy used rather than the desired result, as using too much energy would kill him. However, the book noted, in small handwriting at the bottom of the page:

"This issue of force still applies to The Flametouched; however, because they draw the magic from within and not from around them, unlike sorcerers, the perils of energy loss are greatly lessened as a Flametouched has an endless and continual flow of magic running through their body. It must be noted that while the detriment of using an excess of magic is altogether lessened, the physical toll will be the same."

The chapter continued with three types of solutions to the fire issue, the first of which was the easiest and most efficient, as in it would not take much energy, while the last – stopping the rain altogether – would be almost impossible for a sorcerer to carry out without killing him or herself. A powerful Flametouched, however, might be able to pull it off. Thormir read the underlined, bold text that preceded the end of the sentence. It said that out of all things, the elements of nature are the hardest to destroy, and might kill you in the effort, so it is easier to manipulate them and lessen their effect.

The second thing one would have to do would be to generate heat within the sticks so that they became dry to the point of combustion. The chapter finished off the example with a couple of pronunciation tips and grammatical shortcuts.

Another example asked the reader, "How would you make your enemy choke?" Thormir immediately thought of how he would inflict this choke upon the man with the two scars. He who had the scarred face, the one who had led the group that killed Fern. *He will suffer by my hand.*

As he read on, the book said that one could simply shift the airflow in a man's throat, or make the muscles at the top of his throat close up, but that the latter would probably result in asphyxiation unless the muscles were released immediately.

As Thormir continued to read, he came across many examples of how one would achieve a result, not by doing that exact action, but by accomplishing it through an action that was related, but that was not direct. However, there were exceptions to this principle. Time was a big problem here. The chapter gave an example of a large bonfire. The roundabout way of heating every stick to the point of burning would take more time than just lighting the whole thing on fire instantly. However, at this point the example ended with "See Chapter Twelve".

Curious, Thormir thumbed his way through the book until he reached chapter twelve. Here, the book talked about the need for intent when practising magic. This was especially important when using a direct command. About three pages in, the example of a bonfire was continued. Instead of heating each stick or branch of the wood pile, the speaker simply had to speak the Nolwin word for fire. *Hellesar.* However, the user had to control the type and size of the fire, or object of attention, if they were to be accurate and successful. This was done by focusing and concentrating the mind to the point where the user's objective and intent became as one. For sorcerers and other users of magic, this type of practice was extremely hard, and often perilous to the point of having fatal consequences. In the case of the Flametouched, it was a skill that could be easily mastered over an average of five years. Some of the Flametouched had mastered the skill in two years, but that was unusual. The mastery of the Flametouched's skills were achieved through meditation and becoming proficient in analysing a situation and understanding every possible outcome.

"Therefore, if the Flametouched focuses on the object of attention, in this case the bonfire or woodpile, he or she will be able to set it alight through the use of a direct command; in others words, one can carry out the task by speaking one word in Nolwin, rather than a sentence, which might take longer and yield a less desirable result. Furthermore, by focusing on one's intent, a Flametouched will achieve an exact and controlled result. The downside to this practice is that if the intent of the user or the user's focus is broken, even for a second, the result of the command spoken or thought, can be totally beyond the user's control. Such is the nature of intent. The intent of mind must match the objective of the user."

The passage ended. Thormir read on, and discovered what he had expected; the methods of using intent.

"The use of this concentration and "will of intent" in magic can be designed in two ways. Firstly, I will approach the easiest way. It is indeed possible to use intent as a way to circumvent long and convoluted orders and sentences, and also to use these direct commands (with intent) to make a task easier, but this practice can also take time, as one has first to focus on the desirable result and then, while not breaking the intent, choose a word or command that can form a direct link between your intent and the result.

The second way is the most difficult, but also the quickest, and if carried out well, the most powerful. The user merely has to think of the result while having direct intent and the desired event will happen. Whilst carrying out this practice, the Flametouched will feel a compulsion to lift their right hand in order to direct their focus. Before, during, and for a while after, the scar of the agent will burn white-hot and rise to the surface of the skin."

Thormir stopped. He was thinking of those times when he had been in fights and he had released that energy, and it had achieved what he had wanted, even if it was a bit over the top. The vivid memory of the soldier on his horse came back to him, his bones broken, his skin torn, the flesh ripped from where ribs had punched through to daylight. Thormir remembered how he had not even said a word, and yet the energy had surged through his body, tearing through his limbs until the man had snapped and slumped over the side of his saddle, while still attached to the frightened horse by the stirrups, his muddy boots mangled and jutting outwards.

Maybe I actually performed this . . . magic, I mean I didn't even say anything and yet I got what I wanted. Yet, now I can't perform any sort of damn magic, even if I knew how.

It had been bothering Thormir that now he couldn't rely on his ability. He remembered when he would have considered the loss of his ability as a blessing, but now he just felt exposed, naked to the dangers that might await him.

The page of the book cut his finger as he turned it. Crimson drops of blood lazily dripped down the curve of his thumb. He was immediately startled away from the pain by a scream he heard echoing down the stone corridor. The scream was more of fright than pain, but he did not stop to analyse it – all he knew was that it was of a girl, a girl in desperate need.

He felt his white tunic whip around the corner of his door as he sprinted towards where he thought the screams were coming from. His bare feet slapped against the cold, stone floor as he dashed down the hallway. The screams were coming ever closer. The volume of the screams was dying, but Thormir knew that it was not that the danger had passed, but that her voice had grown hoarse, weak with the effort of calling for help. Thormir felt out with his mind, expanding his consciousness until he found them. He felt the energy of each being. One stood out, powerful and strong, heightened by the excitement of the conquest. The other was struggling, fighting to regain full consciousness.

Thormir's shoulder crashed into the wall as he rounded another corner. Biting his lip in pain, he slid the dagger out from under his belt. He clutched at the bone handle. Soft moans were still coming from around the corner; the sound of someone about to give up the will to survive. Crouching to make himself less of a target, Thormir held his dagger ready at his side. He quickly jerked around the corner. There was no need to look for the attack, as it was taking place right in front of him. A clean-shaven dwarf was pressing a blade to what Thormir knew to be a dwarf child. While this girl could have passed in height as an ordinary dwarf, there was something about her that was unmistakably childlike. Her attacker was wearing a sheet of chest mail and a pale brown tunic. A silver knife flew at Thormir's throat, missing by an inch. The dwarf narrowed his eyes as if making a decision, then took the blade that he was trying to push into the soft of the girl's throat, and threw it at Thormir's chest.

Dodging the expected attack, Thormir raced towards the dwarf. Even though the dwarf was fast, Thormir was faster. Thormir tackled the dwarf into the stone wall just under a torch bracket. The shadows cast a disgusting mask upon the dwarf's face, twists of black crossed his eyes and nose. The dwarf winced in pain as Thormir's shoulder pressed him hard to the wall. Thormir clenched his teeth as he felt a broken link in the mail bury its end into the skin and muscle on top of his right shoulder.

Standing up, he bit his lip as he plucked the metal from his skin. The dwarf was unconscious, slumped on the floor. Using the dwarf's own tunic to fashion binds, Thormir secured the dwarf's hands behind his back and tightened his feet together. *No running away for you, little man!*

Turning, Thormir looked at the girl. She was shivering on the floor and had her arms about her. She drew back as he approached, her eyes wide with fear – Thormir thought it was not the fear of having been in danger, but rather the fear of the unknown.

"It's all right, it's all right. You're fine. I'm here now. My name is Thormir – what's yours?"

The dwarf girl brushed aside a twist of her golden hair and curled it around her ear. "My name is Larna. Are you here to save me?"

"I heard you from my room. Are you okay? Where is your father?"

"Yes, I'm fine – he," she pointed a diamond-donned finger at the dwarf, "he just gave he a shock while I was playing with my toy warriors. I think he was trying to kill me, probably because I am the daughter of Khan Galian. The one time I want to play with my toys without those stupid guards buzzing around my head and I get attacked. Father will never let go of this one."

As if her words had summoned them, Thormir heard iron-clad footsteps marching down the corridor. Thormir quickly sheathed his knife as he saw the Khan of Helmhetter heading the group of soldiers. The powerful dwarf was wearing the same impressive armour that Thormir had seen in the clan meet.

Stopping not feet from them, Khan Galian surveyed the scene: the assassin, his daughter, and finally Thormir, who had his arm around Larna in an attempt to calm her. "Follow me." His order was directed at both Thormir and Larna.

Larna stood up, clutching her wooden soldiers and Thormir followed suit. "And bring the scum." The warriors did not need telling twice, indeed it seemed that it was an expected command, as they had already closed around the dwarf, still unconscious, slumped against the wall, his slackened face a canvas for a dancing shadow.

A little while later, Thormir stood, once again, in front of the khan. Khan Galian was silent. He was looking at Thormir with the kind of attention a winter fox might give its prey. With his fingernail he slowly traced the intricate lines of his golden beard brace, and all the while he stared intently at Thormir. Thormir was sure this was a test of some sort, so he remained still and silent, locking eyes with the khan. Finally the khan stopped his silent interrogation.

"You saved my daughter from a danger that was not yours. It was not your responsibility to care and protect her, and yet you did. For this I can never repay you. *Iza'kum et sercis*."

Thormir recognised the phrase the khan had just spoken. He had learnt it while travelling with Baldur. It was the phrase that the dwarves used when they owed someone their life or a great debt. If spoken allowed, it required of the recipient to ask for anything and their wish to be fulfilled. This law was upheld by all dwarves and had never been broken. *Finally, a way to get the unanimous vote.*

"Come to war with me. Help us fight the enemy, so that your great people can live in peace, whether above ground, or in the stone halls of Baraklemen."

The khan smiled. "You know, most people wait some time before they demand the repayment of the unbreakable debt. Very well, we shall go to war, but if we come back from this hunt with our spears broken and our shields splintered and smashed, remember that it was you who led Dwarvenhiem to its doom. Do not ever forget that this is all for you. Maybe we would have gone to war without you, but your presence here has brought this nation to its feet, ready to fight for *your* cause. Always remember that."

The khan looked around at the six soldiers who were standing nearest to them and, receiving the silent message that had passed between them, all six turned, and with a curt nod to the khan, marched out through the stone door.

CHAPTER TWENTY SEVEN

BENEATH THE SURFACE
Gurda hârnea

Even though Solomon's eyes were shut, Thormir was sure that he was watching him. Thormir was just telling him of his readings and thoughts on what he had done and achieved. While he could never quite read Solomon, he thought he might have impressed him just a little. Indeed, Solomon was impressed to the point of praise when Thormir recounted that a unanimous vote was secured and that the council was meeting again to discuss the logistics of going to war: the soldiers, the horses, the methods of transport, strategy, finance, securities to be left, and the weapons and armour that were to be made and cleaned before they left for the long march east.

Baldur was now sitting in on every lesson that Thormir attended, "I'll bet my beard that every dwarf in Dwarvenhiem knows your name by now." They had become good friends, and Baldur had shown great interest in what Thormir was learning from Solomon. Solomon was not teaching him magic of any kind, nor any kind of deadly skill he could hold over an opponent, but he was teaching Thormir to have a sharper mind and to look at things from many different angles.

It had been three days since Khan Galian had decided to go to war and since then Thormir had been studying with the old man. From the teachings of the flight patterns of the Ruddy Turnstone and the Gyrfalcon, to the weather patterns of the skies east of The Al'Durast, Solomon had taught Thormir a great deal. He had said to Thormir that the knowledge would "aid" him in his travels. In Medani, his schooling had taken much the same form every day, but here Solomon varied the field of study every few hours. Indeed, by the end of the second day, Thormir thought that it was a singularly impressive feat that he could retain so much information in his brain.

Thormir could feel Solomon's eyes upon him as he dissected a rat, cutting down the belly, making sure not to damage any organs that lay close to the surface. Thormir knew that Fern would have dismissed the skill, saying that it was pointless to waste time on such trivial things, but Thormir kept going, carving a bloody slice into the grey fur. As he thought of Fern, his fingers twitched, and for the fifth time his scalpel went deep into the rat's stomach. Thormir could almost feel the pressure of the small kidney bursting open at the sharp metallic touch.

Thormir frowned, the kind of frown a son can only inherit from his father, and picked up another furry lump. Solomon's hand closed around his as he began to make the first incision. "Come with me, you need to let go of your fear, then we will see what you are capable of."

Solomon motioned for Baldur to come and the three of them made their way out of the cosy room and into the dark corridor.

"Aren't you supposed to remain here?" Thormir said, instantly regretting his words. Solomon raised one pencil-thin eyebrow and looked down at Thormir.

"I just talked to the king and he said that it was fine. I did not tell you, Thormir, that with a sharp and well-trained mind, one can practise communicating over long distances. I believe you already know how to do this, but I presume due to the look of unsatisfied disbelief written across your features that your teacher did not know or commit you to the full extent of this skill. If you have no more questions, please follow me."

"Yes, actually I do. Could you go on a bit, I will catch up."

Both Solomon and Baldur gave Thormir inquisitive looks, but Solomon nodded and the two continued up the dark, torch-lit, shadowy corridor. Thormir quieted his footsteps and followed them for a short way. *Oh wow, just what I need now– to be walking alone in another dank, dark corridor. Still, I'd better do it.* Finally he arrived at the place where he thought she was. The same silver eyes turned in the blackness.

"Are you there?"

"Yesss." Her voice came out a weary hiss.

"Was that you who called me, or rather stuck a mental sword into my mind?"

There was a pause. Then came the answer. "Yes. Free me."

"Ha! Well considering what I saw you do to that child and Rake . . ."

"What? I protected that child from one of my own. You should be thanking me."

This new perspective on the situation hit him hard. He remembered the way she had reassured the child in her arms, and the look of care in her eyes. He also remembered the other svay lying dead, with scratch marks around its neck. "Did you . . . were you protecting the baby?"

"Yes."

Suddenly her face appeared out of shadow and through the bars. "If you do not believe my words, Flametouched, then look into my mind. I must warn you, however, that if you enter my mind, you may not be strong enough to leave."

After what felt like a jibe at his character, he reached out with his consciousness and focused it towards hers, just as he had done so many times with Fern both in lessons and when they were exploring the scrub around The Red Hills. Thormir smiled but then gasped as he touched minds with the svay. It was like being plunged into a hot bath on a cold morning. It burned for a second, and then he found himself looking for air. Gasping desperately and holding a hand against a wall so he wouldn't collapse, he opened his watering eyes as he felt her mind.

The only thing close to this that he had felt was the song inside of Selena's mind. But inside this mind there was no resemblance to Selena's requiem for her grandmother. Here the only song was of despair and pain. The notes of the song were so utterly beautiful that the passing of each one seemed like an age, and its end was the end of world, until it began again – an endless cycle of beautiful, wonderful pain and despair. Listening to this song was like torture, but at the same time he wanted to hear more of it. It seemed to be telling a story that he could not quite make out, but understood on some subconscious level.

"Ah, you hear it . . . that is our song, the song of the svay."

And it became apparent to Thormir that even the darkest cell could, on some level, be beautiful. But for now, it reminded Thormir of one thing and that one image burned vividly in his mind. That of the purple flowers that grew before the treeline of Hurst, the same purple flowers that Fern's blood had stained that night. He reached up and wiped away the thick tears that were pouring from his eyes. And yet the song would not stop, it held him there, seeing the colour purple, remembering that moment – the moment when he had lost so much.

It took all his effort to withdraw himself from the svay's consciousness, but before he did, he made sure to see if there was any sort of dishonest thought circulating through her mind. He found none. Gasping for breath in between silent sobs, Thormir tried to steady himself. The svay observed him with a troubled, concerned expression. Despite his predicament, Thormir had the will to notice her eyes. He could not quite make out their detail as they seemed to shift in colour and hue the longer he looked into them. Every time he thought he had the answer, he seemed to forget it and had to start again, searching within deep pools of pain, for her eyes were as such; bottomless wells of yawning memory and sadness.

"What did you do to me?" he said. The breaths between his words were pronounced, and emphasised by the heaving of his chest.

"I did nothing. You looked into my mind, and through my mind, you saw your own pain." The svay blinked at him through the bars. There was something beautiful about the way the torchlight hit her face, the curve of her cheek, the lash of her eyes, and the spill of her black hair. Back at Stockhud she had seemed ugly, even brutal, but here she was vulnerable, even tame.

"Set me free. I can help you to fight my kind. I hate what we do and I want to stop it. The only way I can do this is with the dwarves' help. I can even lead them to our capital."

Thormir raised his own eyebrow now. What he was hearing could indeed lead to every dwarf under Dwarvenhiem being safe from the attacks of the svay in the North. It could also win Thormir the favour of those who doubted him. *I have to try.*

"I promise I will try to set you free, but I fear that if you *are* free you will not be accepted by the dwarves."

Thormir felt that if he stayed any longer the conversation might never end and would turn into a cycle of pleading and denial. So with that last promise he turned to go, and as he did, he felt a gentle touch of slender fingers upon his arm.

"Thank you."

*   *   *

Thormir fought against the wind. It howled like the wargs of legend and shredded the skin on his face like icy razors. The worst thing about it was that it did not come from one direction, it hurled itself at him from every which way, sometimes in one blasting gale that tilted Thormir so that he pitched in the snow like a ship's mast upon a choppy sea.

Squinting through the flying ice, Thormir could see no signs of life apart from Baldur and Solomon. No bird was brave enough to fly up here for their bodies would surely turn to a black and blue crumple of broken feathers. This was Calx Mons, the tallest mountain in The Al'Durast and also the meanest. There was no trick or trade to climbing the peak with ease; this mountain was an unrelenting, menacing brute that gave no mercy to those who chose to climb it. The dwarves had built an endless cycle of stairs that scaled the inside of Calx Mons but it not reach all the way to the brutal peak of the mountain – so now they climbed outside, battling the bitterness of the ranges. The few cairns that memorialised the mountain's kills were barely visible through the ice and snow, but even if they had been, all that would show would be crumbling mounds of rock and rubble.

Countless crevasses criss-crossed the mountain, and each had claimed their victims; too many had fallen into those icy cracks, never to resurface or step on solid ground again. It had been years since the last dwarf had attempted the climb, and set foot on top of the mountain, but for some reason Solomon had had the brilliant idea of climbing to the top, no doubt to give Thormir a sense of achievement. However, Thormir had now decided that one did not have to climb the highest mountain in the range to gain a sense of accomplishment. Why couldn't he just paint a picture, or go for a long run? Maybe he could have shot a bull's-eye for a new record. *That* was an achievement. It wasn't necessary to have to suffer this freezing, cutting wind, and the icy temperature of Calx Mons to feel satisfaction.

Thormir bent his head, still brooding on the thought that this was a useless exercise. He blew his frost-covered hair out of his eyes and pulled his furs closer and further up his back.

"We are nearly at the top, we will . . ."

Thormir only picked up the first part of Baldur's sentence. For some reason this annoyed him, adding to his annoyance that Solomon was leading the party of three, apparently having no trouble at all with scaling the side of the mountain, even with heavy, iron manacles hanging around his arms. Thormir gritted his teeth and thought of the crackling fire that was surely warming every corner of his room. Thormir closed his eyes, *not the wisest move*, he thought, but he needed to distract himself, to transport himself to his room. Within his mind, he could almost feel the warmth of the room reddening his cheeks; or was that icy razors flying downwind? No, he was in his room at his desk. He looked at the book on his desk – it was the one he had been reading not a few nights ago.

Thormir opened his eyes. He thought of all the ways that he could use his power and the lessons learned from the book about intent and objective to lessen his discomfort. He decided that the easiest way would be to divert the wind around him so that the ice would not touch him, thereby offering him the opportunity to warm up. However, Thormir did not know Nolwin well enough to say the right word to match his proper meaning. *Intent*. Maybe he could carry out the last form – no words, just intent.

Okay, think of the result, then of the intent. He closed his eyes and focused on the image of the mountain winds flowing around him, and pronounced his intent through the thought. He opened his eyes as he felt the energy tingling and pulsing within him. The snake-like scar had risen to the surface of his skin. With a gasp he released both the thought and the energy at the same time. He waited for something to happen. For a moment, he thought he felt the wind subside, only to be disappointed when a fresh gust of wind slapped him hard in the face.

Thormir was pleased when he saw the truth of Baldur's statement, for not long after that brutal slap, he found that the wind had died as they passed through a cloud. Thormir looked around, wiping small icicles from his lashes. While the gale had perished, there still remained a cold but gentle breeze that blew from the West and created small twisters of wind and snow. Back bent, Thormir made it to a small flat where both Solomon and Baldur were waiting for him.

Thormir could see the top of the mountain, its zenith towering high into the snowy sky. While ice and snow covered most of Calx Mons, its peak was a singular spear of dark, grey rock. It stuck into the sky, a mark of power. It rent the sky in two, a reminder of the power of nature, of the earth, and while men warred over gold and pride, the peak of Calx Mons remained, towering over the land from which it rose, not caring for the quarrels of man.

Thormir was glad when Solomon said that they would not be scaling the final stretch to stand on top of the peak; rather they were to move around the mountain, taking a narrow path, to their journey's end. Bending down, Thormir took his small knife from his belt and plunged it deep into the snowy flesh of the mountain. He did this two more times until the snow broke and crumbled in his hands, the clumps of soft, newly-fallen flakes, cold and refreshing to his touch. Disregarding the harsh taste of the ice, he lowered his mouth to his hands and ate the snow. Immediately his thirst was quenched, only to be replaced by hunger.

Baldur and Solomon hauled him to his feet. They could see the ledge through the clear, crystal-like ice. The only grips were the few nooks in the stone crag that they had their backs to. Using this and the soft powder of a recent snowfall, they were able to have some hold against the ice as they skirted the rocky ledge that circled the sharp peak. Thormir was thankful for the rough skins on the soles of his boots, without which he would surely have fallen by now – a thought that did not comfort him in the least.

The wind was picking up now, dashing Thormir's hopes that they would ever return alive. To be stuck on a ledge while a gale blew upon them was one in a myriad of ways to die, but they could not speed up their pace, as that could mean slipping and falling onto the jagged stone face below, so they continued, pressing toward, fighting against the fear of ice and wind.

Arriving at journey's end was such a relief that a warmth that defied the cold bristle of the wind spread through Thormir's body. It started from within his heart, and spread outward until it reached the tips of his being. Even his scar felt comfortingly warm at the sight of the summit, heating his right arm considerably more than the left. He thought nothing of it – it was just another enigma of his new power.

Finally, when he and Baldur rounded the corner, they found Solomon staring at great bodies of dark stone shrouded in a blanket of mist that was slowly thinning as the wind picked up. With his back turned to them, Solomon spoke. "There are many things in this world, in this land, that are the way they are because that is how they were intended to be. Streams flow from the snowy caps because they were meant to. The sun rises in the east because that is the way it has always been. A horse can run a certain number of miles a day because that is how they are built. But some things can be altered. And what is responsible for this? It is the science of that which fills all things – the synaptic, the instinctual. The will to use what is around one, to help and aid one, in the adventure of endurance that is named 'life'. But when a stone can be carved through just the use of words, and a peach tree can produce fruit out of its due season, owing to the alteration of its growth, the adventure of life begins to grow old and stale. Living things that once struggled to live, the way they should, become lazy, weak, and dependent. So when a black seed is planted, they no longer have the strength to fight off the weed, they become strangled and lifeless in form, their will and spirit crashes, and they are left to their own, to rebuild themselves out of the ashes of failure and shame." He paused, and even though he could not see them, Thormir could tell that Solomon's eyes were downcast. Solomon continued with one simple statement. "The five broken."

He turned around and straightened his back, reminding Thormir of the clerk, and when he looked up Thormir saw fire in his eyes – something – a look that Thormir had never seen within them before. The eyes that were usually so wise and kind now possessed rings of fire and a power rising from deep within. Thormir saw Baldur step back in alarm, as surely he would have known Solomon far longer. Thormir too felt like stepping back and running away, back along that narrow ledge, even if it killed him. This was fear of Solomon that he felt; it told him to run away, to hide, but the fear also held him in place – unable to move. Baldur must have felt it too, as he was fixed where he stood with the same expression that Thormir imagined he wore. It was in that moment that Baldur and Thormir beheld the soul of Solomon.

Solomon spoke, his voice the same, but the chosen words more powerful and meaningful than ever before. "This is the reason for my desertion. I *chose* not to take part in that battle so, so long ago. I lied to you, Thormir, I was not one of the last. I was one of the oldest and most powerful in the order of the Flametouched. I saw the world, and I deemed it unfit. While the Flametouched did their job for a while and magic was kept in hand, evil still remained, ever present, waiting. It existed right under the nose of those who would have you believe that the world was clean and content. But it was not – it was corrupt and crooked, dishonest to those who looked upon it and claimed it 'good'. So I waited and watched as magic was banished, and the world fell into disrepair. For to get rid of the evil that already existed, all must start again, this time without the aid of magic – for it is that which corrupts the hearts of all men.

"But I was not alone in these plans – the Dragons aided me in my work, for they too, the oldest and wisest of all races, saw the world as it was. So upon The Fields of Celiton, in the last great battle, the elves banished magic from the world, killing their race in the effort. However, despite the elves' efforts, whispers of magic still remained – so the Dragons flew forth and absorbed the remnants of magic and locked its power within themselves. They flew back to their eyries high in The Al'Durast where they sealed themselves in stone, never to reawaken, making sure magic never poisoned the lands ever again. It was my will, me, me alone who put an end to the war. All those who possessed the knowledge of how to control magic, faded in time and so with them did the threat of magic. Even I cannot use my magic properly anymore, I am weak without it flowing through me – and now these cursed dwarves have me chained and bound, forever to remain prisoner, paying for a crime that served to make the world a better place."

Thormir couldn't believe what he was hearing. Solomon, last of the Flametouched, was the betrayer of them all, he was once man's last hope, but it was he who had encouraged the downfall of what was once good and great. "Why didn't you tell me this at the start, why did you hide this?"

"Would you have accepted me like this? Knowing what you know now, how could you ever trust me?"

Solomon bowed his head then turned around and looked at the colossal lumps of rock. The stone was jagged, but that was all they could discern through the mist that swirled around it. The mist was thinning quickly, as the winds picked up across the peak. Soon enough the mist was gone, leaving only a distilled, spectral veil, through which the true shape of the stones could be seen.

Dragons.

Each of them twice as large as The Great Hall, their size as magnificent and terrible as their power. Now that the swirling scarves of mist had been blown away by the mountain winds, Thormir could see every claw, every scale, every detail of the eye that looked at him and cut through him even though it was surely just stone. However, Thormir knew that underneath the stone casing, a real dragon lay dormant, its fury and dominance ready to explode outwards, to remind the world of the true meaning of power.

For some reason, Thormir felt drawn to the stone. He felt himself raising his hand, where his scar was now visible and no longer hiding under his skin. Walking forward so that he was right next to the nearest dragon, he felt and saw his right arm reach out and touch the rough neck of the stone dragon. He felt nothing but the cool sensation of winter-cold rock. Somehow the touch reminded him of the grassy plains on which he used to ride – the large, cold expanse of the Carathron, the lashing of the broken blades of grass blowing downwind, the beat of Shadow's hooves, hunting in the forest, riding past the villages scattered across the harsh countryside, and drinking from the clear, ice-cold streams that ran through the deepest of tundra ravines.

In that instant Thormir felt a horrible sense of homesickness; it wrenched at his heart, reminding him of all that he missed – the stables, all his friends, and even his father. And then there was Fern. And only when he felt a slight pulse run through his hand was Thormir, son of the South, drawn back to that bitter, cold, gusty peak. He stared at his hand, in disbelief. *Was that me?* he thought. He took his hand off the stone and pressed it to his other hand, feeling for that same powerful pulse. Nothing.

He was aware of Solomon talking to him in the background, but he paid no attention. He was still wondering what he had felt. The pulse of the dragon.

Thormir walked away from the three stone dragons, and he made his way over to the others. After some discussion regarding how they would proceed with their relationship, all of them headed towards the path that circled the peak and led to their descent. None of them noticed the deep crack in the stone that had opened up on the first dragon, the dragon Thormir had touched. It had appeared directly upon the carved stone eye, which was now split in two. Flakes and chunks of rock fell away to reveal a single, great, golden eye. Blink.

CHAPTER TWENTY EIGHT

AN ORCHESTRA OF WAR
Lumá Rimôs

Weeks had passed since Thormir had descended from that peak to find the whole of the Dwarven army preparing to march out of Dwarvenhiem. The vivid memory of what had occurred upon the icy peak of Calx Mons had not left Thormir. The realisation that Solomon was not what he said he was, and that he had let the fifth age of Vâryá come to such a brutal end just because he deemed it unfit, was plaguing his mind.

Solomon believes that men are weak and easily succumb to the promise of power, that they do not have the right or discipline to control and govern magic – and if given the chance, the evil that resides within every man and woman will grow strong until it takes hold and spreads, until the world falls under the shadow of cruelty and suffering. That cannot be so. A shadow only falls in one direction and where there is no shade of black or withering grey, there is light, and with light, hope and the will to live free from darkness. It was with that thought that Thormir had decided that it was worth fighting for every soul who had suffered under the emperor's harsh rule. *No more shall villages be decimated because villagers speak their minds; no more shall old religions be forcefully replaced by new ones. I shall brush away the cobwebs of lies and deceit from men's eyes until they see how they have been fooled.* The winds of fate have changed. Hope is kindled.

However, for now it was a mild, northerly wind that played with frayed edges of Thormir's furs as he sat on a flat tree stump, poking at a fire with the blackened end of a branch while the dwarves around him drank mugs of mead, howling at the top of their voices and pounding their chests in an inebriated fury. One of them waved a stick in the air on which was skewered a fat rat. Obviously meant for cooking, it hung limp and dead from the stick between its ribs. It must have been fresh, because Thormir could still make out the pink around its ears and the brush of its whiskers in the breeze. *Vile things.*

Using the rat as a puppet, the dwarf chased around a younger-looking dwarf, who obviously had a severe distaste for the creatures. Thormir couldn't blame him. Finally the younger dwarf turned and tackled the puppeteer to the ground, sending the rat flying off the stick to land in an older dwarf's mug. The circle howled with laughter, the dwarves clutched their armoured stomachs, some of them falling off the logs where they sat, and others pounding the ground, bent on all fours. The older dwarf walked towards the pair, who were still wrestling in the dirt. His gold-braced beard shone warmly in the light issuing from the campfire. The older dwarf picked the pair up by their metal belts that were secured around their waists, and he hurled the struggling dwarves into a bush of thistles. The two howled in pain, sending the others into further gales of laughter.

Considering their reluctance to leave their homes, the dwarves seemed perfectly happy to be outside, free from the mountains. Thormir often heard them commenting on how good it was to roam the free world once more; they were not at all bothered that the secret of their survival had been shattered and that they were exposed to the eyes of the world. When he had asked a particularly fat dwarf, who would have found it easier to roll rather than march, the dwarf had said, "Every sausage needs to come out of the fire sometime."

Watching a wild boar turning on the spit, Thormir smiled as he heard a drunk and crude joke spew from the frothing beard of a Valmar dwarf. This was the fifth large camp they had made since they had left the halls of Baraklemen, which was pretty impressive considering the miles they had travelled in the past month. According to the leading commander, they had arrived at the flats before the walls of Orien. The slightest hills marked these flats and the only trees that pricked the horizon resided in a small wood not far from their camp. This was the passage south – the vast expanse on the borders of Carathron. If held by the enemy, Medani would no longer be secure. *While the emperor sits on the throne of Ironholt, he will send The Crow to do his bidding. If Medani is taken, The Crow will rule in the South, and the emperor will rule in the North, with all lands east of The Al'Durast under his gaze. That's what awaits us if we lose this battle.*

The Master of the Axe was the leading commander on this mission. He took orders from the king and no one else. Thormir had remembered what Baldur had told him about the position. "The Master of the Axe is the position of military commander. He is in charge of all military operations, including all military preparations. How do you think we assembled the army so quickly? The Master of the Axe must have anticipated the khans all agreeing to go to war and made the arrangements for the armies to prepare to be called upon."

And so, when Thormir had met the Master for the first time, he knew what to expect. This dwarf was a clever tactician in battle and a fierce warrior. His strategies were of such a nature that he even took part in designing the weapons that were to fit into his war plans. Baldur had told Thormir that this dwarf's grand sire was the first to find out that whistling a specific tune would call those small powerful horses upon which many of the dwarves in the army now rode.

Thormir heard a cackle and a burp and, seeing Baldur stroll over with the knights, he smiled. *I could do with some company.* Thormir poked at the fire again and a bristle of spitting sparks jumped into the air, touching the boar's belly as the spit slowly turned around and around. Looking up expectantly, he saw the knights peel off and sit with a number of dwarves who were playing some sort of game out of pieces of bone. They rolled them along the ground until they reached a specific point and then either roared in victory or, with red eyes and slack jaws, demanded another go. Thormir couldn't make anything of it.

"Hate tha game, n'er can win." Baldur stomped over, clearly drunk, but in good spirits. He gave Thormir a toothy grin, which flickered as he saw the look of concern that Thormir knew he was failing to hide.

"I'm sure they are still alive, lad." It was as if Baldur had read his mind, although, thought Thormir, it wasn't a far reach, as they knew each other pretty well by now. This friendship was deepened by the fact that they had talked nearly every day on their ride to the camp, discussing battle tactics, how to string bows from woods of various kinds, the types of plants that grew around the mountains, and other useful knowledge any dwarf worth his weight in ale would know. Thormir had also told Baldur of the regular dreams he had had of a great, blinking, golden eye. A golden eye that was ancient beyond time, and possessed knowledge deeper and more ancient than any library. Baldur had offered comfort, telling him that it was just a dream, but Thormir was sure that it was something more – something real.

Baldur seemed to figure that hitting Thormir on the back might knock some sense, if not cheer, into him. "Have up, come of the cup," Baldur said, offering him his cup of mead, sealing the gesture with a grin.

Thormir had no choice to accept, and smiling he put the cup to his lips. He choked, then seeing Baldur's bemused expression, began to laugh. He belched, and fell off his log with a thud on the ground. The dwarves around the circle began to roar with laughter and Thormir joined in. He laughed until his stomach ached with pain, which only subsided when Baldur held chunks of steaming meat under his nose.

* * *

That night was the first calm sleep Thormir had had since leaving Baraklemen – no seizures cursed him, and no troubled dreams visited him. He didn't even mind being woken up by a completely sober but grumpy Baldur in the early hours of the morning. The sun had not risen, so the silent camp was covered in the purple that colours the deep hours of the morning. The darkness that accompanies the hour of the wolf was only interrupted by the moving, orange glows of the watch guards' torches as they patrolled the outer perimeter.

"We have been summoned to the king's tent." Baldur held out his hand and pulled Thormir to his feet with remarkable strength. Holding a torch in his other hand, he guided Thormir through the mass of tents, sleeping dwarves, and horses, and up onto the crest of a hill close to the treeline. The small slope looked familiar, but Thormir could not place it in the dark. As they approached, Thormir noticed the change of the wind and the sudden heat that was now flowing gently through the camp. He turned around and looked out towards the horizon that was not yet visible. *Somewhere out there, I will save them. I will not let them down – no harm shall come to Selena or Maria. I will save them.*

The flap of the king's tent was yanked open and Baldur and Thormir were both hurried inside by two guards wearing blue sashes over their armour. Thormir was surprised to see so many people inside the tent. All dwarf khans were present, as well as the king's guard. The knights stood in a corner with only Hector leaning over a map. All of them were dressed in full armour with their weapons slung across backs or sheathed alongside heavy war belts. Consequently, when Thormir entered the tent wearing nothing more than a riding tunic and undergarments, he felt somewhat out of place. However, no one seemed to care. He felt a tug behind him, was lifted off his feet, and dropped between Hector and the Master of the Axe, whom Thormir had since learnt was called Hoff and liked to be addressed as such. Thormir looked around and saw Rake retreating to the corner, obviously under the impression he had done Thormir a favour, by removing him from Baldur's side and putting him next to a more relevant figure. Hoff was leaning over a roughly-drawn map of the landscape that surrounded them. The East had been drawn as a rough circle, indicating the outline of the city. The enemy forces were an inky block drawn to the northwest of Orien with arrows pointing directly towards at the city.

Hoff leant over the map and sketched a long, diagonal line that led from just north of where Calx Mons would be if the map were larger, down to Orien. The quill Hoff was using was made of a long, grey-white, spotted feather that Thormir recognised as that of a miraki bird. Thormir wouldn't be surprised if he had made it on the way here, as it was nesting season for the birds. He remembered how he had been stung by the thorn of a miraki plant so long ago, and how he had tried to cut out the poison. *That feels so long ago now, as though I was just a boy.* He hoped that the plant had been destroyed and eaten by now. The miraki bird was the only animal that could eat and digest the plant and its toxins, and they did so in abundance, so that at this time of year it was almost impossible to find a miraki plant in one piece.

Tangar had once told him that the birds only digest the berries to the point where the flesh is completely gone, but the inner seed is unharmed. He had carefully shown this to Thormir by cutting open the belly of a miraki bird and removing dozens of crimson seeds. Inside the seeds there is a fine dust, and if dropped on the ground, and only the ground, the seed will explode, expelling deadly powder. Tangar had shown this to Thormir by throwing the seed far off and then watching as a cloud of bright red dust exploded into the air as the seed touched the ground. Thormir wondered if the dwarves knew of the contents of the miraki bird's stomach.

Hoff pulled the map closer to him. "Our spies have counted our enemies' number to be around 45,000, so we must rule out a head-on attack. We will strike at their army at different points at varying times. Remember, there are many ways to kill a wolf other than a spear to the mouth. See this ridge here," Hoff pointed at the outline of a small crag, "we will dispatch 200 archers and 400 horsemen to hide behind this ridge." He took his quill and drew another aggressive line towards the rectangle west of the enemy. "A small unit will then go to the enemy's supply train and destroy everything in sight. Cut the wagons, destroy the wheels, and poison their food and water. An army without food is no army at all."

Thormir was impressed with the strategist's plan, and looking about he saw the other khans nodding in approval as well – all except Khan Roland, who was frowning, but Hoff continued unfazed. "You will notice that the wind and temperature around us have changed in the past few hours. My khans we will be fighting in the midst of a storm. This line here represents wind direction," he traced a long diagonal line on the map with his brutish finger. "By my calculations the storm will reach us before midday. We will use this against our enemy. You see this here," again the Master of the Axe pointed at the map but this time it was at the large, blank space between Orien and the large block that was the 45,000 strong enemy, "this is where the battle will take place. We must take advantage of our height, and the fact we can see our enemy's movement. They will have nowhere to hide so they will advance directly upon Orien. This is where we will catch them." Hoff turned to Khan Stonebridge. "Take 100 of your best riders and make for this place here. However, you must take several large tree branches with you. We will trample the ground and dig up the dirt," Hoff still had his finger on the empty space, "so that when the storm comes and the rains begin to fall, the enemy will be fighting in the mud. Any who cross that space will be trampled and easy picking for the archers."

All the khans looked supremely impressed, all except Khan Roland. "We will not fight against an army of 45,000. Even if your plans work, Hoff, you will barely halve their army. This war is not meant for us – my clan will retreat and Hoff, Viggon," he turned to the king, "I would advise you to do the same." With that, Khan Roland left. By daybreak Roland and his clan would be gone.

The tent fell silent. The atmosphere was like an eggshell – the slightest crack could set off utter downfall and chaos within the Dwarven camp. The departure of Khan Roland was that crack – the slightest doubt could cause all the dwarf khans to take their soldiers and go, leaving Orien and the passage to Medani entirely unprotected. Hoff coughed, regained his train of thought, and in doing so lassoed the khans and secured them once more.

"It is true," he held his quill, tapping the feather on the patch of skin between his forefinger and thumb, "we need to figure out a way to give us further advantage over our enemy or else we will find that the only option is to fight against the significant remainder of the enemy soldiers." He increased his tapping of the feather. Thormir watched the beat of the quill, thinking about how they could destroy the enemy without destroying all the Dwarven factions. One, two, three, the miraki bird's feather flapped up and down, making a blurred shadow on the side of the tent.

"I know!" Thormir felt like a child as he jumped into the air. Everyone in the tent turned to him, and he felt himself blush with the rapidity he only associated with the drawing of an arrow. Regaining his composure, he educated the room about the deadly poison and dust within the miraki seeds. Thormir explained that there were sure to be hundreds of birds nesting in the wood not far from the camp, which would be easy kills considering the birds had a low level of intelligence and nested on the ground. "And after taking the seeds that are found in their stomachs, we can throw them at the enemy!"

The group seemed impressed by his plan, but Hoff said, "And how do you propose we get close to the enemy? We want to keep our distance until absolutely necessary."

The answer came to Thormir so quickly that it surprised even him. "Instead of throwing the seeds we will use those floating lanterns." He had seen the floating lights within the city of Baraklemen. They were easily made of cloth and a few, strong, thin, metal poles. They floated over the city, held up by a small flame underneath.

The realisation that this plan could work, and was so simple to implement, crashed upon them with such power that Thormir could almost feel the vibration of the air. As he finished speaking, the tent exploded into a chorus of shouts, orders, affirmations, and questions.

As the 600 dwarves had already left for the hidden ridge and the supply train, Hector and the knights would follow them with the sacks of miraki seeds and the lanterns that would hold them up, but it would be the hot, east winds that would carry the sacks over Crow's army. Once over the enemy, they would have to be shot down, a role Thormir felt was designed for him, and so he would remain with the main Dwarven army, ready to shoot down the four large lanterns when they were positioned over the enemy army.

Thormir heard orders being given outside and deduced that the 100 riders who had been mucking the land in front of Orien had returned. Thormir and Baldur were now among of the few left in the tent. Tossing aside the tent flap, they were surprised to be greeted by a red sun that was surrounded by scarves of a grey mist on the horizon. Thormir noticed how, as the map had shown, they were indeed in a high position to both look upon the movements of the opposing force and to offer a forceful descent onto the battlefield. Even now he could see the main force of the Dwarven army moving out, and taking a different formation upon the lower slopes of the rolling hills that melted into the plains further off.

*   *   *

Many of the trees at the end of the forest had already been cut down and dragged towards Orien – however, not by the dwarves. *Another mystery – this day is not just a war between enemies, but one of riddles.* He looked towards Orien. He could not tell how long he had been surveying the land. This day he did not just have one enemy. *I have not forgotten you, scar-face.* When he was pulled back to the realm of war and wolves, he could see Orien in the distance. And Orien burnt.

CHAPTER TWENTY NINE

QUARTET
Catro

Great, billowing smoke hung between the houses far in the distance. Black, sooty clouds were towering into the sky, blotting out most of the red sun. The smoke swelled and billowed, bending to the will of the wind. It was so dense that it would easily hide any person who wandered upon the top of the wall.

Acrid smoke enveloped the walls, rolling over the stones and blinding onlookers to the happenings inside the city. The smoke trailed to the south, covering the movement at the southern gate. As Thormir watched the city, he became aware that Baldur had joined him and was squinting hard at the smoke that rose in great, black clouds.

"That smoke is from no ordinary fire. See how there are no true flames at the base of the smoke? This is not a fire that will harm the people inside, this is a smoke screen. You see it is working!"

Thormir followed Baldur's line of sight until he saw a thread of figures slowly moving out of the southern gate of Orien and south towards Brogin. Despite the risen sun, they were barely visible, their path only outlined by the small lanterns they held aloft, guiding them towards the roads and worn paths that led travellers through the wild reaches and bitter cold of the Carathron. *Maybe Selena and Maria are amongst them! I have to ask.*

He turned to go, but Baldur clamped a firm grip around his wrist. "We need you here. I will go and see if they are there – you need to be here. Remember, someone needs to shoot those lanterns and you are our best shot."

Thormir wrestled with the thought for a minute before conceding that it was for the best. He was surprised when he turned to reply to Baldur, only to find him already mounted on one of the small but powerful horses. Upon his saddle was strapped a small spear, several small axes, and a buckler. The horse reared into the air before taking off down the slope, galloping towards the caravan of people travelling out of the city. Not a word of goodbye fell from Baldur's mouth, only a look of determination.

Out of the corner of his eye, Thormir noticed something – some creature – moving on the edge of the forest, its form hidden in shade. He felt the small hairs on the back of his neck stand up, whatever it was definitely looking straight at him. He reached behind his back: *Damn it!* The one time he didn't have his bow. Preparing for a fight, he whirled around ready to charge at the oncoming assailant. It was then that he saw the flanks of a horse that was walking towards him, slowly and deliberately, as if it knew him and had known him for a long time. Thormir dropped his fists as he felt his adrenaline fade, to be replaced by curiosity and excitement.

"Shadow?"

The horse tossed its head and began to trot towards him. He ran towards her. She was a memory of a past life, a happy memory that had returned to him. He crashed into her, hugging her warm neck. He could feel her happiness as well, even in the rhythm of her breathing. "I'm sorry for leaving you," he said, and she tossed her head. She understood. Thormir felt her quivering, and knew that she had missed him as much as he had regretted ever leaving her. The two of them stood together for a long while. It was as if a ripped tapestry of friendship between man and horse was finally being stitched up. Thormir wanted to remember this moment, this perfect moment when his old life had collided with his new one. In that instant, the smoke from the city, the oncoming storm, and the battle were all forgotten as Thormir's joy at having one of his greatest friends return usurped all other feelings and apprehensions.

But it couldn't last forever; a crack of lightning followed by slow rumbles of thunder sounded in the far distance. "Come on, Shadow, let's put some armour on – I have a feeling we are going to need it." As he cast a glance towards the smoking city, he saw movement on the plains. Crow's army was encroaching fast.

A short while later, Thormir was in full battle dress, which was a thin but strong, metal chest plate – the metal of the dwarves. His greaves and bracers were also made up of the same silvery metal. He wore no helmet; he wanted nothing to get in the way while shooting at the enemy. He had never worn one in battle before and now was not the time for practising. He also wore a thick belt over his leather hides, into which he had stuck his hunting dagger. In addition, he attached a small pouch of miraki seeds, just in case. He had a feeling he might need them. Thormir thought that two swords would be a bit excessive, so he had opted for one, casing it in a sheath attached to his saddle. His bow and quiver were strapped across his back. Only when he mounted Shadow did he feel ready. Together they looked out over what would soon become a land of death, burning carcasses, and torn flesh. Thormir could already see the blood spilling in great, crimson pools across the landscape, or was that merely the sun burning fierce in the morning light?

Looking down, Thormir saw that Hoff was also surveying the battlefield. He seemed to take a sudden interest in the land in front of Orien. Thormir squinted, and then he too saw a section of the enemy army running forward, towards the smoking stone walls. Hoff's mud trap had not worked, as the rain had not yet hit, so the enemy advanced undisturbed. Hoff grunted in anger, but when he and Thormir saw a flaming arrow pierce the smoke in the distance and arc towards the enemy, their objections and outrage were cut short. Speeding towards the enemy, the arrow plunged downward, hitting the ground in the midst of the oncoming force. A second passed, and then an explosion erupted with such force that even from where they stood they could feel the rush of hot air. The whole Dwarven army looked to Orien and saw a great, fiery ring encircle the city. There may not have been any flames before now, but now they watched, as great torrents of fire leapt into the sky. The explosion of roaring flames did not just protect the city from any who wished to attack, but it burned any who were still within the ring, including the men who had been running forward just seconds earlier. Thormir winced as he heard horrific screams of pain coming from within the terrible circle of fire.

"Won't the fire blow back to the city when the wind picks up?" Thormir could hardly hear himself speak as the explosion, screams, and wind roared a symphony in his ears.

"No," said Hoff. "See how they have dug the dirt before the ring of fire – it is to make sure that it is not blown back onto the city. I'm surprised they used this technique – usually only the Tangri people have the skill to do this. And look, I was right!"

Thormir looked up and saw storm clouds forming over the battlefield. They rose to gargantuan heights, swirling around each other, their plumage rising and falling, catching red and charcoal in the colours of daybreak. He could almost see the mass of water held within them, their dark underbellies pregnant and bulging with the strain of carrying the oncoming deluge. Surely only the force of the wind kept the clouds up. The gusty wind that had plagued them ever since they had felt the change in the weather in the deep hours of the morning had become a squall, and as Thormir listened he thought he heard a single howl carried upon the back of the tempest. The ring of fire that encircled the city blew to and fro, never quite dying out, but getting a little smaller as each minute went by, crouching and submitting to the storm. More flashes of light bounced between the colossal storm clouds. By their light, Thormir saw Crow's army, still together, still advancing on Orien.

Then came the rain. It was as if someone had opened a door to the heavens, and released a torrent of water that snuffed out the fire ring and turned the ground instantly to mud. Hoff's trap had worked after all; in the distance they could see The Crow's men struggling, helpless in the mud. The forward lines crashed into one another, not expecting the ground to turn instantly into a sea of sludge and muck. Some of the men struggled for a minute and then, under the impression that they should start doing something, drew their bows and began to fire at the walls.

Orien responded with a hail of its own arrows that, from a distance, looked like a moving shadow of something larger flying far above. The spray of arrows seemed to clean up the last of the vanguard of The Crow's army, but the ever-encroaching body of black shapes still marched slowly and deliberately towards the smoking city.

Thormir looked at the gates, and, as he heard Hoff give the order to move out, he saw riders in the distance – about 300 men on horseback, all with bows, riding towards the enemy. Rather than engaging at close-quarters, they circled around and, at the last minute, headed back towards Orien. Thormir realised what they were doing as he saw the horsemen loose more arrows at the army as they rounded and headed back towards the city. Again and again they did this and soon a large portion of The Crow's army had either fallen to the mud, or had been peppered by the arrows that whizzed from the horsemen's bows.

Thormir heard Hoff scream orders above the wind. Then he saw four lanterns, all a warm, golden colour, rise in the distance and begin a deadly journey towards the enemy. In an instant the Dwarven army descended the slopes of Hurst until they too were on the flat, only to see that the enemy were closer than expected. Shadow did not seem frightened. Thormir took great comfort in the fact that she, at least, was not disturbed by the barbed heads of the enemy's spears, the strange chant that issued from them, or the fact that every soldier held a black, metal cage in which something moved – something that neither he nor the dwarves could discern through the acrid smoke and vile wind.

Hoff rode next to Thormir, looking back at his army. He seemed satisfied with his work. Thormir saw that branches were being dragged over the ground behind the last of the warriors, and seeing Thormir's questioning look, Hoff said, "It is always good to look bigger than you are. We are using the last of the dry ground to churn up dirt and dust so that, to The Crow, it will seem that we have a larger force – an old but useful technique. Remember, the more uncertainty an army has, the more likely they will break. See . . ."

Thormir watched as the enemy ground to a halt and formed lines upon lines of armoured soldiers. Before he had time to do anything, they could hear thundering hooves and, searching for the beat, Thormir spotted the 300 soldiers of Orien rush past him, bows raised. But they weren't soldiers, they were ordinary people; only a few of them wore the red and gold of the soldiers' dress. The others wore an assortment of plain clothes, stolen armour, and some even rode in rags with only a leather cuirass to protect them. They rushed at the soldiers, loosing the last of their arrows into the faces and chests of the enemy. As they turned, Thormir was forced to watch as The Crow's soldiers replied in kind: horses fell to the ground, their heads and knees crashing into the mud, crushing their riders. The screams of dying horses were followed by the laughter of Crow's army as the rest of the riders rode back towards the opening gates. In that instant he saw her. Riding like the wind, her hair flying back in silken waves, Maria and her charge were galloping towards the city, the last in the company.

Hoff yelled something in dwarfish, and a second later the archers of the Dwarven army had taken position and had begun to cripple the front lines of the enemy that were within range. The speed at which they drew and loosed each arrow was amazing, but soon they would be out of arrows and it would be time to engage the enemy head on. That time, however, did not come, as they were cut short by several things happening at once. A section of The Crow's army peeled off, heading towards the walls and main gate of Orien. Another, smaller section remained where they were and faced the Dwarven army. Thormir could see them, each of them, each soldier lowering their cages and placing them on the ground. The men began to chant, stamping their boots in the mud, and banging their cruel spears against their armour and shields. Thormir tried to listen above the howling of the wind and the roaring of the rain driving into the mud. The chant was picking up speed, always repeating the same phrase. "*Morscel es var huru!*" Thormir made it out to be some form of old Estarion. He roughly translated it as "Death legion!". Chills ran the length of his spine.

Thormir stood watching as each soldier slid the metal grates open and waited for something – what, he did not know. He felt Hoff grow tense next to him. They did not have to wait long.

The screams of men and horses were nothing compared to what came next. The sound crashed over them, clawing at their ears and tearing at their brains. It was so primitive that it could not be human. It was the scream of an animal in the grips of death, or was it death itself? This was a death scream, high-pitched and vile. It was a gut-wrenching sound that heralded the coming of pure evil. A second later, a flock of pitch-black birds – crows, no less – rose into the red sky. Thormir could feel their jet-black eyes, full of malice, no room for goodness and mercy. As the creatures dived down among the dwarves, Hoff called a formation and, quicker than Thormir would have thought possible, the dwarves had formed a large shell of shields that the sharp, hungry beaks of the crows could not penetrate.

As soon as the crows had been released, rather than dismounting as Hoff did, Thormir turned and rode Shadow back up the hill. Turning back towards the battlefield, he saw the dwarves advancing and the crows being shot down one by one. Yet still the crows came, clawing and fiercely pecking between the cracks between shields. Finally, the few crows that were left gave up and flew off. Tired of their mission of tearing meat from Dwarven bone, they would look for man flesh. It was then that the armies collided. The battle had begun.

*   *   *

The two armies had long since engaged, and limbs now littered the battlefield. The odour of death filled the air. The crows that had flown off had returned for a feast of torn muscle and spilt innards. Blood that had poured crimson was now dark red, mixed in with the mud, sticking in the tread of men's boots and the curved shapes of horseshoes. Weapons were strewn over the battlefield, lost to their former owners and bloodied by those they had touched. The enemy had long since run out of arrows, and the last they had fired they had set alight, so now small spot fires burned in between the fallen bodies and severed parts. They gave off a smell of rotten meat and burning flesh. The field had quickly become a putrid pool of sick, blood, and muck. Wounded men and women lay screaming for their mothers, their faith in their new religion failing them. Some died without a word, lying on the ground listening to their last moments; the last thing they would hear would be the gurgling sound that always accompanied death.

A point of a spear whipped around; the tip of the blade sliced into the first layer of Thormir's shoulder. Beads of blood immediately surfaced. For the first time he jumped off Shadow, landing in the mud, and stared down at the side of a ruffian's worn face that was half-slathered in muck. *Did he have a family? Did he truly believe in the spun, snake-like words of the emperor?*

The clash of metal continued to rattle in his ears as he looked into the eyes of the soldier standing before him. Measuring up the weapon and his skill to wield it took no more than a second. He was no seasoned warrior; this was a man who had been given a spear and told to fight for a cause with no knowledge of the weapons of war. The soldier hefted his spear and, in his moment of indecision, Thormir took his own weapon, his bow, and sent one of his arrows through the man's exposed neck.

Thormir turned and slapped Shadow on the buttocks, urging her out of the battlefield. Watching as she galloped from the blood-stained field and crippled bodies, he drew another arrow from his quiver. He grimaced as he felt his muscles knot, each cord braided with the tension of battle.

*　　*　　*

There had been no place for rest and the battle had been long. Taking a step forward, Thormir felt a row of five ridges embedded in the mud. Looking down, he saw a dying woman stare back at him, her hand outstretched, clawing desperately at Thormir's boot. A blind stare of death was written across the face of the torn soldier and, for a moment, Thormir was reminded of the blind hermit they had left in Hurst. He thought of all the hermit had said and wondered whether it was going to be today that he would see the stone arch and the white horse standing before a crystal sunset. Something told him that he would not be so fortunate.

Thormir felt his neck snap back and his legs give way. As he crashed into the mud, he knew what was happening and fear struck him. His legs jerked back and forth and pain knifed at his back, shooting up his spine. The seizure was taking hold. He could only take short breaths, inhaling between the jerks that ravaged his limbs. Blinking hard Thormir tried to clear his blurred vision. It did not work. Darkness closed in upon him. Staring into the swirling blackness, he wandered beyond time, place, and all eternity. No longer could he hear the movements that made the symphony of battle, only silence blessed this place. Opening his eyes wide, he searched for a face, anyone, anything to help him escape this emptiness – for it was pressing in upon him, constricting his throat. Thormir felt his heart beat rise as he saw a patch of grey emerge through the darkness. Walking towards it, he began to hear sounds again; they were jumbled and seemed to be muffled by an invisible barrier. Thormir stretched out his hand, reaching towards the window of pale grey, and a face appeared through the swirling silver. It was the face of Wed, the greybeard whom he had met when he was captive in Orien. His face looked younger and more at peace than before, but he still looked worried. Wed was shouting at him, his muffled tones becoming clearer and clearer until, "Rise my son, rise. Feel the light and air."

Thormir's heart sank. The grey veil that had been drawn across his eyes had been pulled back and now he felt a burning sunlight like he had never felt before. The sun hovered in the sky like a crimson crystal shining new light upon the world. And there were the horses, white and shining with terrible beauty.

Thormir had joined Wed in death. Looking around him he saw three horses riding hard towards them. Thormir let his mind wander to what the hermit had said about the afterlife, but he could only recall one horse that waited beside a stone arch. These three horses were fierce, tossing their heads, galloping towards them, each baring a rider.

"Rise. Rise Thormir!" Wed's words were clear and strong in Thormir's ears, and they did not betray any sense of courage. Wed was truly scared. Thormir tried to move, to regain any sense in his limbs. Swivelling his head, he looked at the horses' riders. Each had a hood drawn halfway over their face, which was but a swirling mass of darkness under the grey-white cloth. Their cloaks billowed around them as they rode, the tattered material catching in the brutal wind cast forth by the shadowy clouds. The red sun had become victim to the slithering shade, and under the sky's vaulted veil, evil had rode forth. The Pale Riders had found him.

"Thormir! We must hurry!" Wed's words were fading and Thormir felt that same wandering shade closing in upon him once more. He tried to fight it, to warn Wed of . . .

Wed fell forward as the shining sword of a Pale Rider finished its arc.

NO! Thormir screamed but no words issued forth. *Why can't I move!* Three pairs of boots slammed into the ground. He heard the hissing and clicking of The Pale Riders before he saw them. The sounds sent chills down his aching spine. Thormir saw Wed lying in the mud, and he urged his body to move. For he was not dead, but had been delivered back, to lie paralysed in the mud awaiting a horror not worthy of nightmares.

Three hoods appeared over him and he stared into faces of churning evil. The Pale Riders lowered themselves, almost lovingly, ready to suck the life and power from Thormir's soul. Closing his eyes, Thormir waited for the pain. He sunk into the deepest recesses of his mind until he heard the memory of a voice echoing in his ears, "Even the smallest candle can light the greatest darkness". As the voice faded, Thormir felt power and life still in him. Energy surged through him, and one word came to him through his confusion.

"*Hellesar!*" His eyes flew open and he raised his right arm. Flames of blue and green erupted outwards. Unearthly screams came from The Pale Riders as the fire took to their robes. The darkness that the blackened, overcast sky provided meant nothing now. Their horses took off at the sight of the raging inferno, leaving the riders collapsed and screaming in the mud. Finally, with one last ear-piercing torrent of noise, the three collapsed, utterly spent – dead. Thormir felt around and knew he could move. Warily standing up, he looked at the tattered robes of the riders strewn across the ground. Their weapons were shattered and broken – but no bodies remained, only hollow armour and abandoned robes. Somehow they had survived. *They will return for me, but not today, not today.*

Surveying his surroundings, Thormir saw the dwarves take down the last of their opponents and form up, marching on the larger force that stood before the walls of Orien. He saw the gate of Orien open, and another wave of its army and civilians spill out onto the field, thousands of people charging at the soldiers who were trying to steal their minds and homes. He watched as soldiers and the other people of Orien launched themselves into battle; all of them fought with a ferocity that can only be associated with people defending what is theirs. He saw a large, tattooed man tackle a soldier to the ground, followed by his fist smashing into the soldier's nose. Thormir saw another man fighting, flowing through an array of motions, and guiding his sword with deadly precision. He was not as fast as the others, as his leg held him back, but he continued to move, hauling his leg through the mud; swish, thud, swish.

Thormir heard Hoff's baritone voice boom and turned towards him. Hoff's boom was then matched by a cascade of war horns that bellowed somewhere northwest of their position, and from around the ridge in the distance, 600 dwarves were riding hard at the rear of The Crow's army, taking them by surprise. And with them flew the banners of Keleadgurdil, with Khan Roland laughing as he led his army into battle.

Thormir turned to Hoff to see him laughing as well. "Sometimes it is best to keep the biggest secrets from those who most need to know them." Thormir realised what Hoff had done. He had told Khan Roland to act as if he were leaving, but really to join the knights and the dwarves that were hiding around the ridge. Any enemy spies would have been fooled.

The lanterns were now directly over the enemy. *It is time.* Thormir notched his arrow and aimed at the ballooning material that held the miraki seeds. He flexed the bowstring, the tips of his fingers brushing the soft fletching.

He watched as the red seeds hailed towards the mud. The moment they touched the ground they exploded, and red dust enveloped a large section of the battlefield. Thormir shot two more sacks of seed and in each case the seeds burst, blasting out a vast billowing cloud of poisonous dust, killing each section of The Crow's army. The enemy was beginning to break rank, and Thormir watched from the crest of a small hill, as tens of thousands of The Crow's army turned and fled north, back towards the Carabeorn, and the empire. Looking on as the dust cleared, he saw men dying – so many men. Most clutched at their throats, others tried to flee but then fell unconscious, submitting to the embrace of death, while others who had had the sense to cover their mouths and noses with their cloaks, were then cut down by the first dwarves who, by then, had reached the field.

Despite all this, there was something poetic about the way that the three glowing lanterns rose up into the red sky, unburdened by the seeds of eternal sleep. Soon they were high above the field, mingling with the morning stars, looking over the waves of death and pain they had unleashed. But there was still one, a single flushed lantern, blazing in the red sky, still pregnant with its sack of miraki seeds. It floated directly above the front lines of Orien. As he took aim, Thormir saw Maria fighting one-handed, backing away from a brute who was wielding a colossal two-handed sword that he was swinging in great arcs before and above her as she dodged her imminent death. If he shot his arrow, the miraki seeds would explode and release their poison, killing the last of The Crow's force that he had sent forward, but he would also kill many of Orien's men, and Maria too. He frowned, knowing it would be too much to sacrifice. Just as he was about to lower his bow, someone crashed into him. As it happened Thormir released the arrow. It spun towards the sack of miraki seeds and a second later, cherry-red dust covered the ground and hung in the air. Soldiers on both sides began to choke and splutter as they realised death had enveloped them.

A fist smashed into the side of his face and he spat blood out of his mouth. Then another. The second hit was worse than the first; the knuckles buried themselves into his eye. Breathing hard, he was flat on his back and looked up at a crying man who shouted at him, hitting on every other word. "You," *smash*, "killed," *smash*, "my," *smash*, "best," *thud*, "friend."

Blood flooded over and into Thormir's eyes. He knew how the man felt, so he did not object; he lay there and took the punishment, and only when he could see the man drawing a knife with the intention of killing, did Thormir punch him in the temple, knocking him out. Thormir looked sideways at the men and women still choking on the last of the miraki dust. He saw Maria starting to scratch at her throat. She collapsed on all fours and began heaving in the mud.

Running towards her, Thormir dodged the last swipes of swords and the half-hearted spears that sailed his way. He tripped and the ground rose up and hit him hard, throwing him sideways to stare directly into the face of one of The Crow's men. The soldier's eyes flickered and he began to mouth words to Thormir, two of which he caught. "Help me." But it was too late; after the man's last wish he let out a single breath and did not take another.

Rolling onto his shoulder, Thormir wiped away the tears that were running down his face. He felt a dreaded seizure clawing at him but he fought it off. *I will not submit. Not now.* Squinting ahead of him, he saw Maria lower herself to the ground and he could tell that her arms were trembling, weak with the poison. A dark, spectral fog was gathering in front of his eyes, but through it he saw the Dwarven cavalry crash into The Crow's army. He saw Hector ride up to Maria on a white warhorse and, with a powerful arm, lift her off her feet and throw her behind him, bent over the saddle. He rode in the direction of the dark trees and the Dwarven camp.

CHAPTER THIRTY

CRESCENDO
Suélla

Thormir had once been told that every story begins with a scorched map, but now he thought that his story might end with one. The storm that had raged around the battle was gone, but gusts of wind still assaulted the tents and faces of the soldiers that wandered the battlefield in search of weapons or wounded friends. The red sun had painted the sky a burnt sienna, partly hidden behind a grey meadow of clouds that floated lazily in the sky. In the distance was the wink of a golden lantern on its journey into the heavens, sailing to a place where neither man nor bird could reach.

Why oh why couldn't there have been fewer of them? And why did they have to resist? So many wives and daughters will never see their boys again, and it is because of me . . . I killed them. It seemed almost impossible to Thormir as he stood here, surveying the field of battle, taking in the carnage they had inflicted on the landscape, that they had won – and even more improbable that it had been he who had won it for them, or at least driven the enemy from their doorstep; securing the passage of Carathron. *I am just a weapon now, a weapon that will now have to fight and kill so that an emperor will not fight and kill in turn. It just doesn't seem right. How many have died this day? Before the walls of Orien so many have laid down their lives protecting those they love against the shadow of the emperor. And how many more must die? Hundreds? Thousands? This is all because of me – all because of a war begun by my will for vengeance, and the emperor's want for power.*

People have seen and heard what I can do, and I have given them hope – and their hope has turned to anguish, and that anguish into a blazing inferno. Change is coming. Those whose souls have been in peaceful slumber, chained under the spell of the emperor, will awaken to find that they are strong. They shall rise as one, and with time, the iron will of the emperor will bend. The lives of the people who fought before Orien will never be forgotten.

And why should it be me who fights this battle? We have defended the passage of Orien protecting the Carathron, so why should we go further north to fight an emperor who has us severely outnumbered? His empire seems to be happy serving him under the delusion of this new religion, so why should we disrupt that balance? Even if he does manage to raise magic somehow and find a way to control it, what damage would he really do?

The answer to his few questions came in the form of Khan Toshin, who had sidled up to Thormir unnoticed and who now looked over the battlefield just as Thormir did. His black beard, normally rigid, was blowing in the wind.

Thormir looked at Khan Toshin as he heard him speak. "We have really poked the hornets' nest now." The dwarf was not tired, but still he leant on his double-bladed axe rather heavily. However, his voice gave away no sign of weariness. "The emperor will strike at us next, I think." The dwarf paused, drew a long pipe from under his armour, and, to Thormir's amazement, filled and lit it. Letting green smoke spiral into the burning sky, he continued, speaking out of the side of his mouth. "You know, if this emperor succeeds in his plans, whether in taking control of the lands east of The Al'Durast, or raising and controlling the power that is left in this realm, we will all be under his rule. We will be tracked at all times, and any sign of an uprising will not be quelled with reasoned words, but with a noose around the neck or a blade between the ribs. We have just had word that the towns of Grim and Horndean along the banks of The Faeya have been decimated because a few people dared to question the emperor; I will bet my clan's gold that Durnsay will be the next to go. Thormir, *this* is what it will be like. You told the council that Orien was corrupt and evil – well, people will be begging for the rule of Lord Bath and his ugly son if the emperor does seize Orien and rules its people."

A puff of smoke rose up and caught on a sailing current. Toshin followed it as the air took it. "That was a good idea you had with the seeds. It's a pity we can't eat the birds that we killed to get the berries." He let out a deep sigh, "Sometimes you have to sacrifice a lot to gain a lot."

Thormir looked down at Toshin, who was hopping around on one foot, shouting in anger and embarrassment. "Damn it! Look at my beard!" It was so dishevelled that it appeared parted on the right, flowing off in two separate directions. Thormir had thought it impolite to comment. He tried to hide his laughter as Toshin used his fingers to straighten and organise his beard into a more respectable configuration. And he thought that this was why they should defeat the emperor, "So we can laugh."

"What's that now?" Toshin looked up at Thormir from under bushy eyebrows.

"I was just saying that the reason we should fight the emperor is so we can laugh."

"Oh well, I am so glad that my beard is the cause of your epiphany, but this is no way for a khan to look. But, indeed, you are right. Under the emperor's rule, the lines of laughter will fade from the faces of those who once lived free." Toshin resumed finger-combing his thick beard. Thormir turned away from the blood-stained horizon and walked towards the camp.

He would fight.

* * *

Baldur was talking to the king and a still-armoured Hoff, when Thormir entered the tent. ". . . yes, the people were being led, under cover of the smoke screen of course, by four women who called themselves the Sisters of Sa'bil. Much of the military remained to fight the enemy, but they seemed to be under the command of a man named Tangar; he was not of Orien. The soldiers say he is of the Tangri people in the North, which would explain the tactics that displayed in battle. There was no sign of the lords and ladies of the city, although some of the maids said they had travelled to Durnsay days ago, taking some soldiers and slaves with them as well as the . . ." Baldur turned as they all noticed Thormir standing in the corner.

Thormir did not need to say it.

"Thormir, I am so sorry, we think Selena is with them. I have been told that she is one of the slaves that Bath took with him."

He could not think, instead he was tumbling amongst swirling colours of pain and hurt that cut deeper than any sword could, and burnt his insides with the heat of a thousand fires. Another form of pain flew through him as his knees gave way and he crashed to the ground. *It's all my fault. I am so sorry, Selena! I am the one who got you into all of this, I should never have meddled – I should have kept to myself.* But he would not apologise to the world for the way he felt about her. *I would walk to the shores of the Wilderlands and climb the slopes of The Frostfall to get her back. And now she is . . . gone.*

His pain resolved into sudden determination and all tiredness that had previously resided in him was replaced by a burning, smouldering hunger for vengeance. Only one other thought could penetrate his mind, and looking at Baldur, he said, "Where is he? Where is the man with the scarred face?"

Baldur thought that telling Thormir the truth might just finish off his descent into madness, but a misplaced lie could be worse than the truth. "The brute with the scars also accompanied Bath to Durnsay."

"And Lucian? Tangar? Mary? Where are they?"

Baldur bowed his head, "No sign."

Thormir froze. He could feel his limbs shaking with anger, and only when Baldur placed an armoured hand around his wrist and told him to check on Maria did his anger subside as concern washed over him, not quelling the inferno within, but turning the flames into hot coals that would soon rise and unleash a torrent of fire.

He felt his scar beginning to tingle and, looking at his arm, he saw the snake-like burn rise to the surface of his skin. He felt the energy, his power, rise within him as he ran to the medic's tent, but for some reason the power seemed to be fuelled by something else. He closed his eyes and saw the flash of that golden eye that he had been dreaming of so much recently. He shook his head and picked up his pace, hurrying towards the tent where he was told Maria lay unconscious.

One of the dwarves was leaning over Maria, tending to her with a damp washcloth. The dwarf turned and Thormir was surprised but pleased when he saw that it was Khan Jyrell, her face dirty but still beautiful, who was caring for Maria.

"We are losing her," Jyrell said in a whisper, "she mutters constantly and begins to have hallucinations. I have looked into her mind," – this did not surprise Thormir, as he had already suspected all the khans were experienced in the practice – "and all I see is fire and metal. Her thoughts are jumbled at best, but there is one word which I can make out."

"What is it? Tell me quick!"

"'Vengeance.' That is the only word that is clear to my mind. Shall I leave you alone with her? Maybe she will tell you something you will understand that I cannot."

Thormir nodded.

He waited for the tent flap to shut before putting his hand over Maria's. He remembered the girl who had come to him in the middle of that night, remembered her pain, and her suffering, and how when she had been freed he had barely talked to her.

"I am so sorry for what I have done to you."

Maria's eyelids flickered but did not open.

"You have to know, I don't blame you for Fern, I never did."

Her eyes flickered again.

Then he said what he had been thinking about all the people he had met since leaving Medani. "I should have never met you, any of you – all I do is harm people, and wherever I go I leave a trail of bodies behind me. I should have never saved you."

Maria started to shake violently and Thormir tightened his grip around her. *That arrow. If it had never . . . would we have still won?* Guilt seeped through him. He was responsible for Maria's condition and she had barely breathed any of the poison. *How many more have I killed that did not deserve it?* He started as Maria's eyes flew open and she sat up. Thormir was about to say something when he was pushed flat on his back. Maria was on top of him, a wild look in her bloodshot eyes. Somehow she had found a knife and was now pressing the blade into Thormir's throat. She let out a hiss and as she did so, his scar tingled and itched.

"You killed me!" As the words left her mouth, Thormir felt a shiver run down his spine and heard the feeling reflected as the tent took another battering from the wind.

"You killed me," she hissed again, "and now I shall kill you." Her whole body was quivering and Thormir looked on in dismay as he recognised the signs of death by miraki poisoning. But still she had the strength to lift the knife high above her head, and, quick as a summer snake, plunge it downwards. Thormir watched, tears clouding his eyes as she, the one he had saved from a life of slavery, fell from where she rested on his lap. She lay there, still breathing, slow and shallow.

As they looked into each other's eyes, Thormir saw hers soften and her lips twitch with love and recognition as she saw him. "Thormir," Her whisper was not the harsh hiss from before, but an utterance of love and gratitude. She smiled at him again, and then she was gone – at peace.

Thick tears ran down Thormir's face. *Not again. Not again!* "I loved her too," he screamed. "I loved her too!" No one replied; no one came to comfort him. He was alone, just as he had been when Fern . . .

He turned again to look at Maria, so he could close her eyes, to let her rest in peace. He understood that she was acting under one of her hallucinations, but he had already forgiven her. She had done nothing wrong. The pain of her leaving him was almost too much to bear; it twisted in his stomach and, as he turned, it cut even deeper.

His hand jumped to his stomach, even though he knew he would find nothing. But it was there. He looked down and saw the hilt of the knife sticking out from his unarmoured belly. It stuck up like a vertical trophy, glorifying his deadly wound. As Thormir looked at it, the pain he had been feeling doubled. His left hand, the hand that had jumped to the knife, was covered in hot blood. Tearing his shirt so he could see the wound clearly, he looked down. It was ugly. *It is the only way.* With his left hand he took the ripped piece of shirt and stuffed it between his teeth. His scar was burning. Taking the hilt of the knife he pulled, preparing for the rush of blood. Screaming into the cloth was his only outlet, so when the knife emerged he was gasping for fresh air. With his scar still burning along his arm, he spat out the cloth and, gritting his teeth, pressed his right hand to the wound. He felt his blood bleeding through his fingers. *I need help. I can't do this alone.*

"Help!" He could hear footsteps coming, not far off, but there was no way they would be here in time. *At least I will see Fern and Maria and all the others again* . . . As he thought this he could feel the odd sensation of a mind touching his.

He froze. This was a mind he knew. A mind he could never forget. The construction of each thought was so familiar, and yet . . . it couldn't be. Before he had time to decide, he felt a massive rush of energy through his body. It was as though his entire body was set alight, burning with power. Continuing to press his hand to his stomach, he felt an inching sensation of such magnitude that he thought he might tear his stomach out if he did not die first.

And then, as suddenly as it had begun, the power that had rushed through him subsided. Gasping for breath and recognising that his scar was burning so violently that he thought he might explode, he kept his hand on the wound. But as he held his hand there, all he felt was smooth skin. He looked at his stomach and saw that the crimson gash had healed, leaving a red patch of smooth flesh as the only memento of the wound.

He began pounding the ground. "Why could you not have done that for Maria? Why are you being so cruel?" He didn't know who he was talking to, but after a while it seemed pointless to shout. It was only then that he noticed that all of the knights were gathered in the tent, looking on with bowed heads. They too had known Maria at her best, and they too mourned her. Thormir felt a hand on his shoulder as Rake knelt beside him.

Thormir looked at Rake, who was always so tough and hardened to the cruelty of the world.

"I will miss her. She was . . . loving."

It was the first time Thormir had heard Rake speak and even the knights who had never heard Rake talk looked up in surprise. Thormir looked at Rake and noticed that his hard eyes had softened.

"We will get your Selena, and we will get the scarred one. I promise you this."

Thormir looked down at Maria and she seemed at peace. She would be remembered as the girl who fought for love and freedom, but in a dark cell in Durnsay, Selena remembered Maria as the girl who gave her life so that she could have hers.

CHAPTER THIRTY ONE

MIRAKI
Latal acin

Waves of tiredness and pain crashed over him. Slow and steady, they washed him of all other sensations. Even the smells of cut wood, some sort of herbal soup, and damp clothes, were all gone as they were replaced by pain.

He tried to move, but he seemed to be pinned down by rope. He was paralysed, trapped inside his own head. But even his head was in pain; he felt small trickles of blood flow in and out between his canines, flowing out of his mouth, and pooling inside his cheek so he had to swallow painfully.

As he tried to ward off the waves of pain, he began to ask questions, trying to remember what had happened. The last thing he could recall was a sea of purple and a floating sensation, but every time he tried to grab onto the details of the memory it would slip away. He would start with his name and work his way up from there. *What is my name?*

Oh God! I don't know! I don't know my own name! What is happening to me?

A wound, the main wound, gave another stab of pain, and he tried to locate its source. It was his paw – no, under his front leg – deep inside his pit. It felt like a gaping hole that had been healing but still it protested. It cut into him, and at its twinge he clenched his teeth to drive off the sensation. He felt broken in body, but at least he still had his mind. At least he could find out where he was; he just had to remember.

A voice came from behind him.

"Arr, you are awake! 'Tis good, 'tis good. You have been asleep for many weeks, although many has no real meaning; let us just say you have returned after a long absence. Yes, that is good? No? Yes, 'tis good."

The pain cut into him again, and he listened to the madman bumble on about wounds and healing methods. He was about to tune out when he seized upon a piece of information.

"Yes, yes, quite clever, but silly of them really. I mean, smearing a paste made of miraki flesh on an arrow, it could have killed you. But I suppose they also knew that the berry's paste can slow the heart to an almost undetectable beat and induce prolonged sleep. And I also suppose that's how they wanted to take you back to Orien, asleep and harmless – can't blame them, really. I mean, look at the size of you. You know, if I didn't know better, I would peg you as a warg. But then again, you are not." The madman chuckled.

Another throb of cutting pain, and then the memories returned: the escape from Orien, the fight, and the arrow. He had been in so much pain. He remembered talking to someone and the ache increased, this time deep within his chest. The blurry memory of the purple sea came back to him, and the details materialised so that he could make out thousands and thousands of tiny purple flowers.

Haren Gwineth

Printed in November 2022
by Rotomail Italia S.p.A., Vignate (MI) - Italy